No EASY PLACE TO BE

a novel

STEVEN CORBIN

SIMON AND SCHUSTER

New York   London   Toronto
Sydney   Tokyo

SIMON AND SCHUSTER
Simon & Schuster Building
Rockefeller Center
1230 Avenue of the Americas
New York, New York 10020

Designed by Kathy Kikkert
Manufactured in the United States of America

10 9 8 7 6 5 4 3 2

Library of Congress Cataloging-in-Publication Data
Corbin, Steven, date.
  No easy place to be.

  I. Title.
PS3553.064394N6   1989   813'.54   88-29722
ISBN 0-671-65884-0

"Poet to Patron" by Langston Hughes reprinted by permission of Harold Ober Associates Incorporated. Copyright 1939 by American Mercury, Inc.

"We Wear the Mask" by Paul Laurence Dunbar reprinted by permission of Dodd, Mead & Company, Inc., from *The Complete Poems of Paul Laurence Dunbar.*

Reprinted from *Cane* by Jean Toomer by permission of Liveright Publishing Corporation. Copyright © 1923 by Boni & Liveright. Copyright renewed 1951 by Jean Toomer.

Special thanks to

Sherry Robb, my agent;

Malaika Adero, my editor;

and the PEN American Center

for their financial support.

for my mother

Yvonne Kitchens Corbin

and her mother

Eloise Benjamin Kitchens

1908–1968

who, over Bingo

and a cup of tea,

dazzled my childhood by

spinning tales of Harlem

when the '20s roared

SUNRISE

1919

NO BETTER TROOPS
IN WAR

There is a certain Negro regiment

(369th Infantry — "Harlem Hell-

Fighters") over here in France to

whom, were they to march down

Fifth Avenue today, every hat in

New York would be off. They con-

stitute the first Negro force Uncle

Sam has sent to the European

battlefields.

— The New York World
September 1, 1918

OUR HEROES. WELCOME HOME. 369TH FIRST TO REACH THE RHINE.

The homemade pennants and American flags snapped and fluttered in the February wind, hoisted by the assemblage of spectators massed along Fifth Avenue. They were to honor the soldiers who witnessed the sounding of the bugles of peace in France during the November past—the Harlem Hell-Fighters of the 369th infantry who played a key role in the sounding of those bugles. They now marched northward. Home to Harlem. And the atmosphere was charged. Maintenance men pushed their brooms, policemen rode on horseback, and the crowd simmered, as latecomers dashed along Forty-second Street with signs and banners flapping about their necks. Every New Yorker capable of walking turned out, eager to witness history unfold. The soldiers were to march from the recently erected victory arch at Twenty-fifth Street, past the New York Public Library toward Lenox Avenue and 145th Street. The chests of smiling Negroes were lifted with pride as they lined the curb shoulder to shoulder. Some were hopeful and others certain that their participation in World War I—so long as President Wilson had anything to do with it—would not go unrewarded; that now, fifty years after slavery, they'd be full-fledged American citizens. The days of oppression, lynching, and Jim Crow would be forever behind them.

Elvira Brooks, like most Harlemites, embraced this blessed event and its promises with the arms of optimism, making certain that she and her daughters, Miriam, Velma, and Louise, were present.

"Mother," Louise panted, "we're too late. We missed it." They paused at the steps of the Public Library to catch their breath.

"We wouldn't have," Velma said, a trickle of perspiration rolling down her forehead, "if it wasn't for Miriam taking her time."

"That's right; blame it on me," Miriam defended herself. "We could've saved time and stayed uptown and watched this stupid parade."

"We ain't late," Elvira said. "Instead of fussin', we oughta get us that nice spot across the street."

They weaved in and out of the noisy maze of people who buzzed with anticipation. Spectators stood on tiptoe for an unobstructed view. Mothers pacified screaming infants. Toddlers picking their noses and begging for roasted chestnuts were mounted on the shoulders of proud fathers when faint pulsations of a thumping brass band were heard in the distance.

"Here they come!" Elvira said, pointing. "Look! Now, ain't they fine! Gilbert would've been so proud." Her eyes filled as a roar rose from the crowd.

The soldiers approached Forty-first Street and halted. They straightened the lines of formation, and marched in place, sixteen abreast—a formation they had learned from the French, ten neat rows behind each front man. *Hut, two, three, four! Forward harch!* February winds whistled. Confetti rained like paper snowflakes. Granite lions, unmoved by the fanfare, guarded the Public Library's entrance.

"This is so exciting!" Velma shouted to her sisters.

"What's so exciting about standing in the cold," Miriam said softly to no one in particular, "just to watch some soldiers march? Anyway, what makes them think they'll be treated any better than before?"

"Mother, what's a trench?" the youngest daughter suddenly asked.

Elvira pondered a moment, "It's kinda like a ditch, Louise."

"I read in the paper they spent ninety-one days in the trenches."

"A *hundred* ninety-one, young lady," a stranger intoned from behind, smiling down at her as he stood with his wife and son.

"That many?" Louise asked, her youthful, dark eyes wide with wonder.

"That's right," the man replied. "They won the Medal of Honor for their bravery." He paused, studying Elvira, then Louise. "Are *you* her mother?" he asked.

"I sure am," Elvira said. "Is there something wrong?"

"No, no," he said, chuckling nervously. "I was just telling your daughter here that the 369th spent a hundred ninety-one days—"

"Mister?" Miriam interrupted, clearing her throat. "Do you believe social and economic conditions for colored folks will really change?"

"Miriam." Elvira apologized to the stranger with her eyes. Embarrassed, he hurried away with his wife and child. Elvira took Miriam by the arm and led her through the myriad of heavily clothed bodies to a spot beneath a lamppost. "This ain't no place for that kinda talk, girl," Elvira said, lowering her voice. "Remember, if nothing else, your father died in this war—"

"Mother—"

"This is an important day for you and me, for all of us. You should be proud. Colored people done helped win this war. Now white folks know somethin' they didn't know before. Things *is* gonna change. You'll see. It don't happen overnight, Miriam. These things take time. I should know."

"But, Mother—"

"But, Mother, what?"

"I'm twenty-one now and . . . never mind." Miriam shook her head. "I can't make you understand my thinking. You're too set in your ways."

"Like you ain't set in yours?" Elvira replied, one step ahead of Miriam.

A smile crept across Miriam's lips and Elvira laughed, hugging her eldest daughter. "You see," Elvira said, " sometimes the mirror is too tellin'. C'mon, let's go. We missin' the parade."

A formation of soldiers in brown stepped to the beat, while women in white uniforms and heavy overcoats handed out roses to the marching ranks. Children in wool overcoats and buttoned boots waved miniature flags. They grinned and cheered. A one-legged soldier hobbled from person to person shaking hands with people along the curb. Confetti collected on the brim of his hat. Tenants leaned out of their windows, waving, shouting, blowing kisses. People in the neighboring buildings cheered from fire escapes and rooftops.

Elvira shaded the sun from her eyes with her gloved hand and craned her neck. "Velma, you seen him yet?"

"No, I haven't."

"Did you tell him?" Miriam whispered to Velma.

"Shhh!" Velma said.

"Tell him what?" Elvira asked, never breaking her gaze from the marching ranks.

"Nothing, Mother." Velma shot Miriam a scolding look.

Elvira stepped a few paces away from the curb, still combing the columns with her eyes. Miriam seized the opportunity.

"When do you plan to tell him, Velma?"

"I don't know, Miriam," Velma said, refusing to meet her sister's eyes. "Let me enjoy the parade."

Miriam chuckled. "You better. This is all Uncle Sam's going to give us. I don't care what Mother says."

Velma couldn't respond to Mother. Nor did she have any pat answers for Miriam. She stood there, nonplussed, deliberately distracting herself from an impending confrontation she didn't feel the strength to tackle. Not now anyway. She couldn't share her gut-level feelings at this peculiar, awkward moment. She exchanged a glance with Miriam. A knowing glance. She assumed Miriam knew her intentions without having asked. It all reflected in her expression. Velma emptied her mind of commitments she no longer cared to fulfill. She inhaled the crisp air, laden with the aroma of roasted peanuts and chestnuts, and suddenly felt hungry.

Company halt! the platoon leader commanded. On cue, the soldiers twirled their rifles like in a vaudeville show, the heavy steel and wood slapping against their white-gloved palms, and tapped the rifle butts on the pavement. A hush fell over Fifth Avenue at the sight of the troops' skillful execution. Motley heads bobbed in the crowd like apples in a tub of water. The drill complete, the soldiers saluted the spectators. *Forward harch!* The silence filled with the crowd's applause.

"There he goes!" Louise cried, jumping up and down, clapping her hands.

"Here comes Roland, baby!" Mother exclaimed, rejoining her daughters. She flashed Velma a smile. "Be glad yours come back, sugar."

"Roland! Roland!" Louise yelled, cupping her mouth with numbed hands. "Over here!" She waved. A soldier with a cinnamon-colored face turned around and recognized the Brooks family shouting from the sidewalk. He waved, smiling. Marching briskly in the company of his men, he winked at Velma and blew her a kiss to which she bowed her head.

"Well, you jus' gonna stand there an' be a statue! Wave to him, Velma!" Elvira said, waving to Roland. "You and Miriam—um, um, um, I don't know." She shook her head. "Y'all just ain't got no spirit."

"You'd better tell him tonight at the dance," Miriam whispered to Velma.

Velma ignored her. She eyed the Public Library across the street and her mind drifted, her head filling with secret hopes and ambitions. Tuning out the piercing trumpets, the thumping tubas, and the pounding bass drums, she contemplated Dunbar, Browning, Kipling, whose works, she knew, cluttered the dusty stacks of the library's immense marble halls. She imagined her own literary efforts stacked between the dust covers of Baroja and Dunbar. Yes, Velma thought, the 1920s might be promising for the Negro. But even more promising for her. She lifted her eyes toward the heavens as if awaiting a sign of corroboration from God Himself.

"You *what!*"

Roland paced back and forth before Velma, mumbling incoherently under his breath. Velma stood frozen against the wall, clutching the lapels of his army jacket around her shoulders. They stood inside a teasingly lit foyer beneath crepe streamers of red, white, and blue. Music drifted from the adjoining dance hall. "You mean, I waited all this time, I came back home for this?"

"Rolie, honey, I didn't say—"

"What am I supposed to do now, Velma? Huh? What am I supposed to do?" He threw his corporal's cap against the wall. Velma flinched at the thud. "Look out there." He turned Velma's face toward the dance floor. "You see those guys? They're my buddies." Uniformed soldiers danced cheek to cheek with spouses and fiancées. "They think they're going to a wedding. But now you're telling me this crazy jive about not—"

"Rolie." Velma licked her parched lips. She had expected him to be surprised but not livid. "I never said the engagement was off. I just want to finish my year and a half at Barnard. I want to write. Just like you had to fight the war, I have to write. You understand, don't you?" she asked, trying to meet his eyes with hers.

"Stop calling me Rolie."

"I used to call you that before you left for Europe. You liked it then."

"The old Velma used to call me that," he shot back. "I'm not sure who *you* are." He stopped pacing and reached inside his boot for a pack of Camels. He struck a match on his heel and lit one. The foyer glowed, then returned to darkness. He paced, threw up his hands, and slapped his sides. "What am I going to tell my buddies? You're the writer; got any ideas?" The look in her eyes told him that he was frightening her.

"Wait for me."

"Wait for you?" he said, wrinkling his face, as if he hadn't heard her correctly.

"Why not? I waited for you." She spoke slowly, hoping to calm him down.

"That's different, Velma. I'm a man."

"That's not a good enough reason."

"Good enough? You crazy? Lots of girls would give their right arm to marry a war hero. Where you been? I could've stayed in Paris. Colored soldiers got it made in Paris. French girls can't get enough of us. But, no, I came back to you. And now, you got some crazy idea about being a writer. Write what?" He chuckled inside at the ludicrous notion of a colored woman from Harlem becoming a writer. If it were happening to anyone else but him—anyone!—he would've laughed out loud for sure.

"Please take me home," she said softly, realizing she had overestimated him. "I thought you'd understand, but—"

"Ahem." A man, six feet four, stuck his head inside, invading their privacy. A woman, in heels who barely reached his rib cage, clutched his arm. "So, there you are," he said. "We been looking all over for you, man."

"Hey, Shorty," Roland replied hoarsely, staring at the floor. "I'm busy right now. Be with you in a minute."

"I just wanted to tell you two lovebirds that we're going to a rent party down on 116th and Lenox. Y'all comin'?" Shorty's date pulled his face downward, planted a smooch on his cheek, then wiped away the lipstick print. "This your girl?" Shorty looked at Velma, eyeing her head to toe. He smiled, then tipped his cap.

"This here's Velma. Velma, Shorty. We were in France together."

"Pleased to meet you, ma'am. Heard a lot about you," Shorty confessed, flashing Velma a mouthful of teeth.

Velma said nothing. She wasn't in the mood for strangers. As it was, the man pacing before her, a man she had known for some three years, was quickly becoming a stranger.

"Roland, she's even prettier than you said she was, man."

"Come on, Shorty." The woman tugged on his arm, and rolled her eyes at Velma. "Let's go."

"Yeah, man," Roland said, still staring at the floor, wishing Shorty would make himself scarce. "We'll meet you there."

"You don't even know the address, man."

"I said we'll be there."

"Okay, okay. Later . . . maybe." Shorty and his date left. Velma could hear the woman badmouthing her rude behavior as they disappeared.

"Look, Velma, I'm sorry I yelled before."

He guided her by the shoulders, gently lowering her until she sat. Standing above her, he placed a foot next to her on the box and rested an elbow upon his knee. Velma watched him with undivided attention, uncertain if he was about to kiss or strike her. She listened intently as his words fell upon her.

"Velma, baby, I love you. You wanted me to say it; there, I said it." Now that he had gotten that out of the way, the rest was easy.

"I want you to be my wife, the mother of my kids. But I want it now. You don't know the things I saw in Europe. How much I thought about you, day in, day out. Not knowing if I would live to see the sun rise. Every day, I watched death all around me. Men, my buddies, my comrades, falling down dead around me like flies. When I didn't get killed, I wondered why. Imagine wondering why you don't get killed."

He chuckled nervously at the painfully fresh image of flesh and bones exploding and splattering on the European battlefields, appendages flying. The thought made his face twitch.

"But I knew God must've been saving me for you," he said, certain she couldn't possibly refuse him now. "I want children now. I can't wait. If another war started tomorrow and I got killed, there'd be nobody to carry on my name. That's important to a man."

He stroked her cheek gingerly, relieved that she hadn't interrupted him before he got it all out. With a quiet cockiness, he knew he had her now. All women want war heroes and babies, he reasoned. There was no way she'd refuse. He blew the smoke toward the hanging light bulb and awaited her reply. "So, which is it—now or never?"

She sighed heavily. "I don't appreciate your ultimatum," she said.

"Ulti-what? Well, listen to you." He forced a chuckle. "Where'd you learn that word? Is that what college did to you? Teach you words I don't understand? You're a different person. You even talk different."

"Just because I'm a woman doesn't mean I don't have choices in these matters," she said defensively.

"What's a woman without a man?"

"I don't have to listen to this." Velma stood, removed his jacket and handed it back to him. "You've changed too."

"Wait . . . what about that time?" Roland said hastily, realizing he was losing control of the situation.

"What time?"

"The time we . . . you know," he said, groping.

"Yes," Velma said, "what about it?"

"You regret it?"

"No."

"Then why'd you do it?"

"Because. Because I love you. I did it because I didn't know if I'd ever see you alive again. I wouldn't have done it for just anybody."

"Then if you love me, you'll marry me. Tomorrow. Anyplace. Your mother's house, I don't care. Your sisters can be bridesmaids—"

"I can't, Roland."

"Well, who's going to want you now?" His tone became desperate. "Remember, you're not a virgin anymore. I mean, who would want you? A woman's place is with her man. She's supposed to have his babies, stick by him. Not write some damn books nobody's gonna read anyhow." He watched her through disbelieving eyes. "Hey, where're you going?"

"If you won't take me home, I'll go by myself."

"Does your mother know about your plans? What did she say?"

"Doesn't matter. It's my life and I'll do as I please. I won't get married at nineteen and give life to babies before I live my own. I won't repeat Mother's life."

"Velma, Velma, Velma," Roland said, shaking his head in exasperation. He crushed the cigarette butt beneath his heel. "You're weird, girl. You talkin' like a white lady. I ain't never heard you talk like this before. It ain't normal for girls to talk like that."

"Probably because I'm not a girl anymore. I'm all grown up now. Just like you." She turned and walked away. Roland grabbed her by the arm.

"If you walk out on me now, I swear, girl, I . . . well, I never want to see you again. You hear?"

"Another ultimatum?"

"Cut that college jive. Answer my question."

It took every ounce of defiance she had at the moment to look him squarely in the face, her eyes unflinching, when she replied, "I think I already did."

BOOK ONE

1925

CHARLESTON A HIT IN HOME, DANCE HALL AND BALLROOM

"Can you Charleston?" is the question . . . by womenfolk seeking a cook . . . from the ranks of Negro household workers. For the Charleston . . . is all the rage both for ballroom and exhibition, and being of African origin, is naturally best known by darkies.

Proprietors of employment agencies are being importuned to supply cooks, waitresses, laundresses and maids "who can Charleston."

—The New York Times
May 24, 1925

1

"Madam," Velma said, clearing her throat, clasping her hands before her, "I have a degree in American Literature from Barnard, and with all due respect, I hardly think it my lot in life to teach you how to Charleston. It's enough that I polish your silver."

Beyond the immense French doors, she heard the muffled giggles and whispers of the other maids. A lazy breeze stirred the drapes on the arched bay windows. Madam's chest heaved as she fumbled for her monocle.

"What did you say your name was—"

"Velma, ma'am. Velma Brooks."

"Well, Miss Brooks. That's quite a speech for a domestic." Velma stood erect, eyes front, as madam studied the new employee through her monocle. "Why, you're an uppity darkie."

"As I said, ma'am, I'm—"

"Shut up; you're fired. That's what you are."

"But why? Just because—"

"I said, you're fired! Certainly with a college education, you can understand that."

Velma snatched the white cap from her head and crumpled it in her hand. She thought of throwing it to the floor or in madam's face, but decided against it. She unlocked the French doors and stormed down the hall, her footfalls filling it with clicking echoes. The other maids feigned preoccupation with their duties, but as she passed, they stopped to watch Velma take off the uniform as she walked. Descending the marble staircase, she overheard the whisperings. "Didn't I tell you, Leona?" Velma paused on the staircase to listen. "You owe me a dollar, girl. I tol' you that chile wasn't gonna last one day with her dicty self. Think she too good to mop floors. C'mon, Leona, pay up."

At the corner of 131st Street and Seventh Avenue, Velma rubbed a tree stump outside the Lafayette Theatre. The Tree of Hope, as it was called, granted luck and fortune among artists in Harlem. Velma needed that luck. While she had been prolific over the last five years, her efforts to publish her work had proved futile. With no publishing credits to pat herself on the back for and no job, she felt defeated and hopeless.

After receiving her bachelor's degree from Barnard, she had since been getting sour tastes of the real world. As a high school student, she had read books and newspapers to Mrs. Eleanor Dawson, an aging, blind woman who, for years, had been Mother's employer. Indebted to the bright and patient teenage girl who would jump at the opportunity to attend college, Mrs. Dawson made provisions in her will before she died which paid for a four-year college education for Elvira's little girl. When the free ride was over, Velma had to pay her own way through life. She wasn't having much luck.

She had submitted numerous poems and short stories to periodicals and literary magazines since graduating from Barnard. But each submission was returned to her, most accompanied by a form rejection letter. A few said absolutely nothing, leaving Velma to wonder if her work had been read at all. Whatever the reasons, all rejections hurt.

When she had decided at Barnard to become a writer, there were virtually no other Negro women—aside from Phillis Wheatley, Lucy Terry, and Alice Dunbar-Nelson—that she knew of. Where had the notion come from, she often asked herself. Maybe Roland was right six years ago. The only contemporary women writers she knew of as a young girl—published, celebrated writers—were white. But she felt her experience was a galaxy removed from the Elizabeth Brownings, the Edith Whartons, the Gertrude Steins. Where exactly did she fit in, she wondered, her questions echoing back to her unanswered.

She couldn't fight her need to write. She knew in her gut that if she couldn't create, she'd just as soon wither. She would continue her work, despite the odds. One day, she'd show them.

The year was 1925, the year following the premiere of Gershwin's *Rhapsody in Blue* at Aeolian Hall. The dawn of the Jazz Age. The celebrated epoch of Freudianism. The era of unprecedented permissiveness. Prohibition. Gangsters. Bathtub gin. Flappers. Douglas Fairbanks and Mary Pickford were the matinee idols of the silent screen, Rudolph Valentino and Theda Bara the sex symbols. Negro authors were being published widely now. For the Roaring Twenties, they were the new vanguard. Exotic. Primitive. Raw. Provocative. A reservoir of fresh voices. A cultural vogue, this New Negro Renaissance supplied Velma with artistic fuel for inspiration and perseverance. And it compounded her frustration, since her work had scarcely been acknowledged. With the likes of Hughes, Fauset, Cullen, Hurston, and McKay to inspire her, Velma wanted to add her voice to the choir.

A streetcar's clanging bell snapped Velma from her fantasies. She was not in the mood for walking and decided to take the trolley. She stepped on the platform, reaching into her pocket for fare. Instead, she pulled out a weathered copy of *Cane,* Jean Toomer's critically acclaimed novel and her constant companion. She and the driver exchanged quizzical glances. "Fare's five cents, miss." She realized she had no money. But she went through the motion of searching her pockets just the same. "Go on, I got it." Behind her, a dapper elderly gentleman dressed in a dusty pin-striped suit, spats, and a straw boater with a bent brim smiled. A wooden cane rested in the crook of his arm, and his indigo complexion reminded her of her father's. "Go on," he said, "you want to ride, don't you?" Velma thanked him, boarded the streetcar, and sat toward the back. She parted the brittle, dog-eared pages she'd read dozens of times since the book's publication in 1923 and attempted to read them again. During the trolley-car ride through a thriving metropolis, she tried to lose herself in the rural Southern settings of Toomer's backwoods characters. But Becky's one-room shack wouldn't come into focus the way it normally did. Preoccupied with her financial problems, she couldn't concentrate. With no income. Few choices. Bleak prospects. She had applied for an apartment, but without money to pay the rent, she'd be forced to remain at home. But Mother would love that; anything to keep her daughters at home, to fill the emptiness Father left behind. I have to find another job, she thought, and soon.

2

Louise tilted her head, glancing upward at a recently erected skyscraper. The sun stroked waves of warmth on her face and neck. She shaded her eyes with a gloved hand, looking at the address above the revolving door over the Art Deco design. She checked it against the newspaper clipping in her hand and stole one last glance at her reflection in the glass. Straightening her dress, the only good dress she owned, she tightened the bow at the base of the V-shaped neckline. A herd of office workers charged past her. Bankers. Brokers. Shoe-shine boys. She pushed through the revolving door and waited for the elevator. The brass doors parted, unloading a stampede of passengers. A uniformed elevator operator, in strapped pillbox cap, sat in the corner on a stool. "Going up!"

She walked through the glass doors of the seventeenth floor and approached the matronly receptionist.

"Can I help you, miss?"

"I'm here to see Mr. Armstrong."

"You have an appointment?"

"Yes. I telephoned this morning."

"Fill this out." The receptionist handed her an application. "I'll tell Mr. Armstrong you're here. Your name?"

Louise sat, crossed her legs, and filled in the blanks. The Beaute Strap shoe caused her foot to itch and she bent over to scratch it. The shoes belonged to Velma, whose feet were smaller than hers. Sensing she was being stared at, she looked up. A handsome man met her eyes with a smile. He waited for the elevator, puffing a cigar. Hands in pockets, he rocked back and forth on his heels and tipped his hat. Louise blushed, avoiding his gaze. She wrote her name, home address, and date of birth, peeking at the man through the corner of her eye. She found him attractive, admiring his impeccable dress, the gold watch hanging from his vest pocket. He reminded her of Ramon Novarro the movie star. The elevator arrived and a masculine voice announced, "Going down!" The man winked at her, tipped his hat again, then disappeared behind the brass doors.

Though she was attracted to the Novarro look-alike, she had learned through painful coming-of-age experiences, to keep her distance. Men wanted her, she felt, for all the wrong reasons. To them she was ornamental, a showpiece, devoid of feelings and emotions, lacking intelligent thoughts. She regarded herself as more than a cavity attached to a torso and limbs. Unless the men who pursued her did likewise, they didn't stand a chance.

"Have a seat, Miss"— The balding, middle-aged gentleman with a protruding stomach and graying mustache looked quickly at the application— " Brooks. Louise Brooks. Have a seat. I'll be right with you."

She sat in the tiny office. A cloud of stale cigarette smoke hovered above his desk. The walls reeked of nicotine. Sun rays exposed the streaked windows of the crammed room and floating dust particles. The telephone rang.

"Yeah," Mr. Armstrong grunted into the mouthpiece, a cigarette dangling from his thin lips. "Tell him I'm out to lunch. No. Tell him I'm gone for the day. Never mind. Just tell him I'm on vacation . . . What? . . . I don't give a damn what month it is! Tell him whatever you want. Oh, and Miss Thigpen, hold all my calls. I can't get any work done around here." He slammed the telephone down. Louise recoiled. Mr. Armstrong chuckled. "Sorry about that, young lady. Don't be afraid." He gazed at her over the rim of his glasses. He shuffled papers, folded his arms behind his head, and tilted back in his chair. "So, uh, Miss . . ."

"Brooks, sir."

"Yes, Miss Brooks. You're interested in our secretarial position, right?"

"Yes, sir. I telephoned this morning—"

"It says here," he picked up the application and read, "that you type, take shorthand dictation. Hmmm. Had any experience?"

"No, sir."

Mr. Armstrong rocked in his chair, causing the noisy springs to squeak. He looked gravely at Louise, who spoke quickly.

"But that's because," Louise continued before he became discouraged, "I just graduated high school this past January. Class of '25."

"Yeah, I saw that. So, what've you been doing since?"

"Well, my mother's a beautician. I worked for her awhile."

"My wife does that sort of thing, you know. Why'd you stop? Working for your mother, I mean."

"Oh, I guess I just wanted to get out on my own. Get a good job, you know, maybe save some money."

"And you should, you should. Pretty girl like you." He leaned forward and the chair squeaked again. Louise stiffened. Her smile went sour. "Don't be so nervous," Mr. Armstrong said, patting her gloved hand. He laughed, choking on phlegm, his belly shaking. A nervous smile crept into Louise's lips. "Got any plans for college?"

"No. My sister Velma is the brains in the family. She—"

"When can you start?"

"You mean I got the job?"

"I wouldn't ask if you didn't."

"But I didn't take a test or—"

"You want the job or don't you?"

"Oh . . . I mean, yes . . . thank you, Mr. . . . ."

"Armstrong. Remember the name. I'll be your boss."

"Thank you, Mr. Armstrong," she said, reaching across the cluttered desk to shake his hand, businesslike, as Mother told her to do.

"I gave you the job because I like you. You're a nice, serious girl who wants to do something for herself; grab the opportunity; claim her independence. I admire that in a girl," he claimed, undressing her with his eyes. He imagined her naked in a hotel room, on all fours. "Report to Miss Thigpen, our receptionist, Monday morning, eight-thirty sharp, all right?" He extended his hand.

"Yes, sir." Louise stood and again shook his strong hand. Her hands were hot and sweaty inside the gloves. "You won't regret it, sir."

"I have no doubt." He squeezed her hand and lingered a second, then rubbed his hands together as she closed the door behind her.

She stood at the elevator thinking, a smile on her face. Now she could buy this, put a down payment on that, establish credit. Miss Thigpen's telephone rang. "Yes? . . . No, sir, not to me. . . . What on earth makes you say that? . . ."

Louise hummed while waiting for the elevator.

"Excuse me, miss." Miss Thigpen covered the mouthpiece with her hand. "Before you go, Mr. Armstrong would like to speak to you again."

"Certainly," Louise replied, retracing her steps to his office. He probably forgot to tell me about the salary, she thought. I can't believe I didn't have to take a test. But, then Mother was right when she said, *Present yourself like—*

"Miss Brooks." Mr. Armstrong was standing. "Would you please have a seat."

Hands clasped behind his back, he studied her over his glasses before he spoke. His face was flushed. "I was looking at your application here. And, I noticed something I hope you're able to explain."

"I'm sure I can, sir."

"Let's hope so." He lit a cigarette. "I was just wondering about your address."

"Address?"

"Where you live?"

"Yes?"

"It says here that you live on West 141st Street."

"Yes?"

"One, four, one."

"Yes, sir."

He paused, his eyes revealing something she hadn't seen earlier. "Well, unless I'm wrong," he said, "and I don't believe I am, that's not the Bronx, that's . . . Harlem."

"Yes it is."

"Where the . . . coloreds live?"

"I don't understand, sir."

"Neither do I." His ears turned red. "Why do you live in Harlem of all places?"

"I was born and raised there."

"But, you're . . ." His voice trailed off. He grimaced. "You're not colored— what I'm trying to say is that you're not Negro, are you?"

"Yes, sir, I am."

"C'mon, you're white." He removed his glasses. "I mean, you look white. I don't get it."

"What's the problem, sir?"

"What's the problem? I can't hire you, that's the problem."

"But you just did."

"That was before you tricked me."

"I didn't trick you, sir," she said. "I just applied for this—"

"Look, Miss Brooks, if that's your real name, I'm afraid there's been a mistake. We're a respectable insurance firm. We don't hire coloreds, except for cleaning, mopping, that sort of thing. Now, don't get me wrong. It's not my rule. I take orders like everybody else, you know. Besides, I fail to find the humor in a prank of such a bizarre nature. Good day."

Louise walked briskly from his office, slamming the door.

Colored or white, what's the difference? she thought, furious. I can do the stupid job. He hired me, didn't he? Sensing that the eyes of strangers were watching her, she struggled to maintain a cool countenance. How in God's name will I be able to get a job? I enjoyed working with Mother but it paid so little compared to what I could be earning. After all, I didn't get my high school diploma for nothing. Ever since high school, she'd envisioned herself as a hardworking, versatile secretary. She'd have a closet full of beautiful clothes, a handsome boss who gave her raises before she found it necessary to ask and, with any luck, a husband. Mr. Armstrong was refusing *her!* Louise shivered at the undeserved humiliation. Where else could she be a secretary other than downtown in the financial district? Harlem was out of the question.

"Excuse me, miss," Miss Thigpen said, confusion wrinkling her face. "You're not *really* colored, are you?"

The strangers turned their heads.

"Yes. I am."

"Well, I'll be darned. You sure coulda fooled me, honey."

"I already did, didn't I?"

Outside, the afternoon sun irritated her, causing her to feel faint. Nausea gripped her stomach. She pulled off the hat, removed the hot gloves and tucked them inside her purse. The dress was uncomfortable, especially the bow. The wool scratched her dry skin. She wanted to rip the bow from the dress, disrobe altogether, even if it was in the middle of Cortlandt Street at twelve o'clock noon.

A red-haired, freckled boy shouted on the corner, "Lemonade! Lemonade! Get your ice-cold lemonade!" A pale woman and her daughter stopped to buy. The mother removed her veiled hat and fanned herself with it. A string of beads about her neck hung to her knees. The lemonade looked cool, soothing. Louise watched them, licking her lips. She considered exchanging her subway fare for a drink, the last change in her purse. She thought of the long walk home, downtown to uptown. Imagining the distance, she decided she wasn't so thirsty. She watched the woman and the girl turning the cups upward toward their mouths. The girl looked at Louise and grinned as Louise swallowed with her.

She weighed her curse. Living as a colored woman. Looking white. Men lusted for her, propositioned her; boys at school, the blue-black watermelon man, the toothless janitor downstairs with the ill-fitting dentures and chapped lips. They wanted her whiteness, her high-yallerness, the long wavy hair. These physical traits denied her true racial origin, and to most colored men, that was a plus.

She loathed them, especially the ugly ones who flattered themselves at her expense. But they didn't matter. A virgin and proud of it, she was saving herself for the right man.

During her childhood people often had stared at Louise when she was with her sisters. Once when she was playing hopscotch with Miriam, neighboring youngsters stopped as they meandered past her house, but didn't ask to play. They never uttered a word. They just stared at Louise. "Do you want to play with us?" Miriam once asked the youngsters.

A boy with an ashen face and a runny nose stepped forward and asked, "Is that your real sister?"

"Yeah, why?" Miriam asked.

"Y'all don't look like sisters." The children laughed.

"So?" Miriam said. "You're Pee Wee Jackson's little brother and y'all don't look alike either."

The boy stuck out his tongue at Miriam, and wiped his nose with a sleeve. "She's white and pretty. You black and ugly like a African. My mama say she don't belong to y'all. She say your mama pro'bly stole her from the white lady she works for."

"Get out of here before I—"

The children scattered, laughing as they fled. Miriam and Louise could hear them yelling in the distance, "She's a African devil! Ugly black witch!" They repeated it, improvising a singsong until Miriam could stand it no longer. She took Louise by the hand and walked her up the staircase into the apartment where Miriam retreated to her bedroom. Louise ran to her mother.

"What's wrong, sugar?" Elvira hooked an arm around Louise, and buried the child's teary face in her long skirt. "What's the matter with Mother's baby girl?" Louise stopped crying, wiping the tears with dirty hands.

"Is Miriam my real sister?"

"Of course, baby girl."

"Velma too?"

"Uh-huh."

"You my mother?"

"What's this all about, baby?"

"Am I white or colored?"

"You're colored, sugar. What happened?"

"The kids made fun of me, and they called Miriam a black witch."

"Kids don't mean no harm," Elvira said, wiping the child's dirt-streaked cheeks. "They just bein' kids."

"If I'm colored, then why don't I look colored? Why ain't I like you and Father?"

"I don't know why, dumplin'. Colored folks come in all colors, like the rainbow. That's why we so beautiful. You understan' betta when you a lady all grown up."

"I don't want to wait. I want to be white."

Mother's smile became stern. She cupped Louise's face in her hands. "You a Negro chile. You hear, dumplin'? You came from me and Father. Ain't nobody's fault the white blood you got showed up mo' than the colored. Now, you can fool yo'self and maybe other folks if you like." With her thumb, she wiped a suspended tear from the corner of Louise's eye. "But you can't fool God!"

Louise was remembering those words as the train snorted its way into the Cortlandt Street station. She ran to catch it, grateful she'd saved her fare. She could have lemonade at home. I'm a grown lady now, just about, and Mother said I would understand by now, but I don't. Where will I get a job without them knowing? I won't be a maid; I can't. I'm as white as the women I'd be taking orders from. They probably wouldn't even hire me. It's just not fair. I'll have to lie about my address next time.

There were no empty seats on the subway, so she stood. A young blond man reading the *Saturday Evening Post* looked up and offered his. Louise was grateful and sat, crossing her legs. Peering over his magazine as he swayed with the subway's turbulent rhythm, the blond man watched her, unaware that she was living as a colored woman she thought, looking white.

3

Children played gladiators amid the ruins of an abandoned building, using sticks as swords, garbage can lids for shields. A few houses down, others played hide and seek in crates. Little girls in knee socks jumped rope and chanted:

> "Once upon a time
> Goose drank wine
> Monkey did the Shimmy on the
>   trolley car line.
> Trolley car broke
> Monkey choke
> And they all went to heaven
>   in an old tin boat."

Miriam watched a young boy in knickers and mismatched argyle socks drink from a fire hydrant, head bent, tongue lapping the running water. His playmates huddled around him, they pushed and shoved for a chance to quench their thirst. Suddenly, the *Me first!* bickering turned into a fist fight. Two youngsters threw punches and kicks at each other. They wrestled on the ground, rolling and tumbling, as the others cheered their favorite.

"Y'all shouldn't fight each other like that." Miriam broke up the fight, holding the contenders at bay.

"Let me go, lady!" the boy with the bloody nose demanded, swinging at the air, squirming and twisting to pry himself loose from her grip.

"If you want to fight," Miriam said gently, stooping to wipe the blood with her handkerchief, acting as a barrier between them, "then fight the real enemy. This boy is not your enemy. We're all we have. Don't go around fighting with each other."

The children laughed at Miriam, startling her, as if they'd thrown cold water in her face. "Lady, I said let me go!" The boy freed himself of her grip, and the lot of them ran around the corner to finish what they'd started.

Half a block away, a store proprietor stood proudly before his shop, arms folded across his butcher's apron. OUR OWN COMMUNITY GROCERY & DELICATESSEN. Paper signs covered the display window: PEPSI-COLA 5¢. MILK 6¢. 5 LBS. OF SUGAR 22¢. "Leave them be," he said. "Boys gotta be boys. How you feeling today, Miriam?"

"Just fine, Sam. How's business?"

"Could be better, but I won't complain. Your family?"

"Everybody's fine. Velma started a new job today. Mother's still straightening heads."

"How's that pretty little sister of yours?"

"She ain't so little no more, but pretty as ever. Graduated high school this year. And your family?"

"Everybody's kickin'."

"Your store's looking mighty fine, Sam. Mighty fine, indeed." She looked around, surveying the place with a slow sweep of the eye, nodding her head in approval.

"What you need today?"

"I thought to stop by Mother's house on the way home. Think I'll take her a pound of bacon."

"Come on inside. Take a load off your feet."

The store was nearly dark. Wooden floorboards creaked beneath their heels as they entered. Sam moved behind the counter and adjusted the slicing blade.

"Mighty nice thing you're doing, Sam."

"What's that?"

"It's good to see our people doing for their own. We need more stores like this."

"Yeah, but it's hard."

"How you mean?"

"Most folks buy from Murray down the street." He chuckled to himself. "It's funny. I never would've thought it. But colored people rather buy from a Jew instead of their own."

"That's a problem with our people. We never—"

"How's that?" Sam placed a slice of bacon on the counter for Miriam.

"Looks good, Sam. Slice it thick just like that."

"Ain't seen you around much lately. Where you been keeping yourself?" he asked, his eyes focused on the slicing machine.

"Working for the Movement, like always. But, like the white man's Bible says, 'The harvest is a plenty, yet the workers are so few.'"

Sam wrapped the bacon in wax paper. "That'll be twenty cents."

Miriam handed Sam two shiny dimes. "Speaking of workers, how come we ain't seen you lately?" she asked, knowing he'd come up with some lame excuse.

"Been busy—wife and kids, you know, bills. Just don't have the time." He had been wondering how long it would take her to ask. She had a directness about her, an uncanny way of looking him in the eye, causing him discomfort and guilt when he otherwise felt neither.

"Make time, Sam. You got to make time."

"I guess you're right. Just that I figured things had quieted down since they put him in jail. Seems like folks ain't stirred up as they used to be." Why can't she be like other ladies? he thought, giving her his best smile. My brother'd give his right arm to marry this lady if only she'd give that organization of hers a rest. Just don't seem natural.

"You been hiding in this here store, hiding in the darkness, Sam. Folks are just as stirred as ever. You and I both know Garvey ain't no more guilty of mail fraud than those children out there playing stickball."

"But, I ain't heard of no meetings nowhere," he lied, admiring how pretty she was, acting as if she didn't know it.

"Well, we decided not to have an international convention this year. But there's still meetings at Liberty Hall, you know. Matter fact, there's one tonight." She looked at him sideways, anticipating another poor excuse, but hoping he'd attend, and lend them his great organizational skills.

"I'll think about it."

"Don't think, Sam. Ain't no time to think. I'm looking for you at tonight's meeting, okay?"

"We'll see. You take care of yourself now."

"Tonight, eight o'clock. I'll be looking for you. So long."

Clutching the package in her arm, Miriam stepped into blinding daylight. Harlem's foundation was crumbling at the seams around its dwellers, piece by piece, brick by brick. And no one seemed to notice or care, she thought as she strolled. Broken bottles and cigarette butts mixed with the debris lining the curb. Poverty-stricken families, watching the street activity below, the pulse of the community, hung from windows like wet, tattered clothing set out to dry on the ledge. Miriam studied the shoe-shine men near the newsstand popping soiled, dirty rags upon a clean spit shine; the vegetable vendor lazily pushing his cart, singing his pitch:

> *"I got vegetables today,*
> *So don't go away*
> *Stick around*
> *And you'll hear me say,*
> *Buy 'em by the pound*
> *Put 'em in a sack*
> *Hurry up and get 'em*
> *'Cause I ain't comin' back."*

Miriam frowned, yearning for light at the end of the tunnel. In her mind, Marcus Garvey was that light—radiant, brilliant, divine. For her, he was the messiah.

The last time she had seen him speak at a convention held at Madison Square Garden, thousands of dedicated followers had assembled, even those with the slightest speck of curiosity. They carried banners of red, black, and green, sang the Ethiopian national anthem, and "The Star-Spangled Banner." Such a turnout was palpable proof that the Universal Negro Improvement Association was growing and more effectively reaching out to the Negro masses who no longer held faith in the American way of life. UNIA provided concrete alternatives for the downtrodden, the hungry, the dispossessed.

She recalled how the pandemonium had subsided to a hush when
a burly black man with a pug nose and bulging yellow eyes stepped
to the podium. Dressed in flamboyant, dark blue military regalia, he
gazed into the audience. Purple and white feathered plumes drooped
from his hat. There was a red stripe on the sides of his trousers.
Flanked by his quasi-nobility—the Duke of Nigeria, the Overlord of
Uganda—he began to speak. His Jamaican accent boomed through
amplifiers, ringing with urgency and charisma. "Up, you mighty
Race!" burst from his lips, packed with two-fisted emotion. The
crowd roared, standing on their feet, applauding, stomping, waving
banners—the red, black, and green flags. They simmered down,
resuming their seats, and hung upon his every breath.

"Without a desire to harm anyone," Garvey continued, "the
Universal Negro Improvement Association feels that the Negro
should without compromise or any apology appeal to the same
spirit of racial pride and love as the great white race is doing for its
own preservation, so that while others are raising the cry of a white
America, a white Canada, a white Australia, we also without
reservation raise the cry of a Black Africa. The critic asks, 'Is this
possible?' and the four hundred million courageous Negroes of the
world answer, 'Yes!' "

Thunderous applause shook the auditorium walls. Men puckered
their lips to make sounds of piercing whistles. Ambitious reporters
scribbled hasty notes. Lights flashed from bulky cameras. Miriam
remembered thinking the crowd's enthusiasm might bring down
the walls. Jericho had nothing on these folks.

"Fighting for the establishment of Palestine does not make the
American Jew disloyal; fighting for the independence of Ireland
does not make the Irish-American a bad citizen. Why should
fighting for the freedom of Africa make the Afro-American disloyal
or a bad citizen?"

The audience remained motionless, hypnotized by the moving
orator, this magnificent, larger-than-life presence before them. He
spoke of the promises broken to Negroes following World War I,
and urged his followers to make generous contributions—beyond
the forty-cent dues—to purchase additional ships for the Black Star
Line so the *Yarmouth*, and others like it, could sail them home to
Africa. He encouraged trade with the Caribbean and stressed the
need for more volunteers, more money. He then invited first-time
visitors to the UNIA headquarters at 38 West 135th Street.

Then dues were collected. Garvey's loyal assistants, Miriam
among them, labored up and down the aisles and combed the

balcony. Members and nonmembers alike scrambled through their pockets and purses, tossing dollars, nickels, pennies, birthstones, chains, watches, property deeds—anything of value, anything that would help realize the dream.

Such fire and determination! Miriam thought, reflecting upon that memory as she waited to cross West 141st Street. And now they have conspired against our great leader by putting him in prison. The memory of that convention warmed her, stimulated her. She drew upon it for inspiration. Meantime, she read all she could about Garvey, mostly from his newspaper, *The Negro World.* She read little of anything else and found herself memorizing passages from his eloquent essays. It gave her stamina, propelling her to work diligently at the headquarters, to pass out literature in the community, to visit Speaker's Corner at 135th and Lenox and be uplifted by the soapbox orators, or to serve in Garvey's Black Cross Nurses. Between these activities and her work as a nurse at Harlem Hospital, she had little time for anything else.

Walking up the creaking stairs, she heard her mother's rich laughter. Maybe Mother could do some volunteer work for the movement. Probably not, she realized, since Mother was waiting on Uncle Sam's promises and Jesus. Negroes harboring slave mentalities feared organizing themselves, like Sam the grocer. Rather than mobilize their own forces, acknowledge their strengths, their power in numbers, they complained about colored folks buying from the Jew. No surprise to Miriam. If Sam could find time to attend a meeting, to step back and take inventory of himself, to question and challenge what everyone accepted at face value, then maybe he'd understand why folks bought from Murray instead of him. It had been sixty years since slavery, six years since winning the war, Miriam reflected, discouraged, and what had changed? Conditions for Race people, if anything, were worse.

Miriam held the bacon and purse in one hand, turning the key in the lock with the other. Women's voices and laughter filled her ears. Sharp odors of pressed hair and pomade greeted her nostrils.

4

Elvira stood between the sink and the counter. Her hands were soapy, sleeves pushed up, stockings rolled down below her knees. A customer sat in a chair beside her, sudsy head bent backward into the basin, eyes shut. Elvira's nose itched, and with a soapy forearm she rubbed it vigorously as she heard a key turn in the lock. "Well, look what the cat done dragged in," she declared, smiling at Miriam.

"How's everybody?" Miriam placed the package on the table. "Thought I'd stop by on the way home. Bought you some bacon, Mother."

"Thank you, sugar. Just put it in the icebox."

"I bought it from Sam's," Miriam said, placing the package in the icebox when a thought struck her. "Y'all ain't been buying from Murray, have you?" She looked around the room at Velma boiling a large pot of water and Louise cutting collard greens at the table. Both were expressionless. "What's wrong with my two favorite sisters?"

"Oh, hi, Miriam," Louise said.

"Hi," Velma offered, with a wounded expression.

"What's wrong, Velma?" Miriam approached her at the stove and placed a hand on her shoulder. "How'd your job go?"

"It didn't."

"What?"

"You know your sister," Elvira volunteered from the sink, scrubbing the customer's scalp with a brush. "She opened her mouth and got in trouble—"

"The woman I was working for," Velma said, elaborating, as if correcting her mother, "asked me to teach her how to dance."

"Dance?" Miriam didn't understand.

"Imagine, Miriam," Velma said. "She wanted to learn the Charleston."

Elvira wiped sweat from her forehead. "I ain't never talked back to nobody who puts food on my table."

"Mother!" Velma exclaimed, disappointed her mother didn't side

with her. "It's the principle. I don't plan to spend my life taking
orders from rich women."

"Thas yo' choice, sugar," Elvira replied, "but what else you gonna
do? Sell that writin' stuff of yours?" She chuckled, running water
through the customer's hair. "You ain't sold none of it yet."

"Don't worry, Mother, I will." Velma snatched the cut collards
from Louise at the table and threw them into the boiling pot.
"You'll see."

Elvira knew one day, maybe one day soon, she *would* see. The
love she lavished on her girls was exceeded only by her unflagging
faith in them. Not bad, Elvira would think from time to time, not
bad. What she'd accomplished with her girls was not bad at all.
When she left Atlanta with her husband, a young girl with new life
swelling inside her uterus, and joined the great diaspora to the
Promised Land of the northern industrial cities, she never gave it a
thought that she'd have anything but sons. She would have produced a son each time if her husband had had his way. But half the
world's male population couldn't equal the brains, guts, and independence her daughters possessed and sometimes took for granted,
whether she approved their individual endeavors or not. Listening
to Velma outline what she would and wouldn't do with her life
confirmed what she, her mother, already knew. Now all they had to
do was find husbands.

"Maybe," Miriam said, "I could get you a job at the hospital."

"Thanks," Velma said, "but you know I don't have the stomach."

"Why don't you come with me tonight," Miriam suggested to
Velma. "There's a meeting at Liberty Hall."

"No thanks, Miriam."

"What's wrong with the UNIA?"

"Nothing," Velma said, "nothing at all. It's a wonderful organization." She placed the remainder of the collard greens into the
boiling water. "I'm just not the organization type. I fancy myself as
a one-woman band. Anyway, I got plans."

"What's his name?" Louise said. "And where's he taking you?"

"That reminds me, Miriam," Velma said. "Guess who I saw
today?"

"Who?"

"Guess."

"Roland?"

"God no. I ran into *your* old beau."

"Who, George?"

"In the flesh. He asked about you." Velma liked to tease Miriam about her old boyfriend, which usually embarrassed Miriam into changing the subject.

"Didn't he get married?" Louise asked.

"Yes," Velma said, grinning slyly, "and he's still asking about you—wanted to know if you got married yet."

"Whatever happened between you and him, Miriam?" Louise wanted to know.

"We weren't politically compatible," Miriam said.

"What's politics got to do with love?" Louise asked.

"She means," Velma divulged, "that George refused to move with her to Africa."

"Africa?" Elvira said, pausing from her work at the basin, swinging her head around. "Who's moving to Africa?"

"Miriam," Velma said.

"When, with who, and why?" Elvira said, a soapy, dripping hand resting upon her hip.

"Mother," Miriam said, "that's what UNIA's all about. What you think I've been doing all this time?"

"What you gonna find in Africa," Elvira said, "that you done lost here?"

"Liberia," Miriam said, sticking her chest out. "A country established by American slaves."

"Why in God's name," Elvira said, "would y'all leave one country to start another? Sounds so silly."

"Walk around Harlem," Miriam said, "and you'd know why. Besides, Europeans left to start this country. Nobody thought that was so silly."

"Except maybe King George III of England," Velma joked.

"Well, I'll take Harlem any day," Elvira said, wrapping a towel around the customer's dripping hair, tilting her head forward. "This right here is the black capital of the world. Can't beat it for my money."

"Liberia can," Miriam said, turning her attention toward the customer. "How're you doing, Mrs. Ivy?"

"You lookin' good, girl," Mrs. Ivy replied, damp drying her hair with a towel. "What you been doin'?"

"Still working at Harlem Hospital."

"Eloise getting married this Saturday, you know," Mrs. Ivy said proudly. "She the last girl I'm givin' away in marriage. Stop by and say hello."

"Some people got all the luck," Elvira said, sighing.

"I would," Miriam said, "but there's a rally—"

"Miss Miriam here got more to do than the Lord Himself," Elvira interjected, placing a hot comb on the burner flame. She rubbed a dab of pomade in her palms and massaged it into Mrs. Ivy's scalp. "I wish she spent as much time findin' a husban'."

"Good as she look," Mrs. Ivy assured her, "they'll find her."

"Hope they find Velma too," Elvira suggested, playfully sticking her tongue out at Velma.

"When I'm ready for a husband, I'll get one myself, thank you." Velma was annoyed.

"Did I tell you Velma was engaged once?" Elvira turned to Mrs. Ivy. "He fought the war, come back for her and she said no. Now, he married to Jessie Mayfield's daughter with three or four kids. I bet she sorry now."

"The truth is, Mrs. Ivy," Velma defended herself, "I chose to write instead of marrying a man who didn't understand that part of me."

"Well, shut my mouth!" Mrs. Ivy slapped her thigh. "Now, there's a gal with some spunk!"

"I just hope," Miriam said cautiously, recognizing Velma's sensitivity and the delicacy of the issue she was about to raise, "that the fad is still in force by the time you get published."

"It's not a fad, Miriam," Velma replied defensively, as Miriam had suspected she would.

Elvira turned to Mrs. Ivy. "Them two rather take on the problems of the world instead of findin' a coupla husbans."

Given the ambitions of her two daughters, strange as they might be to Elvira, she tried, with every speck of restraint she had to steer clear of their business. Their lives were just that—theirs. She'd already lived hers. No matter what she thought about their passions—Miriam's drastic plans about moving to a part of the world she'd never seen, or Velma's yearning to be celebrated by a public that didn't know she existed—she kept it to herself; discouragement had not been her way with them. But she was, admittedly, vexed about their attitudes toward finding husbands, and couldn't help but speak her thoughts. She didn't want them to be alone in the world. Being alone was something that had happened to her; she hadn't chosen it. And with all the brains and know-how the world had to offer, her girls were *choosing* to be alone. It baffled her. Miriam was already approaching twenty-seven, Velma right behind her at twenty-four. Louise, at eighteen, still had time. She could imagine the relief Mrs. Ivy must feel, with the last of her brood headed toward the altar. But there was always tomorrow.

"I just don't see this age of the New Negro as a fad, Miriam; it's more than that." Velma got her purse, and fumbling with the pack of Listerine cigarettes, shoved one in her mouth.

"And, what is that, young lady?" Elvira asked, a closed fist resting on her hip.

"All the young girls smokin' now," Mrs. Ivy affirmed. "It ain't like when me and you was young girls."

"Well," Elvira insisted, "if you have to smoke, do it in the house. It ain't ladylike to smoke in public."

Velma took a long drag on the cigarette, standing in the corner with her arms folded, her feet crossed. She eyed Miriam, hoping Miriam was wrong about Negro literature being a trend that wouldn't last long enough for her to establish a career. She picked specks of tobacco from her teeth. The kitchen was a battlefield of conflicting odors. Collard greens and fatback fought lye and peroxide. The clashing scents of black-eyed peas, rice and hair pomade curled on the edges of burnt human hair. For reasons unclear to her, lines from a Paul Laurence Dunbar poem came to her.

> *We wear the mask that grins and lies,*
> *It hides our cheeks and shades our eyes,—*
> *This debt we pay to human guile;*
> *With torn and bleeding hearts we smile,*
> *And mouth with myriad subtleties.*

"There you go again," Elvira shouted to Velma, smiling, breaking her daughter's reverie. "I can always tell when you start thinkin' 'bout that poetry of yours."

"How can you tell, Mother?" Her tone was impatient.

"It's all in your eye, sugar."

"Well, you're wrong. I was thinking about something else."

"Mother!" Louise fanned smoke from her face. "Make Velma put out that nasty cigarette. I can't breathe."

"Go outside," Velma suggested, "where there's plenty of fresh air."

"Now leave her be." Elvira came to Louise's defense. "Baby girl done had her a real bad day too. Can't y'all see her sittin' there like a kicked puppy?"

"What happened?" Miriam stared at Louise across the table.

"She almos' had a good job with a downtown insurance company. Till they figured out she was colored," Elvira said.

"White folks and onions," Miriam said, shaking her head in disgust, "make you wanna cry."

"I know where they hirin' colored gals," Mrs. Ivy claimed. "My niece work for Madame Walker."

"I thought she was dead," Miriam said, perplexed.

"Who is she?" Louise asked. "I never heard of her."

"Honey," Mrs. Ivy continued, "Madame C. J. Walker was the first self-made woman millionaire. An' she was colored jus' like us."

"A millionaire?" Louise's eyes brightened.

"That's right, honey. Madame say colored gals gotta right to be go'geous too. She invented all kinda stuff to improve Negro hair. She even invented this here hot comb your mama's about to use on my head right now—"

"She ain't invented no hot comb," Elvira interrupted.

"Did too," Mrs. Ivy rebutted.

"No she didn't. Just made it better for Race hair, that's all."

"You sure?"

"Don't you think I know my biznezz?" Elvira gazed down at her with a look of challenge. She picked up the hot comb from the burner and shook it, gray smoke escaping the steel teeth as it cooled. Parting a handful of hair, she pressed the comb against the scalp, which sizzled upon contact.

"Anyway," Mrs. Ivy continued, "the woman couldn't even read, but she built up this here empire they call it, an' started trainin' people to work for her. My niece work for her now." She turned to Elvira. "You know, Ruthie's oldest girl."

"Yeah," Elvira said. "Now would you be still?"

"What does she do?" Louise demanded.

"First, they train her in the C. J. Walker Beauty System and now she travel all over the country selling stuff for hair. She been a Walker agent since before the war."

"Really?" Louise couldn't contain her enthusiasm. "She travels around just selling beauty products?"

"Around? Honey, she done been to Paris and Rome. Even the West Indies."

"Oh, Mother, that's for me!" Louise said, suddenly feeling better than she had all day. Mr. Armstrong could keep his job. She had Paris and Rome to conquer. "How do I start?"

"I'll call my niece if you—ouch, Brooks! You gonna burn my scalp off with that thing!"

"Now, I done tol' you to keep your behin' still," Elvira repeated. "You the most tender-headed somebody I know. An' thas sayin' somethin' after raisin' Velma." She winked at Velma, who returned it.

"You need a job too?" Mrs. Ivy said, turning to Velma.

"Not until this afternoon," Velma said wearily. "Did I tell you? This lady I was working for saw a Broadway show last night, some show called *Runnin' Wild*—"

"Yeah," Mrs. Ivy said, nodding her head. "I think I heard about that show."

"Well, she said they did the Charleston and that hussy—"

"Velma!" Elvira shot her a look.

"Excuse me, Mother. That *lady* wanted me to teach her. She didn't ask anybody else but me. And, those . . ." She paused, looking at Elvira, careful not to release the foul language at the tip of her tongue. "The maids were laughing and taking bets on how long I'd last. I don't even know how to Charleston myself."

"You don't Charleston?" Mrs. Ivy was astonished. "Everybody Charlestons."

"I'm not much of a dancer."

"You ain't gotta be much o' nothin'," Mrs. Ivy assured her. "C'mon, I can show you the 'uptown' version. White folks do the stiff, 'downtown.' "

"Now I done seen it all." Elvira raised her hands, testifying to the heavens. "Ol' lady Methuselah gonna teach youngblood here how to dance. This I gotta see." She pulled up a chair, sat in it, and crossed her arms.

Mrs. Ivy stood and began humming the "Charleston Rag." Executing simple steps, she paused for Velma to follow. Velma declined, sitting at the table shaking her head and laughing. "No, that's all right, Mrs. Ivy. I'll learn some other time."

"Oh, pleeze, Missy Brooks," Mrs. Ivy mimicked, play-acting with Velma, "let dis li'l ol' slave gal teach ya how t' Charleston. Cuz ef ah can't teach ya, ah wonts be able t' picks ma cotton in de moanin'." She folded her hands beneath her chin and tilted her head to the side, batting her eyelashes.

"Okay." Velma was unable to restrain her laughter. The others laughed with her as Mrs. Ivy lined them up, one by one, and demonstrated the first step.

"You sure you ain't too old to be doin' this here?" Elvira inquired.

"Old? I'm goin' to a weddin' on Saturday, girl. I'm just gettin' in shape; whatchu talkin' 'bout?"

The five women moved two steps back, touched their toes, and reversed the step. One, two, three, kick! They turned around, their arms flailing, touching hands to heels, wiggling their hands in the air. Elvira, having started off on the wrong foot, studied the others a moment. Slowly, she slipped into step and got the hang of it, and she danced with more fervor than the others. The kitchen floor thumped with dancing, shuffling feet. Jumping, boiling pots provided a percussive backdrop to Mrs. Ivy's humming. Downstairs, a neighbor banged on the ceiling. Elvira began coughing and covered her mouth as her stomach contracted. She stopped dancing and gripped her stomach, groping her way to a chair.

"Mother, you all right?" Louise ran to her, helping her into the chair.

Miriam ran cold water over a cloth and applied it to Elvira's forehead. Velma knelt, rubbing her mother's hand. "Just take it easy," Velma soothed her.

"Let me look at her," Miriam said, nudging Velma aside. "I'm the nurse here."

"See how good my girls is?" Elvira boasted to Mrs. Ivy out of breath. "They take good care of me. They good girls."

"You all right, Brooks?" Mrs. Ivy's face was pale.

"You gonna be fine, Mother," Miriam assured her. "You been warned about your high blood pressure before, and you ain't danced in years."

"Hmmm," Velma said, giggling. "I won't mention any names, but a moment ago, somebody was soooo worried about *Mrs. Ivy* being too old."

5

A humid early evening breeze blew through Velma's hair. Heading south on Fifth Avenue, she carried a thick portfolio of neatly typed manuscripts meticulously wrapped in tissue paper, which she sheltered with maternal vigilance. These were her babies. Embryonic ideas conceived in a womb of artistry, they had swirled in her thoughts, and spoken to her in tiny voices. From her need to create, to play God with characters and fate, they came forth, pushing their way into the exterior world. After various stages of rewrites, honing and tightening until she could bounce a quarter off the prose, she wished to share them with the world, to live her life out loud.

Threatening clouds filled the sky. Hearing a rumble of thunder, Velma quickened her pace. The heels of her patent-leather shoes clicked against the asphalt. She stopped at 136th Street, and checked the address in her pocket. She had one block to go. Rain began falling, the sound of silver coins hitting the pavement. Before her eyes, the address melted into a stream of blue running ink. She remembered the address, but not the apartment number. Turning up her collar and holding on to her feathered hat against the wind, she ran, stepping in and over puddles which seemed to have been around for a week. More than herself, she protected the portfolio, clutching it tightly to her bosom. Through the downpour, she located the building and dashed up the stairs of the three-story brownstone. Inside the vestibule, near the mailboxes, she caught her breath. She checked the manuscripts and sighed, thanking God that they weren't wet. Thunder roared across the heavens, in drum rolls that evoked childhood terrors. She brushed her shoulders and hat, attempting to smooth out her appearance, wondering why she had bothered to come at all.

She'd heard through the literary grapevine that women weren't too welcome here. Great, she thought, story of my life. Had she allowed life's obstacles to stand in her way, she never would have attended Barnard; nor would she have embarked upon a career as writer. Tonight she'd find out for herself. She'd never been one to accept hearsay. She ignored the gossip. There were more pressing matters at hand, such as the mess she must look like coming in from the storm.

She studied the scribbled names above the mailboxes, but not one looked familiar. She tried assembling the letters in her mind, but they refused to crystallize. Ascending the staircase, she heard an infant's muffled cry down the hall. On tiptoe, she pressed her ear against a closed door where a couple moaned in intense lovemaking. Now, they're smart! she thought. What else should one be doing during a storm? At the opposite end of the hall, she was startled by a burst of laughter, the overlapping voices of people which emanated from a third-floor room. She climbed the stairs. As she neared the door, she could make out some words. She knocked, and a well-dressed woman with a hand muff and matching hat answered, surprising Velma, putting her suspicions and the hearsay to rest.

"Excuse me, is this the Harlem Writers Workshop?" she asked, nervously fingering the wet hat and her frizzy hair beneath it.

"If it isn't, honey, we're all in the wrong apartment."

Velma entered, removing her hat and scarf. Surveying the apartment, she noticed a dozen or so men mingling among themselves, laughing and engaging in what sounded like heated intellectual debate. The woman who had opened the door was the only other woman present, and Velma was grateful, if only for the one. A few men nodded perfunctory hellos in her direction, but no one introduced himself or asked to take her wet clothing. The majority of them wore three-piece and double-breasted suits like uniforms, and broad, colorful neckties with tiny knots at the collar. Some smoked pipes—the stuffy, college-professor types. They huddled ceremoniously around a lanky figure whose face Velma couldn't see. None of the faces looked famous or remotely familiar.

"We'll begin our weekly meeting in a moment," a man said, speaking from the center of the parlor. "But first we'd like to congratulate Zachary Rudolph." The speaker faced the man whose face Velma couldn't see. "Zack sold his first novel to Knopf a few days ago." There was applause, a few whistles. "We're especially proud as the workshop family of this writer," the speaker continued, "because Zack's manuscript was, in a manner of speaking, born out of the Harlem Writers Workshop." He turned to Zachary. "Anything you'd like to add? Would you like to lend some advice or a bit of the advance money?" The men laughed and patted Zachary on the back, shaking his hand.

"Which one is he?" Velma whispered to the woman. "I can't see from here."

"Who? Zack? He's the slim one. The only one without a jacket and tie."

"There is something I'd like to say." Zachary turned to face the celebrants. Velma could see him clearly now, as the others sat to listen. He was tall and thin; his large eyes seemed warm to her. A pencil-thin mustache spread across the length of his lip. He was dark, smooth chocolate in complexion; his cheeks glowing with mother's milk, Velma thought. His teeth were perfectly aligned. Indeed, he was without jacket or tie, yet he stood out, a flamingo amid a herd of ostriches. His shabby clothes—a wrinkled, fading shirt inside an Army green pullover sweater, uncreased pleated pants with sagging cuffs, baggy at the knees, and a pair of beat-up wing-tip shoes that looked as if they'd belonged to his father, perhaps his grandfather, made him appear informal, unpretentious, bohemian. "I hope," he continued, "that clearing my first major hurdle is encouraging. I can only emphasize hard work, dedication, hustling; to want it more than anything else, because now is the time; the industry is ripe and ready. And, with the talent, dedication and perseverance of some of the writers I know here personally, I feel that many future dustcovers will bear our names; those of us who live and breathe for the written word. What else can I say? Thank you."

"When will the book be out?" a voice rang above the murmur.

"About October or so." Zachary turned away, hands in his pockets, and stood alone against the wall away from the others. Velma watched him, impressed with his boyish good looks, his soft-spoken, gentle manner, his *Aw, shucks!* modesty. She sensed a genuine vulnerability about him that attracted her; a vulnerability she almost never detected in other men. She wondered if he was married, and looked at his fingers for telltale signs.

"What's his name again?" Velma said, nudging the woman.

"Zack. Zachary Rudolph."

"I bet he'll spend that money on his girlfriend," Velma said, fishing for personal details. "He seems the type."

"I hear he's single," the woman said. "I don't know how he manages, cute as he is, don't you think?"

"He's all right," Velma lied, trying to ignore her thumping heart. "Not exactly my type. By the way, what's your name? I'm Velma Brooks." She extended her hand.

"Margaret Johnson. Pleased to meet you."

"Is this your first time too?" Velma asked.

"No, I'm here every week, but this is yours. You write?"

"Yes. Poetry, a few short stories. You know, I must say"—Velma lowered her voice, sharing a confidence with the woman—"I was glad to see another woman writer here—"

"No, no. I'm no writer. I'm engaged to one—Emerson Worth. He's the one who spoke earlier. He lives here."

"May I have your attention please?" Emerson said. "The Harlem Writers Workshop will now come to order." The members huddled in a semicircle in the smoke-filled parlor. They sat on chairs, stacks of books, the sofa, the floor, armrests. An empty chair sat facing the semicircle. As Velma eyed it, her pulse began racing. She suddenly noticed that the room was stuffy. The windows were open, but the wind had died down, rendering the air humid and still. The rain had diminished to a drizzle, tapping faint rhythms on the ledge. The aroma of fried chicken and potatoes from another apartment filled her nostrils, and her stomach growled a response. She shifted her thoughts from food and hunger and hoped no one could hear her stomach. She lit a cigarette, and several heads turned in her direction. Placing the portfolio at her feet, she heard snickering in the room and assumed an inside joke was circulating.

"I would just like to say," Emerson continued, "that we are here to create and discuss serious works of poetry and fiction of contemporary themes, and to keep the readings short so everybody gets a chance. I'm sure you all recall the few instances where some of our past *female* members read long, tedious, so-called short stories about voodoo ladies this and conjure women that and so on." Voices snickered behind Velma, and she turned to see to whom they belonged, wondering about Emerson's emphatic reference and what it meant. "Now I'm certainly not here to tell anyone what to write. But I can exercise control over what's read in my workshop . . . or in my house, for that matter. The point is, we already have one Zora Hurston and that's enough—probably too much for some of us. But, the moral of this story is, everybody can't be her." He looked at Velma. "I see we have a newcomer this evening. You, with the cigarette. Would you tell us your name?" A sarcastic grin was smeared across his face, and she realized that lighting the cigarette had been a mistake. She didn't need to draw attention to herself; especially as the only woman writer among them.

"Good evening. I'm Velma Br——"

"Would you please stand so everybody can hear you."

She stood, convinced she disliked this Emerson guy. "My name is Velma Brooks." She nodded to the others.

"Did you want to listen in or—"

"I have something to read. A short story."

"Good. It's not a long, long short story, is it?"

"Five pages?"

"I trust you heard my opening announcement—"

"Couldn't help it." Velma extinguished the cigarette, opened the portfolio, removed the five typewritten pages, and walked to the chair in the center of the room, sensing every pair of eyes upon her.

"This is a piece I wrote recently," Velma announced, making eye contact with her audience, wondering again about the *past* female members Emerson referred to, and why they hadn't returned. "I think it needs polish and that's why I'm choosing to read it. I call it 'Savannah the Soothsayer.' " Again, she glanced around the room for reactions. A man covered his mouth, leaned over and whispered to his neighbor. A chorus of coughing and throat clearing disturbed the silence. She began reading slowly, fluidly, articulating each syllable. Midway through the page, she heard more snickering. Someone in the back talked in hushed tones, conflicting with her recitation. She looked at Margaret, who was giggling with her beau, Emerson. Enough, they were starting to get on her nerves, and her patience chipped away to the ticking of a clock she hadn't heard until now. Zachary stood against the wall in a corner, his face obscured by shadows. Nevertheless, Velma could see that he was not laughing, but instead listening intently to her story. He stepped forward, out of the shadow into the light.

"Excuse me for interrupting, miss," Zachary asserted himself with the others, "but I think we could show a little more respect for our guest. As her fellow artists, we could exercise more sensitivity. At one time or another, we've all been where she is now, some of us are still there."

As he spoke, she recalled what she'd heard about this workshop. Everything she'd been told, or more precisely, warned against, was coming to pass before her eyes. She could no longer smell the chicken and potatoes; her hunger was gone. Her stomach began to somersault. She felt hot, her damp clothes sticking to her skin, and she wished for a strong gust of wind to sweep through the stuffiness in the room—taking some of these jive niggers with it—and evaporate the beads of perspiration on her forehead. Gazing outside the window, she noticed that the drizzle had become a misty spray when the recollection jolted her. The horror stories she'd been told about this place came from other women, who had vowed never to return, not men. If she could have her way, she would snap her fingers and vanish before their eyes.

"Thank you, Mr. Rudolph." Velma met his eyes with hers.

"But, Zack," Emerson protested with laughter in his voice, "didn't you hear my—"

"Let her finish first. We don't know where the story's going." Zachary shook his head, resuming his corner in the shadows. "Please continue, miss. I'm listening."

Velma resumed, but her attention was divided. Her eyes read the words, her ears tuned into the low murmurs. She wondered whether she should quit, continue, or cuss them out. The snickering grew into raucous laughter, and though she knew that Savannah, her main character, was humorous, she was certain they were laughing at her, not with her. Margaret laughed louder than everyone else. Velma shoved the manuscript inside the tissue paper, folded and tied the portfolio. She grabbed her hat and jacket, turned again to the group, and to what she construed to be forced hysteria. "Let me say that I'm appalled by your behavior!" An instantaneous silence seized the room, and from the expressions on their faces, she knew they were shocked by her outburst. "It's no wonder that you're all still in workshops instead of bookstores. What *is* a wonder, is how someone as professional and considerate as Mr. Rudolph here could've emerged from the likes of you!"

"Hey, Zack!" someone yelled. "I think she got the hots for you, man. Won't you cool her off."

"Don't you think," Emerson asked, "you're being a little too . . . personal about all this?"

"My work *is* personal. It's me. I can't separate the two, but something tells me you're the type who can." She turned and stopped short. "Oh, yeah, and another thing; there could never be too many Zora Hurstons. There's too many of you and not enough of her."

She pushed her way through the jungle of three-piece and double-breasted suits; most of them stepped out of her way. Through the door and down the stairs she hastened into the streets, into the night. She headed north on Fifth Avenue, retracing her steps. No rain fell from the sky. It poured instead, down the slopes of her cheeks.

6

That was no *workshop*. It was a fraternity house, Velma thought, furious with herself for letting them get to her.

The plume in her hat came undone. She stopped at a lamppost, and placed her portfolio and purse on the sidewalk. Attempting to repair the feather, her unsteady hands made it worse. Picking up the portfolio and purse, she continued, crossing 136th Street for the second time, locked into her thoughts.

What was it about men who got their kicks from humiliating women and reducing them to tears? There was something sinister about the human condition where individuals vied for quasi-superiority among one another. She would have expected mortification from a room full of white folks, but when her own people behaved like this, the situation assumed another significance. If they knew how they had wounded her ego and crushed her self-esteem, they might have behaved with a bit of compassion. She expected creative artists to be more sensitive, more thoughtful than most people. These men were insolent and cruel. Why should it matter that she was a woman?

Margaret attended the meetings but obviously kept her mouth shut. She was bourgeois and overdressed, and Velma resented her condescending reference to Zachary as *the only one without a jacket and tie.* She would have liked to ask the woman if they were writers or fashion models on assignment?

Velma didn't know where to go, or what to do. Home was out of the question. She didn't need, and wasn't in the mood for, Mother's well-meaning patronization. The entire day had proved to be one of incessant kicks in the butt. She thought of visiting Miriam to cry on her shoulder. Miriam had a gift for comforting. Then Velma remembered her sister wasn't home. As a matter of fact, she was around the corner on 138th Street, attending a meeting at Liberty Hall. She turned and headed in that direction.

"Hey, miss," a voice called behind her. "Wait up!"

She ignored the plea, and waited for the clanky automobiles with their honking horns to pass. The voice caught up with her, and she felt a tug at her elbow.

"Excuse me," Zachary panted. "You forgot this." He handed her her scarf. She fingered her neck, realizing she'd left it behind. She stared at him, half-dried tears staining her cheeks.

"Thank you, Mr. Rudolph. You're very kind."

"No bother." He placed Velma's silk scarf—a gift from Roland during his service in France—around her neck, and smiled at her. "That was quite an exit."

"I'm so ashamed of myself. I had a bad day and I took it out on them." She placed a cigarette between her lips, which Zachary lit for her.

"Those guys aren't really so bad once you get to know them," he said, embarrassed by their conduct.

"I'm not sure I want to know them."

"You're probably right." They avoided each other's gaze, and a few awkward moments passed before Zachary spoke again. "Mind if I walk with you?"

"No, Mr. Rudolph, not at all." They started walking, Velma nearest the curb.

"Please, call me Rudy. My friends call me Rudy."

"Rudy?"

"As in Valentino."

"But, everyone at the workshop called you—"

"As I said, my *friends* call me Rudy."

"Where're you from . . . Rudy?"

"Jersey City."

"New Jersey boy, huh? Isn't that near Hoboken or something?"

"Yeah, the west bank of the Hudson River. Manhattan's on the east." There was a burning question he wanted to ask, but he had to find a delicate way to phrase it. "Tell me something, I'm just curious. Why did you read your piece about the soothsayer?"

"Well, I was going to read something else," she admitted, deciding he was even more attractive up close, but shorter than she had thought at first. His leanness lent the illusion of height. "But after that announcement, I decided to read 'Savannah.' " They looked at each other a moment and broke up laughing. It felt good to laugh.

"Actually," he said, "I thought the piece was very good."

"Did you really?"

"I think they did too. They're pretty uneasy when it comes to talented females. Especially those with more talent than they have, which is usually the case."

"Did you really like it, or are you trying to seduce me with compliments?" she said flirtatiously.

"Believe me, I really liked it. But, then seduction's not a bad idea either," he said, noticing for the first time how pretty she was. "Are you published?"

"A little, actually very little. A few poems here and there. I'd like to get some short fiction in print."

"Maybe I can help you."

"How?"

"Well, I can read your work, if you don't mind. If I like it, and I have a hunch I will, then I can make a call to *The Crisis* as an introduction, but I can't promise anything."

"DuBois's newspaper?"

"Good ol' W. E. B. himself. I can introduce you to him if you'd like."

"Introduce me? W. E. B. DuBois?" she asked, half flattered, and half intimidated by the suggestion. "You're kidding?"

"No, I'm not." Rudy chuckled. "He's a friend of mine."

Velma stopped walking, and looked him in the eyes, those large, liquid eyes of his. "Don't you think that's quite a bit to offer someone you just met?"

"Maybe. But I have a feeling about you. Anyway, I thrive on meeting and being with writers."

"That's part of my problem. I don't know many."

"Well, you know me. I think our profession is a lonely one, don't you? Everybody needs help; talent isn't everything. People helped me, so I try to help others. What else have you written?"

"Mostly poetry and short stories. I'm dying to do a novel, but I don't have one in me . . . yet."

"I know the feeling."

"Well, you must be walking on air, selling your first novel to Knopf."

"Yeah, but it's one trial after another. Now I'm worried about public reception."

"Take it one day at a time." Velma stopped at the corner. A taxi stumbled past. "Well, Rudy, here's where we part." She held out her hand.

"Could I call you sometime?" he asked, sensing her uneasiness.

She frisked her pockets for paper, and inadvertently pulled out *Cane.*

"You're addicted too?" Rudy asked, indicating the book.

"I love this book. I take it everywhere I go."

"My favorite line is: 'Men had always wanted her, this Karintha, even as a child, Karintha carrying beauty, perfect as dusk when the sun goes down.' "

She was delighted that she wasn't alone in memorizing passages, and jumped in on cue. "Or how about: 'Becky was the white woman who had Negro sons. She's dead; they've gone away. The pines whisper to Jesus. The Bible flaps its leaves with an aimless rustle on her mound.' Is that imagery or what? Whatever happened to Toomer anyway? He disappeared."

"I hear in writers' circles he's passing for white."

"You're kidding!"

"No, I'm not. But then, Toomer was never really around in Harlem, only his work. He lived in Greenwich Village actually."

"Is that right?"

"Listen, Velma, do you have someplace to go?"

"Yes, I have a lot of stuff I should be doing." She wanted to play hard to get, but not *too* hard. She really liked Rudy, whatever his name was. "What did you have in mind?"

"I just moved into an apartment on 135th. It's a bit unfurnished but I'd like to—"

"Like to what?" They laughed as Velma stuffed *Cane* back into her pocket.

"Read your work, of course," Rudy said. "C'mon, you'll be the first guest in my new flat. It's just around the corner."

"Maybe I could come by another time."

"Something wrong? Don't you trust me?"

"I don't know, Rudy. Why do you want to be my friend so quickly?"

"Why?" Rudy laughed again. "Any woman who lights cigarettes and makes scenes at the Harlem Writers Workshop and smokes in public while walking on the outside of her gentleman friend is a woman I want to know. Relax, we're going to be great friends." He offered his elbow, and Velma accepted it. They strolled into the shadows of West 135th Street, into the rain which started again, pouring from the sky with the clamor of hailstones.

7

"**Y**ou always leave your door unlocked?" Velma walked hesitantly through the door as Rudy held it open.

"For one thing, it's easier." He pulled the sweater over his head, unbuttoned his drenched shirt, slipped out of his wing tips and opened a window to air the stuffy room. "Besides, there's nothing to steal."

Velma studied the room, as barren and vacant as the unfurnished apartment she had applied for yesterday. There were a few crates supporting an RCA gramophone and a dusty typewriter. Books were piled in stacks against a wall in need of paint. In the corner, a Murphy bed was visible through the partially opened door that concealed it. Wax candle stubs sat on the windowsills, the mantelpiece, and shelves. Beside the shelves, a vase of roses wilted.

"You'll have to excuse my place," Rudy apologized. "I just moved in today."

"Where'd you live before? New Jersey?"

"Naa, I left Jersey some years ago."

"You left and headed for the big city?"

"I left and headed for Harlem. Would you like to dry your clothes?"

"Uh, well, I," Velma stuttered, patting herself, nervous at the suggestion. "Thanks, but uh, well, I'll be dry soon. Can I take my shoes off instead?"

"Sure. Make yourself comfortable. Sit anywhere." He looked out the window. "Doesn't seem this rain will ever stop. You don't mind the open window, do you? I love the sound of rain."

"No, not at all. Can I ask how much you pay here?"

"Twenty bucks a month."

"Is it cheaper than your last place?"

"Hardly. My last place was the Harlem YMCA down the street. Before that, Hartley Hall at Columbia; boy, was that a mistake," he said, recalling Sambo epithets, the firecrackers slipped beneath his door while he slept, the rotting watermelon that "mysteriously" found its way into his bed.

"What a coincidence! I graduated from Barnard."

"I knew I liked you for the wrong reasons. Hey, listen, I have a bottle of Sauternes I haven't opened yet. Would you like to share it with me?"

"Certainly. Intoxication sounds most attractive after the day I had."

"Keep talking." Rudy walked into the kitchen, and switched on the light. "I can hear you in here," he shouted.

"Did you say Sauternes?" Velma shouted toward the light, unable to see him.

"Yeah. You a connoisseur?" Rudy shouted back.

"God no," she shouted, "I was just thinking what a large advance Knopf must've given you. I mean, Sauternes of all things."

He banged around in the kitchen, and the thumping and clanging upstaged his voice. "You serious? One of the chefs where I work gave it to me as a gift for selling my novel."

"How nice," Velma shouted a little louder. "What do you do?"

"I bus."

"What?"

"Bus." Rudy reentered the room carrying a bottle and two glasses. "You know, I'm a busboy. No, I take that back. I *was* a busboy. I'm not sure now. I have a little money, and I could quit, but it's hard. I could be broke again in a month. Hope you don't mind the glass. The maid hasn't unpacked the crystal yet." The glasses were mismatched, and he handed her a clean one—a jar, actually. The rim of the glass was chipped. "A toast is in order. What to?" Rudy scratched his head.

"Your novel!" Velma chimed in.

"And friendship!"

"To Harlem!"

"Don't forget its writers!" They touched glasses, and sipped the wine. Rudy squatted on the floor. Velma sat on a crate, her legs crossed. The window shades flapped against the panes. Lightning flashed, a skeletal hand glowing against the sky's blackness.

He studied her, turning the glass up to his mouth, not knowing what to say or ask. He thought she liked him, but he had doubts. He was nobody's Romeo, so he'd been told. But he liked her, her straightforwardness, her blithe spirit, and was pleased that he'd invited her for company. Unless he was writing, he spent little time home alone. There was always a party somewhere.

"What made you become a writer?" he asked.

"Birthright, I guess. And I have two other reasons." She sipped the wine. "Hurston and Hughes."

"Really? I just met Langston a couple of weeks ago. Shy fellow," Rudy said.

"Really? Where?"

"At a benefit dance given by the NAACP."

"I admire his work. Don't you?"

"Why?" Rudy asked. "Is he your favorite?"

"Well, his work defies the rigid European structure that both McKay and Cullen adhere to. His work says that poetry is of the moment, like fire and ice; it should just happen."

She sipped her wine again, praying he was impressed and in accord with her observations on literature. She noticed that he appeared as nervous as she was. She wanted to know his thoughts about her, and why she'd been invited. If she had suspected she'd be meeting someone like him, a veritable Mr. Just-sweep-me-off-my-feet-why-don't-you, she would have dressed more appropriately. Clad in a blouse she usually wore when she didn't care how she looked, with her dark blue pleated skirt and oversized jacket, she wouldn't blame him if he thought her gauche. And her shoes, by God, the shoes were so scuffed she was embarrassed, though his didn't look any better. Her hair, thanks to the rain and humidity, was a disaster. She kept fussing with it, out of nervousness, she guessed, and it refused to cooperate. She wanted him to like her—very much, as she did him. Since Barnard, she had cultivated the romantic fantasy of falling in love with a writer, a gifted intellectual who understood her in a way Roland hadn't. Maybe tonight she'd be lucky. She felt a cryptic immediacy in her attraction to him and didn't want to lose him. So schoolgirl silly, she thought, having known him only a few hours, but she could hear and feel the melody he was playing on her heartstrings. When else had she met somebody this handsome, reciting Toomer from recall on a Harlem street corner on a rainy night?

"Why don't you sit on the floor?" Rudy suggested. "C'mon, I won't bite."

Velma slid off the crate, placed her glass on the floor, and tried to squat, but the skirt wouldn't allow her. She folded her legs beneath her, ladylike, as Mother would say. Rudy grabbed a crate and a somewhat soiled cloth. Standing the box upright, he placed the cloth over it, then lit the candles on the windowsills, the mantelpiece, the shelves, and arranged two wax stubs on the makeshift table between Velma and himself.

"I love candles in the dark," he said. "Don't you?" The candles illuminated their faces, which glowed a golden yellow. The flames cast flickering shadows on the wall, and the parlor looked to Velma like a chapel not unlike the one where Mother prayed. The room smelled like good wine, rain, and sardines he must have eaten earlier.

"You always live like this?" she asked, not knowing what else to say. "I mean, do you have furniture?"

"For what? I'm no Jay Gatsby. All I need are the bare necessities. You should've seen the look on my landlady's face when I moved in this afternoon. All I brought were my typewriter, books, some clothes, the gramophone here, and some Bessie Smith records."

"Could you play some Bessie?"

"Be obliged. Let me see." He walked to the gramophone with the horn-shaped speaker and wound it up. He placed the record on the turntable, and spun it while rain played polyrhythms on the fire escape.

"This is perfect!" he declared.

"What?"

"Honoring the rain and thunder, I'm going to play for you . . ." he said teasingly, pausing for effect as he dropped the tonearm, 'Rainy Weather Blues.' " Fletcher Henderson's tinkly piano oozed through the horn-shaped speaker, accentuated by a whining, sliding trombone, and filled the room. Bessie began moaning, the scratches on the record popping in her voice.

> *The rain sho am fallin'*
> *Fallin' down from the sky*
> *The rain sho am fallin'*
> *Fallin' down from the sky*
> *Feelin' wet all over*
> *I could lay rat down an' die.*

Rudy danced with an imaginary partner, sliding his stockinged feet along the floor toward Velma. His eyelids were shut. With the manner and accent of a British gentleman, he asked, "Mahdham, may I hahve this dahnce?" She offered her hand with a smile, and he pulled her gently from the floor. They danced, bodies pressed together, cheek to cheek. Rudy hummed the blues in her ear, his hand firmly cupped around her tiny waist. As she danced, Velma watched the rain, the diagonal ladder on the fire escape, the flat, shingled rooftops across the street, and the lightning glowing in the sky. She wished that the night, just as it was, could continue eternally. Her stockinged foot rubbed against his, and a tingle raced down her spine. Mother wouldn't approve of this, she thought, dancing with a strange man in his unfurnished bachelor apartment. She laughed to herself at the thought. Times were different; it was 1925. Her thoughts shifted from Mother, and she lost herself in Bessie's husky phrasings, as the wine swirled in her head, and the luminous candles flickered. She watched their shadows glide and jerk across the wall, silhouettes in intimate contact, and for the first time that night, she knew he wanted her by the way he held

her waist and hummed in her ear off-key. Not until then did she
relax.

The record finished, and the tonearm sat stationary while the
record spun. A scratching noise repeated itself, but they didn't stop
dancing. Rudy continued humming off-key, leading Velma with
grace and poise.

"Aren't you going to change the—"

He kissed her, and her unpronounced syllables rolled off her
tongue, and flowed into his mouth. He caressed her back, and
pressed harder against her damp blouse. He eased her down on the
wooden floor, his mouth covering hers, removing his unfastened
shirt. Their mouths separated, and they stared at each other, on
their knees, breathing heavily. Velma unbuttoned her blouse, and
peeled the oppressive stockings from her legs. Rudy removed his
socks, unfastened his trousers, and stepped out of them. His shirt
slid down his back. He tossed it across the room, and it landed on
a burning candle. The flame went out.

Birds chirped and pigeons cooed on the building's ledge. A ray of
sunlight shone through the window on Velma's brow. She turned
her face to the other side, hugging the pillow. Her ears filled with a
distant crackling, her nostrils with the smell of frying bacon.
Suddenly remembering where she was, she jumped out of bed and
began clothing her nakedness. She picked up her skirt and wiggled
into it, slipped into the blouse, and fastened her stocking to a garter.
A voice spoke above her, and she looked up.

"Beautiful morning, isn't it?" Rudy, clad in a bathrobe, leaned
against the door frame. Smiling, he held a cup of coffee.

"What time is it?" she said, slightly embarrassed; by what, she
didn't know.

"About nine."

"I didn't know it was that late."

"Coffee? It's burning my hand."

"Oh, I'm sorry. Thank you." She took the cup and sipped the
black coffee. "You didn't make breakfast for me, did you?"

"Bacon, eggs, and hominy grits coming right up."

"Rudy, you're so sweet, but I'm in a hurry."

"It's okay. I'll eat it. But, before you go, don't forget to leave me
your number."

Velma finished dressing, lit a cigarette, and sipped the coffee.

"You smoke early in the morning?" he asked.

"Why not? I'm awake."

"I like you, Velma. You're so full of . . . spirit. I like that in a girl."

"You're not so bad yourself. Thank you for last night." She curtsied. "Best time I had since I can remember."

Rudy went to her and nestled her in his arms. He kissed her lips, her nose, her brow, then turned and headed for the kichen. Velma noticed the candles. What remained were pools of hardened wax. The pile of stacked books against the wall came into her focus. She had a habit of rummaging through people's libraries; their literary tastes revealed much about them. One book in particular caught her attention. She picked it up, dusted it off, and parted the pages.

"Listen, you sure you won't have breakfast?" Rudy reentered the parlor with a plate of bacon, eggs, and steaming grits in one hand, a glass of orange juice in the other. He squatted on the floor.

"No, thank you. I'm sure."

"Okay. That was last call. You're looking at your half on my plate."

"You'll eat all of that?"

"The plate too if I could."

"But you're so slim."

He shoved a forkful of eggs and grits into his mouth. "I see you're browsing through my books. I need to organize them somehow."

"Did you like this book?" She displayed the cover and Rudy looked up.

"G. Virgil Scott's? Yes, very much. I thought it was excellent. I like all his work."

Velma frowned. "I didn't like this one, and I can't say I care for any of the others."

"Really?" Rudy said between mouthfuls. "He's one of the more experimental of the Negro writers I've read. His prose is so lyrical and the tone and mood of his settings so—"

"Who cares." Velma tossed the book back onto the stack.

"I get the feeling you dislike Virgil Scott more than a little."

"I just don't like his treatment of women in fiction, that's all."

"Well, Velma, there are other things to consider."

"His female characters haunt me. They're overwhelming and it weighs the book down. They're always so manipulative, so cunning, even vulgar sometimes."

"Finally! An author we disagree on."

"That reminds me, Rudy. Aren't we forgetting something?"

"I don't think so," he said, feigning a pensive look. "We did it all last night."

"I'm not joking now. Just think about it for a moment."

Rudy thought, continuously stuffing his mouth with food. "Oh, I know," he said suddenly, "your hat and jacket."

"Rudy, I came over last night for a reason," she said, trying not to appear pushy. "Don't misunderstand; I had a wonderful time too, but that's not what I came for."

"Well . . . what *did* you come for?"

"My work, remember?"

"Oh yes, yes." He scraped the last morsel and the fork squeaked against the plate. "I didn't forget. Leave me the pieces before you go."

"I'd rather read them to you myself."

"It's not necessary."

"Yes it is. You understand." She rubbed her hands together, and looked out the window as if distracted. "Another thing, Rudy."

"Yeah?"

"I hope you don't think I slept with you just so you would help me."

"Oh, Velma," he laughed. "You're much too smart for that. What did you want to read?"

"A few poems. I'll leave you two other short stories, okay?"

"Splendid." He plopped the fork and knife on the empty plate and placed it upon the makeshift table. "Listen, I got an idea," he said, making sucking noises, cleaning his teeth. "You read some of your poetry; I'll read some of mine. How's that?"

"I love it!" A man after her own heart. She was falling for this fellow, falling hard.

"Well, you might as well sit back down. Looks like we're going to have a session."

"Good. What better way to spend a morning."

8

If they only knew the truth about George and me . . . Miriam thought, standing in Ward D over Mr. Wilson's bed, wet sponge in hand, her eyes fixed upon the wall clock signaling her shift was about to end. It had been an exhausting day, and she was hardly in the mood for Mr. Wilson's lewd gestures. He'd pulled this stunt each time she'd looked in on him that day, and she'd just about had enough. She wondered what it could possibly be like dealing with this kind of salacious behavior day after day—Mr. Wilson had only been admitted some eight hours ago.

Drawing the curtain to ensure their privacy within the twelve-patient ward, she slid the thermometer into his mouth—not that his temperature reading was necessary, she just wanted him to shut up a minute—then pulled back his hospital gown. There it was again, that one-eyed monster, standing up and throbbing as if it had a life all its own. Mr. Wilson smiled lasciviously as they both focused on his erection. He crossed his legs and folded his arms behind his head while Miriam, with sponge in hand, cleaned him up for the surgery. Gingerly, she held his penis between her thumb and forefinger, pulled back the foreskin, and wiped it, thinking, Some men are just plain nasty. She was sure he'd been told, by his mama, if nobody else, to keep himself clean. She squeezed the sponge in the sink, then dipped it once more into the pan of warm water as Mr. Wilson winked at her. Through clenched teeth, the thermometer dangling from his lips, he said, "The curtain's closed. Nobody won't know." Miriam rolled her eyes, maintaining an aloof professionalism. "Roscoe can't help it," he whispered. "Everytime he see you, it make him wanna stand up at attention and salute. He really quite friendly. Best friend I ever had."

"Would you tell Mr. Roscoe something for me," Miriam replied, struggling to keep a straight face. "Tell him that this here's a hospital and I don't come to make friends. It just ain't that type of party."

Mr. Wilson laughed at her welcome humor. Most of the other nurses took themselves much too seriously and there was no fun for him at Harlem Hospital until Nurse Brooks came around.

She squeezed the sponge once more in the sink, pulled his gown back in place, yanked the thermometer from his lips and pretended to study the mercury reading. She grabbed the surrounding curtain and pushed it open. Mr. Wilson looked at her, disappointed. "What's the matter, Nurse Brooks, don't you like mens?" She smiled, told him to be a good boy until his scheduled circumcision first thing in the morning. "Think you could do that for Nurse Brooks?" she said, and he didn't reply. Besides, she thought, by the time Dr. Shapiro gets finished with you, Roscoe ain't gonna be much in the mood to stand up and salute nobody, unless he likes to hurt himself.

The clock on the wall read 2:54. She picked up the pan of warm water and started for the ward exit. She thought she heard Mr. Wilson mumble something under his breath; something about her being a bulldiker if she didn't want to play with Big Roscoe, at which she smiled, and pushed her way through the double doors.

Heading down the corridor, she wondered where Agnes had disappeared to, and hoped Agnes wasn't avoiding her. She figured that she got on Agnes's nerves occasionally, rambling on and on about Marcus Garvey and the UNIA. But it was her responsibility, her loyal duty, to recruit as many members as possible. Why didn't folks see it as she saw it? Garvey was the best thing to happen to Negroes since the Thirteenth Amendment to the Constitution. But folks in Harlem were too busy going to parties and speakeasies, drinking and humping themselves silly. Not that she had anything against a good time, but there was a time and a place for everything. Elvira had taught her that.

Though Harlem was the most exciting place on the face of the earth, it was still part of the United States, and, in her mind, the political nightmare of that geographic reality grew increasingly bleak with each passing year.

She spotted Agnes approaching down the corridor, a bedpan in her hand, and for a moment, thought she acted as if she didn't see Miriam. Doctors rushed by, barking orders at nurses and technicians, with their unfastened white smocks billowing and flapping behind them.

She caught up with Agnes as she emptied the bedpan. "It's that time, girl," Agnes said, sighing, physically spent after a nine-hour shift. She wiped sweat from her forehead.

"You ain't never lied," Miriam responded. She breathed in the conflicting odors of disinfectants, sickness, and death, and wondered if she should ask Agnes the question now or later.

They strolled down the street. The three o'clock sun felt like high noon. Pedestrians dressed in summer white shaded themselves beneath black umbrellas. Water shooting from an open fire hydrant cooled the bronze and ebony bodies of laughing, jumping, and screaming children.

"I don't know, Miriam," Agnes was saying, shaking her head. "This is short notice, and I haven't checked with Tommy yet."

"I'm not asking you to move in and sleep there," Miriam said, smiling her public relations smile, an instinctive reaction when she tried recruiting folks into something they wouldn't do on their own. "Just tonight, one hour, that's all, and I'll never ask you again."

"Where'd you say it was?" Agnes grew impatient, exasperated, and longed to get home to soak her tired feet in a tub of Epsom salts before Tommy stopped by.

"Liberty Hall's on 138th. UNIA owns that entire six-block radius near Lenox Avenue. If you get lost, somebody can help you." She'd supplied her this information a zillion times, and she'd supply it a zillion more if that's what it took.

"But didn't I already buy that thing you asked me to?" Agnes asked, pausing at the steps of the subway, her eyes squinting from the late afternoon sun.

"What thing?" Miriam asked. "Oh, you mean the stock certificate for the Black Star Line? Well, yeah, but that's not enough."

"I don't think I can be there, Miriam," Agnes said wearily, "not tonight anyway. Maybe some other time."

"That's your choice," Miriam said in a cheerful voice though she was most disappointed. "Just remember, it would only be an hour or two and Tommy ain't going nowhere. How about next Wednesday?"

"I don't know," Agnes said. "Let me check with Tommy and see if he made any plans."

Miriam knew that Tommy didn't have plans for next Wednesday night; nor did he have plans for any night with Agnes. Bedroom to parlor was the distance Tommy traveled with Agnes. She complained to Miriam that all Tommy did was sit up in her parlor with his feet on the table when they could've been dancing and drinking their hearts out at Smalls Paradise or Connie's Inn. Miriam thought quickly of something else to say, anything to detain her friend.

"You know that Mr. Wilson in my ward, he's a fresh somethin'."

"What's wrong with that?" Agnes replied. "He's a *good-lookin'* something."

Awkward moments passed.

"Well?" Agnes said.

"Well what?" Miriam answered.

"You gonna let him take you out or what?"

"He didn't ask me."

"You just said he was actin' fresh with you?"

"But that's different from—"

"Oh, Miriam, girl, even when they do ask, you never go anyway."

Miriam knew Agnes thought it strange that she never dated, and spent so much time with her organization. She didn't want Agnes to think her odd.

"I don't go because it usually ain't the right man asking. Well, guess I'll see you in the morning first thing."

"Yeah," Agnes replied, descending the subway. "First thing, girl."

Miriam watched her back as she descended the subway, her white uniform and cap glowing in the consuming darkness she entered. The sidewalk vibrated from the rumbling of the underground trains. She sighed, turned, and headed for home.

What a nice day for walking, Miriam thought. The avenues were animated with dazzling life, Negro life, spread, like fire-engine red and passionate purple paint, up and down the avenues, around the corners, in the store fronts and buildings overhead. She loved her people, God did she love them! She had decided a long time ago—after World War I and the soldiers' gallant march up Fifth Avenue—to dedicate her life to the cause. It saddened her to watch poverty, oppression, crime, and destitution ravage the community of her birth. But Harlem, like anything else, had its flip side of history, politics, art, culture, theater, music, cabarets and all-night bashes that gave it the needed balance. The greatest asset of all was its people, the grass roots. Yet Miriam could see rather plainly, as she could see that old transient on the corner turning a bottle of cheap wine up to his mouth, that if something wasn't done, and done quickly, Harlem would be sacrificed. Mayor Jimmy Walker didn't care. Neither did Calvin Coolidge. So it was up to them, the grass roots—every able body and thinking mind who drank from the cup of Harlem's prosperity, and picked at the diminishing fruits. Her ultimate goal was to join forces across the Atlantic with a growing Liberia. Why rent a community, she reasoned, when you could own an entire country.

Her apartment felt like an oven. Sweat inched down her face, back and neck, as flies buzzed around her head. She removed her uniform and stockings, and placed them in a tub of water to soak. She thought of George and how Velma had run into him. On several occasions, she tried confiding to Velma about their relationship, but could never conjure the nerve to do it. Admittedly, George wasn't a bad man, it just didn't feel right. There was no meshing of souls. She explained to Velma that it couldn't work with George because, in his own words, he wasn't moving to nobody's Africa, sailing in nobody's ship on nobody's Black Star Line, and Miriam could just forget it. He was keeping his black ass—again, his own words—right here in Harlem, U.S.A. She could go if she wanted to. That was his final answer, and for Miriam, strike one.

George, not unlike Agnes's Tommy, never went anywhere or did anything. He had attended several UNIA meetings with Miriam.

But they had no real social lives to speak of. She didn't mind his visits, or his waiting outside the hospital when she punched out at the end of her shift. Rather, she looked forward to it. But he never spent a dime on her. She cooked meals for him and gave him manicures, sometimes pedicures, because she wanted to. Tit for tat was not her way, but it didn't take long for her to realize she was wasting her time on a man looking for a mother or a slave or both.

It wasn't enough that she cooked and fed him and listened to his boring accounts of life as a Seventh Avenue trolley conductor. Just how many stories could he tell about folks boarding and disembarking from a trolley? But she listened patiently, feigning interest, though her mind wandered to a thousand other things. When he was ill, she personally nursed him, running between Harlem Hospital, her apartment, and his so he wouldn't feel alone and neglected. Caring for him was much like ministering to a nine-year-old. Could you do this? Get me some of that? How about fluffing my pillows? Any more rice pudding left?

Then he began hinting at sex.

Miriam had never given sex much thought. It wasn't that she had no inkling of her own sexuality and needs, she just never took the time. Then George's hints grew into demands. Okay, she thought, why not?

She had had no idea how she'd detest it—spread-eagled while this man thrust in and out of her with no consideration of the pain. She'd told him she was a virgin but it didn't stop him or slow him down. When he finished, her thighs stained with blood and semen, she felt anything but good. She wondered why everyone, namely women, made a big thing of it. She felt pain, remorse, self-debasement. He went off to sleep without so much as asking if she was okay. Strike two.

Two days later, he was back for more. This time he didn't ask. Just grabbed her in the manner she'd seen Rudolph Valentino subdue an unsuspecting nymph—minus the flair—and began placing his hands upon parts of her body *she* didn't even touch. Oh, he sweet-talked and planted sloppy kisses behind her ear, but his approach overall was too raw. She protested and asked what he was doing. He never so much as grunted an answer, but started for the buttons and snaps of her uniform. When she fought him back, he looked surprised, as if she were out of line. His look communicated rather succinctly that she had no right to refuse him—not anymore, since two days ago. They tussled a bit and he threw her down upon his bed, then stopped, dazed, wild-eyed, as if coming to his senses. She decided, at that tense moment, looking up at this stranger looking down at her through sad, remorseful eyes, that this relationship was going nowhere. This mother's son will never, not ever! see me again; not in this life. As quietly as she had come, she collected her things without looking at him, walked calmly across the floor and closed the door forever behind her. Strike three, he was out!

Whatever negative ideas she had entertained about sex beforehand, George fortified them. She resolved never again to give herself to *any* man until she felt it was what *she* wanted.

9

Though the dress was white linen, it still seemed too much in the suffocating heat. Sweat trickled down her forehead, the back of her neck, the insides of her armpits. Louise set down a valise full of hot combs, Wonderful Hair Grower, Glossine hair oil, Temple Grower and Tetter Salve on the hot pavement so she could wipe her face.

Having followed through on Mrs. Ivy's advice—she got in touch with her niece immediately—Louise became a Walker agent. She was excited at the start about selling the products, but after a few months, her sales weren't what she'd hoped for. Most of what she'd sold was stocked along the sink in Mother's kitchen.

At times like this, she drew upon Madame Walker's dream.

A big, black man—according to the Walker training instructors and community legend—had appeared to Sarah Breedlove who later became Madame C. J. Walker the millionaire. She had been worried about losing her hair, when the man appeared to her. He advised a remedy from a plant grown in Africa. Sarah Breedlove sent for it, mixed it, and put it in her scalp. Hair began growing in faster than she could comb. After trying it on her friends, she decided, with an investment of $1.25, to sell it door to door.

This incentive encouraged Louise to persevere, to hold fast to her dreams, hoping they could be her ticket around the country—or around the world. With the same hard work and determination, she could attain what Madame had accomplished.

The products she sold were designed to make Negro women beautiful; to straighten coarse hair and lighten darker skin tones. She considered herself lucky that she didn't need the products. Women tried to become what she already was, by using these bleaching creams and hair straighteners.

Picking up the valise, Louise started up the stairs to knock upon the umpteenth door of the day. In the dark hallway, a cockroach crawled across her foot. She gasped, shook her shoe and the roach fell on its back.

She knocked on a door. Behind it she heard the excited voices of children, the barking and whimpering of a puppy. There was a pause and the knob turned. The door opened, and a homely, worn-looking woman stood against it. Children, more than Louise could count in a single glance, huddled about their mother's skirt. The woman stood defiantly, a baby hugging her neck, and did not smile.

"Good afternoon, ma'am," Louise said cheerfully, knowing from experience this was going to be a difficult sell, very difficult. "Aren't we having fine weather?" She extended her hand.

The woman ignored her hand. "What's fine about it?"

"Well, it is a lovely day."

"Lovely? Not by the looks of that sweat pourin' down your face, chile. Whatchu want?"

"My name is Louise Brooks and I'm a beauty agent from the Walker Company. I sell miraculous hair products of the famous Madame C. J. Walker and I was wondering—"

"Madame who?"

"Walker, ma'am. Of course you know Madame C. J. Walker—"

"Nevah heard of her."

"Well, if you let me come in for a demonstration, I can show you how to make yourself more beautiful with her products. Not that you're not beautiful already, of course." Louise chuckled, part of the slick and polished routine. The woman wasn't going to buy a blessed thing, and she couldn't keep a smile plastered across her face much longer if she wasn't going to invite her in.

"Whatever you sellin', I can't use, honey. Good-bye."

"Well, I'd like to—"

"Look, miss," the woman challenged accusingly, "you givin' away any money?"

"No, ma'am," Louise answered, perplexed.

"Food?" The woman's eyes grew hungry.

"No."

"Well then, we can't talk!"

She slammed the door, barely missing Louise's nose. Good afternoon to you too, honey! Louise thought. She had been about to give the woman a few complimentary samples, something she wasn't obliged to do. Louise felt sorry for the woman and the army of kids clutching her skirt, and thought several free feminine beauty products might lift her day. She was exasperated, defeated. The day was nearly over, and she hadn't made one sale, not unlike the days before, or the weeks preceding that. She'd requested a transfer to another territory but her superiors wouldn't hear of it.

Louise turned around and kicked the wall. She wanted to lie down on that dirty floor and cry. She even considered rushing into headquarters and throwing the valise full of junk in their faces. Mrs. Ivy and the Walker instructors had made it sound so easy. She headed for the second floor and knocked on another door. A man almost twice her age answered.

"Good afternoon, sir. Is the missus at home?"

"Why?"

"I'm a beauty agent from the Walker Company." God, was she tired of repeating these words. "I sell Wonderful Hair Grower, Tetter Salve, and an assortment of our other fine beauty products."

"What's wrong with my hair?" He smiled.

"Why, nothing, of course. But these products are for ladies."

"How I know they work?" His smile was gone. His expression turned skeptical. "Folks is always trying to sell one thang or another."

"If the lady of the house is home, I'd like to give a demonstration."

"You wanna come in?" He eyed her head to toe.

"Yes. If your wife doesn't mind."

"Hell, why don't you just say so. She don't mind. Come on in."

"Thank you, sir. Thank you." Louise stepped inside and fanned herself with her fingers. The man led her by the elbow, closed the door and locked it, smiling. Louise looked around the room. "And the lady of the house?"

"She's inside there. I'll go fetch her. You wait right here and have a seat." He walked into the adjoining room. A frayed curtain hung where a door should have been. Behind the curtain, Louise heard him speak in whispers. She prepared her goods and flexed her sales-pitch muscles. The man reentered, still smiling. "She be out in a minute."

"I really appreciate this, sir."

"Sooooo . . . what you sellin' there, pretty lady?"

"All kinds of products. While your wife's getting ready, maybe you could tell me what she needs. Does she have problems with oily hair, or psoriasis of the scalp? Then again, she may need—"

"Baby, she sho nuff needs all of it. Everythang you got, she need it."

Louise looked up at him. He stood before her, towering above her, the smile glued to his face.

"Well," Louise said, "I'll wait for her—"

"Why wait? You can start now if you like."

"But I'd rather not have to do it twice. As you can understand, I do this all day."

"You wanna sell that stuff, don't you?"

"Yes, I do. But—"

"But, nothin'. If you can't sell me, you can't sell it to her neither. Who you thank gonna pay for it."

"Whatever you say, sir." Louise swallowed, growing impatient with him. "The first product I have here is the most popular with our customers. We call it the hot comb. Madame Walker had the teeth redesigned in France for Race women's hair. The heat of the comb helps the hair to relax."

"What else you got?" He sat near her.

"I'm coming to that, sir," she said, wishing he'd give her a chance to finish one product before jumping to the next. And why was he sitting so close? "While the comb gets hot, we recommend our customers use Glossine hair oil for their scalps. This helps to press the hair better."

"What you use on your hair? You use this here comb and glossy stuff?"

"Actually, sir, my hair won't take a hot comb."

He ran his fingers through the wavy hair resting on Louise's shoulder. She winced and pulled her hair away from his touch.

"Anybody ever tell you you got nice hair, miss?"

"Sir, excuse me, but this is not the proper place."

"Your legs ain't bad neither, if you ask me."

"Sir, is your wife about ready? I have a few more stops before returning to headquarters."

"Don't worry. She'll be here. She prob'bly washin' up or somethin'. Go 'head; what else you got?"

Louise paused to watch the curtain divider, thought she saw it move, and picked up another jar from the case. "If your wife has problems with hair that won't grow, we also offer the Wonderful Hair Grower. This is the product which got the Walker Company established some years ago."

"Let me see that."

Louise handed him the jar. He took it, running his calloused hands over hers, and tried to place her hand on his cheek. Louise yanked it back.

"Your hands so soft." He held the jar, looking at Louise. "You know, you the prettiest thing I seen in a long time."

"Sir, as I was saying, the Wonderful Hair Grower helps ladies with—"

"What will it do for me?"

"Well, sir, I guess it will do the same as it does—"

"What will *you* do for me?"

"Pardon?"

He leaned toward Louise and tried to kiss her. She pushed him away with both hands. "How about a drank," he said.

"What's wrong with you?" Louise screamed, louder than she meant to. She jumped up from her seat. "What're you trying to do?"

"Hey, baby, you want to sell that junk, doncha?" He stood facing her.

"Yes, I do. But, that doesn't give you the right to take—"

"Hey look. You want somethin' an' I want somethin', right? We both have what each other want, so—"

"I'm a Walker agent, sir, not a prostitute."

"What's the difference?"

"Where's your wife? I thought she was on her way out . . . there's nobody in that room, is there?"

He gripped Louise tightly. His hands around her waist, he tried kissing her. She turned her mouth away from him, repulsed, using her knees and elbows to pry them apart. He grabbed her dress and tried lifting it, moving her body toward the sofa. Snatching the neckline, he ripped it, his right hand cupping her brassiere. She bit his hand. He slapped her and their bodies separated. He rubbed his hand, and she saw he was furious. She stepped backward and guarded her upper torso, holding her torn clothing together.

"Now, I'm gonna teach you, you li'l yaller bitch you!"

He took off his shirt, undid his trousers, and pulled them down to his ankles. Louise glimpsed his erection, looked around the room, and not knowing what to do, kicked him in the groin. He doubled over, and fell to the floor. She ran for the door when he grabbed her ankles, causing her to lose balance, stumble, then fall, and pulled himself along her body, slithering like a reptile, and pinned her beneath him. Her thighs crossed, she reached for the hot comb sitting beside the valise and struck him several times over the head with it. It didn't discourage him as he continued struggling to enter her, his strength overpowering. Grabbing the thick jar of Wonderful Hair Grower, Louise smashed it against his skull. Blood and scalp ointment oozed down the sides of his face onto her tattered dress. He lay motionless, his weight trapping her body beneath him. Weak, she freed herself, never letting him out of her sight, and turned him over, checking his heartbeat and pulse. Blood pumped through his veins. Relieved she hadn't committed murder, though she would have felt absolutely justified, she started picking up the valise and her products. Instead, she decided to leave them; something to remember her by. "You wanted to know if that stuff would work on your hair," Louise panted, fingers pressed against her bruised cheek. "When you wake up, you son-of-a-bitch, you'll find out!" She headed for the door, unlocked it, and fled.

10

"An' annudda ting," said a stout West Indian woman, a large mole beside her left nostril, gold teeth glinting from the center of her open mouth. Hands folded at her hips, she reminded Velma of her mother. "We don't 'low no loud music playin', no loud parties an' "— she lowered her voice, looking both ways, making certain she and Velma were alone—"I hope you a decent enough Christian lady not to have no mens sneakin' in an' out of here durin' indecent hours neider. 'Cause me, I'm a deaconess at Abyssinian Baptist an' I won't have it. Eeze dat clear?"

"When can I move in?" Velma asked.

"What kind of question eeze dat? Dat's yo businezz."

"Eighteen dollars a month, right?"

"I know you Americans tink I sound funny, but I don't stutter."

Velma peeled bills from her purse and handed them to the woman, who, in turn, handed her a key.

"I'll probably move in tonight or tomorrow morning. Thanks

again, Mrs. Wigfall. Today is my lucky day!" Velma strutted from the basement apartment. Mrs. Wigfall counted the bills and tucked them in her bosom.

Collecting the mail from Mother's box, Velma found an envelope addressed to herself. She opened it, halting in her tracks while she read. The opening paragraph caught her off guard. She looked quickly to the bottom of the letter for the sender's signature and clutched her heart. She began reading again, her pulse racing as her feet stumbled up the stairs, and she screamed. Running up the staircase, waving the letter in her hand, she opened the door to Elvira's warm, sunlit kitchen. She was with a customer.

"Was that you screaming like a heathen?" Elvira asked.

"Mother! Wait until you read this! Look!"

"Baby, you know I ain't got my readin' glasses on. What it say?"

"Alaine Locke wants to meet me!"

"Who? What? I sure don't know what that is."

"Mr. Locke is a person, a Rhodes Scholar from Harvard. And he's Negro."

"Yeah?" Elvira looked impressed, yet puzzled, awaiting further explanation.

"Well, he's . . . how can I explain it? He's sort of considered the father of Negro writers of this century, or something like that."

"You still ain't said why he wanna meet you."

"He saw my poetry and short stories in *The Crisis*. He thinks I'm gifted. He teaches at Howard in D. C., but he'll be in New York next week!"

"Now, ain't that a blessin'!" Elvira said. "Best news we done heard all day."

"I know who he is," the customer said, opening her eyes. "My son wants to be a writer too. You must be very lucky."

"Luck ain't all of it," Elvira intervened. "Velma work hard. Sittin' 'round here typin' her brains out."

"What have you written?" the customer asked.

"Oh, lots of things," Velma said, pacing the kitchen floor. She read the letter for the third time. "But, lately, my first professional publication was in *The Crisis*. This year, other stuff will be in *Seven Arts*, and *The Messenger*."

"I must tell my son I met you. What's your name again?"

"That's Velma," Elvira volunteered. "She my middle girl, smart as a whip."

"Velma Brooks, huh?" the customer repeated, impressed. "Could you autograph a copy for my son? He'd like that very much."

"No more than I would," Velma laughed.

"That mean," Elvira said, the mirth vanishing from her face, "you still movin' out?"

"Yes, ma'am; probably tomorrow. I just paid my deposit. Thanks for the loan."

"You don't have to," Elvira reiterated. "You can stay here."

"I do have to, Mother. But I'm in the neighborhood and I'll probably be here more than you think. You know how it is for us starving artists." She looked around the room. "Where's Louise? I want to tell her too."

"She gone to another job interview. Poor baby girl," Elvira said. Then, to the customer, "Some folks can't work even when they wants to. It's a shame."

"Oh my God!" Velma slapped her forehead with the palm of her hand. "I've forgotten Rudy!"

"Your gentleman friend?" Elvira asked.

"Yes. I have to call and thank him."

"This the writer? The one I never met?" She placed emphasis on the latter.

"Oh, Mother, please. You'll meet him sooner than you think."

"I hope so," she said to Velma. To the customer, "Velma done found herself a new beau. Been courtin' a few months now. I knew God wasn't asleep." She chuckled.

"Mother, what do you think? Should I call him? No, I'll go over there. Bye! See you later!"

Before Elvira could reply, Velma was out the door. "See," Elvira said, "my girls always wait to hear my advice."

A half-dozen red roses in hand, Velma headed east on 135th Street. It had become apparent over the last few months that Rudy was by far one of the better things to happen to her. They dated, saw each other every week, sometimes twice, read poetry by candlelight, talked politics and literature. As he promised, Rudy personally submitted her fiction to *The Crisis* and put her in touch with Alaine Locke. He never spoke about it, nor did she ask. Until one day Rudy showed her a current issue of the magazine featuring her work and byline. She browsed through it unsuspecting, then screamed and wrapped her arms around him.

There were times she wondered if she was more aggressive than

Rudy. Most of their time spent together was through her initiation. Rudy didn't seem to mind. He was as enthralled with her as she was with him. But he was never again flirtatious and passionate with her as he had been that first night.

The first night they made love—the only night—he became increasingly passive as the act progressed, as if he were stumped by the next move or the shedding of his clothing robbed him of confidence. She couldn't pinpoint it. They had a wonderful time, she thought. The only other experience she'd had to compare it to was with Roland. Rudy wasn't rough and mechanical like Roland. He was gentle, compassionate, caring. But he'd only approached her sexually that night. Maybe he was sleeping with another woman. He really seemed more like her brother than a lover. They were affectionate, touched a lot, shared nuances that suggested the innocence of first love, but it didn't go beyond that, never blooming into the full-blown passion she craved. But Rudy, she decided, was different from other men, even extraordinary by comparison, and Velma felt she couldn't weigh him on the same scale as she weighed others.

She wanted to make love—fierce, low-down, toe-curling love, this afternoon on the bare hardwood floors with Rudy. If she had to be the aggressor, she would. She couldn't wait to tell him about her new apartment. For weeks, she had fantasized making breakfast for him as her overnight guest.

Approaching Rudy's flat, she bade "Hello" and "How are you?" to his landlady.

"What pretty flowers you got there," the woman said from her rocking chair on the porch.

"Thank you."

"Somebody's mighty lucky to be gettin' them roses, I reckon." The landlady smiled and rocked.

"Have you seen him today?"

"No, but I heard that typewriter goin' like crazy this morning. Go on up before they start to wiltin' in this heat."

Velma did just that and paused at Rudy's door. She fussed with her clothes and hair, tugging at her blouse to highlight cleavage. The roses hidden behind her back, she knocked and listened. No one answered. There were no typewriter sounds, no approaching footsteps. She knocked again and realized he was probably not home. So she decided to leave the flowers with a note to surprise him. Knowing Rudy never locked the door, she turned the doorknob, thinking she could leave the flowers inside. Clothes were scattered everywhere, socks on the book pile, pants across the makeshift table of crates, the Murphy bed opened to the floor. Two writhing bodies were embracing beneath the sheets.

"Velma!" Rudy jumped up. "What're you doing here?"

"What am *I* doing here? Who's *that* in your bed?" She could barely get the words out of her throat. "Is that a man?!"

"Listen, Velma. This is really a bad time. . . ." He covered his nakedness with one of the sheets, and struggled to climb out of bed. "You really should've called first."

"Sorry." Velma's eyes filled with tears. "I started to, but I wanted to surprise you. But it looks like I surprised myself."

"Don't get excited. This is no time for dramatics."

"Dramatic? Who? Me, dramatic?"

"You *are* being dramatic! We'll talk later, okay? I'll give you a ring—"

"Dramatic, huh? I'll give you dramatic!" She shredded the roses of their petals and scattered them onto the floor. She broke the decapitated stems in half and threw them too. Tears rolling into the corners of her mouth, she ran, leaving the door open behind her. A gust of wind blew through the room, sweeping the rose petals about the floor. They danced in whirlpool motion like particles of dust.

11

Elvira screwed the caps on open jars, washed excess hair and dirt down the drain, wiped the sink clean, and checked the salt pork and hoecakes, whose aroma told her they were just about done.

This hour of the day, she missed Gilbert, her late husband. He'd be arriving about this time, tired, hungry, grumpy, sometimes argumentative; yet his arrival was the reward of an otherwise tiresome day. Didn't seem like he'd been dead for seven years. Seven years, Lord Jesus! and she could swear she still heard him thumping up the stairs in work boots as if he owned the building.

By now, he'd be in the bathroom washing up, and, contingent upon his mood, relating to her through the adjoining wall, the day's

details, gripes, hopes and disappointments. She'd respond with
Hmm hmm, Is that right? and *Well, I'll be!* When he emerged from
the bathroom, drying his hands on a towel, smelling delicious
enough to eat, she'd be waiting with his slippers, and the day's
Amsterdam News. He'd sit in the parlor, feet crossed on the
hassock, one hand resting on the lace doily Elvira made for his
reading table. Sometimes, she removed his socks, examining them
for mendable holes, and rubbed the feet he stood on all day. If the
mood was right she'd push the *Amsterdam News* out of the way,
plant herself on his lap, and bend down and kiss the nappy hairs on
his chest. Despite his reaction, she knew he loved it. Elvira knew
when their daughters arrived home and sensed when she and
Gilbert could squeeze in a bedroom interlude before dinner.

She knew her man, from the balding spots in his crown down to
the corns and bunions on his feet. She knew his temperament, his
longing for Atlanta and the family he left behind. He was a man of
few words. But she knew of his concerns over his younger brothers
living in Klan territory under Jim Crow and his unshakable love for
her and their daughters. What she didn't know was that he'd go off
to a war she marginally understood and never come home again.
Gilbert, like the Negro masses, wanted to prove his worth as a man
and an American. He wanted to prove his love and patriotism for a
country that could have lynched him. She wanted him alive and at
home.

He left behind a multitude of memorable traits and quirks she
sorely missed: his snoring, his laughter, his inability to hold liquor
or discipline the girls, his good-naturedness. She could still feel him
pressing against her in bed, her body pulled close to him, his arm
wrapped around her waist, snoring against her neck. His smell, after
he was long gone, continued to haunt her sheets and pillowcases.

She yearned for his masculinity. She hadn't had a man since him,
and her body sometimes screamed with desire. She did everything
to repress it, but like the dust on her floor, it returned time and time
again.

She cleared her mind of Gilbert before she got teary-eyed. She
didn't like stewing in self-pity. She dabbed at her eyes with a tissue
and was examining her hoecakes when the telephone rang. A
customer at the other end tried cajoling Elvira into squeezing her in
for an appointment the next day. Elvira told the customer it would
be difficult; she had a full load as it was, but she'd see what she
could do. Actually, she loved being swamped with work. She turned

no one down even on her busiest days. It gave her less time to live in the past with Gilbert.

Besides, she had her daughters to consider, especially Louise. Louise was suffering. Elvira had seen it all before, growing up around mulattoes and light-skinned black folks in the South. Even when you know what you are and take pride in it, it hurts to go through life being mistaken for something else. Though she never told Gilbert, or anyone else, she never forgot that day when, as a child, Louise ran into the house crying, confused as to which race of people she belonged. What is going to become of her? she asked herself. She came up with no answers, and asked God to show her signs.

Louise was just coming in from job hunting. Elvira knew how the day had gone before she asked the question.

"How's my baby girl?"

Louise said nothing.

"You must be starvin'," Elvira said, fixing Louise's plate at the stove. "Look what Mother done fix for you."

"I'm not hungry, Mother. Maybe later."

"I made your favorite. Salt pork, some greens and corn dumplin's."

Louise sat at the table, crossed her legs, and closed her eyes. She massaged her temples, then buried her face in her hands.

"You don't know what you missin'," Elvira signified. "These is the best greens I ever—"

"Mother, what am I going to do?" Louise interrupted, lifted her face from the table.

"Why don't you start with this here hoecake—"

"Mother, I'm talking about my life."

"What's wrong now?" Elvira set down the plate, wiped her hands and sat at the table with Louise. "I know life's tough, and Harlem ain't no easy place to be, but don't worry, you'll find something you like to do."

"I don't know what I want to do. My sisters both have some kind of talent—"

"It ain't like you ain't got no talent. You know how to tapdance. You likes show business and movie stars. Why don't you do that?"

"I'm a quitter, Mother."

"So what if you quit bein' a Walker agent, you can still dream like Madame and make them dreams come true."

"I don't know."

"Honey, it's only 1925 and you only nineteen. You ain't even as old as the century's young. There's lots of colored girls . . ."

Louise didn't want to say it, or be misunderstood by her mother, but now seemed the proper moment. "Why can't I be one or the other?"

"One or the other what?" Elvira asked, knowing good and well what she meant, terrified to even think it.

"Colored this, white that. I'm so sick of it."

Elvira took her hand and rubbed it. She'd suspected this impending discussion would one day rear its ugly head in her God-fearing home. She had to tell the child something. But what could she say that she hadn't said already? "Baby, me and Gilbert had three beautiful girls and each one is different. Miriam dark just like my mama, Velma brown like me and my daddy, and you the spittin' image of your Grandma Brooks. You look jus' like her. It ain't no crime, baby. Just the way things is. Make the best of it. You ain't the only light-skinned gal the Lord done made."

"All I know, Mother, is that when white people think I'm one of them, they treat me like a person. They find out I'm colored, they turn against me."

"C'mon and put somethin' in your stomach—"

"Mother, you remember Marcello the vegetable man who used to come around? Well, he used to stare at me a lot. I never knew why, but he did. One day, I went to get something for you and he asked me who I was. I told him, and that man looked at me like I was a liar. He didn't believe I was Miriam's or Velma's sister. He said I looked like his daughter Luisa. What a coincidence, he said, when I told him my name. And, sometimes, Mother, I wanted to be Luisa. You know what I mean? Please don't misunderstand, but I thought if I could be Luisa, my life would be less complicated. Do you understand?"

"You gonna have a good life," Elvira said, wringing her hands as she grew distressed with this discussion.

"I need to be sure of that."

"What?"

"About my future. I know about a medium who can tell me."

"You know that's playin' with Satan."

"Why not? I got nobody else to play with. All my girlfriends dropped me because they thought their boyfriends liked me too much."

Elvira saw that gleam that usually sparkled in Louise's eye was gone. Resting her elbows on the table, Louise nestled her head between her palms. She didn't touch the food, but sat, a faraway look clouding her gaze. Elvira got up and feigned preoccupation with kitchen chores. Furtively, she studied Louise's expression, worry lines gathering around her own eyes. She felt Louise falling into an abyss, and Elvira couldn't stop the plunge or shield her from it. In her mind, there existed no worse frustration than her inability to shelter her girls from life's poisoned arrows. Lord, she prayed, what am I gonna do? Help her, Lord. Her mind's all twisted up and fulla crazy ideas.

12

"*. . .* An' afta escapin' a hang noose and a mob of angry crackers, I comes all the way to Harlem and old age start to kickin' my behin'. Can't keep one step ahead of everything, can you, Nurse Brooks?"

Mr. Lewis loved telling about his escape from a Mississippi lynch mob and Miriam loved listening to him. He was one of her favorite patients.

She was administering his medication when Agnes stuck her head in the room to say, if it wasn't such short notice, she wanted to attend a UNIA meeting. That made Miriam's day and put her in a good mood that lasted through the late afternoon into early evening.

"How'd you manage to get away from Tommy this evening?" Miriam was curious. Last time she asked Agnes to attend a meeting, she declined, using Tommy as an excuse.

"Well, I didn't tell him, actually," Agnes said.

"Good for you," Miriam said. "About time you stopped letting him own you."

"I didn't say that, Miriam."

"Oh," Miriam said, embarrassed for having been so hasty. She wanted to snatch the words from the air and shove them back down her throat.

"I just decided not to tell him to his face."

"So, what did you do?"

"What I did was," Agnes said, like a naughty girl outwitting her mother, "I left him a note."

"Where you leave it?"

"In the house. He got keys. When he comes, he'll see the note and know where I am."

The two women strolled down the avenue as dusk settled over the city. Miriam pranced down the street with pep in her step that denied her exhausting nine-hour shift.

They turned the corner and she schemed of ways to detain Agnes after the meeting. They hadn't eaten since their twenty-five-minute lunch in the cafeteria. So she thought of having dinner at a UNIA-owned restaurant. This would allow her the opportunity to show off the entire establishment. She wanted to impress Agnes enough for her to join UNIA.

Before the meeting began, Miriam showed off the Liberty Hall facilities as if she'd built them herself. Her pride and joy was the Black Madonna statue. Agnes didn't know what to make of it, staring at the statue with a sour look on her face.

"Well, what do you think?" Miriam asked. "Isn't it beautiful?"

"I don't know, Miriam," Agnes said. "Since when did Mary turn black?"

"Now you sound like my mother."

The auditorium was filling up quickly. From across the room, Miriam waved to fellow Black Cross Nurses and other women members with whiny children clinging to their skirts. They found a couple of empty seats. It's gonna be a great meeting tonight, I can feel it, Miriam thought. Then she noticed him. Oh, Lord, here he comes again, why won't he leave me alone?

"When this man comes over," she said, nudging Agnes, "don't say much and he'll go away as quickly as he came, okay?"

She was speaking of Hiram Woodlowe. He had eyes for her and she didn't have the spit to say his name. Other than their political affiliation, they held nothing in common. Whenever he tried talking to her about anything other than Garvey, she shooed him away like a pestering mosquito.

"Good to see you, Miss Miriam," Hiram said, sitting in an empty chair beside them.

"Good evening, Hiram," Miriam said without looking at him.

"Looks like it's gonna be a good meeting tonight," he said, smiling, waiting for an introduction to her friend.

"Great meeting, indeed," Miriam replied.

"Ain't you gonna introduce me to your friend?" Hiram's eyes widened.

Why can't folks just go on about their business, she thought, as she uttered the words, "This here is my good friend Agnes. She works with me at the hospital. Agnes, Hiram."

"Please to meet you, ma'am."

"Nice meeting you too, Hiram."

"You ladies mind if I sit with you?"

"No, not at all—"

"Yes, we mind very much," Miriam interrupted Agnes. "There's a whole lotta seats in this auditorium; why you wanna pick this one?"

" 'Cause the other empty seats ain't got you sittin' next to them, that's why." He grinned, playing hardball to Miriam's hard-to-get.

There was an awkward pause, and, taking the hint, Hiram politely bade them a good evening. "Well, I hope you enjoy the meeting. If you have time afterward, maybe we can go for a cup of coffee."

"Yeah, yeah, yeah," Miriam said.

"Why you so hard on him?" Agnes asked. "He seems like a nice man."

"Yeah, he's nice. But, he's a . . . a nice nuisance."

"He's cute, Miriam."

"Yeah, and so are midgets," Miriam said, laughing. "Hiram's like a child. He doesn't mean any harm, but he gets on my nerves sometimes, hovering around me like I'm his mama. He just, oh, I don't know, he just goes all through me sometimes."

Agnes said nothing, but kept her eyes front, her stare fixed upon the podium. Miriam asked, "So Agnes, what you think so far?"

"Miriam," Agnes said, "it ain't even started, girl."

A speaker stepped to the podium, shuffling papers before him. A hush fell over the audience as he began to speak. He urged support for the release of their imprisoned leader Marcus Garvey, a victim of governmental conspiracy instigated by J. Edgar Hoover.

In the back of the auditorium, there was a commotion. Miriam glanced over her shoulder and saw a man talking loudly to one of the members, but she couldn't hear the words. The man tried walking around the usher, who stepped in his way, blocking his path. She could see the man was upset, but the words between them were drowned by the speaker's amplified voice. She whispered to Agnes that some fool was giving one of the brothers a hard time.

Agnes didn't budge, listening to the speaker. Miriam watched the intruder glance around the room as if he were looking for someone. Scanning the backs of heads from right to left, his eyes stopped when they met Miriam's. She was surprised he stared at her with some familiarity. She didn't recognize him. He broke away from the ushers and made his way down the aisle. The belligerent so-and-so was coming toward her. She didn't know what was about to happen. UNIA officials trailed him down the aisle. The man stopped at their row and squeezed between the chairs to where Miriam sat.

"Just what the hell do you think you doin'?" he charged.

Agnes snapped her head around. "Tommy, baby, what're you doing here?"

Surrounding members hushed them. Tommy ignored it, grabbing Agnes by the arm.

"I asked you a question."

"I left you a note. I was coming right home after this was over," Agnes said, embarrassed. "This here is my friend Miriam, the one I been telling you about."

Neither he nor Miriam exchanged hellos. He pulled Agnes out of the chair and insisted, "You're coming home with me now!"

"Tommy, it'll be over in about an hour. Why can't I stay?"

"I'm sorry, sir," a UNIA member spoke up. "You'll have to remain quiet or take that noise outside."

Agnes looked from Tommy to Miriam. Miriam hoped that someone would throw Tommy out into the street. Couldn't they see he was disturbing a woman minding her own business?

Agnes stood and grabbed her cap, looking down at Miriam with apologetic eyes. "Sorry, Miriam. I gotta go."

"Why? It'll be over before you know it."

Agnes said nothing, but looked at Tommy, shrugged, and started for the aisle. "See you tomorrow, Miriam," she said, and left.

Miriam couldn't concentrate on the evening's lecture. The woman hadn't warmed the chair she was sitting in. What a waste, Miriam thought. She'd fueled her entire day on the promise that Agnes was attending this meeting. Just ain't fair, women ain't nobody's property. Now, she didn't want to stay for the meeting, the first time in all her years as a Garveyite. Tommy just walked in, raised hell, and stuck a pin in her bubble, and she sat there, helpless, unable to patch it and blow it back up. Agnes wasn't strong-willed enough, Miriam decided, and she flashed on the dinner and discussion that she and Agnes wouldn't have after all.

She'd talk to her tomorrow at work, provided they had the time. They barely had a moment to pee at Harlem Hospital. Miriam was ready to leave when someone tapped her on the shoulder. She looked up into Tommy's face.

"Sorry, I was so rude before, ma'am." His tone was polite, even charming.

"That's all right," Miriam said coolly, wanting to slap his face.

"Think I could speak to you a moment?" he asked so politely she couldn't refuse.

She got up and together they departed. They talked in the hall without disrupting the speaker. She knew Tommy wanted to apologize for his crass manners and an apology was certainly in order. She just didn't know if she'd sincerely accept it.

"Look," he began, "I know you must think I'm crazy."

Think? Miriam thought.

"I didn't want to leave you with the wrong impression, so let's start over. My name's Tommy." He offered his hand.

Miriam didn't accept it. "And I'm Miriam Brooks."

"Agnes told me a lot about you," he said. "But she never told me how pretty you was."

"I'm missing my meeting," Miriam said. "What is it you want?"

"Well," he said, taking a pencil and a piece of paper from his pocket. He scribbled on the paper and handed it to Miriam. "I don't want you to miss your meeting," he said apologetically, "but here's my number. Give me a call sometime. Maybe we could have a drink. Take care, with your pretty self." He winked and disappeared through the door.

Before Miriam could respond, he was gone. The nerve, she thought. He doesn't even take Agnes out for a drink and he's inviting me? Giving me his telephone number? He doesn't know I already got the story on him. She started to throw the telephone number in the trash, reconsidered and tucked it away in her purse.

13

In her bare apartment, Velma stooped to grab a handful of clothes from an old suitcase. Mother had transferred her belongings to Harlem from Atlanta in this suitcase, and Velma regarded it as an heirloom. Stacks of books and unpacked boxes lined the walls. Through a corner window, she looked out into the streets. Happy to be in a place all her own, she hung out the third-floor window and inhaled the fresh air.

The unpacking could wait. She stepped onto the fire escape. Winds off the Harlem River blew through her sheer summer dress. Urban noises rose to the air like fluttering butterflies, then dispersed. Through the open window of the neighboring apartment, choppy, hoarse jazz notes from a wailing tenor saxophone swelled up around her. Smoke fumes of fried porgies and catfish from Leona's Fish Fry on the corner flirted with her nostrils. Eyeing the Bright & Bostick Real Estate office and Green's Employment Agency: Colored Help a Specialty, she acquainted herself with new neighbors. Harlem. Black Harlem. Race artists—writers, musicians, dancers, composers, singers, actors—flocked here from the four corners of the nation to present their polished contributions to world culture. For Velma, there was no other place to be than here. Her birthplace.

She hadn't seen Rudy since that day, and exerted futile attempts not to think about him. She blamed herself for entering unannounced, though he habitually left his door unlocked and bragged about it. She never, not for one moment, expected to find him at home . . . in bed . . . with someone other than her . . . a man at that! The sound of it was harsh to her ears. What a surprise, all right. She didn't know what to make of it. He said he'd call later but her telephone never rang; Mother would have relayed the message.

Juggling the puzzle pieces in her mind, she thought: He likes men and yet he slept with me. What does that make him? She was scared to think it. She should have known. The day she bought him roses was just too, too perfect. No day is that perfect; something had to go awry. Still, she had never expected life to be that jarring and disconcerting. She felt she was growing up.

Rudy wasn't in love with her. How could he be? But loving him so much, she wasn't about to simply give up on him. She had a Plan B. He obviously liked women, so there was hope. She could turn him around and put him on the track she felt his train *should* be arriving on. She hardly shared stockings and underwear when she lived at home with her sisters. She wasn't about to share a man. She humorously daydreamed of branding his behind: Property of V.B. She sighed and mentally scolded herself for getting into this mess.

She grabbed a handful of her dress and thrust one leg at a time over the windowsill. She climbed inside, walked across the floor, and stood in the center of her new parlor. Nothing but space and more space surrounded her. She loved the solitude, the quiet. She could write without distraction. How different it would be from Mother's apartment—the noise, laughter, and chattering. The only threat to her tranquillity would be the fellow next door. Lord, he couldn't play that saxophone a lick, but she could live with that.

She ceremoniously placed her typewriter on a table in the center of the floor. Everything else remained packed. She dusted off the roller, the home-row keys, and the space bar. This would be the spot from where she'd write her great novel. Right here, in the middle of this room.

A faint knock sounded upon her door. She ignored it, thinking it was next door. The knock came again, harder. Approaching the door on tiptoe, she wondered who knew she lived here. She had told no one except her family. It could be one of them, or the landlady bugging her with another annoying house rule. "Who is it?" There was no answer, save the breathing on the other side of the door. "Who *is* it?" She opened the door, unclear how to react to the first visitor in her new home.

"Are you just going to stand there, or invite me in?"

"Suit yourself," she said, walking away.

Rudy entered, his hands behind his back. He walked slowly, scrutinizing the apartment.

"How'd you know I lived here?"

"You'd be surprised by what I know. Here, these are for you." He handed her a bunch of closed yellow roses, hoping she wouldn't throw them back in his face.

She took the roses, wrapped inside tissue paper. "For me?" She sniffed the fragrance. "What are they for?" She wanted him to leave, to give him holy hell, yet she couldn't help but soften.

"Well, recently, I found a bunch of red roses shredded on my floor, just torn to bits. So, I waved my magic wand and, presto! here they are, yellow this time." He snapped his fingers like a magician. "Friends?" Please say yes, he thought.

"Friends," she said, unconvinced.

"I'll put them in water," Rudy said. He found a stained jar, scrubbed it in the sink and filled it with fresh water. He placed the roses inside and set them down beside the typewriter on the table. He took Velma's hand and kissed it. He led her toward the window, and they gazed at street life through the fire escape. For a while, neither of them spoke.

"Rudy—"

"Velma—"

They spoke simultaneously. "Go ahead, Velma." He squeezed her shoulder affectionately.

"No. You go first."

"Well, I came by here today, after much ado with your mother to find out where you live, to say I don't want you to be angry with me."

She noticed that it wasn't exactly an apology. "I'm not angry. I just overreacted, I guess."

"Velma, I told you when we met that we were going to be great friends. Didn't I? And we are. But there's some things you should know about me."

"I think I already do." She couldn't resist the sarcasm.

"Well, that too. But, it's more important that you understand that I'm what I guess you would call a free spirit. No strings, no attachments. I belong to no one but myself. Sorry you had to find out this way. Do you understand?"

Velma sighed. "I'm trying to. But it's hard to swallow. I guess . . . well, I guess I like you too much."

"Like . . . or love?"

"We're playing semantics?"

"If necessary. No misunderstandings, okay?"

"It's probably too late for that." She wanted to, but couldn't look at him.

"What do you mean?" Rudy said.

"Oh, nothing."

"Come on, you're too opinionated and articulate to mean nothing."

"Let's skip it. It's not important."

"Velma, look at me." He turned her to face him.

Her heart pounded so hard, she was afraid he would hear it. She tried to occupy her trembling hands, her back to the window. Plainly, she didn't want to hear any explanation other than he'd made a grave mistake, was hopelessly in love with her, and couldn't admit it. "Okay," she said, "I'm looking at you."

"How do you feel about me? Be honest."

"You're an okay fellow, I guess. Little rough on the edges, but one tends to get used to—"

"Be serious."

"Rudy, why tell you what you already know. Haven't you been flattered enough? Yes, yes, I'm in love with you. There, okay?" She walked away from him, her arms folded across her breasts, and busied herself with the unpacked boxes.

"Don't be," he said, more as an order than a request.

"What do you mean?"

"I can't love you that way and I can't lose your friendship."

"How do you know you can't love me *that* way? You make it sound like a disease."

"Believe me, I've played this scenario more than you know."

"Can I ask you something?"

"Sure, anything." *Oh boy, here it comes,* echoed through his head.

"Why are you that way?"

"What way?"

"Now, who's playing semantics?"

"I don't know."

"What do you mean, you don't know?"

"Answer that and you'll solve the riddle of the Sphinx."

"But, Rudy," she pleaded, taking his hand, "you don't have to be that way."

"Velma, it's not a passing condition or a choice—it's the way I am."

"I can change you."

"Oh boy, here we go. The power of the pussy, right?"

"Rudy!"

"Well, it's true."

"But, you're too masculine . . . too good-looking to be that way."

"I'm sure there's a compliment in there somewhere," he said, realizing it was hopeless. "Let's talk about something else."

"Okay." Velma walked away.

Rudy had thought she was more sophisticated, that she knew the diversely wicked ways of the big, bad world. He had overestimated her, and they were getting nowhere with this. She was denying his reality. A part of him wished he hadn't come. Had he seen how hard she was falling, he would never have let the Sauternes have its way with him. Couldn't folks just go with the flow of life's momentum without gratuitous expectation? He remembered other reasons for which he paid her this visit. "I do have some news for you."

"Good or bad?" She unpacked her boxes without turning to face him.

"You tell me." He yawned and stretched his arms outward. "I think you should enter Amy Spingarn's Poetry Contest. I think you can win."

"Doesn't Countee Cullen usually snatch first prize? Thanks. I don't stand a chance."

"Now, that's not the Velma I know. You have a great chance. And"—he paused dramatically, hoping she'd receive his news with the spirit in which it was intended—"guess where we're going in two weeks? That is, if you want to."

"Where?"

"I got an invitation to one of Van Vechten's literary soirees. I want you to be my date."

"Carl Van Vechten?"

"No, his Uncle Rufus."

"Oh my God! What'll I wear?"

"Do what I do; wear what's comfortable."

"At one of those parties? Are you kidding?" For years, she had wanted an invitation to one of New York's celebrated literary salons. "Who'll be there?"

"Well, don't most starving artists jump at the chance of a free meal?"

"When is it?"

"I didn't tell you why we're going."

"I don't care."

"Someone has published another novel and it's a party in their honor. Guess who?"

"Toomer?!"

"No."

"Zora."

"You're not even hot. Your all-time favorite, G. Virgil Scott."

"You're teasing me?"

"What's wrong? A moment ago, you were bouncing off the wall with excitement."

"Let me think about it."

He didn't want to *belong* to her, Mr. Free Spirit, Velma thought, and yet he was asking for a date. What he said or how he explained himself was utterly inconsequential. She didn't care what he said, she still had designs on him. If she could rinse her system clean of him, she would. She imagined him escorting her to the Van Vechten soiree; walking through the door with the man she loved; the man that wasn't hers. She threw out Plan B. This was going to be a hard one to crack. But he wasn't ridding himself of her that easily.

"Another thing, Velma," Rudy said, clearing his throat, a plea in his voice. "What you saw . . . I need you to promise . . . well, let's keep it between us. I don't want it spread around . . . it's no big thing, but still . . . you understand."

14

The bay windows of a Greenwich Village brick townhouse shed arched squares of golden light on the sidewalk. Overlapping voices and laughter bounced and echoed, spilling into the streets through the open windows.

Guests, bedazzled and jeweled, milled around in an enormous parlor, engaging in forced smiles and contemporary small talk. Ice cubes clicked against crystal glasses. A multisprouted fountain gushed inexhaustible streams of Dom Pérignon. Beside the fountain sat a two-foot swan carved from ice. Between the frozen wings lay a bed of golden caviar merging with the bird's quickly melting back. White-gloved servants carried trays with alcoholic beverages and exotic hors d'oeuvres. Overhead chandeliers were teasingly lit, the dim light mixing with suspended smoke, casting a sensual glow on a group of high-society intellectuals. They laughed, sitting at the foot of a winding, carpeted staircase. They didn't notice Velma's and Rudy's unobtrusive entrance.

Velma held on to Rudy's arm, intimidated by the luxurious atmosphere. "Rudy, you sure I look all right?" She fussed with her hair, tugged at her shoulder straps, the low-cut neckline, looking to Rudy for a reply. "Well?"

"Believe me," Rudy replied, "no one really cares. We're Negro writers, remember? The toast of any party these days."

Thanks so much, Velma thought, considering all her efforts. She wore a calf-length lavender dress, a tied silk ribbon hugging her thighs. The matching headband wrapped around a head covered with tight, glossy fingerwaves; one large curl dotted her forehead, courtesy of Mother. A peacock feather sprouted from the back of the headband. Her lips and fingernails were painted blood red. Rhinestone earrings swung from her earlobes, sparkling as they caught the light. She cooled herself with a tassled folding fan, to give her an air of sophistication she felt had been missing during her quiet entrance. She looked to Rudy, giving him a once-over. "Anybody ever tell you you're very handsome in a double-breasted suit?"

"How about uncomfortable?" Rudy fondled the caramel necktie knot and collar bar. The beige summer suit was new, and upon Velma's insistence, so were his brown wing tips and transparent silk hosiery.

In the far corner, a Negro woman in pink ostrich feathers, sat upon a piano singing sultry jazz, her eyes closed, legs crossed, her head rolling shoulder to shoulder. Her accompanist, a young white man with his hair parted in the middle, played a Steinway. Beside him on the piano bench sat a woman in a barebacked gown. Her stockinged foot caressed his leg. When a servant passed with a silver tray of cocktails, she snatched one, giggling and sipping carelessly, dipping her fingers into the martinis and sucking them. Playfully, she showered the man's neck with her dripping fingers. Six-foot potted palms curved above her head and shaded her face like an eclipsing moon.

"Well, if it isn't Zachary Rudolph!" A baby-faced man with golden-blond hair approached with open arms. He shook Rudy's hand as they exchanged wide smiles.

"How are you, Carl?"

"Marvelous. You?"

"Wonderful," Rudy said, glancing around the room. "Lovely party."

Velma cleared her throat and nudged Rudy.

"Oh, excuse my manners," Rudy said, turning to Velma. "Velma, Carl Van Vechten. Carl, this is Velma Brooks, my date."

"Delighted to meet you," Carl said, pushing his hair away from his forehead.

"Likewise, Mr. Van Vechten."

"Please, call me Carl." He took a sip of his champagne. "What do you do, my dear?"

"Velma's a gifted writer," Rudy volunteered, "you'll be hearing a lot from."

"Oh!" Carl said, impressed. "Do you know Zora?"

"We've never met," Velma said.

"You should," Carl urged. "Her colorful writing is shadowed only by her flamboyant personality, I assure you. Zora's the life of the party, anybody's party. And her intriguing folklore from the rural South, my dear—you simply haven't lived."

"Still photographing?" Rudy asked. He turned toward Velma. "Carl here is a veritable Renaissance man. There's nothing he doesn't do." Rudy stretched his head above the crowd. "Where's our celebrated author?"

"Scott?" Carl stood on his toes. "I haven't seen him in a spell. But then, you know Scott. He may've left already. One never knows."

"I've never met him," Rudy admitted.

"No?" Carl looked surprised. "Well, you should. Fascinating gentleman. A little strange, but then, as artists, aren't we all. I must go; enjoy your evening." Carl lost himself in the sea of mingling guests.

"Rudy," Velma said, watching Carl's back until she saw it no more, "could you please get me a drink?"

"Certainly." Rudy left and walked into the adjoining room. He stopped and admired the sculptured swan. A man with a white handkerchief stood nearby. Every few minutes, he wiped the swan's delicate neck and beak of water, which dripped like perspiration onto the floor. Rudy guessed he was the sculptor, the nail-biting sentry helplessly watching his creation melt into a pool of nothingness as seconds ticked away. With a cracker, Rudy scooped up a dab of the golden caviar. As he walked away, the sentry meticulously wiped the bird's detailed, yet fading, wing.

The air was alive with succulent odors of poultry and other delicacies. Rudy peeked in the kitchen, and watched a band of servants crashing into each other, frantically carrying out duties, as a matronly cook, on her knees, pulled a browned turkey from the oven and sighed with admiration.

Shadows flickered along the flowered wallpaper. Stained-glass lamps and others with fringed shades provided a subdued lighting.

Tall brass lamps, Art Deco figurines, and mirrors tastefully enhanced the room. What a splendid home, Rudy thought, taking in
an eyeful of the eclectic crowd. Negroes and whites mixed and
blended with one another as if integration were the order of the day.
Interracial couples kissed openly or danced the Black Bottom and
other risqué gyrations to the jazzy piano chords. He heard laconic
phrasings and guttural accents pour from foreign tongues. *Who's
playing that marvelous piano?* He eavesdropped on a London art
dealer inviting two American painters to stay in his English
countryside home. Accents leaped all around him from French,
Arabic, Italian, and Swedish throats, imbuing the affair with an
international panache. A distraught woman stood alone in a corner
weeping into a laced handkerchief. Her grief went unnoticed as the
party swirled around her. Her dress was white, layered with silk
spaghetti fringes that shook in unison as she trembled. Jilted! Rudy
thought, and her lover's probably upstairs with the new ingenue he
met twenty minutes ago. He thought of bringing her a drink, and
remembered he was supposed to get Velma one. He wanted to have
a great time with Velma tonight, dancing the Charleston, shimmy-
ing like pagans until dawn. But that was his limit, and he hoped she
expected nothing more from him.

Velma inched through the festive crowd. She was distracted by a
silk-covered wall. Upon it hung a canvas original in avant-garde
strokes and dazzling colorations. She'd never seen it before, but
knew the artist was Aaron Douglas. Below it, on a small, marble
table sat the sculpture of African figures and warrior masks. A loud
cry of laughter broke her concentration as she studied the artwork.
Turning, she saw the guffawing, gap-toothed mouth of a skinny
Ethel Waters. They don't call her Mama Stringbean for nothing,
Velma thought, as the woman talked and laughed with a quartet of
tuxedoed gentlemen, smoking from cigarette holders. Returning
her attention to the sculpture, Velma touched one of the pieces.

"Bonsoir, mademoiselle," a deep, unfamiliar voice uttered behind her. The man was dressed in a smoke-gray suit, matching
leather suspenders, and a pin-striped shirt. His wide tie was dotted
with black, gray, and white specks; the knot at his collar was the
size of a thumbnail. Velma looked down at his white oxfords, then
looked up, resting her eyes on the pearl stickpin in his lapel. A pipe
was clenched between his teeth. If Adonis was Negro, Velma
thought, he would look like this. A part evenly separated his closely
cropped, wavy hair and his eyes became slits when he smiled. He'd

said nothing to her except good evening—that much French she understood—and she felt her composure dissolve.

"I see you're admiring the sculpture. You must have exquisite taste," he continued, nodding.

"Isn't it marvelous?" she replied, not knowing what else to say.

"Hardly as marvelous as you, my dear." He kissed her hand. "But I must confess, I have a weakness for Richmond Barthe. His work is so precise, it's unsettling."

"And primitive," Velma added.

"May I have the privilege?" he asked.

"Velma Brooks. And you?"

"My dear Miss Brooks, would you care to accompany me on a stroll through Washington Square? You'll find it utterly cozy at this bewitching hour."

"Thank you, but I came with a friend," she said, hoping not to discourage the stranger's intentions if he had any.

"Enjoying this monstrosity of a festive occasion, are you?"

"It's quite posh, don't you think?"

"Well," he said, taking the pipe from his mouth, "that depends upon one's definition of *posh*. If you can throw a bunch of people together in a room, whose collective celebrity is, at best, questionable, and kick in a sculpted swan and a fountain of champagne, I don't know, perhaps that's *posh* for some people." He placed the pipe back in his mouth. He studied her intently and decided he wasn't leaving the party without this bronze creature in the lavender headband and peacock feather, this Nubian Pocahontas.

"What celebrities?" Velma asked, regretting her *posh* reference to the party. "All I see is Ethel Waters."

"My dear, the men whose painting and sculpture you're admiring are here among us." He scanned the room and pointed toward the Steinway. "That's Gershwin over there, but of course you know that."

"Yes," Velma lied, suddenly realizing the music did sound familiar. "I knew that."

"And," he said, lowering his voice, "I'm told a motley bunch of Hollyood movie stars are here. Since I fail to share the popular rave of such technological rubbish as moving pictures, their so-called celebrity escapes me completely."

Rudy returned, carrying two drinks in delicate crystal. He nodded to the gentleman with the pipe and handed Velma a drink.

"What took you so long?" Velma asked.

"Oh, I ran into DuBois," Rudy said excitedly. "We chatted and I told him about a friend I want him to meet."

"Where is he?" Velma said, her eyes darting about the room.

"Over there." Rudy pointed, Velma following the direction of his finger. The erudite DuBois stood near an empty fireplace. In his three-piece suit with a gold chain drooping from the vest pocket he was dapper, his graying V-shaped beard distinguished.

"I didn't realize he was such a small man," Velma confessed.

"I don't believe we've met," Rudy said, turning to the man standing with Velma, and extended his hand. "I'm Zachary Rudolph."

"G. Virgil Scott," the man replied, "Scott to most people." He noticed Rudy and Velma's stunned reactions.

"Of course!" Rudy recognized him from dustcover photographs. "So, you're Scott."

"I've been called worse," Scott said, wondering who Zachary Rudolph was, hoping he'd go away.

"You look different," Rudy said, rubbing his chin, studying the man's features. "You shaved your mustache or something."

"When do I get to meet W.E.B.?" Velma asked, thrilled at the thought, considering herself one of DuBois's so-called Talented Tenth.

"Oh, DuBois?" Rudy said. "Now, if you like."

"*Pardonnez-moi, monsieur*," Scott said. "But what did you call him?"

Rudy glanced at Velma. "DuBois," he repeated.

"My dear man," Scott said, "his name is not Du*Boys*. You must be from New Jersey. The man's name is Du*Bwa*. Think you could say that? It never ceases to appall me how Americans butcher foreign names with lazy tongues." He sipped his drink and puffed his pipe.

"Well, that's what everybody else calls him," Rudy defended himself, embarrassed.

"Don't repeat the mistakes of the illiterate masses," Scott replied. "You'll excuse me a moment. Here comes that wretch of a woman, Helena Rubinstein. She simply won't leave without a perfunctory peck on the cheek. Be back shortly." Departing, he kissed Velma's hand and bowed. He walked away, shouting into the crowd, "Helena, dahling, it's utterly marvelous of you to come. So good to see you again. . . ."

"It's too early to tell"—Rudy lowered his voice—"but I don't think I like that guy."

Velma was pleased with what she construed as his jealousy. The soiree's honored guest, indisputably the most gorgeous and refined presence among them, had ingratiated himself with her, and she thought Rudy was jealous; at least, she hoped so.

"I thought he was your idol, Rudy? You're so cute when you get embarrassed," she said, laughing.

"Embarrassed?" Rudy said defensively. "Who's embarrassed? What's funny? You thought that was funny?"

"I find him charming . . . not to mention, gorgeous."

"I thought you hated him so much," Rudy said, his lip curling.

"He swept me off my feet before I knew who he was."

"He's a pompous—"

"Now, now, Rudy. Shhh, here he comes."

"So," Scott said, returning, "what is it you do, Mr. Rudolph?"

"I'm a writer too," Rudy said proudly, getting even. Scott wasn't the only published novelist among them. "Knopf is publishing my—"

"Yes, yes, of course," Scott said, turning to Velma. "And you, my dear?"

"A writer," she said, blushing.

"Fledgling writers, huh?" Scott lit his pipe, his cheeks filling with air as he puffed, tufts of smoke rising. "Bubbling with ambition and larger-than-life notions, you have flocked to Harlem to penetrate the ranks of the celebrated literati—or should that be *niggerati?*"

Velma and Rudy exchanged glances.

"Oh, please don't be put off," Scott said, "I'm just recognizing my younger self in you both. Actually, I'd like to invite you to another soiree."

"To what?" Rudy snapped sarcastically. "Another party in your honor?"

"To a picnic, actually," Scott said. "An initiation rite for young writers in Harlem."

"I love picnics in Central Park," Velma said.

"Not quite," Scott said. "I was speaking of the pedestrian walk on the Brooklyn Bridge."

"You're joking," Rudy said, wishing this man would leave them alone. He'd had about enough.

"My dear boy," Scott said, lightly poking Rudy's chest with a forefinger. "I make it a religious practice never to joke before my fifth martini. Of course you'll both come?"

"Count me out," Rudy said, sipping the last of his champagne.

"We'd love to!" Velma shouted, louder than she had intended. "When, what time?"

"Saturday," Scott said. "Midnight."

"Midnight?" Velma laughed. "Who's on the bridge at—"

"Precisely my point, *ma chérie*," Scott assured her.

"As I said, count me out," Rudy repeated. "I need another drink."

He left abruptly and Velma gloated. Maybe now he'll see what he's passing up, she thought. How could he not want me? Scott blew into her life a much needed breeze—a godsend—showering her with attention and penetrating glances. Romantic rival, huh? With all her Plans A to Z to have Rudy the way she wanted him, she'd never even considered a romantic rival.

She spotted a cluster of people huddled around a small figure. Sporadically, they burst into spurts of drunken laughter. Dominating their attentions, a woman clowned, throwing her head back in laughter, gesticulating with her hands. She was speaking, but Velma and Scott couldn't hear. Again, the huddle laughed raucously.

"Wonder who that is?" Velma said, dying to hear the jokes that were breaking everybody up.

"I'm afraid to look," Scott said, "but by the sound, my guess would be loud, raunchy Zora. Never satisfied unless she's the absolute focus of attention at everyone's party. An amusing excuse of a woman, indeed."

"You know her?"

"Never let it be said, my dear, that I'm proud of it."

"Would you mind introducing me?" Velma asked, grasping at any opportunity to be seen with him or be introduced by him.

"I never refuse a lady's first request," he said, kissing her hand for the third time that evening, and offered his elbow. He counted the moments until he'd have her alone.

Velma hooked her arm through Scott's. As his head turned, she glimpsed his chiseled profile, and her knees weakened. Placing her glass on the table, she fidgeted with the lavender headband and fingered the peacock feather in her hair. Fancying her newly made acquaintance as her escort, she glided along the floor on the arm of the evening's guest of honor, not unlike royalty approaching her subjects.

15

"What a weird place for a picnic," Rudy groaned.

The three of them, Velma, Rudy, and Scott, trod the wooden planks of the Brooklyn Bridge's pedestrian path. A light fog caused the neighboring borough to appear hazy, surreal on the distant shore. Along the Manhattan shore, blinking lights illuminated the jagged skyline. Stars twinkled against the sky's black velvet. Foghorns sounded in the distance. The East River's waves slapped against the New York docks. A tugboat with a single light chugged toward The Bronx, ripples of foam trailing its path. The early September air smelled fishy, reminding Velma of Leona's Fish Fry. The full moon, tinged in burnt orange, hung overhead, omniscient witness to the bewitching midnight hour.

Scott and Velma strolled arm in arm. They'd seen each other several times in the past week. With her free hand, she carried a basket of French breads, imported cheeses, and a bottle of Bordeaux, vintage 1899. Rudy wore a straw hat with a striped band, Scott a cream-colored fedora. They held on to their brims, threatened by a sudden gust of wind. Scott stopped in his tracks, hands on hips, legs spread apart, and surveyed the immediate area.

"How about up ahead?" Rudy suggested, on the verge of turning around and going home.

"No," Scott replied. "Here, in the middle; it's more precarious."

"This is the dumbest thing," Rudy mumbled under his breath. "A midnight picnic on a suspension bridge, for chrissakes!"

Velma spread a red and white checkered tablecloth across the planks, and sat on it. The tablecloth's edges flapped in the breeze.

"Time for our first toast," Scott announced with a scoutmaster's authority. "Hurry, we have about three minutes before midnight."

He opened the bottle of Bordeaux, lifted three fancy glasses from the basket, handing them to his companions, and poured. "To my new friends, Velma and . . . forgive me . . . what's your name again?" He held his glass toward the moon. It shone a filtery spotlight through the glass onto his hand. "May our friendships," Scott said, his arm poised in the gesture of a toast, "be as provocative as the fiction we write. *Santé!*"

"Here, here!" Velma seconded, wondering how Rudy felt about Scott not remembering his name. She herself loved it.

Studying the bridge, she gazed upward at the double-arched monoliths, and got goose bumps at the idea of hovering in space, suspended between Brooklyn and Manhattan.

"*Dix, neuf, huit, sept, six, cinq,*" Scott counted down. "*Quatre, trois, deux, un.* Going up!" He turned the glass toward his lips, emptying it in one swallow.

Rudy and Velma glanced at each other. Rudy shrugged his shoulders, and swallowed a sip, thinking, Enough French! God, this fellow's a pretentious bore!

"Now," Scott said, "that wasn't so bad, was it?" He belched.

"The night's young yet," Rudy retorted.

"Excellent point," Scott admitted. "But then, my dear boy, so are we." He walked to the north side of the bridge, gazed at the majestic skyline, and sniffed salty air. "Everything is devilishly precise: the lights, the full moon, the company. A view like this brings Gershwin to mind. Maybe I'll use this scene in a novel."

"Do change the names," Rudy said.

Velma worried that the rivalry was getting out of hand. Granted, she wanted to make Rudy jealous, but not to deprive him of a good time.

"So you've published, what is it, two, or three novels?" she said to Scott. "Are you busy with another book?" Her summer dress billowing, she crossed her legs, and tried looking demure.

"Yes," Scott replied. "It involves a great deal of research. You?"

"Well," Velma said, fingering the rim of her glass, "I'm gathering ideas for a first novel. Alaine Locke and I had a lengthy discussion about subject matter recently."

"You mean *the* Alaine Locke?" Scott asked. "Compiler of that rubbish better known as the *Survey Graphic?*"

"Yes. We had lunch at the Civic Club."

"I couldn't possibly fathom why," Scott said bitterly.

"What do you mean?" Rudy asked.

"People like him should be deported," Scott said, pouring himself another glass. "I simply have no use for him."

"Why not?" Velma was curious.

"Come on," Scott said. "It's trial enough churning out quality fiction. Then you have this crop of self-appointed, paternal overseers who judge everything written by Negro hands. I understand Locke is advocating that we, as American Negro writers, should turn to our primitive African origins as a source of fresh, artistic ideas. Well, no thank you. I'll write what I goddamn please!" He threw the wine to the back of his throat like a shot of whiskey.

"So what?" Rudy said, offended but trying not to sound it. "They're just critics doing their job."

"Yeah," Velma added, "they're just historians."

"Oh, don't tell me," Scott grunted, "that you two are caught up in the pitiful romanticism of that Harlem Renaissance junk?"

Velma and Rudy looked at each other again. Now Scott was *really* starting to get on Rudy's nerves.

"What do you mean, junk?" Velma asked, disturbed.

"I thought you two were beyond that," Scott said. "Don't you see how ludicrous it all is? We have to be considered in vogue to get a shot at mainstream exposure and success. I can't speak for you two, but I don't need the validation of white publishers and literary circles to certify my existence or worth as an author."

Who else would publish you? Rudy thought in the long, unnerving silence that followed, silence slowly filled with the breaking of waves, the sipping of Bordeaux, the grinding, popping motor of an automobile below, clattering across the bridge into Brooklyn.

"Let's clear the air," Scott suggested. "We're getting much too serious, much too soon."

Velma got up and stood against the railing. Eyes closed, she breathed deeply, held it, then exhaled.

"Anybody ever tell you," Scott asked, "you're absolutely ravishing in the moonlight?"

"Yes," she replied, slowly opening her eyes. "You." *Did you hear that, Rudy?*

"What do you say, old chap?" Scott turned to Rudy. "Isn't she the sexiest mass of human flesh—"

"I say, let's go home," Rudy said, wondering why he had let Velma talk him into this. His head started spinning and his stomach flipped. "This salty air is making me seasick."

"*Mon cher Rudy.*" Scott approached him, cupped Rudy's face in his hand, and stroked the nape of his neck. "Relax, old chap," Scott continued, "I've got just the panacea." He removed his fedora and produced what appeared to be a cigarette. He slid it along his upper lip and sniffed the aroma.

"What's that?" Velma asked.

"Haven't you ever seen marijuana?" Scott was shocked. "Virtually everybody who's somebody in New York is doing it."

Scott lit it, and inhaled the thick smoke. He placed it in Rudy's mouth. "There, now never let it be said I never did my bit to corrupt you."

Rudy puffed, and the lit end glowed. He choked, and handed the cigarette back to Scott.

"Here, Velma," Scott said, smiling.

Velma took it and sniffed the rising smoke. She inhaled it, choked, and passed it back. "That's strong stuff, Scott," she said.

Rudy took it from Scott, puffed it, and had handed it to Velma when the lit end fell.

"The light's on your sweater, Rudy!" Velma shouted.

Rudy brushed the burning ash from his sweater. A hole with brown edges remained.

"Oh, Rudy," Velma said sympathetically, "now you've ruined your sweater."

"I thought it was already ruined," Scott laughed, eyeing Rudy's shabby outfit. All evening he hadn't been able to take his eyes off the young fellow's beat-up wing tips. Weathered and scuffed, they were several clashing shades of brown.

"Well," Rudy shot back, "not everybody can afford silk and fedoras for a midnight picnic on the Brooklyn Bridge, you know."

"You do dress beautifully, Scott," Velma agreed, wondering why Rudy was wearing those clothes. Excepting the sweater and the straw hat, it was the very outfit he'd had on the night she met him months before. "Scott, how do you manage?"

"Easily, my dear." Scott picked up a handful of pebbles he found on the bridge and threw them into the river. "I happen to be blessed with parents who support me. As you can probably tell from my breeding and exquisite taste, I come from money."

Oh, please, Rudy thought. Here's a man who doesn't like himself much.

"Is there any more wine?" Velma asked.

Scott grabbed the wine bottle, and tipped the spout into Velma's empty glass. She hiccupped as he poured. "Most writers," Scott said, pouring, "can't live off royalties. I don't do too badly in sales, but I'm blessed with well-to-do parents. The less fortunate live off patrons."

"I never thought about that," Velma said.

"Well, you should," Scott said. "There are such creatures, you know. White folks on Park Avenue with disgusting amounts of money and nothing to do with it except support the arts, so they say—"

"We know that," Rudy said, interrupting. "But is it like a regular salary?"

Scott laughed, throwing his head back toward the dark waters. *"Mes amis, mes amis,* you're so terribly naive," he said, laughing. "I love it! I have an insatiable lust for innocence. Of course, they pay you a salary. If they find in your work whatever it is in God's hallowed name they're looking for, yes, they pay your bills. It's rather simple, actually."

"Well," Velma said, "I sure don't know anyone with more than a pot to piss in." She sipped the wine.

"Well, you're in luck," Scott said. "I happen to know an abundance of wealthy white folks whose eyes bulge and whose hearts thump for the purple prose of promising literary darkies like yourselves."

"Like who?" Rudy said challengingly, thinking, Is there anything or anybody he doesn't know or have? Jesus!

"Take your pick. But I do have one in mind," Scott said. "She's a very old friend of the family; husband's dead, left her *beaucoup d'argent.* You know, the classic, filthy-rich widow. I could inquire about an introduction . . . oh, wait!" Scott thought a moment, wrinkling his forehead. "If I'm not mistaken, she was on a cruise to Rio. I don't know if she's back. I'll ring her penthouse tomorrow."

"When do you think we could meet this friend of yours?" Rudy asked, calling his bluff. But then, the idea of being supported by a wealthy white woman he didn't have to sleep with sounded rather attractive.

"Whenever it is," Scott replied, "you've got to do something about those clothes of yours."

Rudy looked from Scott to himself, gazing downward at his shoes. The three of them burst into laughter. For the first time, Rudy noticed, in the sensual moonlight, how stunning Scott was.

"So," Scott said, laughing. "The man knows how to laugh after all."

"Ooooooh," Rudy said, flapping his arms like a bird. "I feel so lightheaded, I could fly over this bridge. That's good stuff, Scott."

"Yeah," Velma echoed him, her eyes cloudy from the marijuana and Bordeaux.

"The best," Scott corrected them. "Only the best for my friends."

"Could you pass me the bread and cheese? I'm hungry." Velma took a loaf from the basket. She broke off a corner and chewed it. "Isn't this lovely, Scott? I always have such a wonderful time with you."

She walked toward him, her arms outstretched for an embrace. Scott walked toward her, passing her, and threw his arms around Rudy, who half-heartedly returned the hug. Velma stood motionless, not knowing what to do. A swift gust of wind blew her skirt, and it clung to her body, outlining her knees and thighs.

"I know you like me, Rudy," Scott said, running his forefinger across Rudy's paper-thin mustache: "You're just trying terribly hard not to. Relax, old chap, no need to go against the grain. We're going to be smashing friends, you and I."

They silently eyed each other. From this vantage point, Scott's sturdy arms wrapped about him, Rudy didn't find him so repulsive after all. They said nothing, speaking with their eyes.

Velma walked toward them, separating the two men with her hands, and squeezed herself between them. She circled her arms around their waists.

"That's much better," she said. "I'm part of this divine trinity, too."

She looked to Scott, then to Rudy. Rudy looked at Scott, Scott returned his glance. They stood there, these three bards, locked into a triangle of inebriated passion. Scott held them, and they, him. Everyone smiled drunkenly.

The moon's brightness, a stage spotlight, stretched geometric shadows across their faces. Silhouettes of vertical, horizontal, and diagonal lines concealed the individual motives, lusts, and penchants of the hopelessly romantic, devilishly calculating colleagues sharing their dreams, their wistfulness and a picnic basket. None knew of the others' sequestered thoughts, or how, like a triad of captive butterflies—Harlem butterflies—they were caught in a web; a web they wove in their clever minds.

BOOK TWO

1926

CROWDS STILL TRY
TO VIEW VALENTINO

The public was barred yesterday from the bier of Rudolph Valentino, motion picture actor, because of the irreverence of the thousands who had filed past the coffin in the Campbell Funeral Church ... on Tuesday and Wednesday. But the morbidly curious and possibly some sincere admirers of the film star besieged the funeral parlors despite announcement in the newspapers that the body no longer would lie in state.

—The New York Times
August 27, 1926

1

"Spirit tell me yo' mama sick woman. Got worsa afta she los' her husban' in the war. . . ."

A fragile elderly woman sat at the opposite end of the table, clutching Louise's hands. Her fingers were cold and callused. She rocked back and forth in the squeaky chair. Her face, black as night, merged with the surrounding darkness. Earrings of African warrior masks bounced as she swayed. Her head was wrapped in cloth of bloody reds, bright yellows, and passionate purples. Age had wrinkled her cheeks, her eyes, her forehead. She was toothless, her gums dark. A corn pipe dangled from the corner of her dry mouth. Louise heard howling winter winds slapping against the closed, shaded windows, along with the clanky sound of the old woman's bracelets. Ragtime phrasings from an upstairs piano seeped into the stillness of the unlit room.

"What about me?" Louise asked. "What do you—"

"Shhh!" the old woman snapped. "Ahm gettin' t' that."

The old woman closed her eyes and took a deep breath, exhaling slowly. She tilted her head back; it snapped to one side. She babbled in a foreign tongue. Louise looked away. Beneath a table, a pair of yellow eyes glowed. Uncertain of what she was looking at, Louise blinked, hoping it would go away. The fanged mouth of a feline hissed. Then the cat jumped from the floor onto a footstool and purred while it cleaned its whiskers. The thick billowing smoke of incense curled and rose to the ceiling. The nauseating smell gripped Louise and made her feel faint.

"Spirit tell me," the old woman continued, "a han'som fella wid lotsa money cum in yo' life. You fall in love an' marry. But there be problems." She puffed on the corn pipe and blew smoke to her customer's side of the table.

"What problems?" Louise fanned the smoke from her face.

"It won't cum t'me now. You cum back anotha time. Maybe then."

She released Louise's delicate hands. Nodding at the old woman, Louise stood, buttoned her overcoat and headed for the door. The cat, black as the old woman, hopped upon her lap. The woman flashed Louise a toothless smile and ceremoniously bowed her head. "You cum back anotha time."

A fluffy blanket of virgin snow covered the ground. Naked tree branches glistened with white crystals. Louise trudged in her rubber boots through the neighborhood known as Beale Street. Cold winds whistled and lashed at her olive cheeks. Heading for 142nd Street and Lenox, by way of Seventh Avenue, she passed the Tree of Hope. Stopping for a moment, she wiped the snow-covered stump. The avenue was lifeless, gray, and cold. There were no automobiles, no trolleys, no pedestrians. Who does that old lady think she's fooling? Louise thought. I know she lied and took my money. So, Mr. Tree, I come to you to give me what she promised. She probably preys on young girls like me, telling them exactly what they want to hear. Of course I want to marry a handsome man with lots of money. Who doesn't? She didn't really think I believed that trash for a minute, did she? And she thinks I don't know why she wants me to come back!

A block away from her destination, a cluster of people marched in a circle. They were solemn in attitude, their heads bowed as they marched. Home-made banners hung about their necks: GOD BLESS PROHIBITION. SEX AND RACIAL MIXING A MENACE TO HARLEM. THE VOLSTEAD ACT IS ON THE RIGHT TRACK!

Approaching the group of grim citizens, Louise stopped to look. They stared back at her, blocking the door she wished to enter. An elderly gentleman with earmuffs, reminiscent of her father, walked toward her. He placed a gloved hand upon her shoulder.

"Now, you look like a nice, decent young lady." His cracked lips quivered in the cold. "Why in God's name you want to go in there?" He pointed. The other protestors stopped marching to listen.

"Excuse me, sir. But, I have an audition and you're blocking my way."

"But we beg you, miss," another woman pleaded. "We're trying to rid our community of bootlegging and gangsters. You can understand that."

"I'm not a gangster or a bootlegger," Louise replied. "But I have an audition and you're making me late. Who are you, anyway?"

They looked to each other with questioning eyes and returned their glances to Louise.

"Why," the woman spoke again, "we're the Committee of Fourteen. Surely, you've heard of us. We're trying to save the morals of our children, your children even. You must not go inside. We beg you."

"I mean no disrespect, ma'am," Louise said, grabbing the doorknob. "But I'm hardly trying to corrupt or harm anyone. I'm just trying to get a job. You can't blame me for that."

"Oh yes we can," the old man said. "All these sinful places like the Savoy, Smalls Paradise, the Nest Club, they all the same—Satan's playground. God has appointed us to do His work. What makes you think this place is any different?"

"I just told you, I need a job." She turned the doorknob. "Excuse me."

"Maybe we can excuse you, but what about the Lord God Almighty? How you gonna answer to Him?"

Louise studied the log-cabin facade, opened the door, and climbed the long, narrow staircase. She walked into a dimly lit room. A Negro man with sheet music before him fingered the piano keys. C. Bechten was engraved in gold letters above middle C.

Her skin tingling as her body thawed, Louise removed her scarf and gloves and entered the main ballroom. Plastic palm trees sprouted from the concrete floor. Artificial coconuts protruded from synthetic leaves. The floor was arranged in the shape of a horseshoe lined with eight lampposts. Tables covered with pink and white tablecloths and holding fringe-shaded and stained-glass lamps crowded the small proscenium stage. Booths lined the walls. A mural depicted a slave beneath a tree, strumming a guitar and crooning to his sweetheart beside bales of cotton.

"You here for an audition?" A towering, rotund man with a French accent approached an unsuspecting Louise from the darkness.

"Ooooh! You scared me!" She held her throat, catching her breath. "Yes, I'm here for the audition. Who should I see?"

"Take off your coat," he said. "Let me see what you look like."

Louise shot him a look. The man reeked of whiskey and perspiration. His teeth were stained.

"I'll take off my coat when I audition, if you don't mind," she said, distrustful of the man with the day-old stubble and bloodshot eyes.

"Listen, toots," he said. "If you don't show me what you look like, there ain't gonna be no audition."

As long as you don't touch me, Louise thought, hesitantly removing her coat, and making certain the piano man was still there in case she had to scream.

"Hmmmmm," the man said, stroking his unshaven chin, giving her a quick once-over. "How about your legs? Got pretty legs to match that face of yours?"

"I guess."

"Let me see. Lift your skirt."

Louise flashed her shapely legs before his bloodshot eyes.

"Not bad, not bad. Can you sing?"

"A little."

"Dance?"

"Yes, sir."

"How tall you stand?"

"I don't know. I guess about five-six."

"How old are you?"

"Just turned twenty."

"Report to Mr. Herman Stark backstage. He'll tell you what to do."

"Which one is he?"

"He's our stage manager, the one chewing tobacco. You can't miss him. By the way, toots, what's your name?"

"Louise, sir. Louise Brooks." She started walking away. He touched her shoulder and she winced.

"Any relation to Walter Brooks?"

"No. Who's he?"

"Let's say he used to work here."

"What's your name, sir?"

"Never mind. If you want this audition, you'd better hurry. There's a hundred dames back there for four spots in the chorus line. If you're smart, you'll make it snappy."

2

Miriam guided an elderly patient, Thomasina Lucas, by the arm, as they inched down the corridor for the woman's daily exercise. Recovering from a stroke, Thomasina took steps that, to Miriam, were smaller than a toddler's. Hunched over, leaning on a cane, she told Miriam of her problems. Her children and grandchildren rarely came to see her, she complained, and she was about to die without anybody knowing or even caring.

Miriam had heard the complaints before. It wasn't that she didn't feel sympathetic toward the woman, but her mind was miles away, focused on woes her very own.

She was sorely missing Agnes, who wasn't showing up at work regularly. Miriam worried about her friend's personal welfare and her job. She was convinced the hospital administration would fire Agnes if she didn't do something quickly.

On record, Agnes had been calling in sick daily, until a week ago. Miriam imagined she was using the terrible winter as an excuse. A lot of people had colds or the flu. Agnes could have easily taken advantage of that without raising the supervisor's suspicions. Though Miriam didn't know for sure. She hadn't spoken with Agnes much lately. But her real ailment, Miriam knew, had nothing to do with her physical condition.

Tommy had begun terrorizing Agnes, even beating her. A few times when she came to work, her eyes, nose or mouth were bruised. Agnes lied to Miriam about her bruises. She'd say she fell, or hit her head on something, or tripped down the stairs. Miriam said nothing. She didn't want to meddle. Agnes never asked her opinion, so she never offered one. Whenever Tommy's name was mentioned, though, Agnes froze. She admitted they had some problems, but everything would work out all right. She claimed she loved him, that he indisputably loved her, and that there was no one else in his life. Agnes was usually in a bad mood during these violent periods. She never said much, but was perpetually on the verge of tears, and walked around in a daze. Miriam caught her crying on more than one occasion in the ladies' room. There was nothing Miriam could do for her, except hold her hand, stroke her back, wipe her eyes, and hope her friend would someday confide in her.

Miriam had anticipated going to a special meeting at Liberty Hall all week long. There were new developments in the possibility of Marcus Garvey's release from prison, and she couldn't wait to learn about them.

Before leaving the hospital that day, she performed last-minute checks on the Ward D patients, instructing the nurse on the next shift of their progress or lack of it.

She had her coat and was heading for the elevator, when Agnes nearly screamed her name down the hallway. Haltingly, her head bowed, she asked Miriam, "Do you have a few moments? I need to talk."

Miriam hesitated. This was one meeting she couldn't afford to miss, but her friend obviously needed her, or somebody. Miriam feared that if she didn't take the time, Agnes might do something rash. She sighed heavily and agreed to talk to her.

They went to dinner, though Agnes ate nothing. For Miriam, the restaurant was one major distraction of murmuring voices, knives and forks clicking, soda fountains swishing, waitresses yelling over the patrons' heads, and cold drafts rushing in as the door opened and closed.

Agnes told Miriam that Tommy tried to run her life as if he had papers on her. She admitted to Miriam that she had influenced her to speak up for herself more and Tommy didn't like that. He wondered aloud where she was picking up these new habits. She asked him for her house keys back. He refused. So she decided to rectify the matter herself.

The first day she stayed home from work, she called in a locksmith. Before the locksmith could properly get started, Tommy arrived at her apartment after he'd discoverd she wasn't at work.

"He exploded," Agnes said. "He cussed out the locksmith, and told him to mind his own business. I started raising hell since I was paying for it, and he hit me."

She gazed up into Miriam's face, ashamed. She felt Miriam would never take such treatment.

"Well," Agnes continued, "I should've known then, but . . . I love that man," she said, sniffling. "You don't understand. He used to be so good to me."

"What do you plan to do about it?" Miriam wanted to know.

"What *can* I do?" Agnes said. "He knows when I come and go. And he has a key to my apartment. What you think I should do?"

Miriam couldn't say what she thought. You're wasting your life on a damn fool and you should pack your things and move in with me, she thought. But she knew her motive for wanting Agnes with her was selfish.

"Ain't you got family?" Miriam asked.

"No," Agnes sniffled.

"Friends?"

"How am I gonna have friends? I go between the hospital and Tommy. If I could have friends, wouldn't I see you more often?" she said, her voice rising uncontrollably.

Heads in the restaurant turned. Patrons stared at their table.

"And after that time he come to get me at Liberty Hall," Agnes said, lowering her voice, "that was it."

"Why's he so against you coming to a meeting?" Miriam didn't understand.

"I don't know, Miriam," she said. "I guess he just wants to . . . control me somehow. If I knew that, you think I'd be sitting here asking you?" Agnes checked herself, made aware by Miriam's expression that she'd just said the wrong thing. "I'm sorry, Miriam. I didn't mean that."

"I know you didn't," Miriam said, patting her hand. "Anything I can do?"

"No, nothing . . . you know, he got more girlfriends than the sky got stars," Agnes wept. "Why he want me? Huh? Tell me, Miriam, why?"

"Maybe because—"

"I mean, he could do what he want. I just told him that he can't have them and me too. An' the nigger don't try to hide it none either."

Miriam winced at Agnes's use of the word nigger. She didn't like that word, even if Tommy's personality defined it most accurately.

"Can't you move?" Miriam asked.

"He'll only find out where I am."

"Well, girl," Miriam said, exhausted with the situation and hearing about it, wishing there was something more she could do, like kick Tommy's behind herself. "You gonna have to do something. Look at you, you're falling apart. That ain't the Agnes I know." Miriam lost her appetite, gazing across the table at Agnes. When she ordered the dinner, she could have sworn it was the best-smelling fried chicken she'd seen outside Mother's kitchen. Now, as she looked at the unconsumed portions, the smell of the fried chicken, black-eyed peas, and rice started to nauseate her. "If there's anything I can do, let me know. Anything."

That was the last time Miriam had seen her or heard anything about her.

Getting off the elevator, Miriam walked down the hall, bidding hellos and good-byes to those coming and going, praying for Thomasina Lucas that her kin would come visit her. She thought of stopping by to visit Velma. Her sister had become so busy with her writing career—publishing poetry, short stories, essays, dating some marvelous new beau, what have you—Miriam hardly saw her anymore.

She opened the door to the street and noticed the back of a man near her. She thought of George, who years ago, waited for her in that exact spot. She crossed the avenue to stop by the pharmacy, continuing her brisk walk through the cold streets.

Miriam held her scarf, bracing against the winter wind, and racked her brain trying to think of ways to see Agnes without jeopardizing her safety. Any show of support to her friend—if Tommy was there, and Miriam felt he would be—could threaten him, and she knew he'd take it out on Agnes.

What if she didn't live there anymore? Miriam hadn't considered it before. But she wouldn't be surprised to hear from the landlady that Agnes had moved and left no forwarding address. There was no way of telling.

She thought of how badly she wanted to take care of Agnes, how they could care for each other. They could nurture and love each other in a way men couldn't. While she enjoyed and liked several of the UNIA sisters, they shared no real relationship beyond their political affiliation. Between UNIA and Harlem Hospital, there was no other social time to speak of. To her mind, if it was possible in her day and age to transmit a voice through wires, or turn a set of still photographs into a reel of moving pictures, then there had to be some way to save Agnes.

"Hey, pretty mamma," a man said, suddenly walking beside her.

I ain't your mama, Miriam wanted to answer.

"Do I know you?" she said.

"Yeah," he said, removing his fur hat. "It's me, Tommy, remember?"

"No, I don't."

"Agnes's old man," he said. "I met you at Liberty Hall, remember?"

"Yeah," she murmured, "I think so."

"So, how you been doin'?"

"How's Agnes?" Miriam caught herself asking. "How come she ain't been to work?"

"She got a bad flu. But she be all right. I'm taking care of her."

I'll bet you are! "When she comin' back to work?"

"Listen, sweet thing," he said. "I didn't come here to talk about Agnes."

"Well, what you want?"

"Well, it's kinda cold out here, doncha think? I been walking behind you since you left the hospital. Can't we go someplace where it's warm?"

"Depends."

"On what?" he said, laughing, amused by Miriam's stubbornness.
"Depends on what you wanna talk to me about."

"Oh, c'mon, sweet thing. I just want to—"

"Please don't call me sweet thing."

"Okay, okay. What's your name again? . . . No, don't tell me—"

"Miriam."

"Yeah, well, Miriam, how come you never called me."

"I don't even know you."

"I'm giving you the chance. That's why I gave you my number."

"I threw it away," she said, knowing she had it tucked away in her bureau drawer.

"Well, let me give it to you again."

"I don't want it," Miriam said and started walking faster.

"C'mon now, sweet thing, I mean Miriam," he said, trailing her. "Why you wanna be like that?"

"Like what?" Miriam said, walking as Tommy shouted behind her.

"Oh, come on," he said, slowing down. "See how you actin'."

You better be glad I'm moving away from you instead of running you down like a steamroller, she thought, quickening her pace. She wanted to get away from him before she said or did something she'd regret. Forgetting her trip to the pharmacy, she walked down the subway stairs, and ran to catch the train pulling into the platform.

3

"Ahhh; New York in winter," Scott said, his foot pressed upon the accelerator. *"La neige est très magnifique, n'est-ce pas?"*

He pointed with his left hand, maneuvering the steering wheel with his right. Velma, sandwiched between him and Rudy, marveled at the genuine mohair-and-wool upholstery.

Southbound, they glided slowly through the icy spectacle of Central Park. The automobile cautiously inched around serpentine curves in a path of dirty slush with banks of sparkling snow lining the road. Architectural landmarks like medieval castles loomed beyond the naked trees along Central Park West. Energetic children engaged in snowball fights, snowmen construction, and thrilling downhill sleigh rides.

"I must say," Scott spoke, taking in the fleeting sights, and a breath of crisp air, "this is my favorite season. It brings to mind cognac and a crackling fireplace."

"Well, it's hardly mine," Rudy objected, shivering in his corner. He turned down the brim of his hat over his forehead, blocking his view, and briskly rubbed his shoulders. "It just means hard times and freezing to death in long johns. Scott, could you roll up your window, please?"

"I was just thinking how time flies." Velma lit a cigarette and blew smoke toward the windshield. "A year ago this time, we didn't know each other, and now, life's so sweet."

"Life can be marvelous that way." Scott nodded his head, taking Velma's hand. "Full of unforeseeable twists and turns, like this road we're traveling on." He kissed her hand.

"Rudy," Velma said, "you're so quiet. You look like you've seen a ghost."

"I'm just a little nervous, that's all."

"What about?" Scott asked. "Wearing a jacket and tie, or meeting Mrs. Vanderpool?"

"Both," Rudy replied, fumbling with his bowtie and argyle sweater vest. He was no match for Scott in his salt-and-pepper tweed, raccoon coat, and trademark fedora.

Scott chuckled. "Seems like everybody's got art patrons these days. I was talking with Countee Cullen the other day since he—"

"Does Mrs. Vanderpool support him too?" Velma kissed Scott's hand.

"Don't be preposterous," Scott said. "Countee's a rather proud individual. Van Vechten tried helping him publish with Knopf last year and he wouldn't hear of it. Harper published him. No, the word patron hardly goes over well with him."

"I see." Velma puffed her cigarette.

"Yes," Scott continued, "my kind of fellow. Pride forbids him to stoop for handouts from the wealthy. That's truly admirable considering what one's up against."

"Are you insinuating," Rudy began, "that Velma and I *are* stooping for handouts?"

"Call it what you will," Scott said, chuckling. "Whatever it is, it hardly enhances one's sense of independence."

"But, Scott," Velma protested, "this whole thing was your idea, not ours. I mean, we wouldn't even be meeting your friend if it wasn't for your urging—unsolicited, I might add."

"My dear, my dear, you're absolutely right," Scott agreed. "I did suggest this meeting. However, such a deed on my behalf hardly warrants my approval." He released Velma's hand. "And do yourself a favor and put out that cigarette. You don't want Mrs. Vanderpool to smell that junk on your breath."

Scott parked the '25 royal blue Studebaker Six in front of 860 Park Avenue at the corner of Seventy-seventh Street. As they locked the doors, snow began falling. The uniformed doorman tipped his cap as they walked through a revolving door to the elevator atop a marble staircase. Rudy blew on his hands, and rubbed them until the elevator parted its elegant doors.

Scott knocked on the door and a uniformed maid answered. "Good day, Mr. Scott. Madam is expecting you." Scott flashed Velma and Rudy a knowing smile.

They entered a ballroom-sized living room where domestics were disassembling a twelve-foot Christmas tree. Velma was seduced by the artwork and intricate designs in the ceiling. Gigantic archways and columns, an impressive imitation of ancient Greek architecture, rose above polished parquet floors which, in strategic spots, were covered with royal blue and gold Persian rugs. Before each of the twelve velvet chairs in the dining room were place settings of the finest china, silverware, crystal and twelve unlit candles. At one end of the room hung original oil paintings of what looked to Velma like someone's ancestors. Above the fireplace, hung another—Mrs. Vanderpool as a young girl, Velma guessed—posed confidently on a settee. Bright arrangements of roses, calla lilies, and African violets sprouted from vases that rivaled any museum piece Velma had ever seen.

The voice of a small, gray-haired woman, with a sagging, etched, chalk-white face called from the far side of the room. She wore a flowing satin robe and slippers, and bore a stark resemblance to Alice Gwynne Vanderbilt. Delicate white lace folded about her wrinkled neck and fragile wrists, and a lace handkerchief was tucked beneath her left sleeve. Blue veins and liver spots covered her trembling hands. About her neck hung eyeglasses, resting upon a bosom that had all but disappeared. She sat on a high-back chair of mahogany and satin which, to Velma, looked like a throne. Below her were several footstools.

"Virgil, it's so wonderful of you to come." Her voice was cracked and fragile; her accent New England. She didn't stand. "Please, please, bring your friends and have a seat."

As she drank a cup of tea, the cup and saucer rattled in her hands. On a table beside her was Rudy's novel, *Shadows in the Forest*. Scott hugged the woman and they pecked each other's cheeks. "Please, Virgil, introduce your friends."

"Velma, this is Mrs. Genevieve Attaway Vanderpool," Scott said. "Mrs. V, Velma Brooks."

"I'm so pleased to meet you." Velma offered her hand.

"And, this," Scott continued, "is Zachary Rudolph; but of course you've seen his photograph on his novel."

"Of course, of course. I'm delighted to meet you, Mr. Rudolph."

"Likewise." Rudy shook her hand and grinned nervously. He stood away from the others.

"Well, don't just stand there. Please have a seat." With a drop of the arm, she indicated the footstools beneath her. "Don't mind the noise. As you can see, I've overcelebrated the holidays. This is the price one pays when you're the only person in New York who throws a New Year's Eve party. I just adore the Christmas holidays, don't you?" She rang a gold bell beside Rudy's book. In seconds, a servant appeared. "Yes, madam?"

"Bring tea for my guests and hold any calls which come in the next half hour." The servant bowed her head and disappeared from the room, her footfalls clicking against the wooden floors. "So, now," Mrs. Vanderpool continued, "let us get right down to the heart of matters." She turned to Velma and Rudy, looking down upon them. "I am somewhat versed in both your careers and reputations and I must say you are both immensely gifted, indeed. And, speaking for myself, there's no greater or more profound gift than that of the fiction writer. Now, Mr. Rudolph, I know you've published a great novel. Virgil here, the angel that he is, saw to it that I received a copy. I must confess I'm not quite finished with it yet, but I do have some comments I'd like to share with you. So, we'll come back to that. But, Miss Brooks, I'm compelled to say that your unique talent is only equaled by your delightfully vast imagination. Why, even before dear Virgil brought your work to my attention, I had read your 'Savannah' something or other; pardon me, my dear, but the name escapes me momentarily, but it was in *The Crisis*, if memory serves me. The late Mr. Vanderpool and I have been rather generous donors to the NAACP and all of its functions for many years now. Virgil can attest to that. And, Dr. DuBois, a very dear friend of mine, gave me that particular copy with your story and some poetry. Tell me, my dear, what are your plans?" She sipped her tea, emitting barely audible slurping sounds.

"Well," Velma cleared her throat, looking upward into the aging face, "I'm publishing poetry and short stories in periodicals mostly, but I'd like to compile a book of poetry. I'm also working on ideas for a novel."

"What, may I ask," Mrs. Vanderpool said, "would your subject matter be?"

"It's too early to tell," Velma said.

"Of course, my dear, of course. And, Mr. Rudolph, am I correct in my assumption that this is your first effort with Knopf?" Through her eyeglasses, she glanced at the book, holding it at arm's length.

"Yes, I'm very pleased," Rudy said. "It's being received rather well."

"I imagine that's marvelous for someone with your talent," Mrs. Vanderpool said. "Yet I fail to comprehend the book's success."

"Pardon?" Rudy didn't understand.

The maid returned with a silver tray, the cups and saucers rattling. Placing the tray on the table, she graciously handed the cups to the guests, and bowed to her mistress. "Will that be all, madam?"

Mrs. Vanderpool nodded. "Anyway, getting back to your book, Mr. Rudolph, I must say that you chose a rather depressing subject, if I may be so blunt. Well written, oh, beautifully written indeed, but who wants to be beaten over the head with the voice of protest?"

"Well, Mrs. Vanderpool—" Rudy began.

"Please, call me Godmother. Whether we come to a contractual agreement or not, that's what I like to consider myself, a fairy godmother. Forgive me, Mr. Rudolph, you were saying?"

"Well, I agree that the protagonist speaks with the voice of protest, but then, that's precisely my intention," Rudy said, swallowing, thinking that the majority of Negro authors wrote protest novels. "I cannot compromise reality or truth, at least as I perceive it. But I don't think my work should be judged solely on—"

"I'm not judging at all, Mr. Rudolph," Mrs. Vanderpool interrupted. "I just hold firm to the conviction that gifted Negro writers can find much else to write about than poverty and racial tension and so on and so forth—"

The loud crash of the falling Christmas tree startled them.

"Be careful with that for God's sake!" Mrs. Vanderpool yelled. "Joshua and Rufus, I asked you both several times to hold the tail end of the tree. The others can guide you from the front. But you never trust my judgment, do you? No, you think I'm too old to think straight." To her guests she said, "You know, sometimes, they're like children. They don't mean any harm, but one must constantly supervise them or they're quite lost." She sipped her tea again. "Back to our discussion. Let me say that my ideal of Negro literature centers around the primitive. Gay people, full of music and dance. And that primitive flavor is unique to your race. I see the work reflecting the exoticism of the jungle, if you will. Give me something gay. Keep the protest."

A long silence followed as everyone sipped tea. Through the window, Velma watched the snow falling, and listened to the pop and crackle of the huge fireplace. The woman must never leave this penthouse, she thought. What else do the artists of an oppressed people write about? She tried imagining the thoughts racing through Rudy's mind.

Rudy couldn't help but feel offended. If this fairy-tale sensibility was Mrs. Vanderpool's inexorable contractual condition, Rudy knew he wouldn't be doing business with her. He wondered what Velma made of all this, and why Scott didn't correct Mrs. Vanderpool's mispronunciation of Du*Boys*.

Scott watched his friends grow uncomfortable in the silence. None of what Mrs. Vanderpool said surprised him. He was familiar with her attitudes. But who cared what she thought? He tried communicating telepathically to his friends across the room, Take the money and run!

"Well," Rudy said, scratching his head, forcing a chuckle into his voice, "unfortunately, life isn't always gay and full of music and dance, as you say. Yet life, Mrs. Vanderpool, is the very substance from which we extract and interpret our artistic viewpoints."

"Yes," Velma said. "I agree with Rudy. The writer, especially the Negro writer, has an unshakable responsibility to that and—"

"What I think they're trying to say," Scott spoke up, interrupting Velma, his voice shaky and apologetic, "is that poverty and racial strife are—"

"That's not necessary, Scott," Velma cut him short, getting back at him for the Countee Cullen crack in the Studebaker. "We've already said very plainly what we mean."

Mrs. Vanderpool studied Velma, stroking her sagging chin. "You have a keen spirit, Miss Brooks." She was smiling. "I find you quite provocative and would welcome the opportunity to work with you. You too, Mr. Rudolph. If somehow, we can reach mutual terms on an agreement, I believe we could enjoy a fruitful liaison. Now, my terms and conditions."

"And what, may I ask, are they?" Velma said.

"Precisely this. That you will be forbidden to hold any form of employment other than your writing—"

"Now, I could get used to that," Rudy said.

"I will supply you with a comfortable salary. Perhaps, if the partnership is promising, I can furnish you an automobile, but that remains contingent. You are to provide me a copy of any finished work with the slightest commercial intentions or potential, be it a novel, a short story, a play or a poem. There is to be no mention of my name in print or with anyone outside this room. You write whatever you want, but sell nothing without my approval. There are to be no collaborative efforts with outside parties or between each other without my approval. Naturally, you're spending my money, so it's not peculiar that I have something to say about it. Is that understood? I also urge you to remember that I have many, many friends. Everyone from President Coolidge to any number of distinguished politicians, ambassadors, and statesmen. Alfred and Blanche Knopf are dear friends of mine, as are virtually anyone worth knowing in the publishing industry. So, if you're contemplating the execution of a project against my knowledge, I assure you, I will find out. And surely, you don't want your godmother to become angry with her children."

"Oh, yes," Scott agreed. "Mrs. V has eyes and ears in the most unexpected places."

"So," Mrs. Vanderpool resumed, "Miss Brooks and Mr. Rudolph, I'll give you two weeks to consider my offer. My lawyer will draw up the contracts and forward them to you. I'm aware that I've overwhelmed you with information, but as I pointed out earlier, I welcome the opportunity to work with you both. The sooner, the better. Any questions?" she looked to Velma, then to Rudy who sipped tea.

"Why are you doing this?" Velma looked puzzled.

"My one and only question exactly," Rudy echoed her.

"My dear children, it's rather simple. Whether you can tell or not, I'm nearly seventy years old. I have more money than I can spend in three lifetimes of being seventy. However, that's not the point—" She turned her head to cough. It was raspy, hoarse, and full of phlegm.

"You'll excuse me; I'm catching a terrible cold. The point is that with no children and no rightful heirs to my estate, I give my money to charities of my choosing. Some give money to hospitals, others to colleges and universities. I am a patron of the arts, more specifically, of the Negro artists and institutions designed to improve and uplift the Race. But especially the artists, for they're a unique breed and deserve delicate and special handling. Needless to say, I can provide that special handling. Any further questions?" The room was silent. "So, enough of the humdrum of business and dollars and cents. Tell me, Virgil, how are your darling parents? I expected them at my New Year's party."

"They were abroad for the holidays," Scott said. "Which reminds me, you must tell me all about Rio."

"Rio was marvelous, my dear Virgil. Exotic and primitive beyond my wildest fantasies, just absolutely splendid. I'll tell you all about it sometime." Mrs. Vanderpool raised up from her chair and began descending the slightly raised platform. "But, you'll excuse me. I have another one of those bloody appointments with my physician this afternoon. He should've been here by now, but then the weather is rather ghastly, isn't it?" Through the glasses, she looked out the window. "Again, it was marvelous meeting you both." She extended her hand to Velma, then Rudy. "I expect to hear from you soon. Come by anytime. Godmother is always delighted to receive her children. Virgil, you're no stranger here. You know the way out."

4

Boisterous young girls scrambled backstage at the Cotton Club, chattering and giggling as they disrobed. A tall, confident-looking hopeful flexed her vocals. A group of three, standing outside the ladies' room, polished their time step.

"Sweetie, you better hurry up! The lineup is any minute!" someone yelled to Louise, who studied the multitude of women auditioning for four spots, and sighed at the futility of the notion. She stood dumbfounded, watching the girls remove their blouses, wiggle out of tight skirts, and slip into shiny black tap shoes. Through a partially opened door, she saw an attractive woman with long, shapely legs, adjust her tap shoe. Her leg was hoisted upon a dressing-room chair. "This is your first audition, ain't it?" the woman said, smacking and popping gum.

"How can you tell?" Louise said, entering.

"Sweetie, you look like me when I first started." She switched the position of her legs and fastened the other tap shoe. "You can share this room with me if you like. There's a place for your things over there." She pointed to a dingy closet bulging with feathered and sequined costumes. "Don't be shy. If you want this job, first thing you gotta learn is to push and shove like everybody else. These girls is hungry . . . well, listen to me. You probably wonderin' 'Who's this bossy broad, anyway?' I'm Peaches. What's your name, sweetie?"

"Louise. Your first name is Peaches?"

"My family nickname. My folks from Georgia; what can I say? But, sweetie, you better get some pep in your step. You either ready when they ready or you ain't ready at all."

Louise removed her overcoat, the rubber boots, and glanced into the lipstick-smudged mirror. Panties, girdles, brassieres and stockings were strewn across the makeup table and floor. Sweat and cheap perfume clashed in the air. As she undressed, Louise watched two girls outside the door. They stretched leg muscles along the floor and against the shabby wall. Another practiced her soft shoe, singing a Jimmy McHugh/Dorothy Fields show tune. Louise watched them with intense concentration. It struck her that they all looked blood-related. All had olive complexions with straight or wavy hair. Not one was brown or dark-skinned; there was not a coarse strand of hair. They stood no more than five-six and looked no older than twenty. They could all be cousins, or her sisters. Louise shared a physical resemblance with these strangers that she didn't share with Velma and Miriam. Never had she seen so many mirror images in one place at one time. I'm not so unique-looking after all, she thought, wondering how they dealt with it.

"So, sweetie," Peaches said, applying her lipstick in the mirror. "What brings you to the Cotton Club?"

"A job."

"And a wedding band if you're lucky, right?"

"No, I'm not looking for a husband. I just need a job."

"You're not really a showgirl, are you?" Peaches swung her head from the mirror to face Louise.

"No, but I can be. I saw an ad in the paper and I applied. But after I got here, I nearly started to turn around and go home."

"After plowing through all that snow? How come? Competition gettin' to you?"

"No, those people outside tried to stop me from coming in. Some committee."

"Oh, them, chile? Don't pay 'em no mind. They always out there. Did they really try to stop you?"

"Yes they did. Then after I got inside, some big, rough-looking French guy wasn't too friendly to me either."

"Oh, him? Don't let him scare you, sweetie. That's Frenchie. To us, he's Monsieur DeMange," she said, mimicking a French accent, swaying her hands for effect. "But to the mobsters, he just plain ol' funky-ass Frenchie."

"What do you mean, mobsters? That's what the lady outside said."

"Well, sweetie," Peaches said, lowering her voice, "everybody knows this club's run by gangsters. Last June, a judge closed down the joint for booze violations. Didn't you know that?" She edged closer to Louise. "They keep it quiet, but this place is owned and run by Owney Madden and his people from Chicago."

"Owney Madden, Owney Madden," Louise repeated; it sounded familiar. "Did I read about him in the paper?"

"I'm sure you did. They been callin' him 'Owney the Killer' since he was seventeen. He's the one who murdered Patsy Doyle in some saloon over on Eighth Avenue. Anyway, that's what the word is."

"Now I remember!" Louise snapped her fingers. "The one with the sweet face. Looks like he wouldn't harm a roach. Didn't he date that Park Avenue debutante, oh, what's her name? Dorothy diFrasso?"

"No, you're thinking of Bugsy Siegel. But you'll never guess who works here sort of as a manager."

"Who?"

"Jack Johnson."

"The fighter?"

"The one and only. He owned it when it was called the Club Deluxe. Then Madden's people saw the joint and made him an offer."

"You sure know a lot."

"Sweetie, my boyfriend plays sax with the Andy Preer Cotton Club Syncopators. Besides," Peaches added, turning to the mirror and smoothing the tight finger waves in her hair, "an innocent city

girl should know these things. Come here, I got somethin' for you."
She picked up a bottle of cheap perfume and sprayed it on Louise's
neck, and behind her ears. "I call this my good-luck perfume. You
want the job, you'll get it now for sure."

"Mr. Stark will be ready for you girls in five minutes!" a
stagehand yelled, maneuvering his way backstage. Girls giggled and
teased him. *Hey, girls, he's kinda cute. Whatchu think we should
do about it? Uh-uh, honey, you know what they say about small
feet!* They laughed, and someone threw a silk stocking in his face.

Onstage, Louise stood in a lineup of six dancers. The hot
spotlights caused her to perspire and made it difficult to see the
audience. Her heart pumped out of control. The girls to either side
of her breathed heavily. The Negro man at the piano awaited his
cue. Two men whispered in the audience; one of them cleared his
throat. Herman Stark spoke. Louise could see him now. His jaws
ground against each other as he chewed tobacco while instructing
the girls in the choreography. Louise felt she was no match for these
obviously experienced chorines. Her stomach churned and her
palms were clammy. Her throat felt parched as she tried to
swallow. I'll do my best, she thought. This could be exciting, this
life of a showgirl.

Herman Stark nodded his head toward the piano man who,
acknowledging his cue, laid intricate fingerwork on the ivories.
Louise replayed the choreographic instructions in her head and on
the count of four, she began.

*Two steps front, two steps back. Turn on your toes and shimmy
like you mean it.* Mr. Stark is looking at me, or is it my legs? *Sway
your arms up and down and wiggle those fingers to and fro.* Why
doesn't this female give me more room? God knows I need this job.
Turn around again and tap those shoes. And they call this work?
Return on the count of four, shuffle along and bring it on home!
Please, God, make him choose me.

"Okay, girls, thank you. That was lovely." Herman Stark looked
at his watch, and his expression, to Louise, denied the previous
compliment. He yawned, stretching his arms outward, and patted
his open mouth. "Will the next line come in? And, please, can I
have some quiet back there?!"

Louise retreated to the dressing room, dripping sweat.

"Now that wasn't bad." Peaches stood in the doorway, nodding
approvingly, her arms folded, feet crossed.

"You really think so?" Louise said.

"Sweetie, I seen worse, lots worse. I think Mr. Stark liked you."

"I was as good as those other girls, wasn't I?"

"Maybe, maybe not. But, that ain't got nothin' to do with the price of rice in China."

"What do you mean? I was terrible, wasn't I?"

"You missin' my point. Sometimes, in these kinds of jobs, looks is more important. Remember, this place wants colored gals to look as white as possible. White folks ain't spendin' no money just to watch a bunch of niggas dance even if they are pretty niggas, you can believe that. Why you think they call it the *Cotton* Club? That ain't no mistake, you know. We ain't even allowed to sit in the audience."

"I know. It's stupid, this colored-and-white stuff."

"This here's the only nightclub with the policy of no Negroes in the audience."

"Did you audition here before?"

"Sure did. And, I danced smoke circles around those other girls, but they got the job."

"Why did you come back?" Louise was curious.

"My boyfriend told me they have a new stage manager. Thank God they got rid of Walter Brooks."

"That Frenchman asked me if I was any relation to him."

"Are you?"

"I never heard of him."

"Well, I'm sure that's a point in your favor."

"Johnson, Hayes, Smith," the stagehand shouted. "Williams, Dorsey, McFadden, you're up next! Please line up here!"

"Oh, sweetie, that's me!" Peaches said. "Gotta go! Hand me that perfume, would you please?" Louise handed her the bottle. Peaches sprayed her neck, ears, and jokingly, her crotch, and Louise laughed. She liked this woman Peaches; she liked her a lot.

"If that's your good-luck perfume," Louise teased her, "how come you didn't get the job before?"

" 'Cause sweetie, this is the first time I ever used it in this club. Would you be a sweetheart and hold this?" Peaches removed the gum from her mouth, and handed it to Louise. "There. Wish me luck!"

Herman Stark assembled the girls on the horseshoe stage. Their chatter and cackling had segued to silence. They spoke softly, looking to each other with suspicious, envious eyes, wondering if they, or the girl with whom they shared a mirror or lent a pair of tap shoes, would be called.

Herman Stark stood and walked from the dark audience into the stagelight. Pads of paper in his hand, he drew lines through the names that would not be called, his jaws grinding against each other. Louise turned away. The tobacco in his mouth made her queasy. The hoofers held their breath.

"We'd like to thank you girls for coming," he began, "and you're all so good, it's hard to choose only four."

"I'll bet," someone uttered under her breath.

"The four names I call," he continued, "would you please remain where you are." He tucked the pencil behind his ear; brown spittle stuck to the corners of his mouth. "The others may leave. Again, thanks for coming. Listen up, I haven't finished yet. Would these four people raise their hands as I call their names. McDonald . . . Hughes . . . McFadden . . . Brooks. Would you four please remain."

Peaches ran to Louise and threw her arms around her. "I made it!" she screamed.

"You did?" Louise said, ecstatic.

"Yeah, sweetie. Finally!"

"So did I!" Louise said. "I can't believe it!" They hugged each other as the others headed back to the dressing room.

"Wait till I tell my boyfriend!" Peaches said. "Didn't I tell you 'bout that perfume? Huh? Works like a charm, don't it?!"

5

Winter gave way to spring, the last of the snow melted, and budding yellow and green life dappled the trees as buds and unfurled leaves waited to clothe the naked branches. This was Velma's favorite season. The reward of surviving another dormant winter, a time to prepare for the vivacious summer.

In Harlem, one could always distinguish one season flowing into the next. The streets were perpetually filled with life when the weather was warm. When it wasn't, people remained indoors. They hibernated behind bolted shutters, closed doors and windows.

The trio—Velma, Rudy and Scott—languidly strolled through

Striver's Row. They stopped at 267 West 136th Street, a building more aptly known as Niggerati Manor. Iolanthe Sydney, a businesswoman and artist, had transformed the crumbling real estate into living quarters for bohemian writers and artists. In a brownstone rooming house teeming with hopefuls—half starving for a decent meal, anxious about securing next month's rent, and driving themselves full speed to finish projects designed as their "big breaks"—there was always a party to be found any day of the week.

They greeted a full house as they walked through the door. Up-and-coming talents scattered about the apartment, celebrated the dawn of spring, completed projects, contracts or merely having survived the winter of '26. The guest list read like a *Who's Who* in the community's cultural awakening: writers Rudolph Fischer, Velma Brooks, Countee Cullen, Eric Waldrond, G. Virgil Scott, Zora Hurston, Zachary Rudolph, and Arna Bontemps; the artists Miguel Covarrubias and Aaron Douglas and his wife, Alta; the sculptors Richmond Barthe and Sargent Johnson.

The host was Wallace Thurman, quite possibly the most celebrated of the "yet to be discovered" novelists living at Niggerati Manor. A recent arrival to Harlem from the University of Southern California, Wallace fluttered about the apartment, tending graciously to his guests, holding court in a living room that overflowed with Renaissance men and women. A stout, dark man, he entered the parlor from the kitchen, and paused to whisper to Harold John Stephenson, the only white person present. They spoke in hushed voices. Harold squeezed Wallace's waist and sneaked a kiss behind his ear. A bottle of wine in his hand, and a smile on his face, Wallace circulated the parlor and poured wine into glasses in need of refilling. "Great party, Wally!" proclaimed a man Wallace didn't know, extending his near empty cup toward the bottle.

"I'm glad you're enjoying it," Wallace said. "I owe three months' back rent. Iolanthe may come in at any moment and evict us in mid-drink."

"Amen!" someone else shouted. "Last week, I attended a wine-and-poetry affair over at Jessie Fauset's, but I'm afraid she's heavy on the poetry and stingy with the grape."

"I heard," another voice shouted, "that only French is spoken at Fauset's parties. Imagine, niggers speaking French."

"It's done all the time in Haiti and West Africa," Scott said, a pipe vibrating in his mouth. "Speaking of parties, has anybody been to the Dark Tower?"

"The Dark Tower?"

"Countee, isn't that the name of one of your poems?"

"Haven't you heard about the joy goddess?" Scott asked. "She lives right down the street here."

"The joy goddess?" Alta Douglas inquired.

"A'Lelia Walker Robinson. They call her place the Dark Tower." There was a roar of laughter.

"Well, if you were the sole heiress to Madame Walker's immense fortune, you'd be a joy goddess too," Alta said, laughing.

"She gives the wildest parties this side of the Hudson," Scott continued. "God, you can meet anybody there from writers to racketeers."

"Not to mention," said the voice of a new arrival, "that her parties are usually crowded like the subway at rush hour." He closed the door behind him.

"Lank! I'm so glad you could make it!" Wallace walked briskly toward Langston Hughes, who flinched as Wallace embraced him. "Come in, come in," Wallace said. "Of course you know my friend John Stephenson. You probably know everybody here. If you don't, you will by tonight, or this morning, as it were." Langston nodded his head to the guests. Shy and mysterious, he never sat among them, but stood against a wall, hands tucked in his pockets.

From the kitchen burst a jubilant Zora Hurston, carrying a bowl of piping-hot fried chicken. "Zora, sweetie pie," Wallace said, "you don't have to do that."

"Chile, I don't mind." Zora waved her hand at him and made rounds with the bowl tucked in her arm, handing out crispy pieces of chicken and clean napkins. "In a minute, we're going to pass around the hat for donations," Zora said. "We just about run out of gin. There's cake in the kitchen for anybody who wants some. Langston, I didn't know you were here!" She hugged him. He refused the chicken with a gesture. A copy of *Vanity Fair* in his hand, he conversed with Zora.

"You know, I heard the strangest thing the other day," someone said above the clatter of voices. "Seems that our boy wonder, Toomer, is having an affair with Mabel Dodge."

"Where'd you hear that?"

"Around."

"I hear," someone else said, "that he's a disciple of some Russian mystic named Gurdjieff or some strange nonsense like that."

"That's right. Mabel financed his trip to Fontainebleau."

The floor was open, as individuals added to the chorus of gossip and discussion. Voices bounced around the room, a Ping-Pong of opposing viewpoints.

"Well, I guess that's all we'll be hearing from Toomer during *this* Renaissance."

"Where'd that word come from anyway?"

"What word?"

"Renaissance."

"I'm not sure exactly."

"Who knows."

"I thought it was coined by the *Herald Tribune* critic in an article about the rising tide of Negro authors . . . wasn't it?"

"I really don't know."

"Don't look at me!"

"It sounds so ludicrous. Why Renaissance of all things? Sounds like colored folks been culturally dormant for the past millennium and we're just waking up."

"I never thought about it that way before."

"Personally, I kind of like it; it's apropos. Why not Renaissance? Why should Europe be the only place to have one?!"

"It seems, I might add, that Renaissance is a term familiar only to the artists and intellectuals. Ask the average Harlemite on the street about the Negro Renaissance, he'll look at you like a damn fool!"

Velma's head turned from one side of the room to the other, as if she were watching a tennis match. She was fascinated by the assembled geniuses debating the phenomenon in which they were the force. She sat next to Scott, hoping everyone there noticed that they were an item. She imagined her name linked and tangled in the community grapevine. She felt that Scott was the most charismatic, handsome, and prolific among them. Most of the artists there—established or otherwise—were struggling and looked it. Scott, as always, was sharp as a pin in his starched shirt, bowtie, and cashmere sweater.

Even Wallace's apartment reflected the look of one who hadn't made it. The lumpy couch standing on precarious legs looked donated, perhaps salvaged from the junk pile. All of the furniture was mismatched. Throw rugs were frayed, virtually threadbare, and the walls could have used some paint. It reminded her of Rudy's, except this apartment in Niggerati Manor was Versailles—comparatively, that is.

Approaching Velma and Scott at the end of the sofa, Zora smiled.

"Haven't I met that sweet face somewhere before?" she said to Velma.

"Yes," Velma said, nodding her head, swallowing her wine. "Scott introduced us at Carl's party last summer."

"As in last year?" Zora asked. "Honey, I'm doin' pretty good if I can remember yesterday; no offense. What do you like—leg or breast?"

Scott excused himself abruptly, and disappeared behind the bathroom door.

"Was it something I said?" Zora said, watching his sudden departure. She placed a hand on her cheek, and threw her head back in laughter. "Now I remember!" she said, returning her attention to Velma. "What's your name again?" Zora snapped her fingers.

"Velma."

"Right, Velma. You the same Velma who published in *Opportunity* recently?"

"That's me."

"Girl, that was a lovely poem. What was it about? . . . the darker sister or something like that."

"Thank you, Zora," Velma said, bubbling over inside, yet containing herself. "I'm thrilled you liked it so much."

"Won't you recite it for us?" Zora suggested.

"Oh no, I couldn't."

"But, we'd love to hear it; wouldn't we, everybody? Negrotarians! Negrotarians!" Zora proclaimed, tapping the chicken bowl with a pencil, shouting above the bobbing heads in the parlor. "Can I have your attention please? Wouldn't everybody like to hear Velma's lovely poem?"

"Zora," Velma said, "you're embarrassing me." She was loving the attention.

"Yes," Countee said, "we'd love to hear it."

"But, I don't remember it by heart," Velma lied, knowing every semicolon and comma. "I couldn't possibly recite it."

"That's no problem, my dear," Wallace said, handing her a copy of *Opportunity*. "When you come to Wally's, my precious, we may not pay the rent, but we're sure enough always prepared. Can we have some quiet." He clapped his hands. "Velma's going to share some culture with some of you uncultured folks."

She stood and looked around the room. All eyes and attention were in her direction. Langston put the *Vanity Fair* aside, leaned against the wall, crossed his legs, and folded his arms. There was a distant flushing of a toilet before Scott emerged from the back. He stood in the shadows near the door. Velma's stomach felt queasy. "Well, since you all put me on the spot here," she said laughing. A bit embarrassed by her ego, she playfully pointed a scolding finger at Zora. "I guess I have no other choice, do I?" She parted the magazine pages, shifted her weight to her right side, cleared her throat, and inhaled deeply.

> *"I am America's*
> *Darker sister;*
> *Abandoned, forgotten daughter*
> *Of braided head and*
> *Full lips, swept upon foreign shores,*
> *Against my will.*
>
> *The pyramids I scaled*
> *The language I disseminated*
> *The Euphrates from which I drank*
> *Are lashing echoes in a*
> *Millennium of generational memories.*
> *Umbilical chord to a past now*
> *Severed.*
>
> *"I am America's*
> *Darker sister;*
> *Maimed, raped concubine,*
> *Mulatto bastards suckling*
> *At my breasts*
> *As mine are bargained from the*
> *Auction block.*
> *I am America's*
> *Darker sister."*

The recital was followed by a prolonged silence, then thunderous applause; a few shouts of Brava! Velma placed a hand on her stomach and sighed. She gave the magazine back to Wallace and sat down. Everyone flashed smiles of approval in her direction— everyone except Scott. Velma winked at him and patted the empty spot beside her, motioning him to sit. But before he could do so, Aaron Douglas approached Velma. The dark and handsome man sported a tuft of hair beneath his large nose—an abbreviated mustache—and black, round, wire-framed glasses covered his eyes.

"That was lovely and quite powerful," he said. "My wife Alta and I are most fond of your work."

"I'm flattered," Velma said, her pulse returning to normal. "I'm a big fan of yours too, Aaron."

"Is there a collection of poetry presently in the making?" Aaron asked. "I don't believe I've seen or heard of one."

"No, but Carl is encouraging his publisher to do so," Velma said. "We'll see what happens."

"Well, I'm sure—"

"Excuse me, but you're in my seat." Scott cut Aaron short, standing above him, looking grave.

"Pardon." Aaron rose and maneuvered himself out of Scott's way. "Anyway, Velma," Aaron continued, "if they publish your poetry, I'd love to design the dust cover. I have something rather specific in mind, especially for you." He glanced at Scott. "Perhaps we can talk later." He left and rejoined Alta, who was listening to Eric Waldrond drive home a point.

"What was that all about?" Scott asked, brushing his sweater, staring ahead, never looking at Velma.

"You know Aaron, don't you? The painter? Well, he says that when my book of poems is published, he has some specific ideas for me—"

"I wonder what they are, these specific ideas." Scott couldn't contain his jealousy.

"As they relate to the book's design, Scott," Velma said impatiently.

"He says you'll talk later," Scott persisted, her explanation was insufficient. "What about?"

"I just told you, Scott. Why're you making so much of this?"

"Well, I don't know about you stuffy folks," Wallace said, gliding about the parlor with a drink in his hand. "But what this party needs is music." He clicked on the radio. Flicking the dial, he tuned in a series of back to back static. Suddenly, a jumping rhythm called "Ring Dem Bells" by Duke Ellington escaped the tiny speaker. Some of the guests rose to the occasion. Drunk on wine and bathtub gin, they danced the Charleston and Black Bottom with abandon and ignited the air.

"Let's dance." Velma took Scott's hand.

"No," Scott replied, pulling his hand away.

"Well," Velma rebutted, "you can sit here and pout if you please. I'm going to dance." She walked toward Rudy, who was busy talking to Langston. "Excuse me, gentlemen," she said, mock-curtsying. "Rudy, would you dance with me?"

"Love to." He looked to Langston who nodded. Rudy took her hand, and led her to the floor with fancy footwork. He swung her and dipped her and whirled her about as she tried to keep up. The Duke's upbeat orchestra music swelled and throbbed until the apartment spun before her eyes. She loved the way Rudy held her waist. She pretended, for the moment, that they were lovers again.

"Velma," Rudy whispered in her ear, "you think we did the right thing? With Mrs. Vanderpool, I mean."

"Well, admit it, it's a difficult offer to refuse, and your rent's being paid."

"That's exactly what worries me," he said.

"I must say, I love the freedom from economic worry myself," Velma said.

"So do I, but I have reservations about someone as wealthy and influential as she." He paused a moment, attempting to phrase his next question. "You don't think we're selling out, do you?"

"Selling out? We still maintain our personal and artistic integrity. We're not exactly whoring ourselves, you know. Besides, why should we feel guilty about easy money? It doesn't seem to bother any of the capitalists I know."

"But, she didn't even like my book," Rudy said. "She probably won't like anything I write."

"The contract didn't say she had to like it; just that she has to know about it."

Rudy released the thought and continued to dance and watch the party. The rainbow of ebony to caramel people packed the hot, crowded parlor and began breaking off into smaller groups. The women were gorgeous in their spring skirts, and the striking men, already casual, were becoming more casual as the room got warm and they shed their sweaters, jackets and ties. Langston stood reading *Vanity Fair* while Countee and Eric bubbled over new ideas for upcoming books. Aaron Douglas and Miguel Covarrubias carried on an esoteric discussion of Cubism and Impressionism—Miró, Matisse, Gauguin and Monet, while Alta rested her chin on her husband's shoulder, and tossed in Picasso's name for comparative debate. The room buzzed as people exchanged information about new neighborhood workshops, periodicals and literary magazines looking for fresh material, the names of approachable editors, publishers open to Negro authors, undiscovered art galleries, "must

</a

see" museum exhibits, jazz forms being created in Harlem, the state of theater and dance, and noncommercial bookstores popping up in the Village. Some people sat alone, fell asleep, or studied the groups from a distance. Others drank booze and licked chicken grease and crumbs from their fingers.

"You know what's funny?" Rudy said to Velma. "When Mrs. Vanderpool said, 'I'm nearly seventy years old whether you can tell or not.' I really thought that was a scream."

"That wasn't half as funny as her wanting us to call her Godmother." They chuckled. "Just remember, Rudy, we can break the contract any time."

"I guess you're right. Sometimes, I worry too much."

"Well, don't. Just dance," Velma commanded him.

Rudy began to tango, mimicking Rudolph Valentino. He led Velma across, then back, bumping into several couples in the process. Their cheeks were pressed against each other, their arms erect with drama.

"I couldn't help but overhear your conversation," Zora interrupted, dancing nearby, "but are we speaking of white patrons of the arts?" Not waiting for an answer, she continued. "I won't inquire as to who the little darling is. They're so secretive about which darkies they support. But don't you think it's like a twentieth-century urban plantation? Like maybe we're getting our forty acres and a mule, after all?"

"Sounds like you know the territory," Velma said.

"Chile, do I ever! But then, geography is my business," Zora said, turning, as her partner swung her. "Do what I do. Play little happy-go-lucky darky writer and bat your eyelashes a lot. When I call, I say, 'This is your lil ol' primitive child.' They just love stuff like that."

"Excuse me, Velma." Scott entered the gossiping triangle of drunken dancers. "It's nearly five in the morning. Don't you think we should be going?"

"Scott, I'm having a wonderful time," Velma said. "Why don't—"

"Did I ever tell you," Zora cut in, "the story about the little juke joint in the red-light district of New Orleans when the—"

"No, you haven't," Scott snapped. "And we don't have time to hear it now."

"I'd love to hear it, Zora," Velma insisted.

"So would I," Rudy said.

"Anyway," Zora continued, rolling her eyes at Scott. "This here conjure man was blind as a bat, see, and had a three-legged jackass who couldn't tell north from south—"

"I think I've heard this one," Scott said, not concealing his impatience or displeasure. "Velma, please, I have to be up at nine this morning. As it is, I don't know how I'll manage."

"Okay, okay," Velma said, annoyed. "You'll excuse me, Zora and Rudy, but my date is ready to go." Velma stopped dancing and hooked her arm inside Scott's. They headed for the door, bidding hasty good-byes.

"It always takes stiff-upper-lip Scott to break up a party," Zora said. "Always walking around like he got a pole shoved up his you-know-what."

6

Velma and Scott strolled down Lenox Avenue just before dawn. Her head pressed against his arm, she stifled a yawn with the back of her hand. The two lovers were the only life on the deserted street.

Velma took a deep breath of what smelled like spring in the air. The buildings of a dormant community passed before her sleepy eyes: restaurants, churches, funeral parlors, nightclubs, stores, shops, newspaper offices, real estate firms, lawyer and doctor offices, fortune-tellers and hairdressers. A mysterious mist hung over the city like a net. Twinkling stars in the sky vanished one by one, replaced by sudden hints of sunlight.

A truck passed before a tenement. A man carried a large chunk of ice up the stone staircase. People appeared and moved briskly, their profiles bent against the mild wind. They descended the Lenox Avenue subway near 135th Street. Newspaper boys set up business as a passing *Amsterdam News* truck plopped a tied bundle onto the sidewalk. A bashful sun peeked over the horizon and projected its filtery rays, as building structures and plant life cast shadows to the west.

On West 139th Street, Velma listened to their footsteps against the asphalt, and the pigeons cooing and flapping their wings on an upper ledge. As they approached Scott's townhouse—one in a row of Stanford White–designed houses—she said, "Maybe I should go home."

"Won't you come up for a nightcap, or rather, a morning cap?" Scott suggested.

"Well, you were so grumpy before, I thought you wanted to get to bed."

"I do." Scott inhaled on his pipe. "But not alone."

"You sure?" she asked, excited by the invitation without showing it.

She followed him as he opened the door to his townhouse. Morning sun washed the room in bright yellow. "Have breakfast with me," he joked. "Join me in a gin benedict?"

"I'm so tired, I could drink anything."

Velma plopped down on the sofa and admired the Covarrubias and Van Vechten Negro celebrity caricatures, the African sculpture by Barthe. Framed photographs of Scott with Hemingway and other writers at Le Café Napolitain in Paris, Josephine Baker at a nightclub, and beside it, Pablo Picasso outside his château in Mougins, Cannes, hung on one wall.

The walls were a calming beige against Victorian furniture. Above the fireplace was a red-brick mantelpiece on which stood tall, sterling-silver candle holders with white unlit candles. The ceilings were high-beamed. Lace doilies rested upon the backs and armrests of the royal blue velvet sofa and matching wing chairs. Varnished bookshelves held domestic and foreign books. Velma thought Scott must possess the most extensive private book collection outside of the New York Public Library. Hardwood floors were dotted with eye-catching throw rugs whose hues highlighted Scott's masculine touch. A round Art Deco mirror tilted forward from the wall. For the first time, Velma noticed the Harvard pennant diagonally tacked between photographs of Scott's paternal grandparents, and his Crimson buddies waving and beaming from a model T Ford in raccoon coats. Scott was the only Negro among them.

"You know, Scott, no matter how many times I've been here, I just adore your townhouse. The bay windows, the fireplace."

"I'm so pleased you're pleased." He handed her a drink. "Some party, heh?"

"Yeah, they're a great bunch. Imagine Zora asking me to read my poetry?"

"I can hardly find it within me to like that woman. And, indeed, I've tried," Scott said unapologetically.

"You were very rude to her, you know. Why?"

"I absolutely abhor her pickaninny ways. Not to mention those race stories she passes off as art."

"Race stories?"

"Yeah, she, Waldrond, and Hughes; they're all poor excuses for artists, if you ask me."

"I beg to differ."

"*Ma chérie*, we are a literate class of society. There's no place for dialect or urban ghetto idioms in literature. Perhaps I'm mistaken, but I thought we left that all behind with slavery."

"Oh, Scott." Velma sipped her drink and slipped off her shoes. "That's a part of us. Part of a rich heritage, both racial and literary. For instance, Hughes—"

"Hughes? Your bloody golden boy. You call him a poet?" Scott sat and rubbed her tired feet. "*The Weary Blues* is spotty and undisciplined at best, so I didn't even bother to read *Fine Clothes to the Jew*. Now, Cullen, there's a poet—"

"Not taking anything away from him," Velma cut him off, "but he writes in the tradition of the English romanticists, like Keats."

"Exactly, my dear. Keats is a true poet. The Whitmans, the Sandburgs—"

"So, you're saying that Cullen's work is superior because it adheres to European standards?" Velma asked.

"You said it, not me."

"What do you think of *my* poetry?" Velma sat up straight and placed her stockinged feet on the floor.

"I don't know why you need my opinion." Scott stood, walked to the window, and glanced out into the streets, his back to Velma. "You got quite an ovation at Wally's tonight."

"You resented that, didn't you?"

"Me?" Scott laughed. "Why should I resent it?"

"I don't know. Your mood shifts really puzzle me sometimes. Seems like after I recited, you became, oh, I don't know . . . disturbed."

"Seems to me you're fishing for compliments."

"If it were compliments I was looking for, they came in the form of applause from everybody else."

She thought he was envious, but didn't know why. Here he was a critically acclaimed novelist getting touchy about her "little" poem. It made her laugh inside. And he couldn't really think something surreptitious was transpiring between Aaron and her.

His wife damn near sat on his lap throughout the party. Scott wouldn't share the spotlight. It was either focused on him or turned off altogether. He was the most prolific, and *only* Negro author New York critics compared with canonized white boys like Hemingway, Fitzgerald, even D. H. Lawrence—and he knew it. To an extent, she understood and respected that arrogance, and even recognized it in herself. She didn't really care, in love with him as she was. Just the same, she enjoyed some good verbal sparring every now and again, a challenging match of wits with Scott, who acted like the forefather of the know-it-alls.

"You know Wally and Langston are lovers?" Scott said, leaning against the window, facing her.

"Why're you changing the subject?" Velma asked.

"I'm not. I just think it must be an accomplishment of some kind on Thurman's part. Your precious Langston is such a difficult person to penetrate. He's always so damn aloof, so bloody distant."

"And, I hear Countee's in love with his best friend, Harold," she shot back. "So what?"

"Now you're getting defensive," Scott said, gloating. He loved getting a rise out of her.

"Well, you're always attacking my heroes."

"Okay, okay." Scott crossed the room and resumed his seat next to her on the sofa. "Tell me what you find so special about Langston? I'd sincerely like to understand."

"You really want to hear this or you're just patronizing me?"

"Tell me; I want to know."

"Well, he's one of the few male writers who deals with women beneath the surface."

"He knows how to penetrate women? Hmmm. That's not what I heard."

"Don't be smart. You know what I mean," she insisted, shifting her body to face him. "You and I both experience racial oppression in our lives and in literature, right? For you, that's where it stops. For me, it extends to my life as a woman, as well. I think Hughes is different. He's a male voice in literature that depicts female characters with multidimensions."

"I'm not sure I follow."

"Scott, what I'm saying is that male writers, even Negro male writers, have no more respect for women than white people have for us, and it shows in the work."

"You haven't gotten disrespect from my side, yet." Scott caressed her thigh and leaned closer. She turned her face away from the stench of liquor on his breath.

He was a bit taken aback when she turned away from him, and thought of how often she'd avoided him before. Sex never consummated their most passionate moments. What was going on with Velma? he wondered. Was she bedding down with Rudy? Scott had seen her looking at Rudy wistfully as they danced at Wally's. Scott thought how badly he wanted her, to savor her nude before him, to fill her with himself. That was why he brought her here, even when he needed to be at his typewriter working in three or four hours.

He loved Velma, no mistake. How could he not? She was beautiful, bright, educated, loving, sensitive, loyal, aggressive, and she had the biggest, most perfectly shaped ass in a tight skirt he'd ever seen this side of the Atlantic. Prior to Velma, he'd found no more than a couple of those characteristics at any one time in any one woman. Velma was a gold mine, the Mother Lode! He'd been very patient with her. But if he discovered that she was virginal or asexual, he'd have to find someone else. He loved Velma *and* sex, and had to have them both. Why did she keep her distance even when she was so close?

"How's your novel coming, Scott?"

"Now who's changing the subject?"

"Seriously, I've been wondering about it."

"Not too good, actually. Too many parties, too lazy to get off my ass, I guess. But I was wondering about something which might interest you. Can I get you another drink?"

"I'll drink some of yours."

Scott walked to the alcove and filled his glass with three ice cubes. "I've been meaning to ask you this for a while." He poured gin over the ice. "How would you like to assist me with some research?" He added ginger ale to the gin and mixed it. "You're a terribly bright person. Level-headed, sharp instincts. I could use your talents. Sure you don't want a drink?"

"Sure." Velma stifled a yawn and rubbed her eyes. "What do you need?"

"You're already yawning. I don't want to bore you further." He returned to the sofa.

"I'm tired, Scott. Long night."

"Well, I've been following a particular story in the newspaper. I'd like to fictionalize it. The research would involve gathering the clippings."

"I'd love to. Thanks for asking. I have a notorious weakness for men who appreciate my mind . . . and my body." She laughed and kissed his cheek. "That reminds me. I have to finish my article on Garvey. My deadline's Monday."

"Well, you have time." Scott traced his finger across Velma's lips, alongside her cheek. "Velma, I'm very fond of you, you know."

"Yes, Scott." She took his wandering finger and kissed it. "You know I'm very fond of you too."

"How come you never express it?" He spoke softly, his lips touching her ear.

"I do express it."

"Why then, don't you ever make love to me? You don't impress me as the frigid type." He nibbled on her earlobe.

"I'm not." She leaned her head back and closed her eyes. "I guess, I just want to be sure. I got into trouble that way once before," she said.

"Trouble?"

"Let's just say, I counted my chickens before they hatched."

"Is Rudy one of those chickens?"

She opened her eyes and lifted her head from the sofa. "What makes you say that?"

"Well, is he?" He took a sip, holding her eye contact.

"Rudy and I are just friends. He's like the brother I never had."

"You sure that's all he is?" Scott looked skeptical.

"Yes, I'm sure. I don't even know why you're asking."

"I'm asking because I'm about to make myself vulnerable with you." He leaned closer to her. "And I bet you thought only women were vulnerable." He laughed nervously.

"Vulnerable how?" She wanted to hear him say it.

"I'm falling in love with you, Velma. You're intelligent, beautiful, fun to be with. Why shouldn't I?" He stroked her hair, which sent a tingle across her scalp, and a smile spread across her face.

"Why shouldn't you?" she teased him.

"So I want to be sure there's no one else, Velma. Sometimes, the way you look at Rudy, I can't tell what you're feeling."

"Just consider him a good friend. That's all he is, a friend. Besides, he doesn't really like . . ."

"Doesn't like what?"

"It's not my place to say." She silently chided herself for letting it slip. Rudy had made her promise.

"To say what?" Scott smiled devilishly. "He's freakish, isn't he?"

"I don't know what you mean."

"You know exactly," Scott said, wondering what Rudy liked—men, women, or both. "I saw him flirting with Langston and besides, he never talks about women other than you."

"Scott, if you want to know about Rudy, ask Rudy."

"I don't have to. I read people rather well. I'm not condemning him or passing judgment, if that's what you think."

"What's there to condemn? Who cares what he is?" She surprised herself, listening to the liberal views suddenly leaping from her lips. Where was it, she thought, when I really needed to understand him? "He's one of the best friends I ever had. Next to you, of course," she said, hoping the discussion wouldn't go beyond this parlor.

"He's a delightful chap," Scott agreed. "A little naive and green around the edges, but a cute sorta fellow." You'd just better not be sleeping with him, he thought. "But not as cute as you, my love."

Setting his glass on the table, he took her face in his hands and kissed her repeatedly with half-drunken passion. Mouths pressed together, he lowered her fragile body with an adolescent anticipation, having fantasized this moment time and again. With slow, delayed movements, he lowered his mouth to her neck, shoulders, and breasts. Lifting her blouse, he kissed her stomach, and licked her navel. With a firm grip, he embraced both her legs, inching the skirt hem toward her waist. As he slid her panties down to her ankles, he focused on every inch of her leg. He kissed her body in random spots, slowly and deliberately, then placed her legs over his shoulders and buried his head between her thighs. "Scott! What're you doing?"

He ignored her, his tongue darting into her like a reptile's. Velma moaned rapturously, her hands squeezing his shoulders, pressing him against her. *God, it felt heavenly wicked!* Her smooth thighs quivered against his unshaven face. The prickly hairs tickled the insides of her thighs. Volts of excitement charged through her. She glanced above his head, around the room, focused on a photograph of Scott's family posing outside a church in Sunday finery, and felt a bit of shame that faded as she closed her eyes. She shook her foot and let her panties tumble down Scott's back onto the floor.

7

Bending over the bathtub, Miriam soaped the washcloth in her hand. The water was tepid to the touch, yet heavy curtains of steam rose, thick and moist, and she could barely see Agnes's face.

Miriam soaped Agnes's back in the circular motions she had learned in her training. Her head bent forward, Agnes moaned from the gentle pressure applied to her spine. Miriam dipped the washcloth again and squeezed it along the nape of Agnes's neck and shoulders, the drops falling melodically. Miriam's heart pounded as she timidly focused on a cloud of soapsuds sliding between firmly shaped breasts. Miriam's hand faltered, and Agnes laughed nervously. Embarrassed, Miriam looked away, like a child being forced to acknowledge the broken vase she had been warned not to touch. Agnes slipped the washcloth from Miriam's grip, rinsed and lathered it herself, and gave it back, guiding Miriam's hand across her supple breasts. Once Miriam was comfortable with it, Agnes let go of her hand, relaxed, and allowed herself to be pampered. Miriam's circular massage slid to Agnes's navel. She lifted Miriam's hand again, placed it upon her breast, and laughed again. She dropped the washcloth in the water, and tried to stand. She slipped and slided a bit as she stood. Miriam noticed the iridescent sheen of bubbles between Agnes's legs.

She pulled Agnes closer, wrapped her arms tightly around her neck and held her. It was like embracing Mother, one of her sisters, or any number of women she'd known; and yet it was nothing like those embraces at all. It felt so good taking another human being into her arms. Agnes's breasts pressed against her shot a sensation through her like Fourth of July fireworks. Agnes inched her head from Miriam's shoulder, cupped the woman's face in her hands, and planted soft, bathtub wet kisses along her brow, her eyelids, the corners of her mouth, and ears.

For a moment, Miriam wanted to pull away. But there was no retreat. Her arms were locked around this woman, and she had no key.

Agnes and Miriam were a duet of passion on the verge of

explosion. Miriam wrestled with her own yielding submission as
Agnes inched her face forward. . . .

Rrrrriiiinnnng!
The alarm clock sounded and Miriam jolted awake, wild-eyed. Her
pillow lay on her chest and she wondered how it got there. She
never hugged a pillow while she slept. Then she remembered the
dream. There was moisture between her legs—a kind she'd rarely
felt before—and she felt ashamed.

She attempted to put the dream out of her mind, as she went
through her morning ritual. But Agnes stuck in her thoughts. She
didn't understand what was happening to her. Agnes and Tommy
had reconciled, and Miriam felt a tinge of jealousy. Nor could she
transfer her feelings to George, Brother Hiram, or any other man.

Counterrevolutionary! That's what Miriam thought when she
examined her feelings for Agnes with any objectivity. *What are the
ramifications for a woman like myself? What would my colleagues
think of me?*

The men and women of UNIA were expected to multiply and
flourish, to build the Negro nation. Where did a woman like herself
fit in? She couldn't picture herself with *any* man. Neither could she
fulfill the role of baby-maker that the organization demanded of
women. Officials and members alike had asked her about making
her "womanly" contribution to the cause. *Sister, when are you
starting your family? There's some mighty fine brothers just
waiting for a wife like you.* Miriam could only smile and answer
that she was involved with a man outside the organization and was
making concerted efforts to convert him. They assumed she meant
George, since he'd attended several of the meetings, and she let
them think it. He was the best defense against their prying into her
personal business. But she understood their concern. "One God,
One Aim, One Destiny," they believed, as did she. But she felt her
womb was hers to do with it as she saw fit. She sensed the
interrogating eyes of the other women. They had children climbing
all over them, and wondered why she didn't.

In the system of checks and balances, she felt equal to them.
Her contributions were not one iota less than that of fertile,
child-rearing women. Having children prevented them from working diligently, around the clock if necessary, for coordinating
meetings, parades and seminars the way she could. While they were
home nursing, feeding, changing diapers, Miriam was working her

fingers to the bone, keeping late hours, printing flyers, designing community programs and the like. Did women not serve purposes other than having babies? She got the message, loud and clear. No matter what she did, how much of herself she gave to the cause, she wasn't worth her weight in spit if she couldn't produce a child—from their standpoint, a male child.

Miriam didn't want a husband and babies. She wanted the closeness of Agnes, but shut her mind and simply prayed against it.

Agnes endured Miriam's obsession with Garvey, and Miriam tolerated Agnes's singular vision of Tommy. She couldn't see how unfaithful he was to her. And Miriam couldn't bear to tell Agnes that Tommy had made advances toward her too. She wondered what it was men tried to prove with their promiscuity. Just for kicks, Miriam played it out entirely in her head. If, by some outlandish circumstance, she decided to give in to Tommy, then what? Would he date them simultaneously? Or drop one for the other? Who would get dropped? It was ludicrous to her.

In the hospital cafeteria that day, Miriam sat across from Agnes, but couldn't look her in the eye. Agnes sensed her uneasiness and asked several times what was wrong.

"Nothing," Miriam responded; nothing she could think of. Agnes smiled terminally, as if sharing a joke with herself and held Miriam by the wrist, motioning her to remain seated, the smile wider than ever now.

"Well, ain't you gonna ask me?" Agnes said.

"Ask you what?"

"Ain't you noticed me smiling all day long like the cat who swallowed the canary?"

"No." Miriam really hadn't noticed, not until lunchtime. "So, why are you . . ."

Agnes's eyes lowered and rested upon her left hand. Miriam's eyes followed and she almost gasped at the sparkling engagement ring around Agnes's finger. Miriam's stomach took a dive.

"Well?" Agnes said. "Ain't you gonna congratulate me?"

"You're getting married?"

"That's what an engagement ring usually means," Agnes said. Her smile turned sour, watching Miriam's numbed reaction. "You're not happy for me," Agnes said, "are you?"

"Yes, um, well, of course," Miriam said, straining to smile. "It's just all so sudden."

"Well, it ain't so sudden if you knew how long I been trying to get this nigger to marry me."

There was that word again, but Miriam ignored it. She addressed the more pressing issue at hand.

"Well, Miriam," Agnes said, slightly perturbed, "I was going to ask you to be my maid of honor, but I don't know."

"Agnes, I don't know how to say this . . . or if I should say it at all."

"Well, girl," Agnes said, "you done said it now. Tell me what's wrong." She held Miriam's wrist across the table. "I thought you'd be so happy knowing how you worried about me and Tommy—"

"Tommy asked me to go out with him." She couldn't believe, after six months or so, she'd finally said it.

"What!" Agnes said, recoiling, removing her hand from Miriam's wrist.

"Miriam," she asked, her mirth turning to disbelief mixed with indignation. "Why would you say a thing like that?"

"Agnes," Miriam said, "we'd better go. We can talk about this later."

"We'll talk about it now. Tell me, why would you say that?"

"Because it's true." Miriam lowered her head. She really couldn't face the woman now.

"When, Miriam? Tell me when this happened."

"Well, the night after you left the meeting, he came back in and gave me his telephone number."

"You sure you didn't ask for it? I know Tommy's fine and there's a lot of broads out there after him. What makes you think—"

"Agnes, I'm your friend. I'd never do that."

"Well, so what, even if he did," Agnes said, the issue apparently resolved in her head. "That's when we was having problems. I'd expect—"

"No, Agnes. He asked me again after that. Even waited for me after work a couple of times."

"When, Miriam? Give me dates, and times!"

"Last time was just a couple of weeks ago."

Agnes rose, her palms planted firmly on the table, and gazed down at Miriam with a glare that seemed to pierce her.

"Miriam Brooks," Agnes began, "I think you're jealous."

"Jealous?"

"Yeah, look at you, pushing twenty-eight and all you got to show for it is an organization with their leader in prison. In some way, I feel sorry for you."

"Don't feel sorry for me; I don't need pity. Feel sorry for yourself." Miriam didn't mean that. The focus of this discussion was getting off track. "Look, Agnes, I'm your friend, I care about you. Anything that makes you happy, makes me happy. I just don't want you to get hurt."

"I'm already hurt! By my best friend, no less. Just think, I wanted you as my maid of honor. Yeah, you're right, we should be getting back to work. Sorry I even told you," Agnes said, as she stormed off.

Miriam remained seated, staring after her. But finally accepted the burden of what she'd done and got up to leave.

8

Miriam fanned herself with a menu in Bubba's Soda Shoppe. The heat and humidity were unusually high for May, and an overhead fan seemed to stir only hot air. Dabbing her face with a shredded napkin, she watched people milling about in their Sunday finery, and a young couple giggling and kissing in the neighboring booth. A uniformed waitress asked her again if she was ready yet to order.

"No, thank you," Miriam said. "My party hasn't arrived yet."

"You can't wait much longer." She held the tray against her waist. "These customers are tired from the parade and pretty soon, I'll have to charge you rent," she said, laughing at her own joke.

"I know," Miriam said, returning the smile.

Having marched three miles in a UNIA-sponsored parade, Miriam was exhausted. There had been a divine service at eleven that morning, and there was yet another mass meeting scheduled for eight o'clock that night.

Finally, Velma walked through the door, and she felt as if a life preserver had been cast out to save her sinking spirit. "Over here!"

They embraced and kissed.

"It's good to see you, Velma."

"Good to see you too, girl."

"So, little sister, what's new?"

"Oh, Miriam, I don't know where to begin."

The waitress returned, and on her pad she scribbled their orders of apple pie and milk, tucked the pencil behind her ear, and left.

"So," Miriam began, "tell me about this new beau of yours."

"Miriam, he's a dream. He's everything I want in a man."

"That's wonderful. You deserve it, girl. Tell me about him."

Miriam listened intently, though she had heard most of it. She was happy for her sister, elated that the time she'd spent writing was not in vain, overjoyed with the success of her new love. Moments like this reminded Miriam of when they were teenagers. Velma always had one eye in the books and the other on boys. Miriam would listen to Velma's romantic reveries late into the night when they should have been sleeping. Not that she was fast, she just knew exactly what kind of man could or couldn't make her happy—even at age thirteen. Miriam envied this about her sister. Velma could place her finger on her own pulse. Velma knew herself.

As the eldest, Miriam felt the pressure of being considered an example to her sisters. Mother continued to nudge her about her role as wife and mother. And she couldn't tell Mother that she didn't see that for herself. Velma, the hopeless romantic she was, would ensnare herself a husband or two, maybe three, before her final breath, Miriam thought. Mother didn't have to worry about her.

"I saw you in the parade. You looked grand, girl," Velma said, proud of her sister's dedication to her work.

"Thanks," Miriam replied, wanting to bring up Agnes's name without arousing Velma's curiosity about the relationship. Velma knew her well, and little escaped her.

"So, what's new with you?" Velma's eyes brightened.

"Same old stuff, actually. The hospital and the UNIA," Miriam said, "I don't have time for anything else."

"You still never go out?"

"I go out. There's always plenty to do—"

"You know what I mean." Velma knew Miriam was touchy about her social life. "Don't you go dancing and drinking once in a while?"

"I will when I have more time."

"Dating anybody? Come on," Velma teased, "tell me. Who's the mystery man?"

"No, Velma." Miriam bent her head slightly. "There's no man in my life, not yet."

"Why not?" Velma looked perplexed.

"Where do I find the time?" Miriam said.

"Miriam, don't take this the wrong way," Velma said cautiously.

"But you need to take it easy. You're dedicated to your work, and that's commendable, but don't stop living."

"Okay, you're right," Miriam said. She opted for change of subject. "So tell me, how did you get your stuff published in *The Crisis?*"

"I've told you that story," Velma laughed. "But, there's one I didn't tell you." Velma lowered her voice, and leaned closer. "Remember Rudy?"

The waitress arrived with two slices of apple pie and glasses of milk. She placed them on the table and said, "Were you in that parade today?" She looked at Miriam.

"Yes, I'm a member of Garvey's Black Cross Nurses."

"Well, it's on the house," she whispered, walking away.

"See," Miriam said to Velma. "Your sister's a celebrity in her own right. Now, what were you saying about Rudy?" Miriam cut a piece of pie with her fork.

"Girl," Velma whispered, "I fell madly in love with this fellow, right?"

"Hmm, I remember."

"Well, I dropped by to surprise him one day with some roses, but you wouldn't believe what happened."

"What?"

"I walked in his house and found him in bed with somebody else." Velma paused dramatically, then added, "And that somebody else was a man; what do you think about that?"

Velma expected her sister to be shocked, or at least surprised.

"Well, Velma, you know it takes all kinds. So, what did you do?"

"What could I do?" Velma said. "I let him go. I mean, I can't compete with another man. It was bad enough competing against women for Roland."

"You and Rudy still friends?"

"Oh yes; it was difficult after that happened, let me tell you. But now we're all friends, and I'm convinced that he still loves me. He's got to still like women some, wouldn't you think?"

"Who's *we're all?*"

"Scott, him and myself."

"So, you go around with two men?" Miriam said laughing. "Velma, you're something else."

"It's *très chic* in the '20s to have two beaux. Why not? Men've been doing it for centuries."

"Does Scott know?"

"About what?"

"Well, about you and Rudy or—"

"God no. He already asked me about that. I lied, of course. But, yeah, he said he knew about . . . well, Rudy . . . you know."

"Well, be careful," Miriam advised.

"About what? Scott will never find out—"

"No, you'd better keep an eye on what's-his-name? Rudy? He might go after Scott if he's as fine as you say he is."

"No, I wouldn't worry about that. Rudy's my dear friend."

"Okay. You know what you're doing."

"Don't worry, sis, I do."

Velma didn't admit that she might still be in love with Rudy. She was afraid of what Miriam would think. While she felt fortunate to have found a lover straight out of her wildest fantasies, she sometimes feared that passion, anxiety, and love—mostly love—would probably be the death of her. She lived to love and be loved as the clergy lived to serve God.

She admired Miriam's low-profiled vulnerability. She teased her about dodging suitors but deemed it a talent. Rather than get caught up in the crossed wires and humdrum doings involved in courtship and marriage, Miriam had her eyes set on higher sights. It wasn't as if Velma didn't have objectives, she just made time during her quest to find someone to fit her snugly like a new shoe. Not Miriam. She had a martyrlike spirit about her, the ability to sacrifice herself. Sometimes, Velma would have given anything to share Miriam's indifference to men.

She was ecstatic about Scott now. Given time, if it was in the stars, they would make it work. She hoped for the strength and perseverance to sustain her through whatever trials fate might have in store. But she couldn't worry about that. She was having the time of her life.

"How's Louise?" Velma asked. "I haven't seen her much either."

"Just fine," Miriam said. "She's working as a chorus girl at the Cotton Club."

"Yes, Mother told me."

"Can you believe it?" Miriam said. "Our little baby sister Louise. Out there on a stage kicking her legs up and carrying on like nobody's business. She deserves it. She told me she's never been happier. She'll be just fine."

"Of course," Velma agreed. "Good thing Mother got her those tap lessons." Everyone made a fuss over Louise, but Miriam, Velma thought, really had the good looks. If she wore makeup, she'd be a sure knockout.

Miriam didn't know if this was the appropriate time or not. But she had to ask it.

"Velma, I want to ask your opinion about something."

"Sure."

"Tell me what you honestly think, okay?"

"Shoot," Velma said.

Miriam told her what was happening with her and Agnes—not the incriminating details, but about their friendship, and Agnes's history with Tommy. She described how Agnes announced her engagement, and how she told her friend that her fiancé had pursued her behind Agnes's back.

"Should I have told her?"

"Let me get this straight," Velma said, wiping her mouth and pushing the empty plate and glass aside. "Okay. She's your best friend and her fiancé made advances toward you." Velma gave it deep thought, a prolonged silence passing between them. Miriam held her breath, and nervously chewed the pie she wasn't in the mood to eat.

"Well, if I were your girlfriend, I'd want to know; yeah, you did the right thing," Velma said without a trace of doubt.

"No," Miriam said. "If you were me, would *you* have told her?"

"Of course," Velma said. "Men always stick together; women have to do the same."

"But she won't talk to me, Velma. She thinks I'm making it up."

"If there was a way you could prove it, somehow," Velma said more to herself than Miriam.

"I *can* prove it," Miriam said. "I still have the phone number he gave me."

"Well, then," Velma said.

"I don't know. If she thought I'd lie to her about something crazy as that, she might still think I'm lying."

"Show her the phone number and see, Miriam. How else will you ever know?"

As if windows had been opened in a stuffy room, Miriam breathed in this fresh air of sound advice.

"You think so?" Miriam asked.

"It's what I would do," Velma said, "if my friend meant that much."

Miriam was hiding something, Velma could tell, relating an entire story by starting in the middle. Miriam was no liar, but she had a weakness for omissions. She had had that same look as a young girl whenever she told Mother and Father only what she wanted them to know. Velma knew her sister would fill in the blanks when she felt ready.

"Well, that solves that," Velma said. "Come on, let's go for a walk. We haven't walked through the park together since you moved out of Mother's."

"Thanks for coming," Miriam said. "I feel a hundred percent better now."

They left the restaurant arm in arm. As they walked, Velma described to Miriam the art of oral lovemaking. Miriam was shocked, riveted, and a bit repulsed, as Velma described how Scott buried his face in her crotch. They strolled out into the heat, passing unnoticed through the myriad of parade spectators crowding the Sunday sidewalks, and giggled like teenage girls.

9

In his parlor, Rudy plugged away at the typewriter, munching on a can of sardines and soda crackers. He was struggling through this chapter. The writing wasn't jelling—imprecise metaphors, dangling participles, tenses out of whack, epiphany that wasn't clearly delineated, the voices of narrator and protagonist merging—and he leaned back in his chair, yawned, and wondered if Velma knew about his lunch date with Scott.

She was a swell girl, best friend he'd ever had. What a rare creature, this brilliant Negro woman, an Ivy Leaguer to boot, who lived her life as she damn well pleased. Like him, she bucked convention and lived by her own rules and mores, daring anyone to challenge them. A literary maverick *extraordinaire*. He couldn't imagine traipsing about Harlem without her. But he hoped that she understood and, most of all, *respected* his limits. Occasionally, he noticed her shooting him that sidelong glance—a glance he could no longer reciprocate.

Maybe he shouldn't have succumbed to an impulse strictly of the moment. The morning after they made love, he noticed how her cautious reserve had given way to a subtle possessiveness. He ignored it. In ensuing weeks, he simply wished he hadn't gotten involved with her. But he was drawn to Velma and thought she lived and breathed an urban sophistication he rarely found in his native Jersey City. He had an ex-fiancée back home, but he could no more endure the pressure of giving her what she wanted than he could Velma. No real resemblance existed between Velma and his former fiancée. But when it came to him, they seemed to be alter egos.

Velma had freed him in a way she couldn't possibly know. This alone made it worthwhile.

His academic aspirations and sexual ambiguity in his hometown had catapulted him across the Hudson River into Harlem. Anonymity was sweet. He attended Columbia in his senior year. First three years he spent at Jersey City State College. But Columbia University had always been a goal of his, and during the school year, he earned extra money through odd jobs and by tutoring English. Each summer, Rudy found full-time work and saved his earnings. Even if it was one year; he didn't care. So long as his degree was from Columbia. After graduation, he dreamed obsessively of becoming a published novelist, but he also wanted to find himself; pull himself inside out and scrutinize his interior landscape with a magnifying glass. His physical attraction to Velma he attributed to impulse; the closer they got physically, the more he realized he didn't want to be with her. Though he wasn't impotent, he was certain that the wine, the rain, Bessie Smith, and the moment's magic had pulled him through it and sustained his erection.

As he mounted her, it became clear, like a drug kicking into effect, that he'd rather be with a man. *What am I doing here?* reverberated through him. Entering her, he decided that Velma Brooks was the last word and period in a chapter he was closing on himself. For the first time in his life, he felt in touch with himself.

And, as fate would have it, she interrupted the first adult experience he had in bed with a man. He'd had experiences as an adolescent, but had expected that by adulthood, he would have made the transition into heterosexuality, like a caterpillar metamorphosing into a butterfly. But nature didn't take its course and deliver him from "adolescent tendencies."

Velma claimed she was in love with him. He loved her too, more than any woman except his mother. He just wasn't *in* love. He thought that he would even have to sacrifice their friendship in the face of conflicting needs. But Scott, ironically, kept that from happening. A bargain indeed, to be able to hold on to Velma and take hold of Scott. Scott was easily the most beautiful, most worldly, most provocative man he'd ever laid eyes on. He kept his feelings to himself, accepting the reality that Scott was Velma's friend and didn't share his inclinations. Rudy felt that many people, especially women, ingratiated themselves with Scott for his stark physical appeal alone. Rudy was no different. Scott had the sort of look that made even men want to gaze as he disrobed in a locker room or a Turkish bath. Knowing he could never have him, Rudy lusted from a safe distance, like a fan over a Hollywood movie star. Scott seemed unapproachable, except for that night on the Brooklyn Bridge. Rudy knew that the fine line Scott trod with those dubiously intimate gestures was, at best, vague. Maybe Scott was one of those men who flirted with ambiguity. Classic borderline case. Maybe that's who Scott was. Rudy didn't care. His crush was to savor, to revel in, and to guard as a top secret. This way, nobody got hurt.

Oh God! he thought, snapping from his daydream. He had a lunch date with Scott and he would be late if he didn't hurry. With one stop to make before meeting Scott, he hurriedly put on the beige suit he hadn't worn since Van Vechten's party last summer.

Under the August sun, he removed his straw boater to fan his face. He blotted the sweat with a handkerchief and loosened his necktie. At midday he was on a bustling thoroughfare on the West Side where people shopped and strolled. He stopped in a bookstore to pick up *Nigger Heaven*, the new bestselling novel by Carl Van Vechten, but they were out of stock. Glancing at his watch, he saw he was a little late. Scruffy-looking youngsters played a game of marbles on the sidewalk in Rudy's path. Excited by the game, one of them backed into him, leaving a footprint on Rudy's trousers. Rudy forgave him with a nod. He looked at his watch again, and headed for the subway that would deliver him to Lenox and 135th Street. In his haste he collided with a passerby. "Why don't you watch where you're goin', coon!" Ahead, he spotted a strange sight unlike anything he'd ever seen.

Hundreds upon hundreds of women crowded the corner of Sixty-sixth Street and Broadway, all dressed in mourning. They sobbed openly and some, hysterically. High drama filled the air, as did a battle of perfumes. Profuse tears streamed down white cheeks beneath black lace veils. The street was blockaded. Police barricades clogged the intersection at Broadway. The steps and adjoining street of the Frank E. Campbell Funeral Home were swarming with mourners. "Who died?" Rudy tapped a spectator on the arm. "Don't you know?!" the mourner replied with indignation, and walked away in a huff, wiping a tearless face. The mob was becoming difficult to maneuver through. So he decided to turn back, but that didn't work. Stationary bodies filled every space.

The doors of the Campbell Funeral Home opened, and the crowd closed in. Cries of "Rudy, I love you!" poured from the grieving, twisted mouths. Pallbearers in black shirts flanked the emerging casket. Slowly and ceremoniously, they descended the stairs. A grief-stricken, half-fainting Pola Negri followed closely behind. She was supported on either side by men in wire-rimmed glasses and dark pin-striped suits. A hideous roar issued from the wave of blackness. People pushed and shoved, trampling Rudy's new wing tips. Women uttered high-pitched screams. Some fainted at the sight of the casket. A crowd rushed for the coffin, elongating their arms to touch its shiny steel. Pallbearers and policemen warded off the grief-stricken fans. Horses whinnied, rising on their hind legs, their hooves clicking like castinets on the pavement. It grew hotter. Rudy's heart began to pound. He gasped for air and tried to escape before the ghoulish carnival consumed him. His shortcut had become the long way uptown.

"What the hell happened to you?" Scott asked, wincing at the sight of him. "Looks like you've been in a brawl."

"Sorry I'm late," Rudy apologized, "but I ran into the biggest, most bizarre funeral I've ever seen," he panted.

"They buried Valentino today, didn't they?"

"Yeah, and all these frenzied females wanted to be buried with him."

Resplendent in summer white, silk necktie, gloves, mono-grammed handkerchief, and fedora, Scott crossed his legs beneath their table at a sidewalk cafe. His hand rested upon a sturdy cane, and a white rose camouflaged itself against the lapel. His head turned, and as his profile caught the sun, it so unsettled Rudy that he nearly said aloud, *God must be black!*

"It's bloody hot out today." Scott chuckled after ordering club sandwiches. "Do you realize this is the first time you and I have been together . . . alone, I mean."

"Yes it is, isn't it," Rudy said, repressing a more suggestive remark.

"I know so little about you," Scott said. "How old are you anyway?"

"Twenty-four."

"Just a baby. Glorious youth and innocence. Yes, yes, I vividly recall when I was that age. Tell me a little about yourself." Scott placed the pipe between clenched teeth.

"Okay, well," Rudy began, "I was born and raised—"

"Jersey City. Yes, I'm aware of that."

"My folks—"

"Poor, uneducated, perhaps illiterate migrants escaping the haunting legacy of the great American South, fleeing, as it were, to the superficial promises of the industrial North where they could find unskilled labor while simultaneously blending, and with much difficulty, with the foreign mores of urban life, the absolute culture shock; thus providing their offspring with far better opportunities than themselves. Right so far?"

"Did you rehearse that?" Rudy asked, thinking, Okay, you can drop the pomposity; I've known you about a year already and it's grown old quickly.

"My dear Rudy, don't be put off. I'm the undisputed master of on-target observations. Frightfully ingenious at deciphering character sketches and backgrounds. It's the writer in me."

"How old are you?"

"Twenty-eight," Scott said.

"Where're you from?"

"Massachusetts," Scott said. "But I asked you first."

"What's there to say you don't already know?"

"Let's see. There must be a multitude of secrets I don't know about you. How about the fact that you're attracted to your own sex?" Scott smiled, knowing it caught Rudy off-guard.

"I envy your subtlety," Rudy said. "You have a frightful ingenuity for beating around the bush." How the hell did he know about that?

"Well? How about it?"

"Where'd you pick up this information, first of all?"

"Velma. Who else."

"Velma told you that?"

"She did indeed." Scott leaned forward, patting Rudy on the shoulder. "Relax, my dear boy. It's nothing to get alarmed about. Tell me, do your parents know of this . . . this . . ." He gestured with his hand.

"No, they don't."

"Which explains why you left your one-horse town and fled to Harlem. To escape insurmountable persecution, I imagine."

"Jersey City's not a one-horse town. You should visit it sometime. Give New York a break."

While Rudy sat there boiling over with anger toward Velma, he didn't want Scott to know how it bothered him that he knew. Was this Velma's way of getting even because he wouldn't sleep with her?

Club sandwiches with colored toothpicks piercing the centers arrived at their table. "So, how did you get into this? I mean, what makes a man sleep with another man? Were you the type who wore your sister's dresses?" Scott buried his teeth in a portion of his sandwich.

"First of all, it's as natural as heterosexual attraction." Rudy bit into his sandwich, and talked with food in his mouth, mayonnaise trapped in the corners of his lips. "Second of all, I don't have a sister. And thirdly, I've never had the desire to put on anybody's dress, Scott." He swallowed the portion, and sipped the lemonade. "Not even yours."

"You're very nonchalant about this, aren't you?"

"I have no illusions about who I am. I just make the best of it."

"Okay, let me see if I got this straight. You find your sexual pleasures with members of your own sex?"

"Yes."

"Which negates the possibility that you have similar needs for women?"

"Scott, you're so smart. Harvard, right?"

"Well, I'm baffled," Scott said, ignoring Rudy's sarcasm.

"Why, I'm afraid to ask?"

"Well, if you can't be satisfied by women, why on earth would you sleep with one?"

"I don't follow?"

"Come on, dear boy. Didn't you sleep with Velma?"

Rudy laughed, his mouth full of food. "Some question; have you asked her that?"

"Matter of fact, I did."

"What did she tell you?"

"Well, I'm certainly not the type to betray a confidence," Scott said, dabbing his mouth with the napkin. "But, let's just say she told me the truth."

"And nothing but the truth, so help her God." Rudy laughed again.

"This discussion amuses you?"

"Yes, it does." Rudy picked his molars with a toothpick. "But, what really amuses me is your so-called curiosity. Why the sudden morbid fascination with homosexuals?"

"Admittedly, I know very little about them. Like anyone else, I have natural curiosity. Who knows, I may want to write a novel one day about men in love." Scott wanted to get a reaction out of him. "Even if it involved my taking part in an experience to assure realism, I believe I'd do so."

"I believe you would too," Rudy said facetiously, unsure of where this discussion was headed. Wherever, he was going along for the ride.

"I must say I'd only indulge myself with someone I know rather intimately. I'll try anything once."

"Just who might that be?"

Scott reached across the table, patted Rudy's hand, and smiled. "Well, you never know. There're a lot of writers right here in Harlem who go in for that sort of thing. Although I could probably have my choice, I'd probably pick someone . . . like you." He retrieved his hand. "I trust you, Rudy."

"Should I be flattered or insulted?" Rudy's heart thumped. He enjoyed matching wits with Scott, who had a way of inciting people into conversations they'd rather not have. He loved challenging Scott's provocations, turning the tables, asking him the *unaskable*. It was the only way he felt equal to him. Looking at his soiled beige outfit, then at Scott's impeccable attire brought about no sense of equality.

"I only speak hypothetically, you understand," Scott added. "I don't want to encourage any fantasies you may have or give you the wrong idea." He stuffed his pipe with a fresh batch of tobacco. "Will you allow me to be frank with you?"

"You've never hesitated before."

"You're not as subtle as you like to think, Rudy."

"Pardon?"

"Come on, Rudy. Part of the reason I invited you to lunch today was to clear the air."

"I hadn't noticed the smoke."

"I'm well aware you're attracted to me, who could blame you? And, in some strange way, for reasons I cannot fathom, I'm flattered. I mean, you're not half bad-looking, but my persuasions are not in that direction. Besides, I'm in love with Velma, and, as you can imagine, it could make for quite an uncomfortable situation. I left my ménage-à-trois curiosities in Paris back in '22."

Scott was recalling Paris and Gabrielle, the French-Algerian beauty he met at Gertrude Stein's—or was it along Boulevard St. Germain? He was too drunk to remember. She took him home—he remembered crossing the Seine at Pont Neuf—and headed for Le Quartier Latin. Her flat was a cramped, stuffy three rooms over a boulangerie, and the thick aroma of French pastry hung in her boudoir like curtains. A man was present when they arrived. Scott thought she introduced her friend as a fashion model; her regional dialect was sometimes difficult to comprehend. The predicament, for Scott, was disconcerting. He wasn't sure who the man was, if he was going to leave or what. When Gabrielle and her model friend started undressing, Scott thought, hell, he'd go with it, and see what happened, so long as the man didn't come near him. In Paris, 1922, why not?

While Scott passionately kissed Gabrielle, the model—Scott believed his name was Olivier—started caressing Scott's face and chest, and it felt nice, as long as he couldn't see him. Then the man took Scott into his mouth and he could swear he'd never received such skillful, paralyzing fellatio in his life. It felt too good, too close for comfort, and Scott, with every ounce of restraint he could muster, was forced to suspend the most thrilling oral sex he'd ever had. After reducing the ménage à trois to a pas de deux between himself and Gabrielle, he dressed hurriedly and left, hoping he'd never run into Olivier again on the streets of Paris when he was drunk. Sitting across the table from Rudy, he remembered the occasion. Velma and Rudy, in an odd way, reminded him of Gabrielle and Olivier.

"I'm not as naive as you like to think," Rudy was saying.

"I don't follow."

"You follow precisely. I haven't forgotten that night on the bridge. Or were you too high to remember?" Rudy flashed a smile back at Scott. "You flirted with me right in front of Velma. So don't sit there and flatter yourself."

Scott laughed, wiping his mouth. "My dear Rudy, that was hardly a flirtation. Did you honestly think that?"

"I'm sure Velma thought so too. You saw how she broke up our embrace." Rudy loved the way Scott avoided the issue, walking a tightrope. It intensified his interest all the more.

"It was completely innocent," Scott said. "Anything else, you imagined."

"Don't worry." Rudy patted Scott's hand reassuringly. "Velma's like my sister. I'll have you know I respect that."

"That's what she says about you; that you're like the brother she never had. But, brother and sister being incestuous? That's one for Freud."

"Whether we've slept together or not is none of your business, Scott. She loves you; don't spoil it."

"I've never entertained the notion."

"Listen, I've got an idea!"

"What do you have in mind?"

"Think you could keep a secret?"

"Rudy? What kind of place is this you're bringing me to?"

At the foot of the staircase leading into a dark basement were wall-to-wall men in white cotton shirts with fashionable jackets and neckties. They chattered and sipped cocktails. Others moved cheek to cheek on the dance floor.

"How on earth did you find a dark hole like this?" Scott asked.

"Wally Thurman and his lover brought me here once," Rudy said matter-of-factly. "Quaint little joint, don't you think?"

"By George!" Scott was intimidated. "The things one finds in the crevices of Greenwich Village!"

"Well, you were so damn curious, I thought I'd help you get your feet wet. Come on."

"Uh, Rudy, I'll tell you what—you get the drinks and I'll wait for you here."

"Am I to assume that G. Virgil Scott the novelist is chicken shit? Or that G. Virgil Scott, the worldly, well-traveled intellectual is big on lip service or—"

"It's not that at all." He was whispering. "I just—"

"Just what? They're perfectly harmless, Scott. No one's going to grab your balls or pinch your ass. Think of it this way: you never know if you may write a novel one day about men in love," Rudy said mockingly, relishing the idea of calling Scott's bluff. "Consider this your first source of reference. Well, maybe your second. I'm the first."

Rudy led him by the arm down the staircase. Staying close, Scott surveyed the surroundings with darting, accusing eyes. Friends and acquaintances greeted one another with kisses on the lips. They held hands, embracing each other without inhibition. Against the bar leaned a man with plucked eyebrows. Dramatic eye shadow, like that of a movie star, shaded his expressive eyes. Rouge adorned his cheeks, and cherry-red lipstick covered his mouth. He sipped a drink, smudging the glass with lipstick prints. A silver cigarette holder dangled from his mouth. He nodded to Scott who stood close to Rudy ordering drinks. Eyeing Scott from head to toe, the androgyne winked and smiled at him, sucking on the cigarette holder.

"No, you're mistaken!" Scott said chuckling, waving his hands back and forth. "We're just friends . . . platonic."

Rudy, his back to Scott, laughed heartily. "Scott, just relax.

That's what I like about this place. You can be or do whatever you feel. Nobody bothers you. It's chic, isn't it?"

"If you say so," Scott said, taking the drink from Rudy's hand. "I'm just unaccustomed to dark basements and men in lipstick."

"We can stand over there if you'd like." Rudy led the way, Scott following closely behind. "How long have we known each other, Scott? About a year, would you say?"

"More or less."

"When Velma and I first met—"

"Where did you first meet?"

"At the Harlem Writers Workshop. We discussed everything from politics to history first time we met. We talked about our literary heroes and strangely enough, we agreed on everybody, everybody except you."

"Oh? And what, may I ask, was the consensus?"

"Well, you've always been a favorite of mine, but to put it mildly, Velma was far from being in love with your fiction." Two can play this game, he thought, repaying her for divulging what he asked her not to.

"Is that right?" Scott puffed on his pipe, his eyebrows lifted.

"Anyway, then we—"

"What is it she doesn't like about my work?"

"Let's see if I remember—oh yeah, how could I forget! She criticized your treatment of female characters and—"

"She what?"

"Don't get excited, Scott. It was a valid criticism, I guess. I mean, she is a woman, after all."

"It's unfair criticism!"

"As a female, she has sensibilities we couldn't begin to understand."

"Maybe that's what she meant that morning at my townhouse," Scott said pensively.

"She told you?"

"Not in so many words."

"So, anyway, you're making me forget what I was telling you originally." Rudy sipped his drink. "Then we met you at Carl's, and I'll be the first to admit, I didn't like you at all. Yet Velma was crazy about you."

"What exactly altered your opinion of me?"

"You were pompous and rude to me. Since then, I've figured out why."

"And?"

"You thought Velma and I were romantically involved somehow. When you found out we weren't, you relaxed."

"So, you two *were* involved?"

"I didn't say that, Scott."

"Women! No wonder men turn to each other; not that I'm condoning it, you understand." Scott loved collecting bits and pieces of information on his two friends; information they wouldn't dare tell of themselves. If Velma was there with them, he'd challenge her theory about his fictional characters, and dare her to fail him with inadequate substantiation.

"All of a sudden," Scott said, "I'm overwhelmed by an impulse to get drunk. Rudy, do me a favor?"

"Sure, anything you ask." No harm pretending Scott was his lover.

"Please don't stand so close to me. Nothing personal. I just don't want anybody to get the wrong idea."

"Oh, Scott," Rudy said, laughing. "Your insecurities become you. Want another drink?"

"Bring me anything, but don't leave just yet."

"Why?"

"Don't look now, but there's two pansies standing over there—don't turn around! They've been looking and smiling since we got here."

"I've never seen you so intimidated. You're usually in such control."

"Shhh! Here they come. They're walking over here now." Scott turned, facing Rudy, trying not to be obvious. "Pretend you don't see them. Ignore them, and they'll go away."

"You'll excuse us for this rrrhahther ghahstly intrusion," said a short, pudgy man with a British accent. As he spoke, his slender fingers nervously cut the air with delicate expressions. "My friend Roderick and I were just admiring you two from across the room, and wanted to say it's wonderful to see Negrrroes here! We don't see veddy many. And, you make a smashing couple, don't they, Roderick?" He turned to his friend. "You truly look like movie stars. Wouldn't you say so, Roderick? We hope you find as much happiness as we have. Roderick and I've been together now for five years. Remarkable, wouldn't you say? Anyway, you'll excuse us. We would buy you a drink, but we really must be getting along. We just felt compelled to stop by and say hello, didn't we, Roderick?"

BOOK THREE

1927

LINDBERGH DOES IT!

Lindbergh did it. Twenty minutes past 10 o'clock tonight suddenly and softly there slipped out of the darkness a gray-white airplane as 25,000 pairs of eyes strained toward it. At 10:24 "the Spirit of St. Louis" landed and lines of soldiers, ranks of policemen and stout steel fences went down before a mad rush as irresistible as the tides of the ocean.

—The New York Times
May 22, 1927

1

Andy Preer played percussion from kettledrums to tom-toms to crashing cymbals, and excited the crowd with jungle rhythms. White patrons from every corner of Manhattan save Harlem slummed in the atmosphere of jungle music, as artificial palm trees swayed to the throbbing beat.

Waiters and busboys hustled about ministering to patrons who tapped their feet, popped their fingers, drank scotch, and whistled. Their faces were stretched with smiles, as the Cotton Club Syncopators conjured up images of tribal warriors and man-eating tigers.

Showtime! The master of ceremonies walked center stage, while the band wound up its opening number. Microphone in hand, he smiled at the audience through the smoke.

"Ladies and gentlemen, I want you to join me in welcoming our prized attraction." He paused for effect. The audience murmured and sizzled with anticipation. Above the murmur, ice clicked against glasses, silverware rattled on dinner plates.

"If you haven't seen him, I'm sure you've heard about him. He's the elastic human. That exciting bundle of energy who's part man, part boa constrictor. Join me in a warm round of applause as the Cotton Club proudly presents Earl 'Snakehips' Tucker, and his lovely dance partner, Miss Edith Wilson!"

There were applause and whistles as a plum-colored man appeared from the wings. Clad in a flashy, open-collared silk shirt with fluffy, billowing sleeves, a purple sash hanging from his waist, he led Edith by the hand. Her costume was abbreviated—satin brassiere and panties, feathers around her waist, ankles, neck and wrists, her cleavage bulging—just enough to whet the fantasies of the male patrons. A drumroll sounded, and Snakehips began a grinding motion. His knees bent, as he twisted his haunches and thigh joints into incredible contortions. The crowd gasped and yelled for more.

Edith performed slapstick comedy and sang raunchy songs.

Patrons snapped their fingers at waiters, summoning scotch and mediocre champagne, steak, lobster, Chinese or Mexican cuisine, fried chicken and barbecued spareribs.

Onstage, Snakehips stepped highly to the music, gyrating his waist and belly. His body quivered, his outstretched arms vibrating like rubber bands. Sweat poured down his face and onto his chest as he exuded a pantherlike sensuality. White women gasped with delight at his movements—the tight, bulging trousers, the glistening black skin. Once he had them eating out of his hands, or wetting their panties, he stopped dancing. Sweat dripped from his face to the floor and stained his silk shirt as he bowed and threw kisses to the audience. He took Edith's hand, and they bowed together.

As the spotlight dimmed, the crowd roared for an encore. Snakehips reappeared as the audience screamed, but the tight schedule of the revue prevented him from doing an encore.

"Now, sweetie, that's one helluva act to follow. I don't know why we go on after Snakehips. He's the whole damn show!"

Louise and Peaches stood in line at the wings. Chattering and fluffing themselves, they waited for the applause to subside, and a signal from the stage manager. Louise rubbed her arms to ward off the chill. The grass skirts and leopard-skin brassieres didn't cover much skin.

On cue, they tapped and shuffled onto the stage. The lead singer bumped and grinded her way to the microphone, and belted, "I Can't Believe You're in Love with Me."

Audience response was polite at best. Most of the patrons shoved forks in their mouths, or sipped from near empty glasses. Louise smiled at Peaches who smiled back. While she enhanced her steps with an extra razzle-dazzle, Louise, when possible, scanned the surroundings. Tonight, as every night, women were wrapped in sables, their diamonds catching and throwing the light. They puffed stylishly on dangling cigarette holders. Rubies and emeralds glinted and sparkled from ears and necks. Louise could see the jewelry, the latest fashions, the furs, the enticing opulence. *I should be wearing that sable. And, what I couldn't do with those pearls. I could show her how to really wear them.*

The dance number was midway through when the attention of the crowd shifted to a party of latecomers. Louise watched with interest through the thick smoke as a striking-looking man appeared.

His chiseled features were that of a Roman god. A thin mustache rested on his lip. He was impeccably dressed, in black tails, white bowtie, and spats, with a fur-collared overcoat draped across his broad shoulders; his black, wavy hair was parted in the center, every strand flawlessly in place. Large brown eyes sat deeply in his face, eyebrows bridging under his widow's peak. White gloves and top hat completed the look as he made a conspicuous entrance. Four beautiful women—two blondes, a brunette, and a redhead—hung on his arms. They were draped in sequined gowns and furs and carried rhinestone clutchbags; Louise caught a whiff of the French perfume from the stage. Seated by the maître d', they noisily squeezed behind a large table beside the stage, providing her a closer view. The hazy-eyed brunette, her arms covered with gloves past the elbow, sat next to the man, striking poses. She nibbled his ear, and tried getting his attention. Placing his top hat and gloves on the table, he folded his hands, ignored her vain efforts, and feigned interest in the hoofers onstage.

Patrons gazed at him instead of the revue. Waiters and busboys hurriedly accommodated the party, further arousing Louise's curiosity. Her feet and arms went through the motions, but her eyes were focused on him.

"God! I've never seen a man so beautiful. He's prettier than me," Louise said to Peaches backstage in the dressing room.

"He always comes here. Not with so many broads on his arm, but he's a regular. You never seen him before tonight?" Peaches asked.

"No. I would've remembered him."

"Well, well, well," Peaches declared, a hand on her hip. "Looka here at Little Miss Muffet Louise. First time I ever seen you get all hot and bothered over somebody."

"Who is he?" Louise wanted to know everything about him. Who better to ask than Peaches.

"All I know is Vito. Some dago playboy with plenty of moolah. He's in the society columns with a different girl every week. Tonight, you saw four of them for yourself. Every broad and her mama is after him."

"For his looks or his money?"

"Both, I guess. Which one you after?"

"Tell me about him, Peaches."

"Well, he's single, I know that much. And I think he's twenty-three."

"What's his last name?"

"I think it's somethin' like Kalivoni, or Baloney, or Pastrami; chile, I don't remember. All those guinea names sound alike to me."

"Is he a gangster?"

"I don't think so."

"Married?"

"Sweetie, you just asked me that," Peaches snapped.

"I'm sorry, I just—"

"No, *I'm* sorry." Peaches tossed her stockings across the makeup table. "I'm just a little on edge."

"That's all right." Louise removed her brassiere, and walked to the closet containing her civilian clothes.

"Niggers get on my nerves," Peaches said. "I'm having problems with my ol' man. What is it they have against marriage?" Pulling the last of the flowers from her ankles, she began dressing. "Sweetie, you know, I really like you a lot. You're different from other showgirls I know. They compete with each other, and you know it. We see it every day at rehearsal. But you don't care about being more gorgeous than the next one." She laughed. "I don't know why I'm telling you all this mushy stuff. But it's been real nice working here with you. I just wanted to say that to you."

"Peaches, that's sweet of you. I really like you too. I've told Mother all about you."

Louise hugged Peaches, who sat regally before the mirror. "My whole life has changed since working here," Louise said, studying their reflection in the broken, lipstick-smudged mirror. "You and this club make me feel like I belong."

"Well, you got a friend for life."

"That girl Vito's with," Louise said, getting back to the business at hand, "the brunette, is that his steady girl or what?"

"Sweetie," Peaches said, turning in her chair, away from the mirror, "now, just think about it. She's his steady girl, but there are three other broads pullin' on his arm? At the same time? Whatchu think she is?"

Louise didn't know who or what she was, but she wanted to find out. This Italian playboy—Vito Whatever-His-Name-Was—had her blood pumping. This didn't happen to her every day of the week. He epitomized the man of her dreams. Yet she knew that as a poor little colored girl from Harlem working as a chorus girl at the Cotton Club, she didn't stand a chance. But she could dream.

Peaches saw that faraway look in Louise's eye, and recognized it. "I see you, sweetie. I got my eye on you, honey. You ain't as innocent as you look."

2

Uptown and downtown, celebrations took place as firecrackers and cherry bombs exploded in the street, bursting with the shouts of the Fourth of July. Streamers and sparklers sailed against the blue sky. Lindbergh had landed his monoplane, *The Spirit of St. Louis*, on the soil of Le Bourget airfield in Paris after a trip of thirty-three hours. A ticker-tape parade assembled downtown, and in Harlem the neighborhoods were alive with tenants cheering from their window ledges, people dancing in the streets without music, men banging their wives' pots and pans, children pretending to be airplanes, arms outstretched as wings, their vocal chords revving like motors, outboasting each other that they wanted to be airplane pilots when they grew up; people stood on rooftops, town criers shouting the news, cupping their mouths for megaphone effects, American flags dropping from windows and waving in the breeze, while someone, somewhere on the block, blew no tune in particular on a World War I bugle.

The roar of excitement drifted from the streets into Scott's townhouse windows where he sat peacefully in a bathtub, a glass of gin in hand. Two brown knees protruded through a wet iridescence. Steam vapors rose, and Scott groped for his shaving-cream-covered face.

Velma sat at the edge of the tub. She was reading from her recently published book of poetry, *The Darker Sister*, when Scott playfully splashed her.

"Scott!" Velma pushed away from the tub and held her dress, examining the wet spots. "Look what you've done. It won't dry in time for the parade."

"You should be in here with me like I asked you," he laughed.

"It's not funny."

"Sure it is."

"Not half as funny as that mangy beard on your face." She closed the book and grabbed a shaving mirror. "I won't go anywhere with you looking like that."

"Well," Scott said, sipping his gin, "you're the barber."

Velma playfully poised the straight razor against his Adam's apple. "Splash me again, okay?" She loved shaving him. There was something terribly sexy about a woman shaving her man, especially in a bathtub.

"Come here." He kissed her, holding her head with wet, soapy hands. "I love you, Velma."

"I bet you say that to anybody pressing a straight razor against your throat. Now be still."

Scott held the mirror as Velma braced his forehead. Beginning at the sideburns, she swept his cheek with the blade and rinsed the shaven hair in the tub water.

"You missed a spot," Scott complained, looking in the mirror.

"If you don't keep still, I'll miss something else."

"Sure you won't join me in a gin?"

"You drink enough for both of us; no, thanks."

"Have one on Lindbergh."

"Scott, you drink too much. It takes away from your work. You haven't done a thing with that typewriter in so long, it's looking for a new home," she said. Over her shoulder, she indicated the typewriter on his credenza collecting dust. "Tilt your head; yeah, that's it."

"Good, I can use a new typewriter anyway."

Eve couldn't have loved Adam, Josephine couldn't have loved Napoleon, nor could Juliet have loved Romeo more than Velma loved this man. But Scott drank too much. She didn't mean to single him out. Prohibition produced a generation of career boozers, and, she guessed, until the Volstead Act was repealed, there was little probability of that social pastime fading any time soon.

Scott couldn't hold his liquor, and like most people afflicted with this handicap, he couldn't admit it. He drank and became irritated without provocation; though she'd grown adept at handling him, she didn't like it. Romantic tradition held that famous novelists drowned their woes in bottles of 80 proof. But as long as she had anything to do with it, this custom would never claim Scott.

She wasn't privy to all his personal background, and when she asked, he eluded the subject. She knew as much as he cared to tell her—that he had sprung from an upper-middle-class New England family. His father, if she remembered correctly, was an attorney. Scott had graduated from Harvard, spent some years writing in Paris, and had traveled throughout most of Europe and South America. What she didn't know was what troubled Scott. Despite those smiling slit eyes and drunken laughter a yoke of morosity, the source of which she couldn't quite identify, hung around his neck. It was difficult to detect, it surfaced so infrequently, but in the spirit of the savior therapist, she wanted to help him overcome it, to get on with his life, his work. He was given to moments of ego-inflated temperament, loftiness, and condescension. It wasn't that, it was something else. Velma could identify the symptoms; she wanted to trace the disease.

"How's the research coming?" Scott asked.

"Pretty good. I have a bunch of stuff to give you once I organize it."

"You really enjoy doing this research for me?"

"I do. I wouldn't do it for anybody else, you know." Even researching his novel she found romantic.

"That's strange."

"How's that?"

"Well, for someone who thinks little of my fiction, not to mention my female characters—"

"What?"

"Could you hand me that towel, please?" Scott stood, dripping.

"Who told you that?" Velma was shocked beyond words. She'd forgotten all about it.

"Since *you* didn't have the guts to tell me—"

"Who?" she demanded.

"Come on, Velma. Only one person could possibly tell me that. Unless, of course, you've spread your opinions throughout the literary community." Though Rudy told him months ago, last year even, he'd been waiting for the proper moment to spring this accusatory finger in her face. It hit her like ice water, and Scott loved savoring the reaction. Time was overdue for clarification.

"Well, of all the gall!" Velma moved out of the way and yielded, as Scott emerged from the tub. "I would've told you myself." She was totally unprepared for this. Her defense sounded weak even to herself.

"What were you waiting for? Lindbergh's next flight?"

"No, seriously. I just didn't know how to say it without you taking it the wrong way. You know how sensitive and unreasonable writers can be about their work."

"Sensitive yes. I'm not sure about unreasonable." He dried himself with the towel, sliding it between his legs.

"Exactly what did Rudy tell you?" she wanted to know.

"The truth, I imagine."

"Well, I can speak for myself."

"Why didn't you?"

"I don't know."

He didn't have to run back and tell Scott that. He should've known better; that it was a delicate issue with any writer. Velma remembered saying she didn't like Scott's work. But, at that time she'd only read one of his novels. After the relationship began between them she promised herself to read his other books, but she never found the time.

"Don't fret, dear Velma." He tied the towel around his waist and patted toilet water on his face. "Just tell me exactly what you don't like about my female characters. My ears are open."

"I think they could have more depth."

"Depth, you say?"

"Yes. More complexity, more diversity, I suppose. You seem to write them all the same way. Superficially." She wouldn't dare admit she was referring to just one book. Her argument would be shot full of holes.

"Uh-huh, I'm listening." Scott thrust his arms through a freshly starched shirt, intermittently sipping his drink.

"They could be more positive, that's all," she suggested.

"Positive how?"

"I'm sure you'll agree they're all pretty depressing and stereotypical."

"Well, I'm delighted you've made those observations." Especially someone who has yet to write her *first* novel, he thought competitively. He had three. He pushed his leg through a pair of trousers.

"You're delighted?" Velma couldn't believe her ears. Scott could barely take criticism of any persuasion.

"As a matter of fact, I am." He crossed a necktie around his collar. "You see, admittedly, I never knew enough positive images of Negro women to re-create them in fiction. With you as a point of reference, there's a chance for growth in this area which you find deficient in my writing. Any of this make sense?"

"Oh yes, Scott, absolutely." Velma was smiling, happy he was admitting it. "But, I'm not really the first positive Negro woman you've ever met, am I?"

"More or less." He told her what he thought she wanted to hear.

"What about your mother?"

"What about her?"

"Well, didn't she provide a positive role model for you? I mean, she's well educated and traveled—"

"She's a wretch."

"You shouldn't say—"

"It's true."

He fastened suspenders to the trouser buttons, pulling the elastic over his shoulders. He took Velma's hand, and led her to his bedroom where he finished dressing in the mirror of his chiffonier. She sat down, resting her feet on the bear rug at the foot of his four-poster bed, and listened with undivided attention. G. Virgil Scott admitting he was fallible; this she had to hear.

"There's a lot about me you don't know." He sat on the bed beside her, and the springs creaked as he plopped down.

"Such as?"

"Such as my upbringing, my family, you know, that sort of stuff. You see, I'm descended from one of the most prominently political Negro families of the nineteenth century.

"We had a pretty good life, economically, I must say. But things weren't so great for me, personally. I had an older brother, James, who was probably the most vicious, most unkind person I'd ever met. We never got on well, but what intensified my problem was that he was my mother's favorite. He reminded her of her own father so much that in a large way, I was just ignored. Most of our Scottish blood showed up in him, so I was considered, at least in my mother's eyes, the black sheep, literally. No matter how we fought or for what reason, my brother and I, my mother always took his side. James was always right. I was always wrong. My father was a quiet, and terribly kind man, but he traveled a lot, so I was left to console myself.

"One particular summer, James and I took a canoe ride at a resort where we were vacationing. It was a magnificently beautiful morning; I can still remember it. The lake was calm, the early-morning sun shone golden lights on the ripples, birds chirped signals to each other from opposing treetops, the frogs were croaking, the squirrels dashing, sunlight filtering through the tall pines; just magnificent, I tell you. I even remember imagining that that day was symbolic to me somehow. Instinctively I knew my life would change. Well, it changed all right. That beautiful morning soon turned into one hell of a nightmare.

"By the time we were in the canoe about a mile from the campsite, it started to rain. And I mean buckets. The sky rolled with thunder and the water became rough and jerky. We hit a jagged rock head on, which tore the canoe to shreds. James, who couldn't swim, was too far away for me to grab his hand. Some help I was; I couldn't swim either. Luckily for myself, I had floated toward the rock and held myself there with my eyes closed, holding on for what seemed a lifetime. It's funny, you know; the same rock that almost killed me, saved my life. Anyway, there was poor James, splashing and kicking himself into quite a frenzy. I stuck out my foot so he could grab on, but it just didn't reach and he was floating farther and farther away from me. He kept going down, then he would resurface. When he did, he screamed at the top of his lungs for help; each time the gurgling of water in his throat got louder and uglier. It was the sound of death; death gripping my brother by the throat. I was listening to my brother die. And I clung to the rock and wondered: what happened to the beautiful morning? It was the most hideous sound I'd ever heard in my life. Then finally . . . finally, he never came up again. All that were left of him were his ranger cap, and air bubbles bursting at the water's surface; his final breaths of air. It was over. His suffering had ceased, and he was no longer in pain. . . ." Scott paused, and swallowed. Taking a sip of gin, he massaged the back of his neck before continuing. "It was bloody awful. Bloody awful, I tell you. You couldn't possibly imagine. There were only sounds of pouring rain beating down on angry, raging waters; the thunder and lightning above. I was afraid of being struck down by God for not saving James even though I tried . . . and honestly, I tried to save him.

"My mother, I believe to this day, blames me for his death, which now has to be some, let me see, almost twenty years ago by now. At his funeral, I was so wracked with grief and guilt, I went to her for consolation. It's peculiar, you know, because I cried and cried and cried, and I don't know why. I hated James. He never treated me like a little brother, and I resented all the attention he got over me. Anyway, I walked up to my mother, my face streaked with tears, my voice and lips trembling, and rather than comfort me, or try to reassure me it wasn't my fault, she turned and said very coldly, 'I wish it were you instead. There's nothing to make me believe you didn't do it on purpose. You were so jealous of him.' Well, imagine that? As if that harrowing experience wasn't enough, and I was only about ten at the time. Sometimes, I can't remember one day from the next, Velma, but I've never forgotten those words.

"Life for me got progressively worse with each day. Yet, with all the arbitrary whippings I got and all the tongue lashing, which occurred with much frequency following James's death, I still tried to love her. I mean, she's my mother, I kept telling myself. The only one I could turn to since my father was off globe-trotting. Then, by the time I was about fifteen or so, I decided to kill myself. The misery to end all miseries. At the last moment though, I didn't really want to die. So, I contemplated ways to reach my father and join him. I was all set to run away, but my mother forbade me to write him and calculatingly enough, she made certain I never knew where he was. She destroyed all of his letters.

"One night, I was lying across my bed, staring at the ceiling, considering several forms of suicide. Some form of recreation for a teenager, huh? She called me from her bedroom with a sweet voice; one I hadn't heard since before James's death. I remember it clearly. When I walked into her bedroom, she lay there, conversing as if someone were in her room. On top of that, she had not a stitch of clothing on. Imagine that? Naked as a jaybird. The woman was going mad. I felt terribly embarrassed and couldn't look at her. All of a sudden, she became aware of my presence, as if she hadn't remembered calling me to her room. The expression on her face said 'What the hell're you doing here?' I asked what she wanted and she told me I would rot in hell; that I was a murderer, and she had wasted her life away raising a Cain and Abel . . . and she'd rather have Abel alive. I should've died, she said; it should've been my death and not James's . . . God, Velma, so I . . . please don't cry, Velma. I didn't mean to upset you." Scott paused and sipped more gin. "I just wanted to tell you something about my past. I mean, when you talk about my female characters, I do believe that this is why I write women the way I do. And you're the first person, ever, in all my life, I've ever told this story. I'm not trying to make excuses for myself, but there's a reason for everything. Please don't cry."

Velma sat beside him, holding his hand, tears trailing down her cheeks. Now that she knew, she wasn't sure she wanted to know. How does one survive such a tragedy? It was miracle enough that he sat there, on the bed beside her, telling the story with such courage and valor. No wonder he drank heavily.

"Scott, I'm so sorry," Velma said, sniffling. "I had no idea. You must've suffered terribly."

"Now, Velma, come on. Don't cry. Here." He handed her a handkerchief. Velma dried her eyes, and blew her nose into the white linen. "We're still going downtown to celebrate Lindy, aren't we?" Now, how's that? he thought. Maybe she'll think twice about attacking my work. Who the hell does she think she is anyway? Ask her to do a little research and she becomes a *New York Times* literary critic. She's not even a novelist yet, not a published one anyway. And with one spurious collection of derivative poetry, she wants to stand on a soapbox and criticize my prolific, critically hailed efforts? Me? G. Virgil Scott, the Negro counterpart to Hemingway?

"Let me pull myself together here for a moment," she sniffled.

"That's some story, isn't it?" Scott asked.

"Most poignant thing I've heard in years, and I've heard them all."

"It really moved you, didn't it?"

"Yes, but I don't care to hear any more."

"But, you'll agree, it's not a bad story, is it?"

"Bad story? What do you mean?"

"It's just that. A story. I made it all up!" Scott started laughing, falling backward onto the four-poster bed with the lamb's-wool bedspread, kicking his heels, and rolling back and forth.

"You did what?!"

"Oh, I was just testing the premise of my new novel." He laughed again, uncontrollably, tears rolling down his face, blood rushing to his cheeks. "I'm terribly sorry. I don't mean to laugh, but as you can see, you've given me the desired results."

"Now wait, Scott; let me get this straight. You mean to tell me that none of this is true?" Velma rose, backing away from him slowly as though making a desperate sneak attempt to escape a hysterical murderer.

"I never even had a brother named James." He laughed maniacally.

"You son of a bitch!"

"What's the matter?" He stopped laughing.

"You tell me this . . . this fabricated nonsense about your miserable life, and I believed you. How could you do a twisted thing like that? What kind of person are you?"

"The person who's escorting you to Lindbergh's parade, the person you love. Come on, we're going to be late."

"Scott, if you think for one minute that I'm going to this parade with you, you're out of your mind. I'm leaving."

"Come on, Velma, where's your sense of humor?"

"Humor? That's the worst humor I ever heard."

"Just a moment ago, it was the most moving story you ever heard. Just consider it a sneak peek, or, or, an excerpt from a work in progress from one of the decade's greatest writers."

"Good-bye, Scott." Velma picked up her handbag and headed for the door. Opening it, she turned to him. "You know, it's sad to think a close friend would play on my sympathy like that. It's even sadder that this sick friend happens to be the man I'm sleeping with; the man who could possibly father my children. Instead of making up tragic stories, why don't you try sobering up." She walked through the door and her footfalls diminished down the staircase.

"Velma! Come on!" Scott yelled down the staircase after her. "Can't you take a bloody joke?"

3

"Let's check out Smalls tonight, y'all."

Peaches, perched in the middle of the sidewalk, powdered a face hardly in need of makeup.

"How about Connie's Inn for a change?" Louise countered. "We always go to Smalls."

Accompanied by two gentlemen friends, Bill and Charles, they paused between an all-night restaurant and a storefront church.

"How about you fellas?" Peaches asked. "Where y'all wanna go?"

"Smalls sounds hip to me," Bill declared. "Next to us, they have about the second-best band uptown." He glanced at his watch. "Give us a few minutes and we'll meet y'all there."

"Meet us?" Peaches asked, disturbed.

"Yeah, me and Charles got a stop to make."

"Oh yeah? What's her name?" Peaches demanded.

"*Her*," Bill retorted, "is a bottle of scotch. You know damn well Smalls don't sell nothin' but some bad whiskey."

"And, you're gonna let us walk through those doors without escorts? They'll probably think we ladies of the night or somethin'."

"C'mon, Peaches. Be a good girl. I said we be right back."

"Jive-ass nigga."

The two women moved to a back table at Smalls Paradise. Peaches unfurled her wrap, took out her makeup compact, and fluffed her hair in the mirror as Louise absorbed the surroundings. "Well, sweetie, you like him?" Peaches asked.

"Like who?"

"Charles. He's kinda cute, doncha think?"

"He's all right, I guess."

"He's a good friend of Bill's. I planned this blind date, 'cause I thought you two would make a cute couple. He's a nice guy who spends money. And heaven knows, you could use a man."

Peaches was right, Louise thought, she could use a man. Charles was good-looking and pleasant enough, but it wasn't clicking between them. She hated blind dates. She had had a couple before and they turned out disastrously.

Since Velma had moved out, Louise missed the counseling and confidences she shared with her sisters. Miriam didn't come by as much anymore; her life was busier than ever. Velma was making quite a career for herself, and spending a great deal of time with a beau Louise hadn't even met. If he was as fine and well-to-do as Velma painted him, Louise couldn't blame her. She herself was keeping busy at the Cotton Club between shows and rehearsals. She'd stopped by Velma's and Miriam's apartments unannounced more than a couple of times, but they were never home. Velma, she imagined, was spending more time at her beau's on Striver's Row. Most of what she heard about her was through Mother, or magazines that published her work. She had a new book of poetry which, when Louise found the time, she planned to buy. She couldn't brag enough to Peaches about her sister the writer. She missed her sisters terribly. It was no fun growing up if it meant folks had to move away. She'd never known life without them. Miriam, almost ten years her senior, was Louise's second mother in many ways, an attachment which started to diminish as Louise herself became a young woman. The apartment she now shared alone with Mother, despite the noisy customers, was a ghost town without Velma, who lived life's every passing moment as if it were her first. Velma derived pleasure from the simplest, most mundane facets of day-to-day living. Louise missed that, and as far as she could tell, so did Mother. She had a lot to tell her sisters about her life as showgirl, her friend Peaches, and barhopping to all of Harlem's celebrated night spots. Louise decided to visit her sisters that week, next day maybe.

"How far did they have to go?" Louise asked.

"Shoot, sweetie, by the time they bring that scotch, I'll be ready for breakfast."

"Is it that late already?"

"You could never tell by this place. Is my lipstick on right? I'm too woozy to tell."

"Peaches, don't you just love when they do that?"

Louise snapped her fingers as bouncy and brassy jazz swelled in the air. Waiters and busboys tended to customers dancing the cakewalk, the Charleston, and everything else in between, balancing trays of whiskey and food on their heads to the crowd's cheer. One of the smaller boys set his tray down on the table. Carried away by the music, he danced frantically, as if possessed, an index finger wiggling wildly, his lithe body executing acrobatic feats, somersaulting and balancing himself on the balls of his hands.

"Isn't he fantastic?" Louise was applauding.

"Pretty soon, sweetie, Snakehips gonna be out of a job. But you know," Peaches added, rapping her knuckles on the table, "if one of our busboys tried that, he'd be thrown out on his ass."

"That's true."

"That white trade at the Cotton Club, they likes to keep their distance," she said, gesturing with her hands. "They don't wanna get too close; might rub off."

"Excuse me, ladies." A waiter appeared. A white towel thrown across his arm, he placed a drink on the table. "The gentleman at table number three asked me to deliver this with his compliments."

"Well, how about that," Peaches said, a mischievous purr in her voice. "There's two of us here. Who's it for?"

"I'm sorry, miss, I didn't ask." The waiter looked confused. "The man just pointed over here and I brought it over like he asked me to; but you two look alike."

"What man, honey?" Peaches said.

"He's sitting over there by himself."

Peaches craned her neck.

"You have to stand up to see him from here, miss. But don't worry, I'll thank him for you."

"Don't bother," Peaches said. "I'll thank him myself." She stood.

"What about Charles and Bill?" Louise said.

"What about them?"

"They should be here any minute."

"Well, sweetie, he asked me to wait for him; now he can wait for me."

She disappeared in the smoky haze. Louise picked up her compact and adjusted her makeup by the dim light in the dark corner. Dabbing her cheeks with the powder puff, she decided she could use more lipstick.

She was learning a lot from sweetwise Peaches who, since Velma had left, had become her surrogate sister. There was nothing about Harlem or men Peaches didn't know. They were about the same age, but Peaches, the eldest child in her family, had a protective, big-sister approach about her Louise couldn't resist. She was used to being the little sister, cared for, protected, so their friendship meshed smoothly, both parties assuming their roles.

As a teenager, Louise had found it hard to retain girlfriends. Girlfriends in her past were usually brown-skinned, and frequently, whether they expressed it or not, she learned that they resented her. It had little to do with Louise's personality, which was shy and reserved. Her beauty got in the way, and it was a trial keeping friends who resented her birthright, something totally outside her control. After two or three confrontations, and deeply scarring experiences, Louise learned to be a loner. No friends, no enemies, had become her modus vivendi. She didn't want the straying boyfriends her girlfriends unjustly accused her of stealing, and felt powerless in those sticky situations. She'd been tried and convicted by a heartless jury whose members saw nothing beyond themselves. She was always guilty as charged even before she opened her mouth in her defense.

Peaches was different. Maybe it had to do with the fact that they were of a similar mold. Peaches was just as pretty, her hair as wavy, her complexion as light. There was no competition between them, and Bill, Peaches's beau, who played in the Cotton Club orchestra, never approached Louise as anything but a gentleman. He respected her as his woman's best friend, and behaved accordingly. God forbid she should repeat with Peaches what she'd been through in the past. She was more than comfortable with the friendship—she needed it.

"Excuse me, pretty lady. Mind if I sit with you?"

Louise looked up. "Oh, Charles, it's you. What took you boys so long?"

"Where Peaches go?" Bill said.

"She'll be right back."

Charles and Bill sat at the table, and Bill produced a bottle of scotch from a brown bag. He summoned the waiter for glasses, and poured the alcohol. Charles moved closer to Louise and slid his arm around her. Louise ignored it, and applied her lipstick in the mirror.

"Looks like you ladies ordered early," Bill said, indicating the untouched drink on the table, sent by an admirer. "Knowing my Peaches, it would kill her to wait."

"We were thinking of ordering breakfast," Louise said. "How's the eggs benedict here, anybody know?"

"Hell with breakfast," Bill said. "We're drinking a toast here."

"A toast?" Louise asked. "To what?"

"Well, well, well." Peaches returned. "I'm so glad you both could make it." Bill stood, allowing her to pass him. "Joint like this, two unescorted ladies could be mistaken for floozies. Like we lookin' for johns or somethin'."

"Where'd you go?" Bill inquired, eyeing her up and down.

"Who, me?" Peaches clutched her breast. "The ladies' room . . . to freshen up a bit . . . Louise, can I speak to you for a moment?"

"Sure." Why does she have that strange look on her face? Louise wondered.

"Not here, sweetie." Peaches tried passing a clandestine signal by nodding her head and winking an eye.

"Why not?" Charles said. "Can't we all hear it?"

"Chile, this here's girl talk."

"Could you wait a minute first?" Bill requested. "We're about to have a toast."

"A toast? Sure. What we drinking to?"

"Well, baby," Bill began, "we could've done this in private, but Charles here is my best friend," he said, placing a hand on Charles's shoulder. "I wanted him to be present."

"Sounds so official," Peaches said.

"It is. In the presence of our good friends, I'm asking you to become Mrs. William Jackson."

"What?" She couldn't believe her ears.

"That's right." Bill was smiling. "You been bugging me about it for two years, and I've run out of excuses. Quit the club and be my wife. Whaddaya say?"

"Oh, that's marvelous!" Louise exclaimed, clapping. "Say something, Peaches!"

"Bill!" Peaches covered her mouth with both hands. "I can't believe it!"

"Please believe it. I'm only asking once."

"Well, I don't know; this is so sudden. We gotta have blood tests, send out invitations, find a church and—"

"Who needs all that shit? Tomorrow afternoon, City Hall. I made plans for the blood tests and everything. And, Charles and Louise, we want you two as our witnesses."

"I'd be delighted," Louise said, holding up her glass. "Shall we toast?"

"To the bride and groom!" Charles seconded.

They tapped glasses and drank. Bill kissed Peaches long and hard, as she threw her arms around his neck. "Excuse me, baby," she said, standing. "This is all so sudden and I need to speak to my friend in private. We'll be right back."

"Again?"

"This here is kinda urgent in a female sorta way."

"Okay, just hurry back, baby."

Peaches led Louise by the hand, and headed for the ladies' room. "Sweetie, I don't know how to tell you this."

"Tell me what?"

"That drink wasn't for me."

"What drink?"

"From the mysterious man at table number three. Remember?"

"It's too late now," Louise said nonchalantly, fingering a curl in the mirror. "Charles is back now. I couldn't—"

"Girl, it's him—"

"Him who?"

"That rich dago fella. When I walked over to his table and I found out who it was, my knees got weak. Very politely, he apologized for the mix-up, but he said he sent it to you."

"Is this some kind of a joke?" Louise frowned.

"Would I joke about somethin' like this?"

"What am I going to do about Charles?"

"That should be the least of your worries."

"But, he's Bill's best friend—"

"Look, go on over there and speak to that man. Hurry up!"

"Peaches, I can't go over there. What would I say?"

"You'll think of somethin'. It's probably the first time I ever seen him without any broads on his arm. He's just sittin' there all by himself. So, if you know what I know—"

"He really sent that drink to me, huh?" Louise said dreamily, liking the sound of it.

"No, he sent it to your Aunt Tilly in Hoboken. Girl, you betta go on. I'll entertain the fellas till you get back. Whatchu waitin' for?" She pushed Louise through the door.

Louise walked shyly toward table number three, her heart

beating harder than the drums onstage. She didn't know what to say, what opening line to use. The man turned around, as if alerted by radar, parted his lips and smiled graciously.

"Hello," he said with traces of a Mediterranean accent. Standing, he motioned with his hand. "Won't you join me?"

"Hello."

"May I ask your name?" He kissed her hand.

"Louise." She blushed. "Yours?"

"Vittorio," he said, seating Louise by the forearm. "But my friends call me Vito." He slid the chair beneath her. "What are you drinking?"

"I'm sorry, I can't stay long."

"I was about to leave myself. I didn't know if you'd come over. I saw you sitting with your friend. Are you sisters?"

"No, we're not." She looked away from him. "You come here a lot?"

"Ah, sometimes. I usually go to the Cotton Club, but I come here for a change of atmosphere."

"You like it here?" she said, too nervous to think of anything else.

"Yes, I suppose so. I love jazz, but I'll tell you," he lowered his voice, "the Cotton Club is much nicer. How about you? Have you ever been to the Cotton Club?"

"No. I mean yes. I mean—"

"Relax. You're perfectly safe with me." He touched her hand reassuringly. As he leaned back, his beauty was accentuated by the eclipsing shadows. Louise's heart fluttered, yet she wouldn't release the sigh lodged in her throat, afraid he would realize how attractive she found him. Women must do it to him all the time. She played it cool, and at the same time her whole life seemed to flash before her.

"Does a lovely girl like you always go out unescorted?"

"Excuse me, what did you say?" She was distracted by a million things running through her mind.

"Do you always go out alone?"

"Not much."

"Be careful with these colored men," he said, laughing, looking at Charles seated at Louise's table. "They're liable to corrupt a pretty thing like you."

He'd seen Charles come into the club with the other fellow and approach her table. He remembered feeling he'd wasted too much time while she sat there alone; time enough that he could have stopped by and said hello. He hoped this colored fellow at her table meant nothing to her. With all the interracial dating, especially in Harlem—not that he personally approved—he couldn't be sure. He was certain, though, that he had to have her, this shy creature who couldn't look him in the face.

"I can take care of myself," she said.

"Sure you won't join me in a drink?"

"I really should be getting back."

"I'd like to see you again, Louise. That is if—"

"Oh, I'd like that." Is this really happening to me?!

"What if I give you a call and—"

"No! I mean, what if I call you? Is that okay?"

"Okay? It would give meaning and worth to an otherwise purposeless evening." He stopped a waiter, asked for something to write with, and jotted down his telephone number on a cocktail napkin. "Here. Give me a call. I'd like to see you again . . . when you're alone." He assumed since she took the number that she had no attachment to the colored man. She didn't seem the type who'd take one man's number while another sat at her table. She impressed him as virginal, innocent, untainted by the world's filthy hand. His timing couldn't be better.

"Sure, Vito. My pleasure."

"No. *Il piacere e mio*, I assure you." He stood, bowed, and kissed her hand again. "Well, I must be going. Got a busy day tomorrow. *E stato un vero piacere. Buona notte, cara mia.*"

Louise watched him leave and then examined her hand where he kissed it—his soft lips had pressed against her knuckles. She glanced at the torn cocktail napkin with his telephone number, and nervously tucked it in her purse. Her heart pounded and she exhaled the sigh that had snowballed in her chest for the past five minutes. A uniformed chauffeur in cap, jodhpurs, and black, shiny boots, led Vittorio to the passenger door and opened it. Vittorio stepped on the running board and climbed into the backseat. The chauffeur walked around to the driver's side and pulled away from the curb. The exhaust pipe exuded a cloud of smoke, and like a vanishing dream, the black limousine merged with the black night. *Poof!*

4

A Negro boy at Harvard; don't you know how lucky you are?

Staring catatonically at the photographs on the wall of his townhouse, Scott, a bottle of gin in hand, a near empty glass in the other, looked at the photograph of his family sporting their Sunday best outside the United Methodist Church. His eyes zeroed in on his father's ever present grimace. Scott remembered that expression, the only one his father ever had exchanged with him. He tried obliterating the memory by drowning it in martinis or gin and ginger ale, but like cigarette butts flicked into a murky river, the memory rose again and again, floating to the surface of his consciousness.

Benjamin Scott, Esquire, had made austere plans for the future of his only child, George Virgil Scott, blueprints his son wanted no part of.

From the time he could speak, Scott was nurtured and groomed to fill a position of "dignified responsibility." It meant little to Scott, everything to his father.

Unlike other children—white children who habitually stared at this remarkably beautiful child for the oddity he was—he had no time for baseball, marbles, or leapfrog. Benjamin Scott didn't want his son growing up to be *a lazy, shiftless nigger,* and did everything in his power to prevent it. Scott studied classical piano, French and Latin with a tutor, and attended theater and the ballet.

He was kept away from traveling minstrel shows, and forbidden to read "trash" like *Clotel,* or *Uncle Tom's Cabin.* There was no watermelon, fried chicken, hog maws, chitterlings, or black-eyed peas in his father's house, and Scott's mother dutifully performed these tasks without questioning her husband.

Master Scott—his father's choice of address—didn't see the thematic rigidity of his household, having known nothing with which to compare it. In time, though, it would come to have meaning for him.

Surrounded exclusively by white children at the boarding school, Scott's schoolmaster was personally affronted when Scott explained that he studied Mozart, Chopin, and Tchaikovsky on the piano. Scott related his accomplishments with pride, and didn't understand the children snickering behind him, or why the schoolmaster's chest heaved with ire, his face turning beet red. He suggested, in no uncertain terms, that Scott learn instruments more suitable to his limitations, like the banjo. Scott's father held to the belief that these exquisitely trained instructors taught only what was best. So, while the schoolmaster's angry tone led Scott to believe that he'd blasphemed somehow, he accepted his dictum with blind faith.

At dinner, he reported the incident to his father, whose reaction confused him. His father ranted and raved about how he was not spending hard-earned money to raise a child as an eye-rolling, shuffling darky; that *his* son was destined for life befitting his white counterparts. He banged upon the dinner table, and the silverware and china clicked as his fists landed upon the lace tablecloth. He instructed his son to relay to the schoolmaster that he was being prepped for the law; that his son's fingers were ordained to turn pages of the *Annotated Laws of Massachusetts*, and not to strum pickaninny banjoes.

Scott's mother never interfered with his discipline, but silently sympathized with him. Rather than part her lips, she communicated with her eyes. So, when tucking Scott into bed that night, she reminded him that his father wanted only the best for him. Her husband, she said, worked hard and diligently to practice the law in the state of Massachusetts against incredible odds. All Scott had to do was obey, materialize his father's dreams, and they'd get along. Her way of providing her son an escape from his father's demands was to supply him with books. Thus, Scott fell in love with literature.

He consumed two, sometimes three, books per week—from Robert Louis Stevenson to Mark Twain. The only Negro-authored books he was allowed to peruse were those of Pushkin or Dumas. Master Scott cherished books and became enamored of characters like Robinson Crusoe, Friday, and Cyrano de Bergerac. They occupied his imagination's playground, like the siblings and playmates he never had. And as well as the stories he read, there were those he created. He channeled his creative processes into melodramatic situations where characters were white, fathers who called themselves loving were mean and devoid of compassion, and demanded the impossible; mothers were kind and silent but tipped the scales to balance a growing son's asymmetric world when nobody was looking. More than reading stories, he loved to create them from pathos simmering within him.

His father's vision came to fruition when Scott entered Harvard. He studied political science and English, and longed to stay there forever. It wasn't a particular love for Harvard Yard—especially the racial confrontations—but he didn't want to face what lay ahead in his education—burial beneath a pile of dusty lawbooks and three years of youth down the drain. He abhorred the thought of preparing for a profession which he wanted no association with.

As an English major, he found his literary inclinations were further expanded and fostered by the works of Shakespeare, Flaubert, and Melville. The itch to write burned mercilessly inside him. Senior year found him scratching and soothing it, as he poured himself out in a manuscript that later became his first published novel. As law school loomed, he racked his brain trying to think of an escape. He needed to find a place beyond his father's reach where he could write undisturbed.

France mystified and delighted him, and suggested itself as the ideal spot for producing belles lettres. He had been there once with his family on summer vacation, and walking the centuries-old streets, he remembered thinking they were the streets once walked by Flaubert, Hugo, and Dumas.

He decided, sharing the confidence with his mother only, that he would travel to Paris and determine from there what he wanted to do. He told his father that he would go abroad the summer following graduation, stay for two months, then return to the States to attend law school. Benjamin Scott insisted his son would be wasting time and money.

"A Negro boy at Harvard," his father scoffed, pacing the floor of his study. "Don't you know how lucky you are?!"

"I just want to travel; what's wrong with that?"

"You don't fool me, boy," his father said. "You don't think I know how you detest the law; how you fancy yourself a writer."

"I didn't say I wasn't going to law school, Pop. I just—"

"Who will publish you anyway?" His father stopped in front of him, sticking his paunch into the boy's face. "There's no such thing as a Negro writer. You know of any?"

Scott was on the verge of naming several writers whose faces were as black as his. But this was not the time and place to lock horns with the man who interpreted his impassioned aspirations as insubordination.

"You think that I've worked my fingers to the bone to put you through boarding schools, show you Europe, and send you to Harvard just to throw my money away? Is that your idea?"

"No, sir."

"You remember there's a war going on?"

"Yes, sir."

His father continued pacing, and for the moment his son wished him dead—dead and buried, leaving proper provisions in his will. He never did enough for that man. At that moment, he thought that if he were granted the privilege of spending two months in Europe, his father might never see him again.

Grudgingly—after much cajoling on his mother's behalf—his father agreed, and not three days after Scott marched with the Class of '17, he boarded a steamship destined for a continent across the vast Atlantic. Alone. First time in his life. With a trunk filled with clothes, books, toiletries, a manuscript-in-progress, and the teary good wishes of his mother, Scott set sail on a ship scheduled to dock in Calais, France.

From Calais, he boarded the train which, hours later, arrived at Le Gare du Nord in Paris. He lunched at Le Train Bleu, and appeased his ravenous appetite with escargots, Beaujolais, and cheese. He studied the breathtaking works of Montenard and Maignan, painted intricately in the dramatically arched, gold-leaf ceilings, pleased with himself for having outwitted his father's tenacity; a victory of sorts. Taking another sip of the Beaujolais, he breathed a whiff of newfound freedom, an ocean away from his father's dogmatic grip.

First stop, Notre Dame and her breathtaking flying buttresses. He took a long stroll along the Champs-Elysées from the Avenue du Bois de Boulogne. Turned around and lost in the spiderweb network of poplar-lined Parisian streets, he crossed the Seine at the Pont Alexandre III—his favorite bridge in Paris—then retraced his steps, sucking in the perfumed air and the scent of freedom; finally his feet virtually danced over cobblestones of the Place de la Concorde, once trampled upon by angry mobs, where heads rolled to the beat of the guillotine during the Reign of Terror.

Asking directions at Le Jardin des Tuileries, he headed for the cathedral, marveling at Paris's centuries-old, uniform dirty-gray stones, his own country not quite two centuries old. He passed the

Louvre, and prophesied that much of his idle time would be spent gawking at world masterpieces. Why read lawbooks when he could study the ancient contours of Venus de Milo?

Inside the cathedral, he was overwhelmed by a hallowedness lurking in the dark, dusty shadows of the twelfth-century temple. What sounded like Gregorian chants filled the lofts, and he couldn't figure, for the life of him, where they emanated from. The belfry rang and inevitably brought to mind Hugo's Quasimodo. Kneeling at a pew, beside the stained-glass chapel of Jeanne d'Arc, he prayed for the resolution of his dilemma.

Paris was his city! and he wrote and wrote in an avalanche tempered by discipline, watching the manuscript, page by painstaking page, assume flesh and blood of its own. Corresponding with his parents, he sent separate letters to each one. To his mother, he outlined the unsurpassed wonders of the city, admitting he could remain forever. Betraying himself, he wrote to his father what the old man wanted to hear. His mother wrote back, encouraging him to enjoy it to the fullest, to leave no stone unturned before his return to Cambridge, and to flush the wanderlust out of his system. His father didn't write; his good wishes were enclosed by his mother's hand—good wishes Scott didn't believe for one moment.

He spent the mornings writing. In the afternoons he lunched at outdoor cafés, and meandered through the city where he explored Le Métropolitain, and compared it with New York subways; sat beside and gazed pensively at the Seine, listening to the dingy river lap against stationary, forlorn barges; surveyed tarnished gargoyles, and statues of archangels and cherubs; passed by ground-floor window shutters as the inhabitants opened and slammed them shut; gawked at aloof Parisians carrying loaves of fresh bread; loitered about L'Université de Paris and seduced bright-eyed coeds; held friendly conversations with American soldiers stationed there during the war, many of them Negroes getting drunk in the cafés; fed pigeons in Les Jardins du Luxembourg; and studied the statues of French monarchs and aristocracy, the Eiffel Tower, a grotesque apparition looming through the haze.

Lingering over rewrites in the cafés along Boulevard St. Michel, sniffing the pungent odor of yeast escaping the boulangeries, he was befriended by bohemian writers who approached him out of curiosity and fascination that he, an American Negro who spoke above-average French, was living and writing in Paris. They became his friends, and with them he shared wine and hashish in drafty

one-room apartments, and explored, in heated debate, the nobility
of literary writing by means of which he polished his boarding-
school French, and found his niche, enchanted by a city that, for
him, held no responsibilities.

The promise of two summer months stretched into September,
and his mother sent urgent letters inquiring about his return. He
wrote her back of his decision to remain, and, through sheer
cowardice, wrote his father of audacious convictions that law
curricula at Harvard could carry on fine without him. Benjamin
Scott was outraged, accused him of breach of promise, and threatened to cut him off without a penny. His mother understood,
feeling, in part, responsible, and against his father's knowledge,
continued sending room-and-board provisions until he decided to
return, the prodigal son.

The war ended in 1918, and year by year, his correspondence
slackened.Without selling a book, he could never, ever face his
father. He imagined the old man gloating over his gross lack of
success. Three and a half years in Paris, and he could have been
taking the Massachusetts State Bar. Scott didn't bury himself under
the weight of the pressure, but rather, churned Benjamin Scott's
cynicism into cathartic bursts of writing energy.

He kept himself apprised of the American literary scene. In a
single breath, he could rattle off the names of new, stimulating
talents sparkling on the New York horizon. Friends and contacts in
the Quartier Latin, some of whom were American Negro expatri-
ates, traded hot news about the emerging artistic vanguard; an
increasing number of Harlem writers, who too were launching
reputations, enjoying unprecedented visibility. Until that time,
1921, he'd only published a few pieces, mostly essays, translated for
French periodicals, manuscripts of his novels making the endless
rounds of New York publishers.

By 1922, at age twenty-five, he received his first acceptance letter
from Charles Scribner's Sons. *Hallelujah!* He kissed the letter, fell
back on the bed, and kicked his heels. Time invested had paid off,
not a second unaccounted for—time he might have wasted at
Harvard. Now he could unflinchingly stare his father in the eye.

That night, first time ever, he got drunk on champagne with his
friends, his treat. He met an entertainer of the Folies Bergère,
Josephine Baker, an American expatriate who was quickly becoming the "Toast of Paris." At her insistence, he posed for a photograph
he forgot about completely until she mailed him an autographed
copy through his publisher.

Two days later, still hung over from the champagne binge, he wrote his parents he was coming home—and why. He packed his bags, bade melancholy farewells to his friends and Paris, and boarded a liner to recross the Atlantic.

Scott's father considered it an abomination. His only son was throwing away his life as an author, planting roots in Harlem— Harlem, of all godforsaken places! where the proletariat flourished. Scott forwarded an autographed copy of *Prodigal* to his father as soon as it was published.

Harlem was foreign to him—which was precisely the attraction. His roots were not there, and he somehow felt as if they should have been. He didn't speak the way they spoke, or dress the way they dressed. He'd never heard phrases like "dicty," "jig-chaser," and "sheik." But he loved it. Among native sons, he stuck out in a circle of writers who, among each other, shared something intrinsic and indigenous with their culture, something that eluded him as he scratched his way toward an identity. When he ventured into larger, mainstream Manhattan, his more familiar social milieu, he was reminded of Jim Crow, a social phenomenon he'd never encountered on the European continent.

A displaced zombie, he wandered the four corners of an ethnocentric community that he hoped would put him in touch with who he was and where he was from. But, as his reputation as a novelist skyrocketed, it functioned, in part, to further alienate him from colleagues he believed envied him, his career, his father as practicing attorney, his Ivy League education, his wardrobe, his townhouse, refined manners, bilingual fluency, and overall life of leisure. He missed his mother terribly, and accepted that he might never see her again, so long as his father was alive. He continued to correspond with her, keeping her abreast of his doings, his accomplishments, his triumphs, with whom he had virtually no one to celebrate. She continued to secretly support him, loving the idea of her son as published novelist.

Meeting Velma Brooks at a Van Vechten party honoring the publication of this third novel, whether he admitted it or not, was the first step on a path he'd never traveled. By pulling her into his life, taking her into his heart, he was embarking upon a journey through which, he hoped, he'd find in Harlem whatever it was he felt he'd lost.

5

Sitting at the desk in her den, Miriam's eyes scanned the list of new members resting beside the pile of blank certificates. Memberships were tapering off, with no hope of Garvey's release in sight, but Miriam, unlike other disillusioned UNIA members, retained her zeal even during the organization's dark days. She studied the old stock certificate. She loved the illustration of a Negro man showing the way to a New World, standing beside a globe with Africa at the forefront. The words: Africa, the Land of Opportunity sent a chill through her, as the ship—an SS *Yarmouth* facsimile—emerged from the right side of the illustration, setting sail for the dark continent. Since then, UNIA's fleet had been demolished by repair problems, corruption, and mismanagement, but she enjoyed looking at them. The certificates always brought Agnes to mind. Miriam had sold her one share, at five dollars, years before cajoling her to a meeting.

Work like this usually kept Agnes off her mind.

The rift in their friendship went unnoticed most of the time since she and Miriam seldom worked the same shift. But when they did, Agnes acted as if she'd never seen her before, addressing her only when absolutely necessary, and even then, in the most distant and unfamiliar of tones. Miriam saw the engagement ring, and wondered when Agnes would come to her senses.

Sometimes she wondered if the wedding had taken place already, and if her position in the bridal party as maid of honor had been filled. Miriam had felt honored at the request—inasmuch as one could—but it was like a request to help slip a noose around Agnes's neck. She had been taken totally by surprise at Agnes's sudden announcement—it was the last thing she had expected. Velma's advice, upon further consideration, was hardly the most productive route. Tommy's telephone number lost its value as evidence as months passed, and she kept reminding herself to throw it away. Next time she'd obey her instincts. Had she done so when it mattered, she might still have her one and only friend outside her family. No more meddling in other folks' business.

Miriam shrugged it off. Whenever she heard, or mentioned,

Agnes's name, she tried, in vain, to suppress her emotions. Agnes now treated Miriam as if they'd never been friends or shared confidences. None of the others on the hospital staff knew of the disaster that threatened Agnes if she married that scum. They admired the jewel on her finger. Only Miriam knew that Agnes was walking the plank blindfolded.

She didn't know what Agnes had told people about their relationship, but since that day at the cafeteria, other nurses glanced at her with subtly accusing eyes, as if Miriam planned to jump up at the wedding when the minister asked, *Is there anyone here who feels these two should not be joined in holy matrimony? Speak now or forever hold your peace.* Not that it was a bad idea. Somebody had to stop her. Even Mrs. Greerson, their supervisor, asked if there was a problem between them. She'd have to be blind not to notice that Miriam and Agnes had stopped spending every break together, talking incessantly when time allowed, lunching together, waiting for each other at the end of the shift. Miriam had no explanation. There was no way to discuss the matter without revealing Agnes's secrets. So she kept her mouth shut, and even felt guilty for having told Velma.

Assuming Agnes would report what she had told her to Tommy— Miriam hoped for a confrontation between the lovers—she thought she might find Tommy waiting for her outside at Harlem Hospital when she punched out. He had proved unfaithful, Miriam had reported it, and she wouldn't be surprised if he resolved to downright beat her up either for telling his fiancée, or for not acquiescing to his wishes, or both. Miriam expected the worst, and, to some degree, prepared for it. What else could she expect from a woman beater? The few times she considered the possibility of getting roughed up by a spineless punk, she packed something or other in her bag, like a rolling pin, in the event she'd need it. It was the only language people like Tommy understood.

Her vision blurred, staring at endless lists of printed names. It was too gorgeous a Saturday to be working and sweating behind closed doors. And it wasn't quite two o'clock. She yawned, pushed herself away from the table, and got up to stretch her legs. She'd been sitting there since eight o'clock that morning, and thought of reading some of the recent literature she'd picked up from Liberty Hall, but that was purely leisure, and she had no time for it. By Monday, the officials expected the membership roster completely updated. There wasn't a second to waste.

She considered her negligence in not having been to Mother's house in a spell, and hoped the old woman understood. She'd come home on one or two occasions when Louise had stopped by and left a note. She hadn't seen her baby sister in a while either and wanted to talk with her to see what hand life was dealing her these days.

She remembered Velma's book of poems which she'd only read in parts, and decided to get some of that reading done before her sister quizzed her for a critique. She expressed guilt over neglecting her family and their endeavors, wasting too much futile time with a friend who obviously didn't need her.

She checked the icebox, which told her that it, too, had been neglected, and decided to stop by Sam's market, good old Sam, who had never attended a meeting since last time she saw him in Mother's neighborhood.

She emptied the pan of water from the icebox and made a grocery list: collard greens, rice, black-eyed peas, fatback, chicken, pigs' feet, hominy grits, eggs, a pound of—

Someone knocked at her door. She sighed at the interruption, trying to finish writing a pound of whatever it was that had just escaped her mind, when the knock came again. She dragged her feet across the floor, unlocked the door, opened it, and virtually fainted at the sight of her unannounced visitor.

"Hey girl, ain't you gonna invite me inside?"

Agnes stood in the doorway, smiling, a bouquet of mums cradled in her arm.

Miriam didn't know what to say, but let her in and closed the door. She had plenty to say as Agnes walked across the living room floor, but waited until Agnes spoke first.

"I guess you're still mad at me," Agnes said haltingly.

"You're the one who's mad with me," Miriam corrected her.

"Well, these are for you," Agnes said, handing her the bunch of yellow and white mums.

"Thanks, Agnes," Miriam said, "that's very sweet of you. Let me put them in some water." Miriam was overwhelmed at the gesture, an admission of Agnes's mistake, but said nothing.

"Miriam," Agnes said, "I guess you realize you was right and I was . . . wrong."

"What happened?" Miriam asked, noticing the ring missing from Agnes's finger.

"I broke it off, girl." Agnes plopped on the couch, crossed her shapely legs, and fanned herself with the newspaper.

"You did?"

"Sure did, honey. You know I found him with some other bitch."

I told you so! was at the tip of Miriam's tongue, but she kept quiet.

"I guess I got so angry with you that day," Agnes admitted, "because I knew, whether I said so or not, that you were telling the truth. I didn't want to hear it. I felt I'd come too far with that man. I was finally getting what I wanted out of him, and . . . well, you know the rest."

"Did you tell him about me?"

"Not until a few months later, after I found him with this other broad."

"What'd he say?"

"Well, I could tell he was lying, lying through his teeth when your name came up."

"So, how does he feel? I mean, you breaking off the wedding?"

"He had a fit—what else?"

"Did he hit you again?"

"Sure did. Tried to beat the shit out of me." She stopped fanning herself and put down the newspaper. "I have something to tell you, Miriam, that I ain't told nobody else. You must promise me you won't open your mouth."

"You know I won't."

"Well, I'm leaving him. I went down to Bellevue and got a job. You know they hiring colored nurses these days. Now, I'm planning to move."

Good for you, Agnes! Miriam thought, but listened intently as Agnes unveiled her plans.

"Except, I got one problem."

"Yeah?"

"Well, ever since I broke off the engagement, he keeps coming around and threatening me. I need to move right away but . . . I don't have anywhere to go."

Is she asking what I think she's asking? Miriam thought, a smile almost breaking out on her face.

"And, I was wondering if I could stay here with you . . . just for a while . . . just until I get myself straight—"

"Sure you can stay here," Miriam said before Agnes finished. "I have a den I can turn into a bedroom. There's no bed in there, just a couch. What're you planning to do with your furniture?"

"Well, I ain't got much. But I'll put the stuff in storage. By the way, how much would you like me to pay you for the—"

"You don't have to pay me anything," Miriam said. "Hold on to your money, and do what you got to do."

Agnes couldn't believe that the more she got to know this woman, the more she proved a saint. She stood and hugged Miriam.

"Miriam, I really appreciate this. I won't forget it."

"I told you, Agnes, I'm your friend. Glad I could help."

"Well, I gotta go," Agnes said, "just to pick up a few clothes and things."

"What about Tommy?" Miriam voiced her thoughts. "He knows I'm your only friend. Won't he look for you?"

"Yeah, probably. But he don't know where you live."

Miriam walked her to the door, and in the hallway bade her friend good-bye.

"Agnes, you be careful."

"I will. I should be back in about an hour. If not, call the pohlice." Again, they embraced.

Miriam closed the door, leaned against it, and smiled the widest grin her lips had ever managed. She skipped across the room, sniffed the mums, and busied herself with making room for Agnes in the den. She looked at her desk piled with paperwork waiting for her special touch, and decided it could wait until morning.

In her dresser bureau, she found the piece of paper with Tommy's telephone number. Now she could throw the evidence away. Agnes believed her!

After tidying up the room and rearranging the furniture, she remembered the grocery list, sat down and tried to finish writing what she wanted a pound of. Someone knocked on the door again. She looked at the clock, wondering how Agnes managed to get done in a half hour. She virtually danced to the door. Opening it, she was again surprised by two more unannounced visitors.

"Louise! Velma!" she said, wrapping her arms around them both. The three sisters kissed, hugged, and rocked each other for what seemed a lifetime. They entered the apartment, Velma carrying a brown bag.

"What lovely flowers," Louise said, caressing and sniffing the mums.

"A friend of mine just brought them by," Miriam said proudly.

They parked themselves in the living room, and Velma asked for glasses.

"For what?" Miriam asked.

"Because we're going to have a drink," Velma explained, pulling a bottle of liquor from the brown bag.

"Velma!" Miriam said. "You know that's illegal."

"So what," Velma answered. "It's not stopping anybody else from a good time. C'mon girl, a celebration's in order." She got up and walked toward the kitchen.

If not for Agnes's unexpected visit, Miriam would never have considered it. She hadn't touched liquor since the age of nineteen; even then, it was an experiment spurred on by curiosity.

"What're you doing with this room?" Velma asked, pointing at the den.

"A friend of mine is moving in for a while. She needs a place to stay."

"You mean Agnes?" Velma remembered. Miriam must like this woman a lot. Velma didn't know what to make of her moving in. Again, Miriam was concealing something.

"Yeah, you remember Agnes."

"So, everything worked out between you two?"

"Not really," Miriam admitted. "Not until about a half an hour ago."

"What the hell're you two talking about?" Louise said, getting up from the sofa to join them in the kitchen. "Who's Agnes?"

"Since when you started using words like hell?" Miriam asked playfully. Cutting apron strings even with a younger sibling was a task not to be underestimated. "Agnes is a good friend of mine. Well, girl, look at you!" Miriam said, turning Louise around by the shoulders, admiring her smartly coordinated peach suit, flowered silk blouse, and peach hat cocked to the side of her head. "Velma, look at our baby sister. She's all grown up."

"I know," Velma said, pouring gin into three glasses. "Isn't she gorgeous?"

"Where'd you get that stuff?" Miriam asked Velma, examining the bottle.

"My boyfriend. Who else?"

Miriam grabbed Louise by the arm, hugged her tightly, stroked her hair, and planted a kiss on her forehead. "I miss you so much. You know, I was thinking about y'all earlier today."

"Sure," Velma joked. "And you were coming by my house, right?"

"No, seriously," Miriam defended herself. "I was even going to read your book tonight, girl."

"You were going to read it now that I'm here," Velma chuckled. She picked up her glass, placed the other two in her sisters' hands, and proposed a toast. "This is the first time we've all been together since I don't know when. Let's drink to something, anything."

"Here, here!" Louise said. "Come on, Miriam. I planned my day around you two. I went by Velma's and we knew, without saying a word, that we were coming by here."

They toasted sisterhood, their glasses clicking. Miriam choked as she swallowed. Velma and Louise patted her on the back and laughed. "No wonder they call it alcohol," Miriam said. "That's just what it tastes like."

They moved back into the living room and shared their news. Velma talked about her fabulous beau, her great friend Rudy, who, though she didn't divulge it, was acting peculiar with her lately, as if angry with her about something. Velma felt, conversely, that she had every reason to be mad with him, if anything. She confided to them that Scott had excessive drinking tendencies and she was worried. She didn't know what compelled him to drink, nor did he discuss it.

Louise bubbled over like uncorked champagne with Cotton Club anecdotes, the celebrities, the British royalty, the gangsters that frequented the club, her friend Peaches, and the nightclubbing she'd been doing since she last saw them. The Prince of Wales, she said, wasn't very tall, and Gloria Swanson wasn't as pretty in person. She explained to Miriam what the Nest Club, Smalls Paradise, Connie's Inn, and other cabarets were like, and what she'd been missing. She started to tell them of her tentative date with a wealthy Italian socialite, but caught herself, unsure of what her sisters would make of her dating a man who didn't know she was colored—especially Miriam, overprotective as she was.

Miriam brought them up to date on the Agnes and Tommy saga, filling in the missing pieces for Louise, and saying how ecstatic she was to be getting a roommate.

"Be careful, Miriam," Velma advised.

"What do you mean?"

"Just be careful. Getting in the middle of a domestic spat could squeeze you right into something you haven't bargained for."

"Velma's right," Louise added. "Just watch yourself."

Miriam appreciated the advice, but felt there was no cause to worry. Tommy didn't know where she lived, and Agnes, exhibiting a smidgen of common sense for a change, was swapping jobs. What danger?

They drank, gossiped, traded beauty secrets—mostly Velma and Louise—and decided, on the spur of the moment, to drop by and surprise Mother. Miriam, carried away by the moment's impulse, was on her way out the door with her sisters when she remembered Agnes would be returning in about five minutes. She instructed them to go on ahead without her, but she'd be there within the hour. Velma and Louise agreed hesitantly, not without protest, but promised they'd wait; they were going nowhere until she arrived.

6

A yellow taxi cab screeched to a halt at the foot of Fifth Avenue.

Louise, in a turquoise suit, gloves, and shoes, paid with a five-dollar bill, and instructed the driver to keep the change. He thanked her, tipped his hat, flashed a toothy smile, pulled the automobile away from the curb with a jcrk, and disappeared into the traffic clogging the side streets of Greenwich Village.

Louise admired the gigantic white arch and glanced at the rows of well-kept townhouses; how close together they were. A man on his porch played a guitar, crooning to an audience of oblivious passersby, and graceful, cautious squirrels scattering about on the grass in Washington Square Park across the street. She looked for her date. Her eyes roamed across the green foliage at the park's boundaries from MacDougall Street to the campus of New York University. He was nowhere to be seen. She strolled with languid movements toward a vacant park bench where an old man fed a flock of pigeons bickering among themselves for stale crusts of bread.

Her senses were numbed, as if she were walking in a dream, and she struggled to believe she had met a wealthy man—an *attractive*, wealthy man of her choosing who'd taken an interest in her. As Peaches said, every single girl and her mother were chasing him, yet he was chasing her. His attentions left her with a nagging question: Would she measure up to his expectations of her? Or would he, for that matter, measure up to hers? Too nervous and unable to keep still, she decided to stroll around the small park when a strong hand gripped her shoulder from behind, and she turned abruptly. Behind the strong hand was the stunning face she had met at Smalls

Paradise, his white teeth sparkling in the afternoon sunlight. Tipping his hat, he sat beside her, took her hand in his and kissed it. *"E stato un vero piacere per me il riverderti, signorina."*

"Hello, Vittorio."

"Bon giorno, Louise."

She blushed, and pointed. "Is that for me?"

"E tua, cara mia." He handed her a crisp, freshly cut calla lily wrapped in white tissue paper. Louise handled the long green stem and sniffed the bell-shaped flower with a deep breath, though there was nothing to smell.

"It's beautiful, Vittorio, but you didn't have to buy me a flower."

"I grow them in my garden. Calla lilies are my favorite. When I first met you, you made me think of a calla lily."

"You always give flowers to your girlfriends?" she said, sniffing the flower as she tried to elicit information without being obvious.

"Girlfriends?"

"You must have many girlfriends if what the newspapers say is true."

"I don't know what the newspapers say, but I don't have a girlfriend," he laughed. "But you'd rather believe what the newspapers print, yes?" He was taken by her directness. Women who got right to the point, a rarity, also got to him.

"I don't read them, but people do talk."

"Oh? And what do people say?"

"Oh, that you're a wealthy playboy, the object of every young girl's desire."

"The American press make up stories; they have to sell papers. But nobody ever thinks to ask me."

"I'm asking," Louise said, feeling more comfortable with him now than at Smalls Paradise. Flirting with a millionaire was no different than flirting with a poor man.

"Well, I enjoy the company of beautiful women," he said, wondering how to get off this subject so she wouldn't have the American press's impression of him. "But it means nothing. I want to get married when the right girl comes along, have children, raise a family."

"Have you met her yet?" That might have been too bold, but she couldn't help herself.

"Met who?"

"The right girl."

"I don't know," he said, catching her eyes with his. "Maybe you can tell me. Have I?"

"I don't know." Louise smiled coyly, the yellow powder from the flower's thimblelike center rubbing off on her nose.

In a powder-blue suit, white oxfords, and suspenders, he looked to Louise like the angelic little boy he must once have been, and she struggled with a maternal urge to kiss his forehead. His olive complexion was a shade or two darker than hers; his manicured hands, and the bridge where his eyebrows joined sent a wave of excitement through her. My God, this man's prettier than me! she thought.

"I'm just an average man who—"

"Average? The average man doesn't travel around New York in a chauffeur-driven limousine, now does he?" She giggled, hiding her lips behind the flower.

"You're a sharp cookie." He ran his fingers delicately through her hair. "And, a pretty one."

"Stop me if I'm being too forward, but how did it happen? I mean, how did you get rich?"

"The best way. I was born into it."

"I see. I imagine your parents live on Park Avenue or Central Park West?"

"My parents are from Bologna. When my father became rich, they moved to Sicily, where I was born."

"So, that's where your accent comes from."

"Accent? What accent?" He laughed at himself. "My father's in business and my parents live in a villa along the Tyrrhenian. You should go sometime. Perhaps, I'll take you."

"I've never been to Europe," she said, imagining herself in a fashionable outfit boarding a ship with him, the well-wishers onshore bidding bon voyage as the ship's foghorn sounded. "So, if it's so beautiful and you have money, why did you leave?"

"My father wants to expand his business here in America, and I'm his only son. This country has the potential for great business where one can get rich easily. So he had me educated at Princeton."

He projected himself into the future, bringing her home to meet his parents, his mama rejoicing that he was settling down, his papa disapproving as he disapproved and criticized anything and everything Vittorio did.

"So you're in business with your father?" She wanted to know how rich he was without asking.

"Hmmm, a little, you might say. But, I've made other investments in the stock market. At twenty-one, I received an inheritance and invested it wisely. Now, my money works for me." He glanced at the blazing sun, the swaying trees, her angelic profile, and thought how precise it all was. He'd been counting the days until he saw her again, and it was turning out exactly as he imagined it. "Would you like to take a walk?"

"It's a beautiful day, isn't it?"

"Not as beautiful as you, *signorina*." He led her by the arm, and walked through the narrow, winding pathway. "May I ask you a personal question?"

"That depends on how personal it is," she said.

"Are you married?"

"No."

"Boyfriend?"

"No, why?"

"Well, you were so mysterious about meeting me here today. I wondered."

"Mysterious?"

"Yes. You won't give me your phone number or let me call for you. You insisted we meet in a mutual place, oh, I don't know, you're just a little mysterious." He'd met countless women who lived to be telephoned or called for by him, so, he imagined, they could flaunt him and the limousine before their neighbors and friends. This one was different, a difference that drew him.

"I haven't always had the best relationships with men," Louise said. "Some of them won't take no for an answer. It's better that people don't know where I live, until I get to know them better." She wondered if it sounded convincing and prayed it wouldn't come up again.

"May I ask, do you have plans for tonight?" An afternoon with her wasn't enough.

"Pretty much. Why?"

"I want to take you to dinner at the Cotton Club. We could catch a show and go dancing later at the speakeasies. What do you say?"

"Vittorio, thanks a lot, but I can't."

"So what, may I ask, are you doing that's so important?"

"Well, uh, I have something to do. And, it's too late to cancel."

"Cancel what?"

"To cancel what I have to do," she said, laughing. His persistence made her giddy.

"That's what I mean. You American girls are so mysterious," he laughed again. "Maybe we could meet later at Smalls."

Louise wasn't sure how to approach this. She'd never dated a man who didn't know she was colored. The Cotton Club was Vittorio's

hangout, and she couldn't chance being spotted by him in the
chorus line. She liked him, and the attractive prospect of it all, but
how was she going to handle this? If he saw her, it could be
profoundly embarrassing to them both. For now, she planned to
cross that bridge when she reached it, take it a day at a time, and
pray that he wouldn't go to the Cotton Club that night. The next
two nights she had off.

"May I take you to lunch . . . or something?"

He wasn't about to give up that easily. Dinner, lunch,
anything—he'd do anything or capitalize on any opportunity to be
with her. He was impressed by her directness, her innocence, her
handling of the situation, her refusal to be pinned down and
conquered like most women of his past. She didn't seem overzeal-
ous or overingratiating like golddiggers he'd known, laughing at
anything he said, humorous or not, making themselves too available. She seemed not to care about his money, and he knew this
dark-eyed beauty could effortlessly win his heart. He thought she
liked him too, but there was a flirtatious distance and evasiveness
she maintained which sharpened his interest. The farther she
inched from his grasp, the farther he advanced to capture the
elusive. He was probing and cajoling her to spend as much time
with him as possible, and not the other way around. That in itself
was reason enough to pursue her. She was mysterious, uncommitted, marvelously engaging, and little did she know, with these
hard-to-find qualities, she could have her way with him. Watching
her lovely hair blowing in the breeze, he decided to try again.

"Have you eaten? How about lunch at the Plaza?" he suggested.

"The Plaza Hotel? The one on Central Park South?" She'd never
dreamed of dining there.

"The one and only. Join me? *Per favore?*" He offered his elbow.

"I'd love to, but I'm not properly dressed," she said, glancing
down at herself and making excuses. She thought she looked great,
but needed a compliment to reassure herself.

"You look perfect. Let's go. Taxi!" Vittorio flagged down a yellow
automobile while Louisa waited at the curb. One foot in the street,
one on the sidewalk, he opened the door, and with a gentle hand,
assisted her into the cab, and climbed in the back with her. "Plaza
Hotel, please!"

7

Elvira sat at her bedroom window. First time in twenty years, there were no aromas in the house, no food cooking on the stove, no odors of pressed hair and pomade.

The bedroom was dark. Her eyes bore the wrinkles and puffiness of tearful, sleepless nights, and her stomach growled. A lazy breeze stirred the curtains, tickling her nose. Flies buzzed and hovered about her motionless head and expressionless face. She watched the children play on the pavement below. Hopscotch. Double-dutch. Hide and seek. Their cries of laughter and elation rose to her window, dispersing in her ears, reminding her of her own three girls when they were that age. Stubborn Miriam. Optimistic Velma. Tragic Louise. Her three girls. Her babies. Now they were grown, having assumed their respective roles in the game of life, their own separate identities. Miriam the Garveyite and nurse at Harlem Hospital. Velma the poet and essayist. Louise the showgirl who disappeared. Without trace or clue, she had vanished as if by magic before their eyes. Elvira waited. She got up early in the morning and waited. Bathed herself before praying and waited. Worked her beauty shop without letting on to customers and waited. And still, no word. No telephone call. No letter.

Recalling her baby girl's near brush with a violent rape while working as a Walker agent, she feared for her safety. Two weeks ago to the day, it had been twenty-four hours since she was last seen in her two-piece turquoise outfit with matching shoes and gloves. Velma's advice was not to panic, not to come to dreadful conclusions. Everything will be all right, Velma consoled Elvira, convincing even herself to believe it.

Routine police reports were filled out on a missing person. The responding officers had been patient with Elvira when they should have been alarmed; perfunctory where they might have been polite.

"She's about five feet six," Elvira reported, her eyes stinging with tears that wouldn't fall. "She's lighter in complexion than the rest of us, and sometimes folks didn't believe she was mine—but she is! Her hair's long and wavy like a white woman. Not short and nappy like mine, see? She got a beautiful figure. Prettiest thing you ever wanna see. Look, this here her high school graduation picture. She took it about two years ago now. Ain't she the prettiest thing you ever saw?"

The policemen listened, nodding their heads as if they understood, exchanging perplexed glances when they assumed Elvira wasn't looking. Glancing from the photograph to the anxious woman, trying to reconcile the two, they scribbled notes on a pad which Elvira wasn't allowed to read and told her not to worry. They would find her girl; come hell or high water, they'd find her. But they never did. And, that was two weeks ago to the day.

By now, Elvira had become a daily, hourly voice on the telephone at the police station. She called the same time every day, every hour on the hour. The same presiding desk sergeant answered, repeating the same message as the hour before, the day before, the week preceding that.

"You sure she hasn't run away?" The police sergeant with the Irish-Brooklyn accent sounded irritated, probably because it was that colored woman in Harlem calling again.

"No," Elvira replied, "she wouldn't do a thing like that to her mother. What kind of girls you think I raised?"

"Well," the sergeant mumbled with an indifference that offended Elvira, "you know she's of age. Besides, lady, we get these kinds of reports all the time on a routine basis. Somebody's always missing for one reason or another. Your kid's not the only one missing, you know. I'm up to my eyeballs with missing persons, lady. And, I'll tell you somethin' else; usually we find that the so-called *miss-ing per-son* has just really made themselves scarce, if you know what I mean. And, if they're old enough, like your daughter here, there's really nothing we can do about this kind of Missing Persons report. So, you see lady, our hands are tied."

"What kinda chile would do an ugly thing like that?" Elvira wanted to know.

"The kind who, for one reason or another, wants to sever all past ties, start a new life—that's the kind!"

Elvira slammed down the telephone. She didn't stop there. By telephone or personal visit, she combed the hospitals, and checked the patient lists for a Brooks. She had them check the morgue and instructed Miriam to do the same. Between stripping beds and feeding times, Miriam slipped away to the morgue, inquiring after her sister. There were many cold iron slabs, an endless count of stiff, frozen cadavers, but not one of them belonged to her sister. They had nobody by the name of Brooks, or Louise.

Velma went to the Cotton Club and asked to speak with Herman Stark, the stage manager.

"He's busy," some fat gangster type with a French accent growled. "What do you want with him?"

"My name's Velma Brooks, and I'm looking for my sister, Louise."

"When you find her, let us know. We ain't seen hide nor hair of that broad for almost a month! Who the hell she think she is anyway?"

"Well, sir," Velma said patiently, affronted by his reference to her sister as a broad, "we have reason to believe she's missing."

"Exactly my point," he retorted, "missing from the goddamn chorus line!"

"Can I speak with Peaches?" Velma requested, following through on a lead provided her by Mother. Louise had spoken of a girlfriend named Peaches. "Could I possibly speak with her? I don't know her real name."

"Sure you can, if you can find her," he replied, puffing his cigar in Velma's face. "She quit and married some musician from the band. Every dame we hire ends up quitting to marry some musician bum. Like we ain't good enough for 'em or somethin'!"

"Well," Velma said with her head lowered, "thanks very much for your help."

"Don't mention it," he said. "By the way, toots, you any relation to Walter Brooks?"

Four weeks and the efforts of the three women were futile. In the weeks ahead, they gained about as much as they started with. Nothing. A big fat zero. Panic was setting in. They thought the unthinkable. They would sit together for hours, one of the rare times when there were no words between them, no laughter, no arguments. With bated breath, they waited for a knock, a turning of a key in the door, a telephone ring, a letter in the mail. But nothing ever came. And all they could do was wait and hope.

"Mother, you all right?" Miriam whispered from behind, her hand resting upon Elvira's shoulder.

"About as all right as I'm ever gonna be, I reckon," Elvira replied, releasing the fifth sigh in two minutes.

"Still nothing?"

"You see me sittin' here like yesterday and the day before."

"Well, I thought I'd stop by to see how you were and if you needed anything."

"What I need right now is my baby, that's all. No more, no less."

Elvira didn't mean to sound harsh. Miriam wanted to help, and it certainly wasn't her fault. Just that her heart was on fire, her insides disintegrating, and she clumsily grabbed Miriam and hugged her briefly, afraid if she didn't do it quickly, she might never let go.

"Well, Mother, here's your mail." Miriam placed a thick wad of envelopes on the bed. "You haven't collected it and it's just piling up in the mailbox."

"Put it in there on the kitchen table. I get to it when I can. Ain't nothin' but the same ol' bills."

Miriam sorted the mail herself, knowing Mother wouldn't until she found her baby. Looking at her, the pain clutching Mother's face, she would have given anything, anything in the world to trade places with her. Mother didn't deserve this; she'd lost her husband already and never quite recovered from it. Louise's disappearance, she knew, would put her in an early grave for sure. Then she saw it, and imagined this was the feeling experienced by pioneers during the California gold rush.

"Mother! Here's a letter. There's no return address, but it looks like Louise's handwriting!"

"Hurry, open it up! What does it say? I don't have on my reading glasses!"

Miriam's hands fumbled with the envelope. Tearing it blindly, she partially ripped the letter, unfolded the creases, and a check fell out, twirling like a leaf to the floor. Miriam picked it up, the letter in one hand, the check in the other. "Mother, this here's a check for fifty dollars."

"Would you please read the letter!" Elvira wrung her hands uncontrollably, her lips pursed.

"Okay, Mother, okay, just give me a minute here." Miriam read ahead silently, her big eyes racing down the page, as if screening what she thought Mother should hear.

"I'm waitin'!" Elvira said, rising from her chair, moving away from the window.

"I'm sorry, Mother. Well, looks like she dated it about a week and a half ago, so at least we know she's not—"

"Miriam!"

" 'My dearest Mother,' " Miriam began reading, " 'I simply don't know where to begin. It took me a long time to sit down and write this letter, and even longer to finally send it. Let me say first that I'm fine. There's no need to worry about me. I've never been happier. I know all the worry and heartache I've caused you and I'm aware you're not a well woman, but sometimes in life, we have to do what we have to do. Please accept my deepest, most sincere apologies for any problems I've caused. Also, my apologies to Miriam and Velma. I love them too. And, I imagine they've been worried about me as well.' "

Miriam paused and a tear rolled down her cheek.

"Go on, Miriam. Read!"

Reluctantly, she shifted her attention to the dangling paper, and tried to steady it in her trembling hand. She continued reading, her voice cracking, her insides plunging with every word.

" 'For so many years, I was terribly unhappy, as you know, and now, life is finally cashing in for me. I feel like I'm on top of the world. But it saddens me to say that I can't share it with you just yet. I can't because of the situation. That's about all I can tell you for now. I'll be with you, Miriam, and Velma again. I miss you all so much. And, I love you all so much, but I'm confused and I must work out my problems.

" 'As you've noticed on the envelope, there's no return address. It's better this way. I hope you understand. Please, whatever you do, don't try to find me. I can only say that I'm here in New York, so I'm closer than you think. And, your finding me would only make matters worse. Then, I'd be right back where I started, only worse.

" 'This is the first of many letters to come. I will be writing you about every two weeks to let you know that I'm all right. If I'm not, I'll come back home, but I think that God, in His wisdom and mercy, has opened a lifetime opportunity to me. An opportunity I can't afford to ignore. Please understand.

" 'I'm sure you can use this money. And, I want you to know that there's no reason for you to worry about money anymore. With each letter, I'll send a check. Please take it from me. It's the least I can do for all the problems I'm causing you. If Miriam or Velma can use it, by all means, give some to them. I need to know that my family's all right, that I can help them the best way I know how. Don't be angry. Look for my letters about every two weeks or so. I won't fail to write you or keep loving you and missing you. For I am and will always be, Your baby girl, Louise. P.S. Just give me time. That's all I need. We'll be together again someday, Mother. You'll see. And, someday very soon. I promise you that!' "

"I always knew it would happen," Elvira said, her voice suddenly hoarse, shaking her head, looking out the window, as if speaking with the children who played below. "I knew it. God has a way of tellin' you these things."

"You're thinking what I'm thinking?" Miriam was afraid to ask. The two women faced each other, trying not to reflect the sadness exploding within them.

"My baby got more problems than the law allow," Elvira said. "Just ain't fair."

Elvira looked at her bed. Same bed where Louise was conceived, same bed upon which she was born. A lightning bolt of conflicting emotions ran through her, a sensation exclusively, universally known to mothers, and she didn't know whether to cry or save it for later. Noticing the tear drying on Miriam's cheek, she felt if she started crying, the two of them might never stop. Somebody had to be strong. As matriarch, she was always looked upon as everyone's strength, their Rock of Gibraltar, their mother of steel. But Elvira wasn't made of steel. Her emotions were coming apart like Miriam's. She was just more adept at making it seem like she could hold herself together.

She blamed herself for having no answers the last time she and Louise had their talk. Her baby girl was in pain, pain bred from not knowing who she was, where she was going, if she was going at all. And all Elvira could do was skirt the issue and offer her a plate of hoecakes and salt pork. She'd asked the Lord to show her, to provide her a way, because she had foreseen this day from the time Louise was ten.

The desk sergeant was right all along. He said many *miss-ing per-sons*—to quote his emphasis—wanted to sever past ties, start new lives. Had she been standing within two feet of him when he uttered it so flippantly, she would have slapped him into next week. Considering it now, she accepted that the man knew his business, like she knew hers, and there was something to be said for that.

She knew exactly what Louise was doing. She'd seen it before. Whether her child was safe or not, Elvira couldn't give her up without a fight. Were she living next door, it would have done Elvira no good, having no access to a living, breathing, walking hunk of flesh that had pushed itself out of her womb. What was she going to do?

She thought of Gilbert and missed him more than ever that very moment. While she found it difficult to comply with Louise's written requests, she'd comply nonetheless. Ain't right to tamper with nobody's happiness. Had Gilbert been sitting there with her listening to their eldest daughter read a letter from their missing youngest daughter, he would have been in his shoes and out the door before Miriam was halfway through. That's what Elvira wished for; someone to execute what she didn't have the guts or the know-how to even consider.

Gilbert and Elvira had come North in the hope of providing better lives and flexible opportunities for their children. Negroes in the North were everything Negroes in the South weren't. Her husband read somewhere that New York City had hired its first Negro policeman and assigned him to Harlem. That alone was enough to motivate their pilgrimage, that, and the amazement that colored folks had a thriving community all to themselves where nobody got lynched or woke in the middle of the night to a burning cross.

Sitting in the bedroom, unable to face a quietly grieved Miriam who was doing her best not to fall apart, Elvira wished they'd stayed right there in Atlanta. This problem of a missing child would never have happened had they stayed in Georgia where, she thought again, Gilbert probably would have been lynched, knowing his pride and refusal to be anybody's "boy." To her, Negroes were the most arbitrarily despised, most hunted, most unenviable race of people on the face of God's earth. More so than Jews. No matter where they ran and hid, if their skin was high yellow, brown, or black, trouble found them.

She lost Gilbert. She wasn't going to lose Louise. She gave up Gilbert without a fight only because she hadn't seen it coming. This was different. She couldn't sit there, wasting away, and wait for Louise's return or the sound of her voice. Yet, she was asked *not* to find her which told Elvira exactly what her daughter was doing. The two extremes seesawed inside her. Should she or shouldn't she? How could she possibly sit and wait, or work, or sleep, or eat until Louise's return? She needed her girls, her three reasons for living, but wrestled with suppressing her will to fight. And yet, there was no enemy. Who could she punch or sock in the face for effective results? The man next door? The man on the moon? God? It was a battle of the worst kind, where the enemy dodged her blows, slipped between her legs, climbed over her shoulders, sat on top of her head, and laughed behind her back as she tired herself silly with a futile exercise in shadowboxing.

She had to find Louise. She needed her. If not, Elvira knew she might not live to see Christmas, knew it like her own name. Like a whole needing all its parts to comprise itself, she was profoundly, viscerally, missing something. One-quarter of her familial strength was gone, not to be replenished until that one-fourth reappeared. Until then, she'd waste away, day by day, heartbeat by heartbeat, tear by tear, and for her to see New Year's 1928, she knew, would be another of God's wondrous miracles.

8

In the Studebaker, Scott swerved down Morningside Avenue, and slammed on the brakes at the 110th Street traffic light. Their bodies jerking forward, Velma and Rudy shot him dirty looks. Scott explained to Velma, in slurred speech, that the clutch was jamming, and he needed to have it examined by his mechanic.

Velma rolled her eyes at him and said nothing of the clutch, but thought Scott's head needed examination the way he was driving like a madman with a half pint of gin in his belly. She'd just this side of begged him not to get drunk after they left the cinema, but her pleas went unheard and unheeded.

Everyone was in a rotten mood. Since they had left the theater uptown, barely three words passed between the three companions. Before the light changed to green, Scott turned Velma's face with brute force, and kissed her with drunken, sloppy passion. The kiss was so prolonged that the light changed to green, back to red, and Scott's tongue continued exploring her mouth. She was embarrassed, since Rudy sat squeezed in the corner beside her. She pushed Scott away when he began biting her lips and neck, an amorous technique he delicately practiced on her frequently and that she loved, but tonight, it felt like he was trying to draw blood—not to mention that he smelled like a distillery.

Now there, Scott thought, his head bumping slightly against the window from Velma's light shove, let's see if Rudy can kiss you like that. The entire night, he had noticed Velma and Rudy tiptoeing around each other, and he could swear, had he not known them personally, that the two were engaged in a nonverbalized lovers' quarrel. He couldn't discern any other explanation for Velma's bloody mood—nothing had transpired between himself and her, and she wasn't having her period.

He'd just about had enough of those two. Sometimes he couldn't tell if she loved Rudy more than him, if she was still sleeping with him behind his back. His blood curdled at the thought of them committing debauchery and laughing at him. They only *claimed* Rudy was homosexual. He was as masculine as Scott himself or any other man on the street. Was this their ploy? Or the reason why Rudy never spent time with other women? Would they pal around with someone just because he had the key to elevated worlds and people they wouldn't otherwise have access to?

He knew Velma loved him; she made no bones about it, and substantiated it, the romantic she was, every chance she got. He'd never known a woman as romantic, not even in Paris, and got chills at the thought of losing her. But even he, with all his self-proclaimed liberalism, had limits.

Rudy filled with sympathy watching Scott's pitiful drunkeness, and disgust witnessing Scott plant a sloppy kiss on Velma. He derived no pleasure, as an outside, nonparticipating third party, playing voyeur in the front seat, listening to wet tongues and saliva swish around in a cramped automobile while the windows fogged. Similarly, if it were him Scott had kissed, he never would have pushed him away like Velma. She didn't know a good thing even when its arms were wrapped around her and its lips pressed against hers.

All night she had acted as if he'd insulted her and forgot to apologize. During the entire movie, Rudy wondered what the hell he'd done to her. She spoke to him only when necessary, in the flattest of tones, and her perfunctoriness—she spoke with an affected distance, as if she'd just met him—was starting to grate on his nerves. She had everything that women like her thought they were entitled to, and she still wasn't satisfied. Hell, she had the coveted prize. Lots of folks would take Scott, namely himself, if she was all that bored. And so what if he got drunk occasionally. She acted as if the world owed her something, something she, least of all, could define. The way he felt about her in the Studebaker, if he had his way, Scott would put her out on the next corner, and they two could enjoy the remainder of the evening alone. Looking out the window as the Studebaker zoomed down Madison Avenue at fifty m.p.h., he didn't know which passed in more rapid succession, the nocturnal city sights or the ugly thoughts in his head. He would have given a dollar—a dollar he didn't have—to know Velma's.

She couldn't shake Louise from her mind. The more she tried to dispel her sister's image and her mother's alarmed, wounded expressions, the more indelible they became, pressing against her consciousness. Discussing it with Scott might have helped and maybe she should have told him what was wrong when he kept asking at the theater while he was still sober. She chose not to discuss it with either of them. It was family business and there were things she needed to solve herself before she could openly analyze them with anyone not blood-related. She wondered if her sister was safe. The letter gave every indication she was, but until Velma could see her, hold her, and hear the words herself, it was the same as if she'd been abducted. She was vexed with Mother's predicament, feeling guilty for riding around aimlessly with two friends who wouldn't so much as talk to her—one of them roaring drunk—instead of sitting at the bedside of a woman who, unless she found her daughter, was as good as dead.

As if that wasn't enough, Scott was getting on her nerves, glancing at her surreptitiously throughout the evening, getting drunk despite her protests, and driving his automobile as if he were trying to kill them all. He wouldn't talk to her, yet he could grab her at a stoplight—an audience in the automobile, mind you—and force himself upon her as if she were a tramp. That was hardly romantic; it was . . . oh, she didn't know what it was; she just didn't like it.

And what was Rudy's problem? She felt she was bending over backward to get along with him at the cinema. He had little to say in general—less to say to her in particular—and she thought about what she'd possibly done to him; Rudy was so sensitive sometimes. But he ran back and told Scott about her unflattering opinion regarding his fiction. She didn't ask him *not* to say anything— neither of them personally knew Scott at the time—but, God, he'd have to be an imbecile not to have better judgment. And, if this was his haughty way of dealing with it, he could just take his sullen ass home. Now. What was he doing anyway, perennially hanging around without invitation? Didn't he know when three became a crowd? If he liked men so much, why wasn't he with one? She wasn't about to forgive him as long as he was in his dismal mood. He owed *her* the apology, and until he opened his mouth to her

like the friend he was supposed to be, she had nothing further to
say.

"Well," Scott said, deciding to break the silence, maneuvering
the steering wheel with a passive grin on his face, "did you two like
that or what?"

His friends remained silent, breathing and sighing ambiguous
responses. He tried again. "I asked," he said, his speech slurring,
"what you two thought about it."

"Thought about what?" Rudy said, irritated. "The way you
turned that corner on two wheels?"

"Don't be a wise-ass," Scott said, then belched.

"I'm still debating," Rudy said. "Anyway, why would they call it
the first talkie when the talking was minimal?"

"I myself haven't been so insulted since Griffith's *Birth of a
Nation*," Velma added, not in the mood to discuss an overrated
movie. "Just who does Jolson think he is, pulling off a blackface
stunt like that?"

"I found it amusing myself," Scott said, pleased they were at least
acting marginally civil with one another.

"Amusing?" Rudy retorted. "But, then you *would* find that
entertaining, wouldn't you, Scott?"

"I agree with Rudy. What could you possibly find amusing about
a black face in white lips singing 'Mammy'?"

"Oh, you two are always so judgmental, so bloody, goddamn
serious. I thought it was just a kick."

"Well," Velma pleaded, "how about the title, *The Jazz Singer*?
The cantor's son never sang any jazz that I heard. Did you ever hear
jazz like that in Harlem, Rudy?"

"With all the publicity surrounding this picture, I expected more.
You'd think that October 1927's a milestone year for the artistic
advancement of motion pictures. But tonight, the only advances I
saw were purely technological."

Velma noticed the numbers on the street signs descending
rapidly. "Where're you taking us, Scott?"

"For a ride." Scott intensely studied the dark road.

"Where?" Rudy echoed Velma.

"Oh, I thought we'd stop by Nazimova's penthouse for a bit,"
Scott said.

"The movie star?" Velma gasped.

"No," Scott growled. "The chief of police."

"Wild party?" Rudy's voice sprang from the darkness.

"Sort of."

"Sort of?" Velma asked.

"You kids didn't like *The Jazz Singer*, so we can take in some artsy films. You're both cultured, aren't you? Certainly you appreciate good cinema." His tone was suspicious, condescending, and the tires screeched against the asphalt, fleeting shadows passing over their faces.

"Be careful, Scott!" Velma turned her head to watch the automobile Scott nearly hit, then faced him. "Please slow down. Now, what kind of films are you talking about?" she asked, one eye on him, the other on the road.

"Flesh films."

"Flesh?"

"Yes. Flesh. You know, as in human bodies? Nudity?"

"You mean pornography?" Rudy sat up erect.

"I don't care to see that," Velma protested. "Please take me home."

"Don't be so bloody Victorian!" Scott yelled in Velma's ear though she sat beside him. His voice was loud, raucous, not unlike that of other drunks she'd heard. "You're too damned cultured to watch people fuck?"

"I'd rather not go there," Velma said. "That's all."

"Why? You never want to do what I want to do."

"Scott, you know that's not true. We always do whatever—"

Scott jerked the Studebaker abruptly toward the curb. The tires screamed, and his passengers lurched toward the windshield. Without facing them, he barked, "Get out!" He leaned across them and unlocked the passenger door.

"Right here in the middle of East Fifty-second Street?" Velma asked, shocked.

"If that's what the street sign says!"

Rudy opened the door, and emerged from the automobile, Velma following. Scott extinguished the motor. The three of them walked along Third Avenue, quietly and separately. October winds blew the coming of winter in their faces. Their polyrhythmic footfalls clicked against the pavement. Scott broke the monotony by hopping upon a brick wall. He balanced himself unsteadily like a tightrope walker, his arms spread.

"Rudy," Velma said, in a final attempt to bring Rudy out of his trance, unable to tolerate the silence any further, "did you know the *New York Times* raved about your second novel today?"

"Yeah."

"I'll bet you were pleased." Don't give me one-word answers either!

"I guess so," Rudy said, thinking how easily people forget their betrayal.

"Rudy, what's the matter with you lately?" Velma said. "You've hardly said two words to me all evening. Did I do some—"

"Nothing's wrong."

"Did I say something you didn't like?"

"No." He wanted to tell her, scream it into her face, but thought it would've been a petty outburst; possibly even, a misconstrued admission that he was ashamed of being homosexual when he wasn't.

"Then what's the problem?"

"There's no problem. You've been quiet with me too, you know." He chuckled to himself, hoping she'd ask what was so funny.

"What's so funny?" she asked.

"Nothing." He lowered his voice. "I was just thinking how the *Times* critic compared my work to Scott's."

"You're changing the subject," Velma insisted.

"No I'm not—"

"I heard that!" Scott said. "I read the newspapers too, you know. So what, now, Mr. Rudolph, you think because they made a minuscule comparison, you're as great a writer as I am? Huh? Is that what you think?" The way Velma pampered Rudy and paid him more attention, he'd been wanting to pick a fight with the little pansy for quite a while.

"I didn't say that, Scott," Rudy said smugly. "The *New York Times* did."

"Well, well, well. Do you know," Scott said, looking down at Rudy and Velma with a twisted expression, and jumped down from the wall, nearly falling. "Do you know it took me three—not one, not two, but three goddamn, bloody works of fiction to even get a snort of approval out of those low-lifes at the *Times* who so fittingly call themselves critics, that it took three painful efforts for those bloody bastards to even spit in my direction?" He pointed in Rudy's face, his body swaying. "Did you know that? But, then how could you? Coming from a city which lies at the bowels of the Hudson River, who could blame you? Certainly not I! And here comes this skinny, undernourished lad, fresh out of—where did you say you were from? Jersey City? Ah yes, Jersey City, indeed! The little, skinny, bohemian, homosexual fellow writes two ersatz, sopho-moric pieces of mediocrity, probably the remnants of an exercise he had in creative writing at Columbia, encouraged, no doubt, by some idiotic, liberal professor who felt sorry for the darkie, homosexual fellow. He writes a piece of commercially celebrated crap, and he thinks he can be compared with the likes of me because the *New York Times*—"

"Scott, stop it!" Velma nearly screamed, plugging her ears. "You're drunk!" Nice going, Scott. I already asked you not to repeat what I told you about Rudy—repeating it to his face, no less, Velma thought.

"You'll wait your turn, Miss Woman of Letters." Scott released his grasp on Rudy's wrinkled jacket and turned to Velma. His face was one she didn't recognize. "Or how do you prefer to attribute yourself? Miss *Negro* Woman of Letters? Huh? Don't you say anything to me. I haven't even started on you yet!"

"You know, Scott," Velma said calmly, "I still haven't forgiven you for that story you made up about your family. And, I'm getting a little—no, I'm getting more than a little impatient with you!" She began shouting. "One minute you're fine, the next minute, you're a raving lunatic! One day—"

"It's nothing personal," Scott interrupted. "Don't get excited because you're not as talented a writer as you think. Oh, I know you're excited about your first novel about to go to press. But I've got three, remember? Besides," he said, chuckling sinisterly, "I wouldn't be surprised if Van Vechten's photography and Aaron's dust cover illustration were the best things about your so-called work of fiction. You know, you get me, you women writers. People like you, Fauset, Larsen, and let us not forget Hurston the pick-aninny; you all think you're pretty damned clever, don't you? Riding on the coattails of more established, more credible writers like myself. Not that I'm invalidating your worth, you understand. But, *Negro* women have nothing really substantial enough to say. They're just along for the ride. Isn't that a correct evaluation?"

"You're being insolent!" Velma screamed, her echo bouncing off the buildings around them and back to her. "And I hate you when you start drinking!"

"Oh?" Scott stumbled back against the brick wall, his shoulder slipping. "Did I say something to offend you? I was merely stating a fact. Don't get angry with me because I'm *gifted*. All you two have is mere talent, if that, and there's a bloody world of difference." He belched, then hiccupped.

"Please take us home!" Velma demanded. "Are you going to take us home or not?"

"*Ma chérie*, Velma. Of the three of us, you're the only native New Yorker. Certainly you know your way about this ghastly, claustrophobic island. You're the goddamn independent woman. Oh, pardon me, the independent *Negro* woman."

"God! I don't believe this!" Velma looked from him to Rudy. "You're angry because we don't want to watch some white folks fucking on the screen. The only time you're happy is when you get your way. Did you ever think to ask us what *we* might want to do for a change? Rudy and I have some ideas of our own. We can think too, you know."

Yes, Rudy thought, and some of the ideas I have don't include *you.*

"Oh, *pardonnez-moi*," Scott said, his hand pressed against his lips like the shrieking woman who's just seen a mouse. "Did you want to visit Roscoe's Hog Maws and Pig Feet Joint instead of basking in the delights of Nazimova's luxurious penthouse suite? Or perhaps, oh, let's see, maybe we could buy three watermelons and eat them in the middle of Park Avenue as we speak in Negro dialect? Hmmmmm? Rudy, how's your buck-and-wing? How does that sound to you, Rudy?"

"You're pathetic, Scott." Rudy moved away.

"Not pathetic, *mon ami.* Just honest without compromise! I'll have you know that I've been educated at the best schools this country has to offer. Traveled extensively throughout Europe and South America. Can either of you claim that of yourselves? How dare you question my itinerary or tastes for that matter? You should be honored just to be in my company. Nothing's ever said about how I descend from my social station to pal around with the proletarian likes of yourselves. A girl from a Harlem tenement who's never so much as stepped outside New York, and her bohemian sidekick who wears century-old wing tips, mismatched socks, and doesn't even know a salad fork from a dinner fork. Wouldn't you say I'm doing you both a grand favor? Huh? I could be biding my time with *real* luminaries like Hemingway, Lawrence, Mann; the great intellectual talents of the twentieth century. But, no, instead I—"

"Scott," Velma said, calmly, shaking her head, "you're disgusting! You're full of self-pity and hatred. You're mad at the world because you're Negro. Like a dirty trick played on you when your back was turned, right, Scottie? Then, shit, go on and be white! Nobody cares—"

"What did you call me?"

"I didn't call you anything yet. But I have a few choices—"

"Don't ever call me Scottie! Ever! Scottie sounds so bloody feminine!"

"Feminine? That's the last thing I had in mind. I just thought it fitting for a little boy grappling the threshold of puberty!"

She looked around them, disbelieving her ears. She wanted to keep quiet before she said something she *really* regretted; something that probably had nothing to do with either of them, but she had one last comment to make.

"Mr. G. Virgil *Scott*! What does the G stand for? God?" Velma said, walking toward the subway. "Rudy, you coming?"

"Where do you two think you're going? You can't leave me here by myself!" Scott stumbled away from the brick wall. Supporting himself upon a lamppost, he shouted into the night. Velma and Rudy slowly disappeared from his intoxicated view—four people moving briskly away from him, their footfalls fading beyond earshot. "Before I introduced you to Mrs. Vanderpool, you both amounted to nothing. Not a grain of dirt. Now, you think you're too big for your britches, but I'll fix that. First thing tomorrow morning, I'll give Mrs. V a call and see what she has to say about it! And, no matter how you beg or plead, she'll listen to me; she always listens to me. I've known that woman since I was about ten years old. Can either of you say you grew up around the affluent?" He shook his fist, perspiring profusely. His voice became hoarse and whiny as if he were sobbing internally. "Did you hear that, Rudy? . . . Hey Velma! . . . Where are you? . . . Are you two hiding from me? . . . Don't leave me here by myself!"

Descending into the subway, Rudy couldn't help gloating. He didn't enjoy Scott's making light of his critically acclaimed efforts; nor did he like being called a homosexual at a volume sufficient to wake the neighborhood. But he did like watching Velma and Scott quarrel.

Sitting beside her on the subway, as they resumed their former silence, he felt anyone running around shooting her mouth off about his sexual preference didn't deserve Scott—she obviously lacked the sophistication. Scott had his problems—who didn't?— but Velma had grossly mishandled the situation and abandoned a man who desperately needed her. The pain he screamed into the night said it rather clearly. As he held onto Rudy's jacket during his jealous outburst of the *New York Times* review, rather than spit in his eye, Rudy wanted to cradle and comfort him. And, maybe he would have, had Velma not been around. Now that the "homosexual" part was out in the open, he was tempted, in his shitty mood, to confront her, right there on the subway, and raise the complacent eyebrows of the elderly couple sitting across from them, and the young man buried behind the *New York Post.* He knew Velma might never speak to him again if he released his dark thoughts in front of the passengers. He'd let this one blow over. If Velma had any conscience, Scott's having said it should suffice without his rubbing it in.

Velma felt uncomfortable sitting beside Rudy as the subway jerked, and the lights intermittently went out and came back on. He didn't have much to say to her although she'd tried breaking the ice. Watching his dulled reflection in the opposite window, she knew there was some attraction left in her toward him, and she loathed herself for it. Two years and still she hadn't wholeheartedly shaken him. She wanted to apologize now that Scott had revealed Rudy's private life to everybody who cared to listen at East Fifty-second and Third. Except she felt she'd been apologizing all evening in her own way; pride wouldn't allow her to form the words in her mouth. And, just as well, he should have apologized first.

The memory of Scott supporting himself upon the lamppost had to be one of the saddest sights she'd ever seen. Poor man. Though she viewed it necessary to defend herself—and Rudy—the need for vindication turned to pity and guilt. She felt sorry for Scott looking like an abandoned, unloved little boy caught up in a tantrum, and she might have exercised more patience and understanding had the night not been one of an all-time low. She couldn't handle his inebriation, his insolence, and his superciliousness. Not tonight. She had too many other things on her mind.

9

"Brooks! Chile, what done happen to you?" Mrs. Tinsley exclaimed.

"Nothin'. Watchu talkin' about?" Elvira said, knowing good and well what the customer spoke of.

"Chile, lemme look at you." She examined Elvira with a disapproving eye. "Girl, you done los' so much weight. I heard you been sick, but sweet Jesus!"

"My blood pressure been actin' up again," Elvira admitted in an effort to dismiss it.

"You sure that's all it is?" Mrs. Tinsley eyed her head to toe, her mouth gaped.

"Ain't that enough?! Come on over here and have a seat." Elvira patted the chair before her, standing at the sink. Her frail arms leaned against her side as if they weren't hers. "What can I do for you today?"

"Chile, it's my tenth weddin' anniversary, an' for the first time in years, I'm goin' out. Needs to get my hair done first before . . ." Mrs. Tinsley's voice trailed off, watching Elvira supporting herself against the sink as if she didn't have another breath to spare. "Brooks, you feelin' good enough to work? 'Cause if you ain't—"

"I'm fine, chile." Elvira waved her hand. "Just fine."

"I hear your shop been closed for a few weeks. What's wrong?"

"Ain't nothing wrong. An ol' lady just get tired sometime."

"You look like you done los' a good twenty pounds there."

"So, where you goin' tonight?" Lady, please talk about something else.

"Evah since it opened, Jessie been promisin' to take me to the Cotton Club. Tryin' to raise four kids, it ain't easy, I can sho tell you that. But, tonight's the night."

"They ain't gonna let you in, you know that?" She just had to bring up the Cotton Club, didn't she?

"That's what you think, but my sister, you remember Evie, well, she go alla time. She yalla enough, ain't she? If you got the right complexion, those folks don't know if you white or not. I'm gonna take my chances."

"Well, good luck. But you still ain't tol' me what you want done with your hair."

"I need it washed for one thing. And, you know," she said, smoothing her hair back with the palms of her hands, "those finger waves would be somethin' different. That'll make me look white, doncha think? A few spit curls here and there. Whatchu think?"

"Waves coming up." A pain passed in her chest, but Elvira refused to falter.

"And, you know what, Brooks, I'd like some of that Glossine hair oil to make it shine. You know, that Madame Walker stuff. All my friends say it work like a champ." She turned her head toward the shelves along the basin and pointed. "Yeah, child, gimme some of that stuff right there."

Elvira looked at the jars above the basin. The jars Louise sold her. Her vision became blurry, her head spun. She had never felt so debilitated in her life except after giving birth. She hesitated, as if afraid to touch the jars.

As she predicted, no sign of her baby meant no sign of her health on the upswing. Closing the shop down for about a month, she felt forced to reopen for business, and quickly. The unnervingly endless silence of the haunted apartment drove her crazy and, at times, she felt on the verge of throwing her window open and shouting to the world the anguish festering in her bones.

She discouraged Miriam's and Velma's thoughtful visits. Their presence only sharpened her awareness that one-quarter of the Brooks family unit was still missing. She'd even taken to blocking their entrance when they appeared at her door, insisting, in as sweet a voice as humanly possible, that she'd rather be alone. They didn't scare easily and Elvira's heart felt consumed with iniquity, as she watched their dejected backs descend the dark stairway. They too were in agony and had a right to solace, except she lacked the strength to console herself; there was none to spare for them. Everything in her wanted to summon them back as her polarized wants and needs fluctuated between desiring their company and needing to be alone. Studying her despair mirrored in their eyes was enough to bolt her door shut until Armageddon, or the Rapture, whichever came first. Though she never doubted for a moment the promise of Jesus' return to earth, she found herself speeding it up in prayer, asking for the Lamb of Peace to take her away with him as he singularly annihilated a world reeking of evil.

Miriam insisted she put herself in a hospital; high blood pressure was nothing to fool with, and even tried bodily forcing her one night until Elvira screamed and kicked like a child getting her first doctor's needle. She begged Miriam to leave her be, frightened of hospitals, the disinfectant odors made her queasy, the rotting smell of death all around her. If she was going to die, she wasn't about to do it without dignity, expiring before bedridden neighbors she knew for all of two weeks. If she had to die, her apartment on the second floor facing West 141st Street in Harlem, New York City, was as good a place as any.

She took to digging out old photographs: Louise as infant in a carriage while a beaming Miriam and snotty-nosed Velma proudly held on to the buggy, Miriam appearing as the mother; Louise on her third Easter, all bonnet, lace, ribbons, and pigtails, with a big grin; Louise and Gilbert . . . no, she couldn't look at that one; Louise nearly grown up, posing for her high school graduation picture. And, oh, she'd forgotten all about the lock of Louise's hair stuffed away in the bottom drawer beneath the weight of twenty-five years of photographs. She didn't want to examine them, necessarily, but they sure beat the heck out of having nothing at all to cherish. From the lace handkerchief, she unfolded Louise's hair, strands Elvira had cut herself and saved, unaware it would be retrieved at such a poignant moment. She sniffed it, pressing it against her nostrils as if for its restorative powers, then exhaled. She could still smell the fifteen-year-old shampoo and pomade she used that day.

Then there came a period when she boycotted any reminders. She wouldn't look at the pictures, or smell the hair, or glance at the unused products she'd purchased from Louise. She stayed out of her bedroom, the door shut as if Louise were safely inside, asleep after a late night on the town with her girlfriend Peaches and Elvira was to wake her in another half hour.

Letters continued to arrive, as promised. But Elvira had given up reading them. Rather than consoling her with the knowledge that Louise was alive, kicking, and happy, they deepened her depression.

And just as she was about to resume her daily routine, to try not thinking about Louise—along came Mrs. Tinsley, unwittingly dredging the whole thing up again. She had to finish with Mrs. Tinsley, break her own record for speed, and get this sweet, churchgoing, God-fearing woman the hell out of her house.

"Don't one of your girls work over there at the Cotton Club?" She turned around to face her beautician.

"Not anymore she don't."

"Ooohhh," Mrs. Tinsley sighed regretfully. "And I was lookin' to see somebody I know dancin' up in that chorus line."

"You a little too late for that."

"Where she workin' now?"

"If I'm gonna give you these here waves, you gonna have to keep quiet and still."

"Oh, I'm sorry, Brooks. I'm just sittin' here runnin' off at the mouth."

Running off at the mouth, indeed, Elvira thought, ashamed of her short temper. The woman was only trying to make conversation as all of her patrons usually did while Elvira worked on them.

She wrapped a towel and bib around her customer's shoulders, and tilted her head under the running water before applying the shampoo.

"Brooks, you should see this here dress I'm wearin' tonight. Girl, it's gonna knock 'em dead. First new dress I done had in years, and they might have to call out the fire squad." The woman giggled to herself, the warm stream of water dripping down the sides of her face. "You know, sometime it make me madder than hell that this here club is up in the middle of Harlem and us Race folks can't even spend our own hard-earned money there. Ain't that somethin', Brooks? But, they got us doin' all the entertainin' 'cause without us, they really have to close down business. Am I lyin' or am I tellin' the truth, Brooks?"

As she rambled on, she could feel Elvira's hands leave her scalp as she turned away from the sink. She heard a thud, and wondered what the hell it was.

"Brooks, you listenin'? . . . Brooks?"

She lifted her head from the sink. Holding the towel around her wet, dripping hair, she glanced around the kitchen. There was no sign of Elvira. She stood, wrapped the towel around her head and spotted a strange sight sprawled across the floor; an expression of horror gripped her face. She stopped short and screamed. "Brooks! What happened? Brooks! You all right?! Somebody, heeeelp!"

10

Little Italy bustled with crowds cramming the narrow streets. Louise and Vittorio strolled arm in arm and turned into Mulberry Street. Vendors showcased their merchandise and wares to interested, bargaining customers. Children watched the street circus from fire escapes. Big-bellied men with deep voices bellowed their sales pitches in Italian, selling vegetables, fruits, pasta, sausage, salami. Walking past a cart loaded with apples, Vittorio took one, rubbed it against his jacket and handed it to Louise, who smiled before biting it. Elderly, white-haired women, in black dresses and veils, rolled-down stockings, and rosary beads gossiped among themselves in their native tongue. Louise's attention was caught by a monkey jumping across a green awning. In a red vest and strapped hat, it bounced with animation on a leash extending from its owner. Its long tail curling behind, it collected money from an audience who sat at their windows. They patted the monkey's head and fondled the tail. The portly owner with his stained T-shirt and handlebar mustache, smiled approvingly, his pot belly protruding from the T-shirt, exposing a hairy navel. Grinding music from his hurdy-gurdy, he rewarded his monkey with a banana as passersby tossed coins into his hat. The sidewalks were too crowded. Louise and Vittorio took to the street where the bulk of traffic was composed of vegetable trucks and pushcarts. An open, gushing fire hydrant showered the impish bodies of fully clothed children who shrieked with delight. Young girls jumped rope, chanting a sing-song as they bounced. Boys in tattered knickers ran toward Vittorio and Louise. One of them collided with the lovers, fell back, and landed on his bottom.

"They remind me of when I was a boy in Palermo." Vittorio offered the child his hand, and brushed the dust off his bottom.

"Does this section of New York remind you of Italy?"

"Yes. I suppose that's why I come here so often."

"I bet you'd be a great father."

Since their meeting in Washington Square Park, the lovers had been inseparable, so much so that it became increasingly difficult for Louise to continue dating while living in Harlem.

Following their date in the Village, they had proceeded to the Plaza Hotel for lunch, after which Louise had instructed the cab driver to drop her off at Bleecker Street in Greenwich Village. Waving good-bye to Vittorio, who blew kisses through the back window, she walked through the door of a building she'd never seen in her life, and waited in the vestibule. Hearing the taxi pull away, she looked to see if it was safe, then flagged down another which delivered her home in time to get to work at the club.

One night, Vittorio inquired about her address. He returned to what he believed to be her building on Bleecker Street. Since he didn't know her surname, he rang every bell or knocked on every door in the building.

Louise's stomach churned, her heart pounded, her palms sweated, as he told her, with lifted eyebrows, what she already knew—that no one lived there who fitted her description. He had checked with the superintendent, who didn't know what or whom he was talking about. He explained that no Americans lived there. The building was rented predominantly by Italian immigrants; one Czech. To his knowledge, unless one of the tenants harbored someone he knew nothing of, there was no one under thirty living there. The landlord suggested that Vittorio had made a mistake; he had the wrong house. But Vittorio insisted it was the building he'd watched her enter.

A long silence followed Vittorio's account, and he waited for an explanation. Louise's mouth went cotton dry as her mind clicked with plausible accounts of why she didn't really live there. She reiterated what she'd already told him; that she wasn't in the habit of letting men know where she lived until she knew them better. Vittorio remembered, but thought himself an exception and said so. Without hurting his feelings, she confessed that she liked him a lot, but still, it was their first date. She impressed upon him that she did this habitually when dating men she just met.

As their relationship intensified, so did Louise's trepidation that Vittorio would spot her face in the chorus line. She followed Peaches and quit her position as chorus girl to gamble on her blossoming affair. Her next step was to relocate, to sever all past ties, painfully so, but nevertheless inevitably, to give this relationship everything she had. She was certain of the seriousness of Vittorio's intentions. And since most of the city's Italian citizens settled within the boundaries from Little Italy to the Village, she knew what had to be done. She preferred the ethnic community.

Having saved most of her earnings during her short-lived career as showgirl, she went apartment hunting, not informing anyone of her plans—not even Peaches. It was easy. Perhaps too easy. Like a sign, an omen from the gods. The landlord was gracious and accommodating, despite his inability to speak English. Falling over himself at Louise's beauty, he saw to it that she got what she wanted—the proper apartment with the precise view overlooking the arch in Washington Square, where she and Vittorio shared their first moments alone.

She lived as a white woman. Among white neighbors. In a white neighborhood. Where no one knew her, or her name, or where she was from. Once settled, she gave Vittorio an address and telephone number, so that the mystery about her would subside, and there would be no further need to lead a double life. She pulled it off with the finesse and expediency of a Houdini escaping a safety vault. She made it appear as if she'd lived in her Village apartment for almost two years, where she could receive his calls, invite him in for a late-night drink, entertain him at whim, or be available for surprise visits if he chose to make them. On many occasions, he did. She delighted in this new life. Looking like a white woman. Living as one.

Though she missed her family, her sacrificial lamb, her decision was easy to arrive at. Following their lunch at the Plaza, they rowed in a boat in Central Park where Vittorio kissed her and mumbled passionate words in his language, as her hair blew in the breeze. The mystery of comprehending the gestures, if not the words verbatim, made it for Louise all the more romantic. No matter where they went or what they did—Coney Island to scenic drives to Connecticut—he was always the gentleman, constantly attentive to her and her needs, treating her like royalty though she claimed no crown, never uttering a harsh word or raising his voice, never touching her where she didn't want to be touched, or asking her to do what she didn't want to do. The respect he paid her was a reverence she'd never known. There must be something to these European men, she thought frequently. Whenever they met, and wherever, he presented himself with a broad smile, strong embrace, a barely audible whisper of *"cara mia"* in her ear, and freshly cut calla lilies, one more for each successive date. He said they reminded him of her. Lately, they reminded her of him as well.

A knight in armor, Vittorio di Bolognese of Palermo, Sicily, had rescued this damsel from her distress. She wanted and needed him.

He epitomized her preconceived notions of a romantic affair. Though there had been no physical consummation as such—she remained a virgin—her body ached for him. His mere touch raised goose pimples on her arms. His soft, seductive Mediterranean accent caused her heart to pause a beat or two. And, when the proper time came—if it ever came—she had determined to give herself to him. At various times of her day—lying in bed or shopping on Madison Avenue—she fantasized him seducing her, her body opening up to him; the fanning of a peacock's feathers. But he never did. Vittorio was too much the gentleman.

Inside Giuseppe's Ristorante Italiano, Vittorio's favorite eating spot in Little Italy, he and Louise sat quietly at a candlelit table. Louise gazed at Vittorio, who gazed at the floor. They were speechless. No sounds emanated save the distant clicking of china, glasses and silverware. The throaty tenor of Enrico Caruso singing *Rigoletto* floated from the scratchy-sounding radio behind a swinging kitchen door.

"Vito, you haven't said a word all afternoon," Louise said. "You haven't even touched your linguini, and Giuseppe makes it especially for you. Is anything wrong?"

"No."

"Are you mad at me?"

"Of course not," he laughed. "It's just . . ."

"Oh, Vito, please tell me." She touched his hand across the red and white checkered tablecloth. "It's awkward seeing you like this. You've been so quiet these past few days."

"It's just that . . . aahh, never mind."

"Please."

"It's not important."

"Yes it is, Vito. It is."

"It's just that . . . well, this is difficult to say, but I think we're getting too serious."

Louise stopped chewing her food and slowly withdrew her hand. A knot formed, tangled in her stomach. "What's wrong with that?"

"Nothing, *cara mia*." He forced a chuckle. "But, I'm looking for, how would you say, a certain, special kind of woman."

"I'm not special?"

"No, darling, that's not what I mean."

"So, tell me," Louise said with a dash of flirt to camouflage the hurt. "What kind of woman is special?"

A nervous smile crept over his face. "This affair of ours—how do

you say it in English?—it's getting, or should I say, *I'm* getting a bit
. . . *involved* I suppose is the word." His smile turned solemn.
Again, his eyes shifted to the floor.

Louise pondered this a moment. "I understand exactly," she
heard herself say, not knowing what he wanted her to say, or to
where this was leading. "I'm . . . involved too."

"You *are!*" Vittorio was smiling again.

"Of course. What did you think?" Louise resumed chewing her
food, washed it down with a sip of wine, and exhaled a sigh of relief.
"Are you saying you're in love?"

"Yes," Vittorio said. "That's what I'm saying." He looked into
those big chestnut eyes of hers. "If you don't love me, I can't see
you anymore."

"Well, I do . . . love you, I mean," she confessed.

"And . . . I'm just a little curious about something else too."

"Yes?" Oh, God, please not now. Please don't let him say it.

"An Italian girl named Louise; where did you get that name?"

"That's not my real name, silly boy."

"Then, you must tell me. I can't go around with a woman for
almost four months without knowing her real name," he said
jokingly.

Louise combed her mind for a name undeniably Italian. She
remembered the anecdote she confided to Mother; the Italian
vendor who once compared Louise to his daughter. "Luisa," she
said, surprising even herself. "That's my real name. Anna Luisa."

"Does Anna Luisa have a last name?"

"Yes . . . Carcionne."

"Then, why do you call yourself Louise? It sounds more American, no?"

"My parents died when I was very young." Her insides felt as if
they were tied in a knot. "I was raised in an orphanage. They
shortened and Americanized my name. It's nothing really. It
happens to all the children." Her smile was crooked. A nerve
caused her upper lip to twitch, and she sipped the wine to conceal
it.

"You have no brothers or sisters?"

She indicated no with a slow nod.

"You don't speak the language."

"I did as a young girl. But, it wasn't spoken in the orphanage, so
I've forgotten it."

He paused, swallowed, looked Louise in the eyes, and cupped her face in his hands. "Now you have a family. I want you to be my family."

"What?"

"I want you to become Mrs. Vittorio di Bolognese. We're perfect for each other. Just meeting you has changed me so much." He looked away from her, fearful of her rejection—embarrassed by his vulnerability, his cries of desperation—and studied the waiter in the rear, his arms folded behind his back, rocking on his toes and heels near the swinging kitchen door. "Will you?"

"God! Vittorio, I don't know what to say! Let me think about—"

"Don't think; just say yes." He kissed her. "That's all I want to hear—the word yes." He kissed her again. "It's such a beautiful word in the English language, don't you agree?"

"But of course! Of course I'll marry you. Is this happening?"

"That's what I said when I first laid eyes on you. Yes, it's really happening, and it's real, and what perfect timing." He exhibited a toothy smile. "My parents are sailing from Palermo to spend Thanksgiving with me next month. They may be staying for a while. I was hoping to introduce you as my bride-to-be. I can see it now. Mama will adore you. She'll take you in as the daughter she never had. You just wait and see. You know, this is the happiest day of my life!"

"I'll be perfect for Mama."

"Well, then, I think this isn't out of order. I'm so excited, I almost forgot."

From his pocket, he produced a diamond engagement ring. Its dazzle blinded Louise, bringing a smile to her lips, tears to her eyes. Her hands trembling, she allowed him to gently place it on her finger. It fit like their complementary personalities.

"From this day forth, you are no longer Louise. I shall call you Luisa." He hesitated, then added with emphasis, "*My* Luisa. From now on, life for us will be very different from anything we've ever known." He lifted her ring finger and pressed it to his lips, without a clue to the irony of what he prophesied.

11

"Do you know a woman named Agnes Brown?"

Miriam looked over the official's head at the hanging photograph of Marcus Garvey in military regalia. The American flag and the red, black, and green flag were faded and needed to be replaced. A brass spittoon on the floor beside his desk nauseated her. She had no idea why she was called in, or why the official asked the question, but she sorted out her thoughts, hoping her reply would be the one for which he was searching. On either side of his desk, two men stood, their arms folded, legs spread, and gazed down at her. She could hear members outside in the larger hall congregating, and she wondered how they even knew Agnes's name.

"Yes," she replied, her eyes clouded with question marks, "I know Agnes Brown. Why?"

The official deliberated, tapping a pencil on his desk. She watched his Adam's apple bob and felt that whatever he had to say, he would say with much difficulty.

"We want you to understand," he began, "that we're very aware that you're an outstanding asset to this organization, and we feel that if we could have ten like you, we would without question."

She was pleased, nearly euphoric with his flattery. Seldom, perhaps too seldom, were her tireless efforts lauded, and she knew the official wasn't one to distribute insincere compliments. The other two men nodded as he said it. One of them moaned an Amen! which should have put her more at ease with them. Except, she felt a *but* was coming; it had yet to leap from his throat.

"You're an exquisite example of the kinds of people we want in UNIA," the official continued. "We know of few women who work harder than you, the time you give of yourself, your dedication . . . but that's not why we called you in today."

Miriam had given thought to why he asked to speak to her. On her way to headquarters—she went directly after work, the letter she'd received sounded *too* official—she surmised that she'd been chosen to head, or supervise, or organize a UNIA function of one sort or another. She hadn't anticipated the praise, but neither had she expected to hear Agnes's name. According to him, none of those were the reasons. So, she figured, the bee was allowing her a good, long lick of the honey, before he stung her.

The interrogating official wore round wire-frame glasses—Flowers was his name, Miriam remembered, but then she always confused him with someone else—and his salt-and-pepper hair receded, exposing a bald spot that shone in the light. His clothes were conservative but dusty, and she guessed he didn't take care of himself. She was studying the hair sprouting out of his ear when he folded his hands, and leaned forward at his desk, his voice dropping to a whisper.

"It's been brought to my attention," he said, glancing at both men on either side of him, "that you're involved in, how can I delicately phrase this; that you're involved in an illicit affair with another . . . female."

"What?" Miriam couldn't believe her ears. It was the single most preposterous charge she'd ever heard. "Where in God's name did you hear that?"

"I'm afraid I have to ask you, Miss Brooks, is it true?" He studied her, his Adam's apple bobbing again, and waited for her reply. The other two men stared at her with the intensity of prison guards. The heat of the spotlight seemingly shed upon her in the small office made her sweat, not knowing what else they had allegedly discovered.

"No, it's not true. Of course not. Where did you get that—"

"Are you living with her?"

"Well . . . yes . . . I mean, yes, I am," her voice weakened.

"May we ask why you live together?"

"I don't know that I have the right to discuss her business—"

"We believe," the official interrupted, raising his hand like a stop sign, "that it would be in your best interest."

"She needed a place to stay," Miriam began, the guilt clutching her by the throat as she told things she swore she never would. "Her fiancé was . . . harassing her . . . and beating her up, and she needed a place to stay. That's all."

The room grew quiet, and Miriam could hear someone laughing outside in the auditorium. She wished it was her laughing, anything—anything except sitting here being accused of something of which she knew nothing.

One of the men standing bent down to whisper into the ear of the interrogator. A knock fell upon the door. The official told the person to enter. He stuck his head inside the room, and upon realizing it was occupied, excused himself and closed the door.

"May I ask," Miriam said, "where you got this misinformation."

The official didn't answer, but looked at the man who whispered in his ear.

"I demand to know!" Miriam said. If they could waste her time by calling her into the office to defend something she knew no more about than the wino on the street corner, she wanted answers, just like them, and she wanted them now. "I deserve to know. This is a serious charge."

"Yes it is," the official agreed. Again, he looked to his associate who nodded.

"Do you know a man named Thomas Jenkins?"

Miriam had never known Tommy's full name, so she wasn't sure if he was who the man spoke of. But suddenly it made sense; not that the shock value of hearing his name held any less weight. She felt her face cracking into a zillion pieces.

"Tommy?" she said.

"Yes, you know him?"

"If it's the same one . . . yes, I do. Did he really say that?"

"Miss Brooks, how would we know of any Agnes Brown unless this man made the charge?"

How dare they? she thought, considering all the work she'd done and the exemplary, sterling character she exhibited among them. And Tommy? Was he that desperate? How dare he make such an accusation. Just because his former fiancée lived with her, how could he possibly draw those conclusions?

She had him pegged. He was a weasel, a worm, a walking . . . scum of the earth, that nig——— ! she stopped herself from thinking it.

Arriving home, she busied herself with something, anything, so she wouldn't think about it. She hoped to see Tommy once more. Just one more time, Lord. She wanted to hear those accusations. Let him say that to her face. It sounded a bit hysterical. She and Agnes sleeping together like lovers. Since she moved in, Agnes had slept in the den Miriam prepared for her, and Miriam slept in her own bedroom. She'd never so much as seen the woman naked.

She thought of calling Mother. She wanted to tell somebody. Her outrage wouldn't permit her to remain calm. Reconsidering it, she

didn't need to bother Mother with something as petty and inconsequential. She dialed Velma, whose line rang and rang.

She started cleaning her living room, picking up dust and dirt,
wiping the coffee table, and straightening the doilies on the sofas
and chairs when Agnes walked in. She must have known Miriam
was enraged by her curt hello, and abrupt, jerky movements in the
living room as she bent over on the floor, and cleaned the room
with a frantic abandon.

Miriam was glad she was home. Who better to tell than Agnes.
While she related the story, Agnes began undressing. She climbed
out of her uniform, and in her brassiere, slip, and garters, threw the
white uniform into her room. She slipped out of her shoes and
white polish marks stained her heels. As Miriam told her the punch
line, the reason she'd been called in, Agnes peeled the stockings
from her legs, and flexed her toes. She was listening to Miriam's
account, and responded with a "Hmm hmm" here and there, but
didn't react as Miriam expected.

As Miriam wound up the story, punctuating it with the name of
the person who had made this outrageous allegation, Agnes never
so much as blinked an eye. She shrugged her shoulders, balled her
clothes up, tossed them into the hamper, and headed for the
bathroom.

Miriam stood in the center of the living room, wondering why
Agnes was acting so strangely. She wanted a reaction. She needed
corroboration that she was not committing or living in sin, that her
character was upright, and she thought Agnes might be as discon-
certed as she was.

She crossed the room, and knocked on the closed bathroom door.
Agnes told her to enter, and Miriam asked point-blank for a
response. Agnes claimed it sounded like something Tommy would
do. He was mad that she moved in with Miriam, and frustrated
because he had no address. He couldn't go by Harlem Hospital
anymore to harass her.

Miriam nodded her head, about to close the door, leaving her
roommate to her privacy, when Agnes shed one final ray of light on
the situation. He probably suspected as much, she said, and she
couldn't blame him. When he met her, she was living with another
woman, long ago and far away. Therefore, it didn't seem farfetched;
he probably assumed she was sleeping with Miriam. She told
Miriam there were a lot of things Miriam didn't know about her
past, but one day, she'd tell her. Okay, Miriam replied, baffled by

Agnes's nonchalant admission to having lived with a woman. The idea of women lovers wasn't strange. But in Agnes's case—craving men the way she did—it never would have occurred to Miriam. She tried not to appear shocked, and suggested that Agnes start telling her some of these things she didn't know about her. Velma's and Louise's warnings of *Be careful* and *Watch yourself* rang through echo chambers in her head.

12

"**V**ito, you sure I look okay—"

"Stunning as always." He embraced her, planting a kiss on her forehead. "More beautiful than the day I met you."

"This is no time for romancing," Louise said, steadying her hands. "I'm too nervous."

"Then you need a drink." Vittorio snapped his fingers to summon a servant. "What will you have?"

"I can't drink now. What will your mother say, smelling liquor on my breath before dinner? Are they here yet?"

"They arrived yesterday. I told them all about you, but I didn't tell them the news."

"When will you tell them?"

"At dinner."

"Where are they?"

"Upstairs. They'll be down in a moment. Relax. I'm going to check with my cook and see how the dinner's coming. Have a seat."

Vittorio headed toward the kitchen, unable to confide to Louise that he needed to follow his own advice. Regardless of his father's reaction—which he expected to be the worst—he was proceeding with his marriage plans. Not that it would hurt to receive his father's blessing; his mother, he knew, would approve.

Lucia di Bolognese loved her only son without reservations. He did nothing wrong in her eyes, and she, knowingly or unknowingly, singularly embodied the gap that was ever increasing between himself and Papa.

From day one, Vincenzo said no, Vittorio rebutted with yes; Vincenzo thought high, Vittorio contradicted with low. It established a locked pattern, a cycle they'd spin around in and perpetuate throughout their lives.

Vittorio attributed their triangular dynamics to the mere fact that Mama loved him, maybe a bit too much. Vincenzo loved his wife, but the two men couldn't love—not really *love* one another because, Vittorio was convinced, Vincenzo acted insanely jealous of his wife's overindulgence of the boy from the time he could walk.

He understood and accepted early on that he was destined to give his life to the family olive oil business. The export commerce didn't bother Vittorio nearly as much as Papa dictating his every breath and move.

He thought he'd be doing them both a favor by attending Princeton in America. It would allow him autonomy; their line of division the Atlantic Ocean and then some. Papa could have his wife all to himself and Vittorio could fulfill obligations to the family trade. But it didn't work out that way—no, that was too easy for Papa.

Lucia was commissioned by her son to intervene on his behalf. She didn't care for America any more than her husband; Italy was their universe. But she read between the lines of her son's request, and interpreted his wish beyond that of a young scholar wanting to attend the university of his choice. He needed to establish independence, and that she encouraged.

Vincenzo conjured up a litany of reasons why the boy shouldn't go. He was spoiled rotten, Vincenzo insisted, and Lucia was giving into another of his whims. First, he wanted to be a priest, then a movie star, and now he wanted to attend Princeton? No, he could do the family good by staying put right where he was; end of story.

But Vittorio couldn't give up on his New World vision. Student and mother agreed that the son was made up of the same components which constituted the father. The fruit doesn't fall far from the tree, Lucia insisted, and they joined forces to gently win him over.

Vittorio actually thought Papa jealous of the adventures awaiting him down the winding road of life. Once a dapper, stunning young man himself, Papa envied the prospect of a son pioneering on another continent, planting roots. He didn't accept the story that Vincenzo deplored America, since he had never been there. Who could dislike America? Papa shivered at the thought of Vittorio gaining independence, escaping his authority. New York teemed with beautiful, eligible women. Had he made his millions during his youth, given similar opportunity, Papa would have been the socialite playboy he suspected Vittorio would one day be. The biggest flirt this side of the Tyrrhenian Sea, he didn't have the outlets or the strength to exercise it; Mama substantially cooled him off, casting a watchful eye upon him.

And how often in one lifetime could Papa reiterate that *he* had earned their wealth, and *he* alone. He hadn't had the opportunities available to Vittorio, and wanted him to get his hands a little—no, a lot—dirty with the business, rather than gallivant around an Ivy League campus, in expensive clothes and drive up to New York on weekends.

They hadn't come downstairs yet—he knew Papa was postponing it as long as possible—and Vittorio was in no hurry. He anticipated Papa's refusal of permission to marry this strange woman with no family and no money. And he felt prepared, his fangs sharpened. So what if the old man refused. Vittorio had done rather nicely by channeling his inheritance into sound investments. He could count on Mama, he knew, but seeing how nervous and intimidated Luisa was at meeting them, he couldn't tell her the whole story, not then. She was timorous enough, and one of them had to be composed, confident, even headstrong, if necessary.

Louise parked herself on a lounge sofa in Vittorio's study. Crossing her legs, she scanned the titles of classic books on the shelves. The fireplace was lit, warding off the November chill, and she concentrated on the jerky flames which normally soothed her. She was unable to sit still. She rose, paced the floor, and constantly checked her appearance in the lavender Art Deco mirror. She fussed with her hair and picked pieces of lint from the formal, beaded gown Vittorio had bought her especially for this evening.

She couldn't wait to meet Mrs. di Bolognese. Vittorio assured her she'd be the daughter Mama had never had. As the youngest in her family, Louise had grown accustomed to being babied and looked after. Unable to be with her family, she looked forward to having a mother-in-law who would coddle her until she could be with Mother again. It was hardly the same, but it was better than having nobody.

The French doors to the study opened, and Vittorio entered, escorting a man to whom he bore a striking resemblance. In black tuxedo, the older man was every bit as dashing as the younger version of himself, and Louise could tell what Vittorio would look like in middle age. Vittorio led him by the arm, and with formal gestures, Vincenzo di Bolognese bowed before Louise and smiled. She found his receding gray hairline virile and distinguished. Vittorio introduced him, speaking English for Louise; Italian for his father.

"*Parla lei italiano?*"

"No, Papa," Vittorio said, and turned to Louise. "He thinks the whole world should speak Italian."

"Where's your mother?" Louise asked.

"She's coming. Ah, there she is. *Mama, venite, venite! Mama, questa e Luisa, la fiore bella mia.* Luisa, this is Mama."

"I'm so pleased to meet you, Mrs. di Bolognese." Louise extended her hand, and Lucia shook it half-heartedly, eyeing Louise head to toe. Her hands clasped, she looked to her husband, then to her son. The fleeting moments were awkward.

"*Quando mangiare, Vittorio?*" Lucia said to her son.

"*Un momento, Mama.*"

A formally attired servant appeared at the door. "Dinner is served."

The guests moved toward the dining room, where a golden brown turkey, as centerpiece, rested upon a table that sat eight. Above them hung a crystal chandelier that swayed in the wind from the open window, and its melody made Louise think of chimes. Turkey was the only American entree. Piping-hot dishes whose looks and aromas were unmistakably Italian, made up the bulk of the menu. A calla lily sat across the plate beside Vittorio's. Louise forced smiles and grins, letting the elderly couple pass before her. She tugged Vittorio's elbow. "I don't think your mother likes me," she said, biting her lip.

"Of course she does," he said, cupping her shoulder. "She just has to know you first."

"But, Vito, she didn't say a word to me."

"Luisa, you know how mothers are when they're about to lose their sons to another woman. American, Italian; it's the same everywhere. Now don't worry."

Four servants stood erect and lifeless. Upon a silent cue, they stepped forward. One hand behind their backs, they slid the chairs outward with gloved hands. Seating the guests, they moved one step back, another to the side, and clicked their heels. Uniformly, they executed a right turn, then disappeared. Louise was fascinated by the precision of their movements.

"Papa will say grace first," Vittorio said.

They bowed their heads and closed their eyes—all save Lucia who watched Louise out of the corner of her eye. Vincenzo mumbled in Italian, and after they had blessed themselves with the sign of the cross, the meal began. Vittorio informed his guests that he would act as interpreter for the flow of dinner conversation.

"*E bellissima, Vittorio, bellissima,*" Papa began.

"Papa says you're beautiful," Vittorio translated, disarmed by Papa's admission.

"Thank you, sir," Louise said.

"The word is *molto grazie.* Say *molto grazie* to Papa."

"*Molto grazie.*"

Vincenzo spoke again, and again, his son translated. "Papa wants to know how you can live in a city as big and complicated as New York?"

"Well," Louise said, "I was born in New York. And while you're here, I'd love to show you around. Is this your first time in the city?"

"He says yes and he hopes his last."

"How long do you plan to stay, Mrs. di Bolognese?" Louise turned to Lucia.

"Mama says they might go back after the Christmas holidays. It depends on how she feels. She has arthritis, you know."

"Well," Louise said, "in a month, I can show you a good time. I'll show you all around."

"Papa would like that very much. He'd go anywhere with a pretty girl." Vittorio couldn't believe Papa's charm, but welcomed it nonetheless.

Louise laughed partly from pleasure, partly from anxiety. She could tell that Lucia had once been a beautiful woman. She was dressed in dark colors, her gray hair pulled back in a bun, a string of pearls around her neck, worry lines gathered about her eyes—Vittorio's eyes. Sipping her soup, staring fixedly at the bowl, she dined as if alone.

"Mama and Papa," Vittorio said, grabbing Louise's hand for support, he couldn't stand the tension any longer. "I'm pleased you could be here to spend this holiday with me . . . rather, with us. I have some wonderful news to tell you, and now's the best time while we break bread."

"What're you saying to them?" Louise whispered. "Why're they looking at us like that?"

"Shhh! *cara mia.* I'm telling them our plans."

"Not now, Vittorio. It's too early."

"Sweetheart, I know you mean well, but they're my parents and I know them." He turned to his parents. "For years, you both haunted me about getting married and settling down to raise a family. Luisa has agreed to be my bride. I would like to marry her with your blessing."

Vincenzo's face lit up. He mumbled something congratulatory to his son, and dabbed his mouth with the linen napkin. Rising from his chair, he went to Louise. They embraced, pecking each other's cheeks. Yes, Vittorio thought bitterly, you'll embrace her, but not me, old man, your own son. Vincenzo spoke again.

"Papa says you will be the daughter he never had. He welcomes you into our family with pride."

Vincenzo resumed his seat, and proposed a toast to the bride and groom. Everyone raised their glass of red wine—everyone except Lucia. Oblivious to the festive atmosphere, she sipped her minestrone.

"Mama, what's the matter? I thought you'd be happy." Vittorio gestured dramatically with his hands.

"Happy?" It was the third time Louise had heard her speak.

"Yes. We've decided to get married in December while you and Papa are here with us, before you sail back."

"Then I'm happy," she said, communicating compromise and defeat with her hands, the tone of her voice.

Vittorio and Louise exchanged glances. "I told you she didn't like me," Louise said.

"Oh, but she does, *cara mia*. She does."

"How long have you known this girl?" Lucia said in an even, controlled voice.

"Long enough to know I want to spend my life with her."

"Is she Italian?"

"What's she saying, Vito?" Louise mumbled without looking at Lucia.

"Of course, Mama. Just look at her; can't you tell?"

"She doesn't look it to me," Lucia said. "She's a gypsy or something."

"What did she say?" Louise wanted to know.

"She said she's a little surprised we're getting married so soon." He laughed nervously.

"No, Vito. She didn't say that."

"Just like that," Lucia said calmly. "You don't ask Papa or me first? Who is she, this woman? Where's she from? Who's her family? How do you know she's not marrying you for money? I don't trust these Americans. They worship money."

"Mama says that maybe we should wait—"

"Since when, Vittorio, since when do you make this decision to marry an American? Huh? Have you buried me and Papa already? Don't we have anything to say about anything anymore? What makes you think we'd be happy to see you get married in a foreign country? To a stranger, no less."

"Mama, what is it you want exactly?" Vittorio asked, consciously maintaining a cool countenance, not wanting Luisa to be further upset. If she hadn't been there, he'd be throwing a tantrum by now. "You complain when I date a different girl every week. You tell me I'm spoiled, I need to settle down, take a wife, have babies, take responsibility. Well, now I'm doing it. Mama, you must give me your blessing."

"How can I give you my blessing when I don't even know this woman? She's a stranger. She's American. Is she Catholic? Have you asked her that, Vittorio? Does she take Holy Communion? You ask for my blessing. I don't even know if this woman believes in God. To me, she believes in money. I may be old, but I'm not stupid. And, she's no more Italian than this cooked bird." She turned to Louise and smiled graciously.

"Mama says maybe she's upset for nothing. She—"

"Vito, why're you lying to me? Your mother isn't happy about our plans. Look how she stares at me."

Louise had lost her appetite. She wanted to excuse herself, run into the bathroom, and vomit. Even better, leave this beautiful house until Lucia was gone. She sympathized with Vittorio and his gallant efforts to handle a situation out of his control, juggling personalities and translations, yet trying to keep her at ease in the face of the opposition. She loved him for that.

"Mama, you're making Luisa nervous. Please be nice. Please? For my sake?"

Vittorio didn't understand what was happening at the table. Prepared for Mama's blessing and Papa's opposition, he was baffled. Their responses were confusing him. Since Papa obviously liked Luisa so much, he wondered why the old man wasn't discouraging his wife's objections. He's doing it—or not doing it—to spite me, Vittorio was convinced.

He'd never seen Mama behave so rudely, and now when he most

needed her characteristic charm and support, she was abandoning him. No matter how she felt, in his home she had to speak to his *cara*, make her feel welcome, and not shame and humiliate him. Luisa, whenever she looked at Mama, gave him the impression she wanted to get out—out of the dinner, out of the house, and possibly out of the engagement.

"Mama, talk to Luisa; she's a very nice girl. Please, Mama, for me." As he made the request, he saw Papa smile furtively, and wondered why he'd remained silent throughout the bitter exchange.

Lucia turned to Louise. "You look lovely in that dress, like an angel," she said through Vittorio.

"*Grazie*," Louise said, and held her breath, noticing the woman wasn't finished.

"Tell me, Luisa," Lucia asked through her son, "what do you do?"

"I'm a secretary," Louise lied, as she had to Vittorio. "I work for an insurance company."

"What part of Italy does your family come from, Rome?"

As Vittorio translated, he knew Mama's reference to Rome was snobbish; a put-down that he hoped went over Luisa's head.

Louise repeated her contrived background of the young girl who lost her parents and was placed in an orphanage, at which Lucia winced as she wiped her mouth. Louise preferred talking to Papa. The distinguished, gray-haired gentleman in his tuxedo hadn't stopped smiling at her since they met, and Louise was becoming quickly bored with Lucia's conversation which was, if anything, an interview. Men adored her; it was the women she always had to worry about.

"You have no family?" Lucia asked, and managed a perfunctory smile.

"No," Louise replied.

"We're going to be her family," Vittorio jumped in to save Luisa who, he saw, was sinking in the quicksand of highly personal questions.

"So, you've made your decision? You're going to marry this girl? And, Papa and I have nothing to say about it?"

"Mama, listen to yourself. Doesn't this sound familiar? Your own parents forbade you to marry Papa and leave Bologna. And look how your marriage turned out. Besides, Papa approves; it's only you who doesn't."

"Is this girl in trouble?"

"No, Mama—"

"How much does she want? I'll pay her. What does she want?"

"Mama, we love each other."

"All right, then. I wash my hands of the whole thing. Mary, Mother of Christ in heaven. Look what this depraved country is doing to my son."

"What's she saying now?"

"She's just a little nervous. She doesn't think we've known each other long enough. But, don't worry; it won't change a thing—"

"Even so," Lucia chimed in, "when I married your father, I was sure of two things: he's Italian and Catholic. Vittorio, my son, you will forgive my behavior this evening. May God's angels in heaven look down upon me with mercy. But a mother knows things she cannot explain. And suddenly, I have a terrible headache; I must retire. Papa, come." She wiped her mouth, and rose from the table. Taking her husband's hand, she turned. "Whether you and Papa love her, I won't give this marriage my blessing. God as my witness, there's something strange about her."

She turned to Louise and, forcing a smile, shook her hand, bowed, and bade her good night. To her son she said, "*Buona notte, figlio mio. Mi scusi.*"

13

Through Elvira's bedroom window, Velma watched the funeral procession, a caterpillar in mourning, slither languidly down the gray avenue. Late December rain showers fell, washing debris from the gutters into rushing streams. An unprecedented turnout of Harlem dwellers crowded the sidewalks; women sniffled, dabbing their eyes and noses with handkerchiefs, men removed their hats and bowed gracefully and reverently with a sense of loss. A horse-drawn carriage, not unlike those transporting the remains of deceased presidents, was the focal point of the dreary parade and bore the floral-wreathed casket of Harlem's divine goddess, Miss Florence Mills. The horses' hooves clopped against the pavement, and the carriage wheels squeaked as they turned. The steady, haunting beat of a distant bass drum pounded against the rain.

After returning home two months before from a successful European tour, Miss Mills was stricken without warning. A clutching, sudden death. The star of successful Broadway shows—Blake and Sissle's *Blackbirds* and *Dixie to Broadway*—she had captured the imaginations and loyalties of fans as never before. Her name was a household word, and her achievements brought hope and encouragement to her people. She gave them pride, a sense of accomplishment they had never dreamed possible; she broke racial and sexual barriers, allowing Race people, Race women in particular, to reach for the stars. And now, their brightest star had fallen. All that remained were the memories, the legacy, the phenomenal funeral procession, unlike any the community had ever witnessed, winding its sullen way down the broad avenue.

The horses halted, snorted, and bared their teeth. Countless black umbrellas bobbed above the mourners', spectators', and marchers' heads with piercing melancholy. From behind a window shade, Velma watched the procession with a tear-streaked face. The umbrellas struck her as an army of defeated mushrooms. Raindrops, manipulated by the wind, fell in a slant, tapping light rhythms upon the umbrellas and window pane. "You all right?" Miriam's voice distracted her.

"Yeah, I'm okay." She sniffled, and blew her nose into a shredded tissue. "How is she?"

"Sleeping peacefully for a change." Miriam's tone was whispery and complacent.

"You think—"

"No, she's breathing all right. I've been checking her pulse."

"Oh, Miriam," Velma broke down, "what're we going to do?" She collapsed in her sister's arms. Sobbing uncontrollably, the tears splattered upon Miriam's blouse. "I don't want to live without Mother."

"Shhh, shhh," Miriam consoled her, patting her back, and smoothing out Velma's hair. "Let her have some peace and quiet." She rubbed away her sister's tears. "Don't watch that funeral. It'll only make you feel worse."

Miriam pulled the shade closed, and walked Velma from the bedroom into the kitchen. Sitting her in a chair, she took the one opposite, and waited patiently for Velma to pull herself together. Miriam looked around the room at the stove, the sink, the basin, the hair pomades, the dyes, the hot comb, the special chair used by the customers. "Are you okay?"

"Yeah, Miriam. I'm all right."

Velma wrapped her arms around her shoulders, and rocked herself in the chair. She and Miriam communicated with their eyes, not a word spoken. A stroke was the medical diagnosis for what was killing their mother. But they knew it was really a broken heart. They had watched Mother waste away, day by day, month by month, and there was nothing they could do.

Miriam wanted, like Velma, to let go, release it, break down and have a well-deserved cry. On top of everything else, not three weeks ago, the government had released Garvey from prison on false charges of mail fraud, but deported him to Jamaica. Insiders had it that a handful of the ambitious were bucking against each other for positions of power left vacant by their leaders; 1928 looked bleak.

"She's waking up. I think Mother just said something." Velma rushed from the kitchen, her sister following behind. Entering the bedroom, Velma saw Mother tossing, her frail arms trying to move. She coughed, turning her head to the side. "Yes, Mother," she said, "can I get you something?"

Elvira raised herself with difficulty, and Velma stacked pillows, then placed them beneath her head. Kneeling at her bedside, she took her hand. "Where's Miriam?" Elvira said in a raspy voice.

"She's right here," Velma said as Miriam walked in.

"Mother, why don't you let us take you to Harlem or Bellevue? Please!" Miriam pleaded. "You don't have to give up. Come on! We're gonna dress you and take you whether—"

"Miriam . . . Miriam," Elvira replied weakly, and coughed, turning her head to the side. "I done tol' you before, the hospital can't do nothin' for me. I don't want to be in no hospital with no bunch of strangers. That ain't no easy place to be."

"But, Mother, I don't want you to—"

"Sweet chile." Elvira chuckled the faintest chuckle Velma ever heard. "It ain't about what me and you wants; it's the Lord's way—"

"Mother," Miriam interrupted, "why don't you eat something? I can make—"

"Just come on over here and sit with me. I got my girls, don't I? Velma, you listenin' to me? Velma. Stop cryin' and listen to me." She took Velma's chin and raised it lovingly, wiping the tears inching down her cheeks. "Will you promise me one thing?"

"Yes, Mother, anything."

"You is twenty-seven now. You wanted to be a writer, and God bless you, you a writer for sure. But you hold on to that fella of yours. I know I've said this over and over, but when you get older, chile, you needs a man and some young'uns in your corner. I know, 'cause I been there. And, Miriam?"

"Mother, please don't—"

"Now, just listen to what I'm gonna say first. I need you to promise me that you'll settle down too. Now, can you promise me that?"

"Yes, Mother."

"Yes, Mother, what?"

"I promise."

"All right. Now, look over there and hand me that envelope under my pocketbook, would you please?"

"You feeling any pain?" Miriam asked.

"Not so much in my body." She moved about to make herself more comfortable. "You know, I'm so tired of laying up in this here bed." She exhaled. "All my life, I ain't never spent so much time in a bed; tied down to it the way I've been these days. You got that envelope? Good. Now, this here's the checks your little sister . . ." Her mind wandered. "Wherever she is, this is what she been sendin' me every two weeks just like she promised. I want you girls to divide up my furniture and belongings, and split this here money. Louise been sendin' it, so I guess the only proper thing for somebody to do is spend it."

Louise's bedroom door had remained closed, like a shrine, for months. But as Elvira's strength had waned, and her weight dropped, she had spent more time in the bedroom where Louise no longer slept—until then, it had been off-limits.

She'd lie down in her bed, smelling her child's scent among the blanket and bed linen. When her daughter disappeared, she took not a stitch of clothing with her, and Elvira opened the closet, rummaging through the beautiful, forsaken clothes and costumes which hung, she thought, looking sad because they missed the shapely body of their owner as much as she did. She pressed the outfits against her own body, and stood before the mirror trying desperately to picture Louise in them, recalling the life and body that once filled these outfits. She perused her high school yearbook, and reread the lines beneath the photograph. While others were off to conquer the world, Louise's ambition was to marry a wealthy Prince Charming, and Elvira hoped to God she'd found him. There were her dolls and teddy bears neatly arranged on her bureau the way she left them. Elvira wished they could speak, and tell her of Louise's whereabouts. She'd had them since early childhood and they must have shared secrets. Her vanity table was buried under any number of exotic cosmetics and Parisian perfumes. Elvira sprayed the perfume throughout the house, recreating the scents Louise left behind on her way to work every night.

Elvira couldn't tell if it was a dream or if it was real. Occasionally, she heard Louise laughing down the hall, and when she got out of bed to investigate, she could swear the laughter emanated from behind the closed bedroom door. She looked in, and there was no one save the dolls and teddy bears, staring as blankly at Elvira as they always had. She closed the door, and climbed back into bed.

Sound asleep an hour later, she could have sworn she heard Louise. Again, she got up, opened her bedroom door, and there she stood, sparkling and beautiful as ever in her turquoise outfit with matching shoes and hat cocked to the side. Elvira loved that ensemble; she'd helped Louise pick it out for some mysterious date she didn't want to tell Elvira about. She half walked and ran toward her daughter; Louise's hand poised on the doorknob. When she got there, it was just the door, and pitch darkness. Elvira sat a moment, listening to the late autumn wind howl, and slap wet tree branches against the closed windows. She chuckled to herself. Louise was playing hide and seek with her. She always did it as a child. For now, she'd let the girl have her fun. Elvira was too old and exhausted to be searching her out all over the house. She'd find her first thing in the morning, probably hiding in the broom closet; her favorite spot.

The last day she spent in Louise's bedroom before retiring to her own—she'd become too debilitated, and walking around the apartment was a major accomplishment—she went through Louise's bureau drawers. There were Hollywood magazines, a few yellowing want ads with penciled leads where Louise sought work. Elvira wondered who Vittorio was. Louise was forever telling Elvira stories of folks she met at work. She found a Smalls Paradise napkin with the name Vittorio, apparently stashed away for safekeeping—she could tell by the way it was tucked deliberately in a corner of the drawer. She didn't know what it meant—a name, a street, a city. If it was a man, he sure wasn't colored with a name like that. Louise met different people every night, Elvira thought, and whoever it was, she probably met that fellow once, and he never saw her again and knew no more than Elvira where her baby was.

"Well," Elvira said to the daughters at her bedside, "all we can hope is that she's happy. Just too sad she couldn't live like a colored person."

"Passing . . ." Velma mumbled. The first novel she'd authored, about to go to press any day, was a tale of a woman passing for white. She'd gotten the idea before Louise disappeared, and shook at the thought that her story was actually being lived by a sister she might never see again.

"In so many words, she told me she was gonna do this one day," Elvira said.

"You think we'll ever see her again?" Miriam asked.

"God is good. I just wish I could see her one more time and then—"

"Mother, why don't you try and get some rest now?" Miriam suggested.

"Where I'm goin', I plan to get plenty of it."

"I think you should calm yourself down. Talking about Louise is getting you upset again. I can see it." She helped Elvira lie down, pulled the blankets, and tucked them around her shoulders. "There, now ain't that better? Velma, can I see you a minute?" She waited until they were in the kitchen before she spoke.

"How you want to divide this furniture and stuff?" Miriam asked.

"I don't know. Your apartment's bigger than mine."

"What about Louise's things?"

"Miriam, I don't know . . . I just don't know."

Velma was saddened by the state of the apartment. The kitchen which had sustained years of laughter, good times, bad times, and growing up, was now dark, the shades drawn, layers of dust collecting on everything. Mother's house had always been spotless. The house was no longer "lived in." It had already succumbed to the death that Mother herself anticipated.

"Louise! . . . Louise!" Elvira called from the bedroom. "Where's my baby? Gilbert! Gilbert! Is that you there in the kitchen? It's raining outside. Go and find the baby before she get all wet and catch cold! Tell those gals the shop is closed today. I ain't feelin' well. They come back tomorrow. Did you go get my baby like I asked you? Gilbert! You hear me talkin' to you?"

"You hear that!" Velma said. "She's calling Louise and Father . . . dear God."

"I wonder," Miriam said more to herself than to Velma, "just where she is, if she's all right." She looked to Velma, who continued rocking herself in the chair. "I wonder what Louise's doing."

On the other side of town, inside an immense Gothic cathedral, a bride walked down the red-carpeted aisle, sprinkled with petals by a flower girl. In an embroidered white satin gown with lace appliqué and pearls, Louise clutched a bouquet of calla lilies to her breast. Her painted, manicured fingers fussed with the veil covering her face, trailing down her back. The veil and gown combined formed a three-foot train which staggered haltingly behind her.

A hundred wedding guests—none of whom were family, friends or acquaintances of the bride—smiled, nodded, and sighed at the bride who inched her way timidly down the aisle. An unseen choir, tucked somewhere in the cathedral's loft, sang a hymnal march in quintet harmony. Their angelic voices caused a lump to form in Louise's throat.

At the altar, an archbishop stood with hands clasped in prayer. He was draped in lavender and white cloths of the clergy, the silver chalice before him. Dark-haired altar boys with large brown eyes carried lit candles. Ceremoniously dropping to their knees, they made a sign of the cross before a twelve-foot replica of Christ at Calvary. Louise stared at the likeness, and with each step, it sharpened into focus. A crown of authentic thorns pierced His head. Painted blood trickled down the sides of His face. His mouth twisted in agony and despair, His teary eyes were aimed toward the heavens. As she approached the altar, the fragrance of hundreds of fresh flowers awakened Louise's nostrils, and her eyes became sensitive to the flames of burning candles. She looked up at Jesus. He *seemed* to look scathingly down at her.

". . . Dearly beloved, we are gathered here, in the sight of God, to join this man and this woman in holy matrimony." The archbishop paused to cast holy water upon the couple who kneeled before him, their heads bowed. "If there is anyone here with reason why these two should not be joined together, let him speak now or forever hold his peace." His eyes shifted, scanning the faces among the pews.

It wasn't Louise's choice to be married without the honored presence of family and friends. Vittorio, with the understanding that his bride was an orphan, and without close friends, urged female acquaintances to participate as bridesmaids—all expenses paid. Though some of them—one-nighters and old flames—might have preferred to be the bride, they complied, jumping at the chance to take part in the former playboy's wedding befitting the royal family.

Louise requested Peaches to be her matron of honor. Her sole friend. The only person who knew of Louise's whereabouts. Peaches was honored at the request, crediting Little Miss Muffet Louise for landing the man she first watched from the proscenium stage at the Cotton Club. But when she understood completely, she nearly snatched the compliment back.

"I don't mind bein' your matron of honor," Peaches said. "But, you askin' for more than that, sweetie. How can you ask me to be in your wedding, when your own husband don't even know who you are? I'm sorry, but I can't pretend to be white. I'm much too colored for that. Not even for one day. Not even for you. You know what you gettin' yourself into?" Peaches said, her eyes growing angrier as she spoke. "I know thousands of folks are passin', but somehow it don't fit you. I mean, marryin' a white man who thinks you white too? Hmmm, hmmm! I don't know about that. Now, I never said I wasn't a broad who liked a little danger every now and again, but sweetie, that's a little steep, even for a broad like me; many skid marks this here body done collected. You used to have good sense. Somebody I call a broad with her head on straight. And you come and ask me this? I thought you was smart, girl. You done lost your mind?!"

"But, I was your maid of honor. I came through when you needed me," Louise shot back. "I'm not asking you to do anything but be by my side. For obvious reasons, I can't ask my sisters. Believe me, Peaches, you don't have to say anything. It's the most important day of my life, and I need to have someone close to me. Please, can't you do it just this once for me?"

Accepting Peaches's refusal to participate, Louise was forced to examine what she was doing. It occurred to her more times than she cared to remember, but she allowed herself little, if any, time to ponder it. If she let it overwhelm her, she knew she'd call the whole thing off. And how could she possibly do that to the man of her dreams? Why tamper with happiness? Didn't Mother always say that?

Dear Mother. She ached to see her, Miriam and Velma, prayed diligently for their understanding and cooperation, and hoped they would not misjudge her. But they were all happy, having found their places in life. Now Louise had found hers and needed their support more than ever. Christmas was in two weeks; the first she'd spend without her family.

She wished they were here with her, witnessing the first marriage of the second generation. The importance of it was paramount, but it also meant slitting her own throat. She'd lied enough to Vittorio and his parents, and lying wasn't her way.

She pictured Miriam in her white uniform, Velma behind the typewriter, and Mother bent over the sink. She missed them terribly and wondered how long she could take it before she reunited herself with them out of desperation. Meanwhile, kneeling at the altar with the man who would father her children, she questioned what her family was doing at this moment, uptown on a cool and rainy Saturday afternoon.

"Do you, Luisa, take this man to be your lawfully wedded husband? To have, to hold, to cherish until death do you part?" the archbishop whispered with a grave expression.

"I do."

"And do you, Vittorio, take this woman to be your lawfully wedded wife? To have, to hold, to cherish until death do you part?"

"I do."

"The ring, please."

Vittorio turned to his bride, and placed the brilliant Tiffany wedding band with its marquise-cut diamonds on her finger. Mr. and Mrs. Vincenzo di Bolognese sat in the front pew. Vincenzo beamed. Lucia was stoic.

"You are man and wife; you may kiss the bride."

Vittorio looked at the archbishop, then to Louise, then to Mama who avoided his eyes by looking away. Louise helped him lift the lace veil from her face, and, pulling her body closer to his, he kissed her. The organ struck a startling note through the pipes, and briskly, they marched up the aisle, followed by the bridal party. The ring bearer and flower girl fell into the procession behind the twelve couples, as the archbishop and altar boys descended from the altar and the choir sang.

Outside on the cathedral steps, spectators—guests and curiosity seekers alike—threw grains of rice at the newlyweds. Three bridesmaids feigned smiles and congratulatory hugs with Louise as they fussed with the trains of her gown and veil.

Vincenzo embraced Vittorio with a bear hug, and pecked him proudly on both cheeks. Turning to Louise, he showered his new daughter-in-law with wet kisses to the forehead. Lucia kept her distance, and stood erect with unfaltering pride. She said nothing, tears streaming down the slopes of her cheeks, and clutched a lace handkerchief to her red, runny nose. Vittorio and Louise attempted to kiss her, but she stepped back, turned her face away, and mumbled under her breath. Embarrassed, Louise looked away as cold drops of a hovering thunderstorm splashed upon her face. Gathering a handful of her gown with a quick sweep, she was assisted into the backseat of the limousine idling at the curb, Vittorio following closely behind, the group cheering, throwing kisses and rice.

With a grunt from the motor, the Rolls-Royce crawled into the traffic, honking its horn down the long gray avenue. Tin cans tied to the back of the fender clanked and rattled in its path, mixing contrapuntally with the slanting raindrops hitting the pavement, the sound of loose change.

BOOK FOUR

1928

POET TO PATRON

What right has anyone to say

That I

Must throw out pieces of my heart

For pay?

For bread that helps to make

My heart beat true,

I must sell myself

To you?

A factory shift's better,

A week's meagre pay,

Than a perfumed note asking

Any poems today?

—Langston Hughes

1

Chameleon, the first novel by Velma Brooks, was received with high praise by both white and Negro presses from the *New York Times* to the *New York World*. She had been published by a major house, with a moderate first printing, and the New York literati embraced Miss Brooks, poet/essayist, as a raconteur of paramount gifts. The dustcover illustration by Aaron Douglas, the author's photograph by Carl Van Vechten, the dedication to the memory of Elvira Brooks, and the acknowledgment to Zachary Rudolph moved Velma to stare countless moments at her book, telling herself that the dream lay materialized in the palms of her hands. Her elation transcended passionate sex.

One main ingredient was conspicuously missing though—Mother's hugs, kisses and praise, but she consoled herself that Mother, wherever she was in God's kingdom of heaven, beamed proudly upon her nonetheless. She could just feel it.

Her editor reassured her that she'd achieved the magic of good, clean writing. With all the distractions she encountered during the writing of the novel, Velma wondered how she ever pulled through the project at all.

Forced isolation was the first step. She struggled through passages which, in outlined notes, she'd worked out thoroughly beforehand to the minutest detail. But when she was faced with the cold indifference of a typewriter whose keys stuck, the prose and dialogue declined to spring forth, as if their maturation and deft juxtaposition had all but dissolved. As she sweated it out at the typewriter through late nights and into the early-morning hours, twirling tufts of hair around her index finger, contriving a thousand and one distractions, smoking countless cigarettes she extinguished midway through, a riveting tale and fleshed-out characterizations finally began to emerge. Life drew its first breath on the empty page. Frequently, she pushed herself away from the typewriter, closing her eyes in deep concentration. The narrative rang with more verity and plausibility than even she could tolerate, and she wanted to escape and relinquish the worlds, real and fictitious, where Negro heroines passed for white, and singlehandedly engineered their doom. Immersed in the tale-spinning techniques, she overlooked the frayed edges of her work, manifested in dangling prepositions and participles, split infinitives, and superfluous words, none of which was important until the fourth or fifth draft.

It had been weeks since she last saw Scott or Rudy.

Rudy called with congratulations, and insisted upon a celebration, thrilled that she cited him on the acknowledgment page.

For those very rave reviews in the New York presses, she didn't expect to hear from Scott. She knew Scott shared the limelight with no one, including the woman he slept with. She imagined him cringing as he read the reviews. DuBose Heyward of the *New York Herald Tribune* reviewed *Chameleon* as "a stunning debut," and stated that "Brooks, the poet has given us a first novel that marks the opening of a career well worth watching." Babette Deutsch, who critiqued it for *The Bookman*, called it "the outstanding book of the month." *Opportunity* lauded the work as "craftmanship of the highest order." And rarely did both white and Negro presses agree upon any one author.

She thought about Scott, and sorted through the jagged pieces of their relationship. There were times she wished to discard him as she did poorly composed passages in her manuscript.

He possessed cryptic powers that bordered on insidiousness which he cast over his victims like a net. With everything going for him, there were dark sides to him upon which she wanted to shed light. She continued to be stumped by the fabrication of a brother's death in lurid circumstances, and his rancorous character assassinations of his two best friends, for which he had yet to apologize.

His wrath was misdirected, Velma thought. He aimed poisoned arrows at the wrong targets. An unassembled puzzle, he searched for something or someone to piece him together. After all, he was extraordinarily brilliant and *gifted*—to use his word—and derangement and insecurity were the prices one sometimes paid. With all that near perfection, there had to be profound shortcomings. If she could ascertain the method to his madness, her diagnosis would be half the work.

Rudy and Scott were increasingly indulging in each other's company without her. It occurred to her that Rudy possibly held amorous intentions for Scott. Who could blame him? She was the last to deny Scott's magnetism. She dismissed the thought as her own insecurity and unwarranted paranoia. But she noticed Rudy, time and again, looking at Scott with eyes that only she was supposed to have for him. She tried not to give way to absurd, emotionally invoked suspicions which could rock her stability. Yet it hardly required clairvoyance to discern where friendship left off and flirtation began. Rudy exuded an energy toward Scott that he once had directed at her; an understated . . . something that Scott reciprocated. This worried her. Was Scott the hunter and Rudy the game? In her self-imposed mission to bring order and coherence to Scott's disheveled nature, the last thing she needed was competition from an outside party. Miriam had warned her about Rudy. She possessed no strategy for dealing with competition from another man. Nor did she know how to prevent it. Prevent what?

She wondered why Rudy had betrayed her to Scott, and why he had revealed their ephemeral sexual liaison. Was Rudy so desperate that he stooped to undermining her? Did he, behind her back, paint an unflattering portrait of an opportunist who slept her way into the most desirable of social circles? She didn't calculate Rudy as such, but then he did leak confidences that ricocheted back to haunt her. Then there was the Brooklyn Bridge picnic.

When the two men had embraced each other as if she weren't there, she felt reduced to an intruder eavesdropping on an intimate moment. The searingly vivid image was one she couldn't dismiss. If there existed an implicitness in that embrace, she had no way of telling. Time, and only time, did, which is what she placed between herself and her gentlemen friends; time, space, and her hermetic concentration on writing *Chameleon*.

Seated on the downtown subway, she couldn't fathom why Mrs. Vanderpool had summoned her to the penthouse. Their relationship, thus far, had proved productive, and she thought it one of the wisest moves of her career. If she held a job, she couldn't be nearly as constructive or able to complete ongoing projects. She'd still be writing *Chameleon* at night and on weekends if Mrs. Vanderpool hadn't paid the bills. What a godsend! She'd heard a tome of horror stories regarding patrons and their selfish, unreasonable demands on writers, the oblique manner in which they operated, throwing around their weight and power in ways that benefited neither party. She and Rudy were lucky. They only heard from the woman monthly, in their mailboxes, her illegible signature scribbled across the check. That's the way they wanted it; low profile, no interference with the artistic endeavor. As long as she sent the money, they continued to produce, and hopefully, grow. Infrequently, she called for updates, status reports on current projects, just as the contract outlined.

Today, however, the old woman had called and said she wanted to speak with her. It wasn't the words, but the urgency in her voice that Velma recalled, not knowing what to expect when she arrived. Maybe she wanted to pan Velma's novel, as she had panned Rudy's. And, her line of defense was clearly delineated, taking shape in her head as she rode the subway. If the woman wanted to assault her contribution, Velma wasn't about to retreat.

"My dear," Mrs. Vanderpool said, characteristically perched upon her thronelike chair, sipping a cup of tea. "You should feel most accomplished with this work."

"Excuse me, Mrs. Vanderpool? My thoughts are somewhere else today." She was wondering where Scott and Rudy were— particularly, if they were together.

"Your book, my dear, the book. You've written one of the finest this year."

"Thank you. I'm glad you're pleased."

"Indeed I am. And you?"

"Yes, very much," Velma said, distracted, her thoughts everywhere except the penthouse.

"You have an unorthodox way of expressing enthusiasm."

"Just a lot on my mind, I guess." Velma shrugged.

"Well, if it's any consolation, I'm certain your dear mother is happier than she's ever been. My understanding is that the afterworld is a lot more promising than we'd like to think. I lost my mother as a young woman too." She leaned forward and squeezed Velma's hand. "I understand."

"That's very kind."

"Tell me," Mrs. Vanderpool said, withdrawing her frail, liver-spotted hand. "Is it true as you've written it in your book?"

"True?" She couldn't possibly mean Louise.

"Does that kind of thing really happen in New York or is it just an extension of your vast imagination?"

"The story and characters are imagination, but the situation is quite real." If the old woman was suggesting Louise, Velma had nothing to say. Purportedly, she had ears and eyes all over New York; no telling what she might know. Velma hadn't told Scott or Rudy, and certainly, she wasn't about to confide family business to Mrs. Vanderpool.

"My word. How positively fascinating! What will people think of next?"

They sipped tea, simultaneously glaring at each other through silence. Mrs. Vanderpool set the cup and saucer upon the table beside her. From her bosom, she produced a key, and swung it in Velma's face like a pendulum. "Do you know what this is?"

"A key."

"But to what?" Mrs. Vanderpool was smiling.

"I have no idea." She was in no mood for guessing games. Hopefully, the woman would proceed to the reason she'd been summoned.

"How does owning a roadster with leather seats sound to you?"

"For me?" Velma gasped.

"Can you drive?"

"Yes, but—"

"Well, it's settled. I promised you that if our liaison was fruitful, I could furnish you an automobile."

"But, Mrs. Vanderpool—"

"Please," she interrupted. "Call me Godmother."

"But, Mrs.—"

"Remember, I'm your fairy godmother. I wave my magic wand and, presto! I make life easier for my children. Is there a problem?"

"No, I guess—"

"Then, it's settled."

"Don't you think—"

"Please, Miss Brooks. I'm an old lady who derives happiness from giving gifts and pleasures to her children. Surely you won't deny me this pleasure."

"I'm at a loss for words."

She had plenty to say, all of which would have offended the old woman. She didn't mind the "gifts"—who would?—but Velma feared that a price tag came with them. She didn't feel she was selling herself or jeopardizing her integrity, but the woman, she thought, gave too much, and she wondered about her anticipated return. It caused her the discomfort of the consumer sinking deeper into debt with the creditor. And how, when, where, what, and how much she wanted in return for her free money and "gifts," Velma didn't know. She couldn't sell herself and reputation down the river, yet the temptation was relentless. She imagined it was how Eve felt, picking the apple from the tree.

"It's no secret your godmother enjoys having her way."

"Thanks again," she said, thrilled to get an automobile, but not letting on. "You're very kind, Mrs. Vanderpool."

"I've asked you not to call me that."

"If you insist."

"I do."

2

"Great dinner, Rudy."

"Thanks, Scott." Rudy rose from a squatting position on the floor and carried two empty plates back to the kitchen.

"I didn't know you cooked so well," Scott said, wiping the corners of his mouth with a napkin.

"What?" Rudy yelled. "I can't hear you from in here!"

"I said," Scott shouted, "I didn't know you could cook." He lowered his voice as Rudy reentered the room, carrying a bottle of cognac.

"There's plenty you don't know about me," Rudy said.

"Perhaps. But, I never would've figured a bohemian like yourself for a good cook." Scott picked his teeth with a thumbnail. "Usually, you guys throw a meal together with a can of sardines, no?"

"C'mon, Scott, I'm not quite so bohemian anymore." Rudy gave himself a once-over, surveying his clothes. "This is what happens when people like me are influenced by the likes of you."

"You learned how to cook because of me?"

"Don't be funny. But, I picked up this bottle of cognac especially for you. Hope you like it."

"Hmmmm, let me see," Scott said, studying the label. "I've had better."

"I don't doubt it."

"Actually, I had something different in mind."

Scott unfolded his wallet, produced a marijuana cigarette, and slid it across his upper lip as if he were sniffing a Havana cigar. "You remember this, don't you?"

"Every time I see the Brooklyn Bridge."

Rudy couldn't tell Scott how many times he had relived that night, or the frequency with which he dreamed about him, or that Scott was the constant subject of his masturbatory fantasies. Nowadays, Rudy couldn't look at other men and a few months ago stopped picking them up and bringing them home.

The one time he tried dispersing the spell which held him captive, he brought home a white, Yale-educated, athletic type who was slumming around Harlem as Rudy headed home. Their eyes met, they smiled, and Rudy noticed the pink carnation pinned to his lapel. The pink carnation was a clandestine code which said, for those in the know, *I am, are you?* He'd never been with a white guy before and embarked upon it as a new adventure.

They tumbled and rolled and grunted in primal lust, and Rudy imagined Scott was his partner. Halfway through the act, he stopped. He couldn't go through with it, and regretfully asked his friend to leave; furious with himself for wasting this beautifully Nordic creature whom he'd probably never see again, but would want somewhere down the line, without knowing where to find him. Perplexed, the man got dressed, left his telephone number, and headed for the door. Before stepping over the threshold, he stopped, turned, scratched his head, and asked, "Who's Scott?" Rudy didn't understand. "You called me Scott while we were . . . you know. My name's Julian." Rudy apologized, embarrassed by his slip, and promised to call, knowing he wouldn't.

A week. That's how long it took. For seven days he groped through life, fighting the urge to ask Scott to dinner. Now that he was there, and the preliminaries were out of the way, he mused upon subtle maneuvers to seduce him. His morals, as they pertained to Velma . . . well, libido was taking over for the moment, and he made no excuses.

"Is the Brooklyn Bridge the last place we smoked together?" Scott laughed.

"I believe it is."

"Well, hopefully, you've improved your gagging technique."

"I know. Velma and I choked our guts out, which reminds me, have you read her latest book?"

"Can't say I have." Scott lit the cigarette.

"I haven't finished it yet, but it's absolutely wonderful."

"Is that right?" Scott sucked in a lungful of smoke, held his breath a few seconds, and spoke through his nose. "What's the title?"

"C'mon, Scott, you know all about it," Rudy said, convinced he was full of shit. Scott just never wanted to give it up. "How could you not know?"

"Seriously, I don't." I have more important things to do, he thought.

"Shame on you. It's called *Chameleon* and, I might add, it's quite possibly one of the best novels this year." C'mon, Scott, give it up.

"The year isn't over yet."

"Doesn't matter. Our friend has produced an original, trenchant work and frankly, it's a hard act to follow. Haven't you spoken to her lately?"

"No, I haven't." He passed the cigarette to Rudy. "I've been busy with my novel too, you know."

"Don't you think congratulations are in order?" Rudy inhaled the smoke.

"Why should I congratulate her if I haven't read it? Bit premature, wouldn't you say?" He took the cigarette back from Rudy.

"She deserves it just for getting published."

"I don't agree."

"Why haven't you spoken with her?"

"I guess we need time and space apart right now. You know how that is." Take a hint, Rudy.

"Can't say I do. She supports your work. No reason why you can't support hers."

"Have you seen her lately?" Scott was bored with this conversation.

"No," Rudy said. "But the minute I read the reviews, I called her immediately. She seems to be doing fine."

"Good," Scott said. "Now that I know, I don't have to call myself, do I?"

Scott couldn't figure him out. He felt certain that Rudy was sexually attracted to him, but feigned naïveté. As long as Rudy maintained a safe distance, he didn't care. Let the homosexual indulge his deviate fantasy; just make sure it didn't cross the line into reality. He wasn't interested.

What threw him was Rudy's ambivalence. He seemed to ache for Scott, but then he spoke on Velma's behalf. He acted like her defense counsel or watchdog. If I don't want to see Velma these days, that's enough; it's my business, Rudy. Now, bloody butt out, he thought.

Scott wanted the literary high Velma was floating on to pass over.

He couldn't stand her flaunting the critics' hyperbole in his face. And he remained disgruntled at her feelings for Rudy, distrustful of her motivations.

Sitting in this ghastly excuse of an apartment, Scott wondered what the hell Rudy wanted from him. He generally thought himself quick to pick up on seductive schemes. He'd been pursued enough. However, the signals were inconsistent.

He pondered the sincerity of Rudy's concern for Velma, and decided, looking at Rudy looking at him, to flirt just a little. Test the water.

"You know," Rudy said, chuckling. "Sometimes, your stubbornness makes me want to just wrap my hands around your throat."

"If you want to wrap your hands around something, you could start with my shoulders. There's a year's worth of tension sitting in there."

Rudy walked over in stockinged feet, extended the cigarette to Scott, and took hold of his shoulders. "Can I ask you a personal question?" Rudy said.

"What is it?"

"It's about Velma."

"What about her?" Scott closed his eyes, and tilted his head backward. "That feels bloody marvelous. Could you press your fingers harder . . . against . . . oh yeah, that's it."

"Do you love her?"

"Who?"

"Don't be a wise-ass."

"Yes, I suppose if one could make any sense out of the past two years or so, I imagine one could call it love."

"You're not sure," Rudy paused.

"Yes, I'm sure."

"Well then, why—"

"C'mon, Rudy. Massage my shoulders first, and I'll answer any questions you may have."

Rudy moved his hands from Scott's shoulders to his biceps, across his chest, and back again. His head was tilted back toward Rudy; his closed eyes and inviting mouth faced him head on. "Why don't you lie down," Rudy suggested. "You'd be more comfortable."

Scott lay down and Rudy took the extinguished cigarette from his fingers. Kneeling on the floor, he massaged Scott's thigh—*how Freudian*, he thought—and applied intricate thumb work on his muscles. He concentrated on the tight calf, then reached down to the balls of Scott's stockinged feet, and sneaked a peek at Scott's serene face. His hands moved back to the calf, then to the thigh, and the temptation dizzied him. He suspected Scott was flirting with him again, but didn't know how far he should or shouldn't go. Massaging his body as he lay there limply spread-eagled on the floor sufficed for now. Studying the perfection of his sculptured features from that angle, he listened to Scott's breaths, which came long and easy, and Rudy thought he'd fallen asleep.

He wanted to stop, he was getting aroused, but his hands continued to move with a mobility of their own. The pacing of his own breathing changed pattern, and he didn't know if Scott felt his hands trembling. For years, he had imagined a scenario like this, with Scott all to himself and Velma somewhere else, and yet he was blocked, or afraid, he couldn't say which. An opportunity this golden didn't shine very often, and lured by the marijuana, the setting and the momentum, he crawled around to the upper part of Scott's body, leaned over, his face hovering above Scott's, and bent forward. His lips brushed soft kisses across Scott's forehead, his eyelids, the bridge of his nose, his lips. Scott jumped up and pushed him away.

"Rudy, what're you doing?" He stood, and wiped his mouth with a sleeve.

"You know what I'm doing," Rudy said, without a trace of remorse.

"Well, not with me you don't." He grabbed his shoes and shoved his feet into them.

"Scott, why can't you be honest?"

"About what?"

"You wanted me to touch you; admit it."

"Rudy, I've made it very clear that I don't like you that way," Scott said, trembling. "You just want to imagine something that's not there."

"You seemed to enjoy it." Rudy noticed him shaking. "What're you afraid of?"

"Could you get my jacket? I must be going."

"Scott," Rudy said with a nervous chuckle. "Why didn't you stop me when I first kissed you? Does it have anything to do with my view from here?" He eyed Scott's swelling crotch, as he struggled, almost tripping over himself, to get into his shoes. "Well, well, well, not only are you good looking," Rudy said, savoring his crotch unabashedly, and the power he held over him, "but you're talented too." *Velma, that lucky bitch!* Rudy thought ironically. *No wonder she's in love.*

"Thanks for a lovely evening, but I must be going." Scott walked to the door and opened it.

"Why don't you spend the night?" The marijuana gave Rudy courage; made him intrepid.

"No, Rudy." Scott turned to leave.

"Wait, Scott."

"What?" Scott said, standing within the door frame.

"No hard feelings." Rudy laughed inside at the unintended pun.

"No, Rudy. No hard feelings." He smiled crookedly, and closed the door behind him.

Velma sat in the darkness of her parlor, her legs and feet curled beneath her. Sipping a glass of wine, she listened to Bessie Smith on her new gramophone. As she stared through the fire escape, her face lit up in intermittent green and red hues from the neon flashing across the street, whose incessant buzz conflicted with a moaning, jilted Bessie.

> *I woke up dis moanin'*
> *Wid a awful achin' head*
> *I woke up dis moanin'*
> *Wid a awful achin' head*
> *My new man has left me*
> *Wid a room an' a empty bed.*

She planted a cigarette in her mouth and struck a match; the room glowed. In the tentative light, her eyes scanned the newspaper clippings of various reviews, and she smiled, tidal waves of warmth rolling and washing over her. She blew out the match; the room went dark.

A knock on the door distracted her. She placed the glass of wine on the table, slid into her slippers, and tiptoed across the floor. Pressing her ear against the door, she listened. "Who is it?"

"It's me, Velma. Open up."

"What brings you here this time of night?" she said, struggling with the lock.

"Long time no see," Scott said, entering. "Turn on some bloody lights."

"You know what time it is?" She closed the door and switched on the light.

"It's after midnight. So what? The clock can't stop me from

visiting my favorite girl." He pulled Velma to him, and pressed his mouth against hers hard and long.

"I would accuse you of drinking," she said, wondering why he was calling so late at night, "but I don't smell liquor."

"Why're you surprised to see me?" Scott unlaced his shoes.

"I haven't seen you for a while—"

"I know, I know." He looked at the pile of review clippings. "But, it's not every day my woman publishes her first novel." He unbuttoned his shirt, and flung it in a corner.

"Have you read it?" Velma said. "My book?" She so badly wanted his praise.

"I most certainly have, my dear. And, I must say it's a trenchant, original piece of work, and frankly, it's a hard act to follow."

"Do you really think so?" She was delighted. She'd trade all of her rave reviews—including the *New York Times*—for a grunt of approval from the young master.

"Like it? *Ma chérie*, let me say in sheer confidence, that it's a piece I wish I'd written myself." Now I've said enough; let's not get mushy.

"Oh, Scott! I was afraid you wouldn't like it. Wine?" She walked into the kitchen and turned on the light.

"Better. I'd like a glass of you." He unzipped his trousers and stepped out of them, wanting her so badly, he couldn't imagine why he had stayed away for weeks, despite her book.

"I missed you," she shouted from the kitchen, pouring him a glass of wine. "Last week even, I started to call and ask you to meet me at the museum, but then. . . ." She turned around, reentered the parlor, and stopped, frozen in her tracks. "My goodness!"

"What's wrong?"

"Well, it's not every day I find a man stark naked in my house. Trying to say you missed me?" she said, gazing ecstatically at his erection.

"Next week, let's go to the museum. I'd bloody love it."

Velma crossed the room and handed Scott the glass. He sipped it, put it down, and took Velma in his arms, kissing her repeatedly, running his tongue across her raisin-sized nipple. Like the groom with his bride over the threshold, he picked her up, carried her to the unmade bed, gently deposited her body, and climbed in with her, as Bessie, on the gramophone, wept into her gin.

3

Standing at the top of the winding staircase, Louise wrapped herself inside a silk robe, and tied the sash at her waist. Stifling a yawn with the back of her hand, she descended in satin slippers, holding on to the railing. At the foot of the staircase, domestics carried out duties. "Good moanin', Mrs. B," they said, as she walked toward the kitchen.

Strolling through the foyer of parquet floors, passing several looming potted palms that swayed from the breeze stirred by her passage, Louise entered the stark brightness of the early-morning kitchen. Vittorio sat at the head of a polished table. He sipped cappuccino, his head buried in the *Wall Street Journal*. Sara, the head maid, stood by the stove scrambling eggs. Upon hearing Louise enter, she turned and bowed her head. "Mornin', madam." The table was clear save for a breakfast plate opposite Vittorio upon which rested a calla lily.

"Why didn't you wake me, you sly devil?" Louise asked, rubbing her eyes.

Vittorio, in starched white shirt and polka-dot bowtie, looked up from the newspaper. "*Bon giorno, cara mia.* Did you rest well?"

"Until I realized you were out of bed." She sat on his lap, wrapped both arms around his neck, and kissed his forehead.

"You looked so peaceful, I couldn't wake you." He kissed her nipple through the robe. "Look at this," he said, stabbing the newspaper with his finger. "My aviation stock rose tremendously. Thanks to Lindbergh."

"All that Wall Street mumbo-jumbo. How could you think of that on a beautiful morning like this?" She glanced out the kitchen window, enjoying the view of the garden. "I feel bad your parents don't want to stay here," she said insincerely. She knew Mama didn't think she was good enough. Vito could have told her that at Thanksgiving. She knew that's what Mama was saying; he didn't have to lie, but she loved him for it.

"It's not your fault," he said, folding the newspaper and setting it aside. "If they can't respect me or my marriage, then too bad."

"But, still."

Sara extinguished the flame on the burner, and carried a steaming plate to Louise.

"Aren't you going to feed my husband?" Louise slid from Vittorio's lap into the chair.

"He said he wasn't hungry, madam," Sara replied, a private reporting to her sergeant.

"Well, he is," Louise contradicted. "Please make him something to eat, Sara."

"I can't do that unless he tell me—"

"*I'm* telling you, Sara." She looked from Sara to Vittorio, then back. "Make him something to eat."

"Well, madam, I been working for Mr. —"

"I don't care; I'm the lady of the house now. And, you'll learn to take orders from me too. Understood?"

Sara didn't reply. She stood erect, hands clasped, eyes front.

"Did you hear me?" Louise placed her hands upon her hips.

"It's all right, sweetheart," Vittorio interrupted, getting a kick out of watching Luisa protect him like a tigress protecting her cub. "She's just in the habit—"

"It doesn't matter, Vito," Louise said. "She has to learn that she'll take orders from two people in this house, not one. Is that understood, Sara?"

"Yessum." Sara took two eggs, cracked them, and emptied the shells onto the griddle. The egg yolk and white bubbled and crackled. She peered at Louise through the corner of her eye, her face without expression, and hummed a gospel melody, rocking to and fro on her heels.

"Sara," Louise said, shoving a mouthful of eggs and toast into her mouth. "Why do you always look at me that way?"

"What way, madam?"

"You know what way. You're always staring at me from some part of the room. Why's that?"

"I'm sho I don't know whatchu mean, ma'am."

"The way you're looking at me now. It's not a smile, it's not a frown either. But you have a way of looking through me like you resent me. I can't explain it."

"I'm sho I can't neither, madam."

"And that constant humming. Would you please stop humming. It's about to drive me nuts."

Louise didn't want to be this way, but after several months, Sara didn't acknowledge or respect her as the lady of the house. Louise tried to ignore it, and didn't want to raise the issue in front of her husband, but enough was enough. She could understand that the woman had worked for Vittorio a long time and was still getting used to two supervisors, but she wouldn't stand for insubordination.

The woman acted as if she hated Louise at first sight. Every woman connected with Vittorio, it seemed, was giving her a hard time. First Lucia, then two or three of her bridesmaids at the reception, and now Sara . . . who was only the maid.

It was peaceful now with the in-laws gone to another part of town. During the time they stayed, Vittorio and his father stepped around and barely grunted at one another; the mother remained upstairs in her room most of the time. She was pleased to be rid of that quiet tension in her new home, and she wasn't going to have Sara pick up where Lucia left off.

What was wrong with Sara anyway? Why did she continuously stare at Louise without parting her lips? It dawned on her that Sara might know who or what she was. She could have been one of Mother's friends, a member of her church. She behaved as if she knew something Louise . . . or somebody didn't. She decided it might be wise, for her own intents and purposes, not to react so vehemently to the woman, especially in Vittorio's presence, and call attention to herself. Except, she didn't know how to treat the staff, all of whom were Negro except the chauffeur. Treat them as a white lady would, she told herself, but she had had no dress rehearsal or guidance on being a white lady. This was all new to her, and meantime, she'd try to communicate with them so that everybody got along, but nobody got real close. Isn't that how a white lady would behave?

"Is something troubling you this morning?" Vittorio asked.

"Nothing."

"Are you feeling all right?"

"Yes, I'm fine. Now what about your parents? Where are we taking them today?"

"I was thinking of a ride to Coney Island." He folded the newspaper, pushed it aside and clasped his hands. "Mama likes the sea air and says it's good for her complexion."

"What about Papa? What does he like?"

"Who knows? Who cares?" Vittorio said. "He'll go where I take him."

"Vito, that's not right."

"Luisa, you don't know how difficult that man is."

"At least he likes me." More than I could say for Mama. She turned her head, as Sara cleaned the breakfast table. "Sara, didn't I ask you just yesterday to finish up in the kitchen after my husband and I have had our breakfast? Our privacy's very important while we're having breakfast. You could do that later when we're through," she went on coolly, wanting to scream at the woman. Sara played stupid, but Louise knew she wasn't.

"Mr. B say he don't mind if I cleans up here while y'all—"

"How many times do I have to tell you things are different now, Sara?" Louise said. "Mr. B's married and has a wife now. Don't you think that changes things?"

"I don't know, madam. All I know is what Mr. B here tell me."

"Well, *I'm* telling you, Sara," she said, rising up from her chair, determined to put an end to the woman's willfulness. "If you have a problem with that, then you'll have to find another job."

"Luisa, you're being too hard—" Vittorio said.

"No I'm not, Vito. I'm sick and tired of the way these servants treat me. They act as if I'm a stranger, and maybe I am, but they've got to get used to it." She turned back to Sara. "And, I don't need you to tell me what Mr. B said. You'd better listen to what *I* say. Do I make myself clear?"

Sara looked at Vittorio, who nodded. "Yessum."

"Good. Now we understand each other." Louise turned pale. A wave of nausea swept over her. She placed a hand over her mouth, and ran from the kitchen.

"Luisa! Luisa! Are you all right?" Vittorio shouted, running after her up the winding staircase. Sara smiled gloatingly, humming "Jacob's Ladder," as she cleared the kitchen table anyway.

Hours later, just before dusk, Vittorio walked down the staircase in a tailored smoking jacket. He looked around several rooms. The house was quiet. Most of the help had gone home for the day. Walking to the kitchen, looking through the window, he watched Sara in the garden with a pair of snippers. Humming, she snipped recently bloomed flowers, and placed them inside a newspaper. Vittorio started to call her, changed his mind, prepared himself a cup of espresso instead, and sat at the breakfast table. He was stirring the espresso when Sara reentered the house through the back door.

"Ain't they beautiful, Mr. B?" she said, inhaling the fragrance.

"Beautiful, Sara. Where're you going to put them?"

"Oh, I don't know. I just knows how you likes fresh cut flowers an' all, an' these was so pretty. I just knew you'd want them—"

"Sara, could I speak to you for a moment?"

"Sho, Mr. B. Anything wrong?"

"Won't you sit down."

"Sho. What is it?" He had never addressed her in that tone and she was afraid she was about to be fired.

"Now, you've been with me almost since I first came to this country, right?"

"Right."

"And, while I was a bachelor, we had our way of getting things done around here; am I right?"

"You right."

"You're only used to answering to Mr. B, but now we have a Mrs. B too, you know, to run the house, get things done, you know, that sort of thing."

"Yessir."

"Well, it's really my fault for not telling you sooner, but from now on, Mrs. B's in charge. Whatever she says goes. Whatever decisions she makes, I want you to pretend it's me. Does that suit you?"

"Suits me jus' fine."

"Then, we should have no more problems after today. 'Cause I'll tell you, Sara, I married one fine woman and when you get to know her better, I'm sure you'll agree that Mrs. B's a very nice lady. And, you're a nice lady too. There's no reason you two shouldn't get along. Understood?"

"Understood."

He felt sorry for Luisa, moving into a house that must have been twenty times the size of what she was used to. Having to be in charge of a home this immense was no easy task. He understood that if not for Sara, his household would be in trouble. He wouldn't know the first thing to do, and all his life, he'd lived in villas and châteaux. It must have been triply intimidating for Luisa. He'd watched her since their marriage, struggle with her new status of employer, instructing servants whose jobs she knew nothing of. In time though, she'd be fine. She had to learn that colored people guarded their menial jobs with a fierce, autonomous pride.

He sympathized with Sara too. Caught in the middle of the domestic crossfire, she wasn't sure where her orders came from anymore. She was a hard worker, loyal, punctual—Vittorio wouldn't know what to do without her. Women in his life were always fighting each other under the guise of *his interest,* and this was just another manifestation of that theory. He had never expected Sara to be so overprotective of him. What was it about women that they couldn't get along, and scratched and hissed like felines over a man? In part, it was comical. Imagine if Mama was still there. Then his lovely wife would have two opposing forces with which to contend. He didn't want Mama staying outside his home in a strange hotel. But she couldn't stay in her room all day and disregard his wife's hospitality. Happy it was his parents' idea and not his, he realized they were better off, for everybody's sake, staying at the Plaza. Much as he adored Mama, he wouldn't stand for that behavior. Luisa was his wife; he hadn't begun living until he met her, and Mama had to get used to sharing him—as did Sara. As for Papa . . . he could catch the first thing smoking back to Palermo for all he cared.

"I'd like to apologize for her behavior this morning," Vittorio said to Sara. "She didn't mean it, you understand."

"Sho I understands, Mr. B."

"But, what I'm really trying to say, Sara, is that Mrs. B was a little, how do you Americans say 'on edge' this morning, and for good reason."

"Oh? What's wrong wid her?"

"Morning sickness I believe you call it."

"You don't say."

"We had the doctor in this afternoon, and pretty soon, there'll be three in this family."

"You sho mus' be happy, sir."

"Go easy on her, will you?"

"No problem here, Mr. B. I knows how it is. Got five o' my own."

Sara complied and acquiesced, grinning from ear to ear, although she didn't like that rail of a woman he married. Comin' in here actin' like she Queen of England an' wuz pro'bly poorer than a church mouse when he pick her up outta the gutta. Sara noted he had rarely dated wealthy women, those from his own social milieu. His girlfriends usually didn't know a place setting procedure or that the wine was poured from the right, but they always treated her like she was their dishrag to wipe up the messes they created. No trainin'!

This one, wife or no wife, was no different, and Sara had nothing against the woman thus far. But she had to learn to stay out of her business. Mrs. B had her job, and she had hers, and she wouldn't tell that woman any more about being the wife of a wealthy stockbroker than she would tolerate being told how and when to make breakfast. What was wrong with straightening up the kitchen, as she always did, while Mr. B sat there at the kitchen table? The woman had no idea what all she had to do. Like she had time to come downstairs, backtracking to rooms she'd already cleaned. Just wasn't enough time.

In some way that she couldn't figure, maybe there was something different about Mrs. B. She was more nervous than the parade of women she'd seen march into and out of the master bedroom over the years. It went beyond the newlywed jitters. If she said Boo! the woman jumped sky-high. Even when she fussed at her that morning at the breakfast table, shouting in front of Mr. B, she was fussing about more than scrambled eggs or the table being cleared.

4

Miriam stood back and admired the night table near her bed. It had originally belonged to Mother. Most of Elvira's possessions were stored or sold, but what Miriam had space for in her apartment, she kept.

God, did she miss that woman! Father's death wasn't easy, but Mother's passing seemed impossible to accept. She didn't always remember Father being around. He was either going to or coming from work, or a war, and Miriam cherished many family memories that didn't include him. Mother was always there. She rarely left the house, and was the one constant in their lives. She was so accustomed to the woman's presence, unsolicited advice, scolding, praise, unconditional love and laughter that not a moment passed when she didn't think of her.

She and Velma were proud when the pastor eulogized their mother as two hundred or so mourners paid their respects before placing Elvira in the frozen ground. They had to do everything. Select her clothes, pick out a casket—which Velma flatly refused to do—and make funeral arrangements. These things happened all the time, but it was the first for them. When Father died, Mother handled the particulars. Miriam discovered that funeral expenses were as high as giving birth, and she thought, either way, whether one's coming into or going out of the world, one must pay for the entrance and exit, not to mention all the bills in between. She was outdone when the funeral director quoted the price of the casket she had her heart set on. It happened to be the best, and Mother deserved nothing short of it. During the haggling and bargaining to get the price down, they ended up with the cheapest box he had. As it was, she and Velma were forced to sell most of the furniture to cover expenses. It was unbelievable. And the money Louise sent— God bless her—also helped. It was just difficult cashing a check endorsed for a name other than theirs.

Now it was all over; the suffering, the heartache, the bouts with delirium, the headaches, fainting spells and dizziness. Yes, it was all over. Like the end of an era, Miriam thought. She couldn't remember waking up in a house that didn't reek of burnt hair, pomades, and shampoo. Those odors lingered longer than any seven-course meal Mother made. But now, the last of the human hair in that kitchen had been burned, and there were no longer overbooked appointment lists and clients waiting with bated breath until Mother found time to do them; no more soapy hands buried in somebody's dirty scalp; no more laughter, gossip, and "bull sessions." Though Miriam had moved out years ago, she missed it as if she were still living there.

She had to learn not to speak of Mother in the present tense. Most times it was habit, other times, deliberate. She couldn't let go, and refused to accept it, but she knew it was unhealthy, and forced herself to live with the tragedy. Life had to go on.

She was happy to have Agnes as a roommate with all that was happening in her life. Agnes didn't even know about Louise, but her being home when Miriam got there each day was a comfort. If Miriam's training as nurse helped her to console folks in trouble, as Mother said, then it must be true of Agnes as well. She was attentive, and compassionate. Agnes held and rocked her, wiped her tears, and painted soothing pictures of Mother being better off now than she ever was.

Miriam wasn't altogether comfortable with this roommate arrangement. She was tired of always cooking dinner for them. It was a bad pattern she set. Agnes was used to hot meals awaiting her after work, though she never so much as mopped a floor, cleaned the bathroom, or dusted the house unless Miriam told her to. Agnes was living rent free and still wasn't compelled to pick up a loaf of bread from the store after she had eaten the last slice, or empty the pan of water from the ice box. She loved Agnes, enjoyed her company, and was grateful not to be living alone. But often she felt that Agnes didn't respect her home.

One night, Agnes arrived home complaining that she was fulfilling more duties than she could possibly manage at work. She removed her shoes, rubbed her tired feet, then sniffed the air.

"I would say what's cookin'," Agnes said, "except I don't smell nothin'."

"That's right," Miriam said.

Agnes caught the tone, and asked, "What's that supposed to mean?"

"Just means I get tired of doing all the cooking and cleaning around here, Agnes, and you're going to have to start carrying your load."

"I know, Miriam. I've just been too tired to do anything around here after running around the hospital all day."

Miriam knew that was enough, she'd made her point, but continued lashing out at her.

"I mean," Miriam began, "what you think, you got a maid here? I don't feel like I should have to remind you when to do this or buy that."

"I know, Miriam," Agnes said, growing impatient. "I heard you the first time."

"Well, just do it," Miriam said. "Make sure this is the last time." She couldn't believe she'd said that. It wasn't Agnes's fault she was feeling the way she was.

"Are you okay?" Agnes said.

Miriam looked at her and their eyes locked, the tears clinging to the rims of her eyes. "Yes. I'm sorry. I didn't mean that." She started crying, and pushed some literature she was reading from her lap to the floor. Agnes crossed the room and comforted her.

She quieted her down, and again apologized for her oversight. Agnes explained that, growing up, she never had any real responsibility, and seldom did she stay put in one place.

"Your folks moved around a lot?" Miriam asked, sniffling.

"They moved around all right," Agnes said, "but forgot to take me with them."

"What?"

"I was raised with orphans," she said, remembering there were things about her background she wanted to tell Miriam; now seemed as good a time as any. "But I always ran away."

"Is this one of things you wanted to tell me about . . . "

Agnes nodded. Miriam had never personally known a child abandoned by parents, though she had heard stories. She stopped crying to listen.

"I had a crazy life," Agnes said, staring at the floor. "I still can't believe I've made something of it, to be a nurse."

"How did you meet Tommy?"

"Well, going back a bit, I used to live with an older broad who I met when I was in training. She liked me; she liked me a lot, and she was really good to me. But she liked young girls, and did things with me that she'd do with a man . . . if you know what I mean."

"You just let her? Didn't you say anything?"

"Miriam, you had folks who loved you. You got sisters who love you. I didn't have any of that. This woman was the first person in memory who I knew loved me and wouldn't give me up or put me out in the streets. So, I went along with it, got to like it, even," she said. She decided she was going to have a drink and rose from the chair. "And one day, I got to meet her family who stayed away from her because of what she was." She walked into the kitchen, dragging her stockinged feet. "Will you join me," she said, pouring herself a glass.

Miriam declined; that was another of Agnes's bad habits she didn't like. Liquor was illegal and she didn't want it in her house. It seemed like ever since the day Velma brought it over with Louise that Saturday afternoon, it never left. "Tell me the rest of this story," Miriam said.

"Well anyway," Agnes said, reentering the parlor with a glass in her hand. "Guess who her nephew was?"

"Who?"

"Tommy."

"What?"

"Yeah, and he was real sweet to me, too. I'm telling you, Miriam, the things you'll do for people who're nice to you . . . anyway, he was real fine, and had eyes for me. His aunt saw that right away, and she tried keeping him away from me. But, he convinced me, not that I'm so convinced anymore either, but he said that I was living in sin with his aunt. I was a pretty girl wasting myself on a bulldiker. I needed a good man to look after me. He said I needed him, and I probably did, you know. I can't tell you how good that man was to me in the beginning. So, one night, I let him have his way with me. Next thing I know, I'm the nigger's property."

"What did his aunt say?" Miriam asked, riveted by this bizarre threesome. If anybody had weirder stories to tell than Velma, it must be Agnes.

"Well, she didn't know at first. But she caught on. And, let me tell you, them two had one of the biggest fights I done ever seen. To this day, they don't speak to each other. Wasn't until around the time I met you he started acting up."

What a life! Miriam thought, feeling somewhat guilty for bringing up petty things like housecleaning when this woman had never really been loved. The pushover in her wanted to forgive Agnes, apologize for jumping all over her when she came home, but she knew it was necessary. Whether folks were loved in their childhood or not, there was responsibility.

"So you still like women . . . you know . . . that way?"

"I guess so," Agnes said, shrugging. "That's what I meant by I'm not convinced Tommy knew what he was talking about. There's something . . . oh, I don't know how to say it, but women are sweeter by nature. His aunt never beat up on me, and never tried running my life. Women are softer, I guess. I know this sounds weird, but you understand?"

"I think so," Miriam said.

"I mean, I didn't realize how good I had it until he came along and ruined it; that's what he did, ruined a good thing."

"But I thought you loved men so much?"

"I do." Agnes took another sip. "But it's more the sex. But then, there's some things he can't do in bed as good as his aunt could . . . if you know what I mean."

Miriam was bewildered by this barrage of information. She hadn't really thought about how two women did it. Contemplating her own sexuality, she didn't know what she was. And whether she'd slept with a woman or whatever, at least Agnes knew what she liked. Miriam couldn't say that much. She'd been with men—a man, anyway—and didn't like it. She hadn't been with women, and couldn't picture herself trying it. There was that dream, however, and to this day, she couldn't figure out what it meant.

Then it struck her! If the dream, as portent, told her that much about Agnes, then did it implicate *her*? Miriam didn't know. Most times she felt asexual. She recalled her feeling from the dream, and remembered loving it. Except that, awake, she couldn't see herself sleeping with Agnes. Sex, she felt, in any form or persuasion, was the least interesting side of life. She wanted to tell Agnes of the dream, but felt Agnes would misconstrue her intention.

"Miriam, what do *you* like?" Agnes said, taking a sip.

Oh my God! Miriam thought, completely unprepared for this. "What do you mean?"

"You don't like men, do you?" Agnes's eyes narrowed.

"I like them."

"How come you ain't never with one?"

"I don't have time—"

"Don't give me that," Agnes said, laughing. "You likes women, don't you?"

"Agnes!"

"Well, what, then?"

Miriam wanted this moment, and everybody taking part, to evaporate.

Agnes didn't realize she was putting her on the spot, or she wouldn't have persisted. But Miriam was a puzzle to her. She never knew what she liked or if she liked anything at all. She didn't impress Agnes as frigid, and she wondered if she were still a virgin. Whatever she was, Agnes had her own ideas. She had to come up with a rescue tactic for her friend who sat frozen stiff before her.

"I know what," Agnes said.

"What?"

"Let me take you out to dinner tonight. And I promise I'll make dinner tomorrow. How's that?"

"Well, I don't know."

"Miriam Brooks. You can't sit up in this here house, crying your eyes out all the time. You remind me of myself when I was having my problems with Tommy. Crying and feeling sorry for myself. Well, honey, that ain't gonna cut it. So come on. My treat, and I don't want no lip."

This was what Miriam loved about her. The woman cared. She could talk harshly, straightforwardly, without compromise, and Miriam knew she was telling the God's honest truth. She got her coat and handbag, and stepped out into the streets with a woman who was becoming more enigmatic each day. Upon first meeting her, Miriam had thought her demure, quiet, soft-spoken, with a simple life. But Miriam had lived more life through Agnes than she'd probably ever live herself. Life with her was never dull. The more complex she became, the more Miriam adored her.

5

Rudy pushed through the doors of Grand Central Station with a big smile, feeling giddy. He loved his and Scott's game of cat and mouse, tit for tat, I'll show you mine if you show me yours. He'd lived it before, been through the motions countless times. What Scott most lacked was courage, the willingness to try anything once. Though even after those awkward moments they'd had, Scott looked Rudy unflinchingly in the eye. Yeah, Rudy thought, I got you figured like an algebraic equation.

What was so goddamn special about Scott? he asked himself repeatedly. Beyond the brilliance, the dapper threads, and the drop-dead beauty, what was it? He had long ago stopped chasing men who couldn't decide whether or not they wanted to be had and instead went after men who, like himself, knew what they were and celebrated it.

Dear Velma. Where did she fit in the canvas Rudy was sketching for himself and her man? He had no more answers for that than for why he was consciously entangling himself in the spider web their overlapping friendships weaved. Whether his plan infringed upon Velma's sense of monogamy no longer concerned him. Not that he felt amoral, or without virtue, but there was little he could do about his feelings. If he had possessed a control panel that manipulated his desires, he would willingly have turned the switch off. He knew he was headed for murky depths, given Scott's tortured makeup, and without his writer's bent for tasting life with all its jagged, sharp angles, he couldn't march into an emotional labyrinth. To mesh souls, and whatever else, they would have to enter each other's worlds as first-time passengers, a price he was willing to pay.

Whom else did Velma shoot her mouth off to about his personal life? They were still best friends, and their competition took on a dimension other than that of literary contemporaries. And it came as a relief that he could loosen the ties of his loyalty to her. It was apparent everyone was out for him- or herself, and he felt it was open season, where there were no rules, no right and wrong. Much of this, he believed, was solved for him during Scott's last visit to his apartment. After their brush with whatever it was that happened on Rudy's floor, his finger was on the pulse of something beating, throbbing, something alive, and his, if he wanted it badly enough. All that he'd suspected about the man's irresolute flirtation proved true. The signs of arousal on Scott's trousers told him more surely than any eye wink or gentle touch that it was too late. Pandora's box had been opened and he, of all people, wasn't about to nail it shut.

The train roared and snorted into the station. Rudy unfolded the *Amsterdam News* from beneath his arm. His eyes couldn't advance beyond the first line, because this afternoon's conversation with Scott clanged like a bell in his head. Newspaper headlines and small print didn't register loud enough to drown out the reprise of their eye-opening conversation.

Today, they had planned to meet in midtown for lunch. Traditionally, Rudy was the latecomer. But this time, he waited twenty or so minutes for Scott, and telephoned him to inquire whether he simply forgot or just plain chickened out. But Scott hadn't forgotten their date, or so he said.

"While I should've been on my way to midtown to meet you," Scott continued, "it occurred to me: Why don't we have lunch here? You were courteous enough to have me over for dinner. I'm sorry, Rudy. I didn't mean for you to travel all the way downtown for nothing. Don't know why I didn't think of it before."

"That's okay," Rudy replied, his voice calm and forgiving, listening to the radio playing on Scott's end. "What time should I meet you?"

"Come right away," Scott said. "I'm whipping up something special for you." It was the suggestiveness, the undertone of the last comment which set Rudy's mind reeling, but experience urged him to inquire further.

"What do you mean by that—"

"Let me put it to you this way, *mon cher*," Scott interrupted in a way that was vintage G. Virgil. "I'm here in my townhouse waiting for you, and the only thing I'm wearing at the moment is a smile."

By the time Rudy could squeeze another question in edgewise, to be sure he interpreted the remark the way it was intended, Scott hung up, laughing.

This was the confirmation, the charge Rudy needed. With a

folded tissue containing marijuana he had obtained from an uptown street source, he was prepared. He noticed that whenever Scott decided to let down his guard, to flirt either covertly or subtlely with him, devil weed was always present. This, Rudy conceded, was Scott's Achilles' heel, not the gin and ginger ale he was most noted for, or the occasional brandy or cognac.

"Come in, the door's open!"

Rudy knocked again.

"I said come in!"

Opening the door, he surveyed the surroundings. There was no one in sight. Ma Rainey's heavy voice growled from the radio somewhere in the apartment. A trail of scattered clothes formed a path across the floor, leading into another room. If, in fact, Scott was cooking lunch, there were no aromas igniting the air to evidence such; not even a pot of water boiling on the stove. "Scott, where are you?"

"I'm in here, old chap," Scott shouted. "Back this way."

Rudy followed the voice down the foyer and around the corner. Scott smiled from the bathtub, buried in suds up to his chest, and Ma Rainey came in loud and clear. "See," he said, splashing water with the vigor of a toddler playing with toy boats. "I told you I was wearing nothing but a smile."

"Well, no wonder you didn't show up," Rudy said, trying not to look directly at him, wanting to climb into the tub with him.

"My, my, aren't we dashing and bloody handsome today." Scott leaned over and picked up a glass of gin sitting on the floor. "I'm a terrible host. Won't you make yourself a cocktail?"

"You like my suit?" Rudy was ecstatic he approved.

"Love it. What turned you from pauper to prince?"

"Pardon?"

"You dress better these days than when I met you. Have you burned those antebellum wing tips yet?"

"Well," Rudy said in the voice of a child praised by his schoolmaster, "clothes were always something I never cared much about. At least, not until I met you."

"It's bloody marvelous to know I still have the touch."

"I thought we were having lunch," Rudy said, glancing every way except at his friend. "You cooking?"

"My dear fellow," Scott said, laughing, "I'm not sure I know how to boil an egg. Why, are you terribly hungry?"

"Well, I guess—"

"For food . . . or me?" Scott said, nearly purring.

"What do you mean?" Rudy's heart thumped.

"C'mon, Rudy, don't give me bloody innocence; you don't wear it well."

"I just don't want you to play games with me."

"You'll find that's all life is made up of, my dear boy, a series of never-ending, stamina-challenging games. And, only those with teeth sharp as mine get to play again and again. It's the euphemism for survival." He growled and flashed his teeth.

"Well, anyway, I—"

"Could you hand me that towel, please?"

"Sure." Rudy turned. Behind him, a white, fluffy towel rested on the doorknob. He handed it to Scott, deliberately keeping his distance. Scott rose from the water, the suds sliding down the sheen of his brown skin, liquid clouds descending, melting into the sea of dirty water, and Rudy tried his damnedest not to look.

"Go on, my dear fellow," Scott dared him, holding the towel away from himself. "Sneak a bloody peek if you please."

"C'mon, Scott, don't play with me—"

"No, really, it's okay. I imagine you've wondered on several occasions what I must be like underneath it all." He climbed out of the tub, and briskly dried himself. He tied the terry cloth around his waist, walked from the bathroom into the bedroom, miniature puddles forming a path behind him, and sat on the edge of the four-poster bed. "Make yourself comfortable. That tie around your neck is choking me. Sure you won't have a drink?"

"No, thanks. I never drink on an empty stomach." Rudy spotted a calligraphy-penned invitation lying face up on the table. "What's this?"

"Oh," Scott said, chuckling, "of all the improbable things. You'll probably hear about it sooner or later anyway. I'm worried about Countee, you know."

"What's wrong with him?"

"That, my friend," he said, pointing, "is an invitation to a wedding. Countee's wedding, of all people."

"He's getting married?" Rudy laughed.

"Have you ever? And, to Dr. DuBois's daughter, Yolande, no less."

"And, you don't think it'll last?"

"How could it? Harold Jackman is the only person Countee's ever loved. But I guess he can't marry Harold, now can he?"

"I imagine Harold's rather heartbroken."

"If he is, he certainly has a priceless way of showing it. He's the best man, scheduled to accompany them on the honeymoon, if you can believe that! That's far better irony than I could ever dream up." He patted the spot next to him on the edge of the bed to ease a nervous Rudy standing in the doorway, his hands thrust in his pockets, jiggling change. "Come, Rudy, rest yourself. You must be tired."

Rudy sat beside him. Scott lay back, sprawled across the lamb's-wool comforter, and sighed. "So," Rudy said in a fading voice, turning to stare at Scott's hairy navel, waiting for a few strategic moments to pass, and for his quick breaths to subside. "What're we going to do? About lunch, I mean."

"Anything you want, dear boy, any bloody thing you want." He ran his fingers across Rudy's back. Rudy's head turned around slowly at the touch and met Scott's diabolical smile.

"Make yourself comfortable," Scott said. "Take off those dashing threads before you ruin the creases."

Rudy began disrobing before someone could wake him and say it was a dream. His hands shook violently at the mere unbuttoning of a shirt, the unbuckling of his trouser belt. His heart pounded frantically. Turning to face Scott, he stroked his hairy, athletically proportioned calves, and worked his way up toward the damp towel. For a moment, he rested his hand upon Scott's flaccid manhood beneath the terry cloth. Yes, Scott was talented indeed!

Scott closed his eyes as Rudy cupped his face, kissed his brow, the slope of his cheekbone, and closed eyelids.

Little did he know that Scott was granting him these liberties with his body, in part because he liked the pampering, and that because of his mounting frustration and jealousy, he'd come up with a scheme born of wicked curiosity coupled with desperation.

For reasons known to him, Scott found Rudy sexually fascinating—but not to the degree that Rudy did him. The writer and curiosity seeker within him urged an exploration of male sexuality, and Rudy functioned more as a convenience than someone with whom Scott shared romantic or sentimental overtures. Beyond that, Rudy was Velma's man, her secret heartthrob, and Scott didn't mind at all utilizing him as his boy, to teach them both a lesson.

He could not visualize himself kissing a man, committing sodomy—worse, being sodomized—or even holding hands with a man. Never! Scott admitted to his friends though, whenever the topic arose, that he was very oral. He loved to eat; he loved to kiss. And there was nothing like nestling his nose in the whiskers of Velma's "Miss Kitty." Velma had the spirit and an eagerness to learn and please. But considering the earth-shattering fellatio he received in Paris from Olivier—God, he still remembered his name!—he had every reason to believe Rudy commanded a similar virtuosity. He guessed that a man would know best how to push another man's erogenous buttons.

He relaxed and let Rudy press his dry mouth slightly against his own gin-soaked lips, gently brushing them back and forth. Scott's eyelids were half-drawn shades in a whorehouse. As Rudy pressed his mouth harder against his, he turned away, and forced Rudy's head downward. He loosened the towel from his waist and slid it toward his bare, ashen ankles.

6

Velma grinned in the mirror as she dressed for her date with Scott.

Last time she saw him, he'd shown up unannounced and swept her into bed. And what they did could only be choreographed by two people held captive by a spell called love.

Admittedly, at first, she had been annoyed and had to be persuaded to forgive him. He had insulted her. But what had gone wrong was nothing Scott's tongue and imagination couldn't rectify. Isn't that what love is? Clawing each other's eyes out one minute, licking each other like kittens the next. God, she loved that man! Every inch of him—from the capricious to the impenetrable—she adored.

She remembered her promise to Mother. If Scott didn't propose soon, she'd pop the question. She wanted to sleep and wake every morning in his arms. Every night could be New Year's Eve. He wore provocation as a nun wore a habit; it was the shot in the arm she needed.

She dressed for this museum date as if it were their first one. She put on his favorite colors, tightened the finger waves in her hair, and wore the French perfume Louise had left behind.

Too bad, she thought with melancholy, that Mother wouldn't be around—and perhaps Louise either—to enjoy the beautiful and bright children she and Scott would someday have. Her son, with his father's rugged, square jawline and slit eyes, would study at Harvard and travel throughout Europe *and* Africa before becoming a celebrated poet. Their daughter, a facsimile of Velma, with a smidgen of Scott, would follow Mommy's footsteps to Barnard. She would be encouraged to do any and everything her brother accomplished, and then some—anything but early marriage and child rearing. She could just picture them: Elvira Louise and Scott, Jr. She and Scott would buy a home on the Connecticut shore where they would write. They'd be one happy Ivy League Negro family, licking their lips—despite the dictate of times—from their hefty slice of the American pie.

She sat in the parlor and awaited his knock, watching the clock that read five minutes of two. He instructed her that if he hadn't arrived by two, to come by his townhouse. As a result of his crack-of-dawn writing sessions, which spilled into the afternoons, he might be late, in which event, she was to come by—calling wouldn't be necessary—and pick him up instead. He said he might be in the tub, or shaving, or getting dressed. Whatever, he instructed, the door would be left unlocked so she could enter.

She knocked on Scott's door and there came no reply. Per his instruction, she turned the doorknob, and walked in. Noticing the clothes sprawled carelessly about the floor, she heard the sudden flutter and thud of feet landing on the floor. She walked toward the bedroom, and looking over her shoulder, saw a virtually naked Rudy and a completely naked Scott who fumbled with the towel, hastily trying to fasten it around his waist, his nervous hands causing it to continuously slip from his grip.

Velma's jaw dropped, as the double dose of erections came into focus. Rudy struggled, turning shades of blush, thrusting his legs into trousers which didn't cooperate. Scott smiled nervously. Rudy painfully avoided her gaze, turning away from her as he zipped himself up. She threw her handbag to the floor in disgust, crossed her arms, and paced the bedroom floor.

"Velma, what're you doing here?" Scott asked, gloating inside.

"We had a date, remember?"

"Did we?" He slapped his forehead, and feigned forgetfulness.

"What the hell's going on here!" Her lips began trembling. Her arms folded, she tried retaining composure when she wanted to break a lamp over his head. "Somebody better tell me something!"

"I want you to know," Scott said, trying to appear embarrassed and humiliated, his voice becoming hoarsely convincing, "nothing happened." He refused to meet her gaze.

"I guess not," she said. "It was about to."

She wanted to ram their heads together, slam that crooked smile down Scott's throat; castrate the bastards. How dare they? Her instinct was to kick and scream and wreck Scott's apartment like a bulldozer with them in it, but she maintained an artificial coolness and waited to hear the tenuous explanation before she annihilated them both.

"Velma, please calm down," Scott said, wondering if she'd caught them in the precise position he'd intended her to see. "Let me fix you a drink?"

"I don't want a goddamn drink!" she snapped, her voice trembling. "I'm sick and tired of you trying to patch up all life's misfortunes with a drink!"

"Well then, I'll make one for myself. Join me, Rudy?"

She looked to Rudy who continued to avoid her gaze. "Long time no see, Rudy."

"Yeah, Velma. Good to see you again." Like recurring syphilis, Rudy thought; why's she smelling like a New Orleans bordello?

"Somehow, I fail to find the sincerity in that. Maybe you mean it's a *surprise* to see me again." She waited for a reaction that never came. "What do you have to say for yourself, Mr. Rudolph?" Now her nostrils flared, as she paced like a lioness contemplating the jugular of her prey.

"Say for myself?" He looked up and faced her directly for the first time.

"I mean this . . . " she said, pointing toward the unmade bed with disgust.

"Should I have something to say?"

"I think you should," Velma said.

"Now that I think of it," Rudy said, buttoning his shirt. "You do have an uncanny nature to come calling at life's most inopportune moments. Second time we're meeting like this, isn't it?"

"This is no time for your fucking sarcasm, Rudy!"

"And, this is no time for your fucking ill timing either!"

"Come, come now, you two." Scott crossed the room, having mixed himself a drink at the alcove, loving every minute of it. "We're all adults here and—"

"If we're adults, then maybe we should try acting like it," Velma said. "Look at this, I mean, Rudy, I can't believe you'd do this to me!"

"Do *what* to you? Don't pull that victim shit on me, Velma. It works in fiction, but it hardly—"

"I thought you were my friend!" You fucking, amoral bastard! she thought, as tears rolled down her cheeks and she bit her lip.

"I *am* your friend. Just that—"

"A friend of mine, I mean, a real, true friend wouldn't do this," she interrupted, her voice unsteady and wet with tears.

"Velma, it's life. What can I say? You want me to say I'm sorry and I'll never do it again? I can't say that."

"May I remind you that Scott's *my* lover! Find your own!"

Maybe I have! "I didn't force him to do anything he didn't—"

"Well, maybe it wasn't force, but—" Scott shouted above their voices from where he sat, disappointed that Rudy had barely got started when she walked in, on schedule.

"Oh, Scott," Rudy interrupted him, "she can see for herself that what she walked into can't exactly be construed as rape, you know. Don't make me the villain. Besides, Velma, you can stop huffing and puffing. Nothing happened. Really." Thanks to you!

"Why does everybody keep saying that? Obviously nothing happened. But, then, you didn't expect me to walk through that door either!"

"Maybe you should learn to knock sometimes," Rudy said under his breath.

"What was that, Rudy?" Velma said.

"Nothing. Forget it." You heard me loud and clear.

"Well," she said, beginning to pace again. "Of all things, I find my lover in the arms of not another woman, but another man!"

"Velma, for bloody sake," Scott said, stirring the ice in his glass. "We could go to the bloody museum anytime. I'm sorry. I forgot, okay? Forgiven?"

"You know damn well the museum isn't the issue here!"

"Then would you be so kind as to tell me what is the issue—"

"Let's get this straight now!" Velma shot Scott a deadly look. "Who do you want, Scott? Me or Rudy? I'll tell you right now, you can't have us both!"

"What kind of question is that, Velma?" Scott said.

"Don't you patronize me, you cunning little son-of-a-bitch! Who do you want? I'll admit, I don't have the temperament for ménage à trois!"

"Now you're babbling," Scott said, sipping his drink. "What do you think—"

"Is this the first time this has happened between you two? . . . Tell me!"

Rudy and Scott looked at each other, but neither replied. Rudy sat at the edge of the bed, tying his shoelaces.

"Well?" She looked to Scott, then to Rudy. "I'll tell you what. You two decide which way it's going to be. When you reach that decision, give me a call." She picked up her handbag from the floor, and tried battling an outrageous impulse. She gave into it and placed her handbag on the floor. She grabbed framed photographs and smashed them back against the wall. She wrestled with the Art Deco mirror she loved so much, yanked it from the wall, and threw it across the room. It shattered with a crash that must have caused the neighbors to wonder what was going on in there. Scott and Rudy winced, guarding their faces from flying, jagged pieces. Velma noticed blood dripping from her finger onto his carpet. "May you motherfuckers have seven years bad luck . . . apiece!" she blurted through a sudden upheaval of hysterical weeping. Through her tears, the two of them became blurred mistakes she'd made out of poor character judgment. They were lucky she hadn't thrown the mirror directly at them. She turned, picked up her handbag and headed for the door, slamming it with a bang so fierce that it disengaged a hinge.

7

"One in lavender, one in white, please," Louise instructed the clerk across the Bonwit Teller counter.

"Shall I have these delivered with the rest of your purchases?"

"Yes, thank you."

"Certainly, ma'am. Will there be anything else?"

"No, thank you."

She stood on the avenue deciding whether or not to have lunch with her in-laws at the Tea Garden, or to buy the Lilly Daché hat she saw in Bruck Weiss's window.

Eyeing a taxi as she stepped into the street, she toyed with the idea of sneaking up to Harlem. A nagging temptation. It was nearly a year since she had been even remotely near the community. She was puzzled as to how she could grow up in a neighborhood for twenty years, knowing virtually every side street, alley and obscure corner, only to be away from it for months, and feel as if it all took place in a past life.

Mother's face perpetually crowded her thoughts. She wondered whose hair she could be doing now? With whom was she conducting her bull sessions in the kitchen beauty parlor?

Many times, she was tempted to telephone. A couple of times, she did, but hung up while the telephone rang. She hoped, until she saw her again, that Mother was doing well, and that the checks she sent were helping to carry the household load. The guilt she felt for abandoning her mother and sisters sat undigested in her stomach. As the baby of the family, she never would have believed that she'd one day pick up and walk out of their lives. It knocked her virtues down like sitting ducks in an arcade. But she thought her family would understand. Flesh and blood, they loved her unconditionally.

Much was lacking in her life. She could be part of one family, but not the other. One day, she promised herself, as she promised Mother in her letters, she'd rejoin them, and unite the two families. Before that could happen, Vito had to know who and what she really was. That thought was enough to make her sit right down on the curb and fan herself into a frenzy so she wouldn't pass out. It made the baby stir inside her.

She wanted her baby boy to know his maternal grandmother and aunts. How could he grow up and not know them? The thought frightened her as much, if not more, than Vito finding out about her before she could tell him. If Lucia's attitude toward her was any indication of how she'd regard her first grandchild, Louise wanted the woman never to come near him.

She wondered about Velma, her writing, her beau, if they'd gotten married; Miriam, her organization, and her new roommate— Louise couldn't remember her name. Every night, she prayed for her mother and sisters, their welfare, their happiness, and their understanding and forgiveness of what she'd done. She had done right to obey her instinct and not tell her sisters of her date with the Italian playboy. If she'd told them, they could easily have tracked her down. Velma's recall was incredible. She remembered leaving the Smalls Paradise napkin in the back corner of her dresser bureau; the napkin with his name scribbled in his handwriting. To her, it was an autograph in case she never saw him again. Luckily, she had torn off the telephone number and called him from a public telephone. Everything else remained there at Mother's—her clothes, Cotton Club costumes, cosmetics, jewelry, magazines, teddy bears, and favorite dolls she'd had for years. Who could have known that the day she and Velma visited Miriam with a bottle of gin, it would be their last time together. And weren't they celebrating sisterhood—never again to be apart from each other?

She wanted more than anything to jump into a taxi, run uptown for a quick moment and touch them and smell them and kiss them and hold them and beg forgiveness, and let them know she was all right. Missing them was like a migraine that never went away.

But just one visit could ruin everything. And though she loved her family, nothing in her life exceeded the joy and pride of being Mrs. Vittorio di Bolognese. She let the last available taxi pass her by and went to the department store.

At Bruck Weiss, she saw a rotund man in a black derby and tight-fitting pin-striped suit. The same man she'd seen earlier in Bonwit. She watched him avoid her gaze, pretending to read a *Saturday Evening Post*. She caught him stealing glances at her. Something about him was very strange.

She entered the millinery department of the store. She started to purchase the Lilly Daché hat when she had an idea. Strolling around the aisles with half-interest, glancing over her shoulder intermittently, she slipped through another exit and flagged down a taxi at the corner of Fifty-seventh Street. "Plaza Hotel, please."

Two and a half blocks away, she pressed the driver's palm with a five-dollar bill. She surveyed the immediate area before dismissing the cab, which idled at the curb.

"Did you want Plaza Hotel, lady?"

"Yes, but I wanted to wait a minute if you don't mind."

"Hey, for five bucks," the driver said, stuffing the bill in his shirt pocket, pulling the hat down over his eyes, slumping in his seat, "you can sit here all day if you like."

She opened the door cautiously. Her head swung northward, then southward, before she planted her feet on the ground. She waited beneath a lamppost before entering the lobby. People coming and going, climbing into and out of idling limousines and taxis, camouflaged her. Waiting five minutes or so, she decided her suspicion was unfounded, and proceeded inside the hotel.

Another taxicab came from the direction of Central Park South and stopped. Hidden by throngs of people crowding the lobby, she watched the rotund man with the black derby reappear as the door opened. Amid the rushing crowd where he couldn't discern her, she watched him, her heart beating like a drumroll. He stood at the curb, derby in hand, and scratched his head. He looked in every direction with apparent frustration distorting his puffy face.

8

"Well, Rudy," Velma said, walking outside of him nearest the curb, as they left the theater. "What do you think?"

"I enjoyed it. Did you?"

She paused beneath the marquee and lit a cigarette. Blake and Sissle's *Blackbirds of 1928* flashed on and off in bright lights, as theatergoers chattered and laughed among themselves, spilling from the lobby out onto the sidewalk.

"Well," Rudy repeated. "Did you?"

"Yes, especially Adelaide Hall and Bill Robinson. But, there's something seriously lacking." She glanced up and down the street. "Come on. I'm parked around the corner here." Arm in arm, they strolled away from the noise and bright lights into the silent darkness.

"How nice of Mrs. Vanderpool to furnish free passes," Rudy said, picking something from his eye. "How do you like your roadster?"

"Very much. It's nice to have an automobile in this city."

Velma was happy to be alone with Rudy. After their last meeting or, rather, confrontation, she wrote their relationship off and accepted, painfully enough, that they'd no longer be friends. She left there that day, went home, threw herself across the bed, and cried herself a reservoir, her thumb throbbing and bleeding onto her bedspread. Once the storm of tears passed, the fury dissipated, she thought out the event clearly.

First of all she never should have taken it out on Rudy. Scott was the culprit. After it was over, she thought of a million and one things she should have said and done to Scott. Her reaction to Rudy, she thought, was typically female; punish the rival, not the lover. She prided herself on being above such nonsense. Anybody would jump at the chance to sleep with Scott. It was *his* responsibility to keep them at bay. She and Rudy owed each other an apology, but she took the first step toward mending the tear in their friendship.

She suspected that the entire scenario at Scott's had been staged. Not once did he appear genuinely surprised at her intrusion, and how could he have forgotten their date? Scott remembered license plate numbers he saw in Paris. And how about his instructions and the unlocked door? She wouldn't put it past him to sabotage her friendship with Rudy and whatever ties he believed they had. What was he trying to prove? Were he and Rudy lovers, and she "the other woman"? Or was this Scott's way of saying he was bored with her?

She thought of old times, pre-Scott, when she and Rudy led comparatively simple lives and never scratched each other's eyes out, even after she had caught him in bed with the first man. She decided that Scott was their problem. He was dividing and conquering them like the Portuguese ravaging Africa. Because of their blind lust for him and subsequent competition against each other, they didn't even see it. Scott could be gone tomorrow, sailing back to Paris. Lovers came and went. Friends were another matter entirely. And she wasn't foolish enough to lose a best friend over a blemished man just because she loved him and he had the most magical tongue in Manhattan.

She refused to see him until she could figure out her next move. There was so much she had to find within herself to forgive him.

She decided that Rudy shouldn't see him either, at least for a while. Let Scott stew in his own gin-soaked misery and realize what good friends he had, instead of pitting them against each other.

She called Rudy and apologized, then invited him to the theater as a peace gesture. Rudy apologized as well, and listened intently to her theory and proposed course of action. They agreed. Scott, their bone of contention, was now the subject of their truce.

What she didn't tell Rudy was that she wanted *him* to stay away from Scott since she discovered Scott couldn't be trusted. Sitting beside him in the theater, she wondered what thoughts reeled inside his head; if he was replacing her in this game of romantic musical chairs. Yes, she was sorry for what was happening between them, the disintegration of their link to one another.

"What were you saying before?" Rudy asked. "What's seriously lacking from *Blackbirds*?"

"Well," she said, exhaling the smoke through her nostrils. "While I'm happy to see Negroes working in theater, I wish they were doing something else."

"Comedies don't go over well with you?"

"No, I enjoy a good laugh, but all they'll allow us to do is comedy."

"You're right," Rudy agreed. "All Negro shows are either remakes of established white shows or musical comedies."

"Exactly!"

They stopped in their tracks and looked at each other. Simultaneous grins crawled across their lips. "Are you thinking what I'm thinking, Rudy?"

"I'm sure."

"Rudy, you and I could write a serious drama. Imagine it: no music, no comedy. What do you think?"

"I'd welcome the opportunity to work with you, Velma. You know that."

"You and I could write a marvelous play together. I mean, we're established writers; that must count for something," she shouted over the chugging motor, driving away from the lights and crowd outside the Lafayette Theatre.

"We could do a piece about a family facing real problems plaguing Harlem—"

"And make it uncompromisingly honest. No frills, no thrills. Drama with real social, political content, of course. Oh, Rudy, I'm getting excited," she said, punching the steering wheel. "What would you like to write about?"

"How about an impoverished family, whose sons died in the war. You know, the broken promises to Negroes following World War I?"

"Great! Or how about a piece stressing our case in point." She shrugged her shoulders.

"What do you mean?"

"Well, we're kicking around ideas because of the dearth of serious Race art on Broadway. We could do a piece about that."

"Velma, that's great! I like that! But, if we're contemplating a mortal sin in this business, we'll need a big name to back us up. Someone who has box-office draw, yet sympathizes with our cause." He watched night shadows pass over her face.

"Let's take a step at a time. We'll write it first. Tomorrow, we'll throw around some ideas. Do some character sketches and premises that would draw the most discriminating viewer to the theater."

"You know, Scott may not like the idea of being excluded from our project," Rudy said.

"That's not true. He'll be a great contact to people we might need behind us—like Paul Robeson. I know he'll help us." A long silence followed. Velma downshifted the gears and stopped at a traffic light. She fumbled through her purse for a cigarette, lit it, and inhaled deeply.

What better way to make up, Rudy thought, than to write what could be a historical breakthrough in New Negro theater. It was great to be out with Velma again, alone, laughing it up and flexing creative muscles. The moment was reminiscent of the days before they met Scott. She was absolutely correct. They were doing fine without him, and their plan to stay away from him for a while made more sense than their scheming to co-author a Broadway play.

He couldn't believe Scott.

The afternoon Velma walked in on them, not two minutes after she left, Scott started laughing, maniacally so. He glanced around at the mess on the floor and asked Rudy if he was okay. If that wasn't enough, he suggested they pick up where they left off. As desperate as Rudy was for him, he couldn't have gotten it up again if someone drugged him with Spanish fly. He'd wondered why Scott had moved so quickly from the bathroom to the bedroom. It was no more an act of spontaneity than Scott's impromptu invitation. If she was right, he was glad nothing happened between him and Scott—well, somewhat.

He agreed not to see Scott. But if Scott approached him, called his house, or stopped by, he wasn't going to snub him either. Scott embodied his weakness, the vulnerability he wore on his sleeve. He was furious with him, but not to the degree Velma was.

He wondered why Velma had received an automobile and passes from Mrs. Vanderpool when he hadn't. Was Mrs. Vanderpool, like Scott, also undermining them? Was divide and conquer an integral ingredient of her patronage?

"Rudy," Velma said, "do you mind if I ask you something?"

"What's that?"

"Did anything really happen between you and Scott?"

"Velma, we've been through this before," he said.

"It's just a question."

"Velma, we chose tonight as a means of rekindling, remember? We said we'd burn old bridges, didn't we?"

"Yes," she said reluctantly. "We did. You're right. But you—"

"But nothing. Now don't go and spoil a perfect evening."

"Hey, I've got the perfect idea!" she said.

"What's that?"

"Let's drive by the Tree of Hope."

"Sounds great."

Velma parked the roadster at the corner of 131st and Seventh Avenue. They walked arm in arm toward the stump and planted their palms on the bark. "May we have the best of luck with our play," Velma said, her eyes closed.

"And may our friendship, prosperity, and success flourish like the population in China," Rudy echoed her.

"I know this tree works," Velma said, turning to seat herself. "The last time I was here making a wish was back in '25. Same day I met you, in fact."

"Really?"

"I was so disillusioned that day. I got fired from my job. Nothing was happening with my writing. So I came here and made a wish. I guess the tree began working its powers right away, because, later that night, I attended the Harlem Writers Workshop and you know the rest."

"I'll never forget that night," Rudy said, his head craned backward, watching the stars twinkle, trying to discern the big dipper and Orion's belt.

"Neither will I . . . but, you know . . . there's something I need to talk about—"

"Velma, we just said we wouldn't—"

"No, not that," she said, contemplating whether she should tell him or not, wondering why she hadn't visited the tree in three years. She must have felt she didn't need the luck. "I never told this to anyone, Rudy, but I feel I can trust you. I have to tell somebody or I'll explode." She paused, lit another cigarette, picked a speck of tobacco from her teeth, blew the smoke toward the lamppost light where moths fluttered, their wings beating a tinkly melody against the bulb. "Rudy, I have a younger sister, Louise, I never told you about and . . . I really don't know where to begin. Anyway, right before my mother died, she was working at the Cotton Club as a chorus girl and . . . never mind. Forget it."

"Go ahead, I'm listening."

"No, that's all right. Come on, we have a busy day ahead of us tomorrow. Tonight, we need our rest." She tossed the cigarette to the ground, and crushed it with a twist of her heel, not in the mood for opening old wounds. If she started talking about Mother and Louise, her tears might float them and the Tree of Hope down into the dark shadows of Seventh Avenue.

9

Miriam fidgeted in her seat as Mrs. Greerson, her supervisor, studied her from the opposite side of the desk.

"Miriam," Mrs. Greerson began, choosing her words discriminately. "Are you having problems?"

"No, ma'am," Miriam replied, avoiding her eyes.

"We're aware of your mother's recent passing," she said, fingering the desk calendar. "So, we thought . . . maybe, you're still shaken by it."

Miriam said nothing. There was nothing she could say. She had expected to be called in sooner or later.

"You do understand," Mrs. Greerson reminded her, "that we can't tolerate tardiness and absenteeism."

"I know, ma'am."

"You're one of the best we have. The doctors constantly request you. But you must understand our position."

"Yes, ma'am," she said, then sighed. "I just . . . "

"Yes?" Mrs. Greerson leaned forward.

Miriam shook her head, and decided against defending herself. The situation was either black or white, no grays in between. There was no defense.

"May I suggest you take a couple of days off," Mrs. Greerson recommended. "I'm certain you've accumulated vacation time."

"Thank you, ma'am," Miriam said, rising from her chair. "I'll be back to work on Monday."

Mrs. Greerson watched her leave when a thought occurred to her. "Excuse me, Miriam."

"Yes?"

"I'm just wondering. Are you and Agnes still friends?"

"Yes, we are."

"Do you still see her?"

Miriam thought for a moment. The confrontation with the UNIA officials, though the charge had been dismissed, made her cautious about giving unnecessary information. It was none of Mrs. Greerson's business anyway.

"No, I don't," Miriam replied.

"Well," Mrs. Greerson said. "If you need someone to talk to, I'm here. I know it's difficult and sometimes, we need someone to talk to. Know what I mean?"

"I do, ma'am."

"See you on Monday. Get some rest. You don't look well."

Miriam gathered her things. She'd arrived at work not a half hour before Mrs. Greerson called her in. She could tell a reprimand was impending by the way other nurses glanced, embarrassed for her. They whispered, seemingly stepping on eggshells around her, and she figured Mrs. Greerson asked for her or wondered out loud why she was an hour late, third time this week.

She didn't know what was happening to her. With Mother gone, the foundation of her world was shaky. She felt uprooted. From the moment Mother took ill, until the time they laid her in the cold, wet ground on that gray December morning, she had had to be strong. Velma leaned on her heavily and had many good cries, unburdening herself of grief. Miriam didn't have that luxury. She was the big sister. In a peculiar way, she regarded Louise's absence as a blessing. She and Velma together would cause her an emotional overload. In addition, innumerable telephone calls from neighbors, friends, and associates offering condolences, unexpected visitors bringing food, money, and advice on everything, and dealing with the mortician and the pastor made her want to lie across Mother's casket and let the gravediggers bury her as well.

She could have reached out to Velma, as Velma had to her, but felt she would be infringing upon her sister's valuable time. She thought Velma had more pressing matters at hand than consoling an elder sister who was just beginning to sense the aftershocks of her mother's death.

Agnes was seldom there when Miriam needed her. She was either at work or asleep.

Miriam thought about the gin Velma brought by the house. It had calmed her nerves. Agnes and Velma drank it like water, but Miriam couldn't get past the smell. She felt like her patients when she dosed them with castor oil.

Walking down the street in the early morning, she was numbed, zombielike. Her feet and eyes operated automatically from familiarity. If it depended upon her faculties, sense of direction, and motor abilities, she'd be walking around in circles within a community she knew like the back of her hand.

Several blocks away, a group of men stood on a corner and furtively passed around a bottle enclosed inside a wrinkled paper bag. She saw them and didn't see them. Stepping into the street to cross it, she heard her name called. She heard, yet didn't hear, her feet operating and ignoring the signals from her brain to stop. She continued walking, and realized someone was suddenly trotting beside her, chuckling and panting out of breath.

"Long time no see, sweet thing," he said. She knew, without looking, that it was Tommy.

"Hey, mama, slow down," he complained, trying to keep up. "Have you seen Agnes?" She lacked the strength and focus to respond. All the vitality in the world couldn't part her lips to speak to him.

"Where's Agnes living now?" he asked, interpreting her silence as willfulness. "She get fired? What's the matter, cat got your tongue?"

Tommy began slowing down, gazing at her through baffled eyes. Discouraged, he turned around, headed in the opposite direction and rejoined his friends on the corner who laughed at him being ignored by the pretty woman.

At home, as she climbed out of her uniform, she sensed an explosion of tears churn in her stomach, move its way up to her heart, then to her throat, where it stuck. She wouldn't allow it past the throat, but held it there like vomit. She bent over the bathtub, turned on the hot water and watched the tub fill. Sitting on the bathroom floor, she laid her head sideways along the rim. As curtains of steam rose, she climbed in, sat motionless, and stared catatonically. Exhausted from scattered patches of sleep, she closed her eyes, and listened to the noises of her neighbors' lives through the walls.

When she woke, the sun had crawled across the sky, and she wasn't feeling any better; just wet and cold. She poured herself a glass of Agnes's whiskey. With each sip, the whiskey tasted better and better. She finished one small glass and began nursing another.

She heard Louise's voice, laughing and talking inside her head.

She rubbed her head to rid it of the voice and considered putting something in her stomach.

The sight of food nauseated her. She thought she should force herself to eat, but the room started spinning, and she closed the icebox. Holding on to the kitchen counter, the doors and furniture, she guided herself into the bedroom where she plopped upon her bed, and fell into a drunken sleep.

She woke with Agnes's key turning in the lock. She looked at the clock. It read an hour past midnight. She wanted to get up, but her body didn't. She thought of calling out to Agnes in the darkness, but didn't have the strength. She heard the bathroom light click on and Agnes run the water to wash her hands. Her mouth was parched and she licked her lips at the sound of it. Rolling over, hugging the pillow, she went back to sleep.

When she woke again, Agnes was shaking her. The pillow was wet with her tears and Agnes was in a nightgown. The clock read almost three-thirty. Agnes sat down on the bed, and told her she was wailing and thrashing in her sleep. A thousand tiny needles pricked Miriam's head, and a hangover settled over her like a swarm of locusts. Agnes brought her a glass of water from the kitchen. She drank it in one gulp, and asked for more. Agnes suggested something stronger, but Miriam refused. As Agnes returned to the kitchen, Miriam bolted out of bed, ran to the bathroom, and vomited. The smell repulsed her, and pangs shot throughout her body. She writhed in pain against the cold floor. Agnes rubbed Miriam's back, picked her up off the floor, and guided her back into the bedroom.

Tucking her in bed, she climbed in and nestled Miriam in her arms, singing softly as she stroked her hair.

"I want my mother, Agnes."

"Shhh, shhh, I know," Agnes said. "But you still got me."

"Why did God have to take her?" she asked, her words slurred. "He had no right to take my mother, did He, Agnes?"

"No, baby, He didn't," Agnes said. "Now you try and get some sleep."

No sooner than Agnes said it, Miriam rolled over, Agnes still holding her, and fell asleep once more.

She was having that dream again. Agnes was standing before her naked. She touched Miriam in places she'd never been touched. She kissed Miriam softly, and held on to her firmly. They were floating on a melting iceberg in the middle of an immense sea. Agnes kept reminding her to hold on so she wouldn't fall in the water and drown. The ice was melting fast and there was no sight of land. Agnes insisted that as long as they held on to each other, the water could not threaten them.

She woke again and Agnes's face was pressed against hers; her nostrils filling with Agnes's perfume and the gin on her breath. She wanted to push Agnes away but couldn't. She'd never felt so warm and comforted.

Agnes kissed her tenderly. She inched down and kissed Miriam's nipple, tracing her tongue around the contour of her breast. She darted her tongue into Miriam's navel which contracted her muscles and made her want to laugh. Miriam could feel Agnes breathing against her vagina and felt embarrassed at the moisture collecting around her thighs. She stiffened while Agnes parted her legs. She moaned, thrashed her head side to side, and bit into the pillow. An explosion sent shudders from her knees, over her shoulders, past her spine, down to her buttocks, and her thighs opened wider of their own reflex.

When it was over, Miriam emitted laughter that fringed on delirium. Agnes's face popped out of the darkness and was suddenly gazing into her eyes. She smiled, asked if she was all right, and whispered, "You feel better now, don't you?" at which Miriam blushed. Agnes bent down and kissed her, and Miriam, disbelieving her impulse, made a vague, awkward attempt to return the kiss. Then they both fell asleep, Miriam cradled in her arms.

The next morning, she jumped out of bed, then remembered she had the next two days off. She turned off the clock, looked beside her, and wondered where Agnes had gone. Crawling back beneath the blankets, she pulled them over her and remembered the preceding night. She wasn't sure if she could face her roommate now.

Agnes came into the room in her uniform. She smiled and whispered to Miriam to remain in bed until she felt like getting up; she would take care of everything. Kissing Miriam on the forehead, she asked again if she felt better, then turned around, and headed for the kitchen. She returned with a tray of eggs, bacon, grits, toast, orange juice, and a rose protruding from a vase. Miriam was surprised, since she hadn't smelled any food cooking. She was ravenous, and sat up in her bed. Agnes set the tray down, fluffed her pillows, and balanced the tray on her lap. Sitting beside her, she encouraged her to eat and asked what it felt like to be on the other side of the bed for a change. Miriam grinned, a little ashamed about last night. Agnes told her she looked better this morning than she had in weeks. The dark circles were gone from her eyes, and she seemed to glow.

Agnes gathered her things to leave for work and reminded Miriam to get plenty of rest. "Go out, do something, get your hair done, buy something for yourself, you deserve it." With that, she left, locked the door, and Miriam wondered how she could act as if nothing had happened between them.

Now she knew what Velma meant about oral techniques.

No longer did she find it repulsive.

10

As the di Bologneses sipped cappuccino, the aria from *Pagliacci* floated through the warm air. The tenor soared dramatically, dipped with delicacy, spilling into the garden from the gramophone inside the drawing room of the mansion. Gentle breezes caused the trees to sway in lazy rhythms. Bees and butterflies buzzed and hovered over beds of blooming flowers. Blue skies and white puffy clouds painted, with impressionistic strokes, an idyllic afternoon.

Vittorio sang with the music. Mimicking Caruso, he stuck out his chest and contorted his face. Louise laughed and applauded. She picked a flower, shredded it, and threw the petals at Vittorio who continued, undaunted.

While he swung her in the magnolia-grounded hammock, she stared into the field of blue sky and green, listening to the buzzing of insects. So lulled by the perfumed spring air and her loving husband, she could have fallen asleep. She thought about the man in the derby who followed her. She hadn't seen him since, but then, she hadn't ventured outside her door since. She couldn't decide whether or not to tell Vito about him. It occurred to her once or twice that her husband was having her followed. Unfamiliar with the eccentricities of the wealthy, she suspected he didn't trust her, and wanted her free time away from him monitored and accounted for.

But what if the man following her was a maniacal murderer who stalked pretty girls as they shopped along Fifth Avenue? She felt compelled to tell Vito. What if something happened to her and she hadn't seen it fit to warn him?

"Sweetheart," Louise began, her voice deliberately soft. "The strangest thing happened to me recently."

"I know. You married into a strange family."

"I'm not joking. I was shopping at Bonwit Teller one day when I noticed a little, fat man. Well, I didn't think much of it at first. But, then I saw him again in another part of town."

"And?"

"That's what I said at first. Except the second time I saw him, he kept staring at me when he thought I wasn't looking."

"He fell madly in love with you at first sight. Not unlike myself."

"Sweetheart, please be serious. Anyway, I decided to find out if he was following me. So, I left the store and hailed a taxi. When I got to the Plaza to meet you and your parents for lunch, there he was again."

"Can you blame a man for watching poetic beauty in motion?"

"Watching is one thing; following is another."

"What does this fat man look like?" he teased.

"He was wearing a three-piece pin-striped suit," she said, shooing away the bee circling her head. "It looked worn and faded and much too small for him. He had gold watch chains hanging from his vest pocket and he wore a black derby. Don't you find that strange?"

"There are lots of strange people in this city. What can you do?"

She was getting nowhere with this. She had to pursue a more direct approach.

"Vito, I'm going to ask you an even stranger question. I don't want you to misunderstand, okay?"

"I could never misunderstand you, *cara mia*."

She paused, sensing the weight of what she was about to ask. Taking a deep breath, she released the words from her lips without listening to them. "You're not having me followed, are you?"

Vittorio laughed. "Sweetheart, why should I have you followed?"

"I don't know. That's why I'm asking."

"No. I think you're overreacting. Probably—"

"Overreacting?" She rose from the hammock with a start. "Vito, the man was following me. It's kind of scary, you know."

"Why should he be following you?"

"I don't have a secret lover on the other side of town."

"I'm sure you don't."

"Then why is—"

Sara appeared with the silver tray, carried it to the table on the patio. Louise continued the conversation the moment Sara left. "I know it sounds strange, but I can't think of anything else."

"Sweetheart, nobody's following—"

"Somebody hired a private detective!"

"Why are you so sure it was a private detective?"

"God, Vito, it was written all over his little fat face!"

"Now, you're getting upset."

She wasn't handling this well at all, and wished she hadn't brought it up.

"Yes, I'm upset. I don't like being followed, do you? I don't even know why he's following me."

"Right now," he suggested, "you should have lunch. Sara made us a special—"

"I don't care what Sara made. How can I eat with that on my mind? For God's sake, I'm afraid to go out anymore."

"Shhh, shhh." He stroked her face and hair. "It's no good for you to get yourself all worked up or go without food in your condition. Remember, you're eating for two now. Sure you don't want to try that delicious veal Milanese. It's got homemade sauce like Mama makes and—"

"You're not taking this seriously, are you?"

No, he wasn't taking it seriously, but rather attributing it to a pregnant woman's hysterical imagination. He could see she was terribly upset but assumed it would pass, like morning sickness.

Watching her get angry and flustered as he swung her in the hammock, made him want to disrobe in the garden and play Adam and Eve in Eden.

She was a unique flower; the finest he'd picked among his bouquet of ingenues; loyal and trustworthy, untainted by hard, lower-class living, unimpressed by his wealth. She loved him, not the image, and that was of paramount importance. She didn't beg him for nights out on the town, where she could thoughtlessly spend his money, or flaunt him on her arm as showpiece. She was shy, unaffected. He couldn't even get her out of the house, and rubbing elbows with the celebrated and notorious at the Cotton Club didn't interest her. She took no spectacular joy in being chauffeured or pampered by servants. It wasn't that she didn't like it, she just didn't live for it. That was why he had decided to marry her. They shared similar notions of life, marriage, home, and family. And to be in love, completely in love, was true happiness. She blended maturity and innocence, a woman who'd lived and been around several corners without showing the scars. She knew what she wanted and went after it; he could understand that.

She had something, something he was yet to identify, something subtle, inarticulate. A deeply embedded element glowed within her that matched his passion. He had dated mostly WASP women, socialites with rich daddies, and found them flat, nondimensional, rigid, spoiled, boring, their passion and zest for life no match for his. With Luisa, he could throw it and get it back threefold, whatever *it* was. Their inner connection went beyond the definable and tangible.

No, he wasn't having her followed, a preposterous idea at the suggestion of which, had she not been carrying his child, he might have been insulted. If he had even once believed there was any reason to have her followed, he would never have married her.

"*Cara mia*," he said, realizing he had failed at lifting her spirits. "I just think you're a little nervous about the baby and all. Sure you won't eat just a little?" He poised a forkful of veal at her lips.

"Food is the farthest thing from my mind right now," she said, refusing it.

"I'll tell you what, then. I'll have Sara draw you a nice hot bath. It's very relaxing."

"Where will you be?"

"Wherever you want. In the bathtub with you if you'd like or just waiting right here in the garden or," he said, tickling her stomach, which he couldn't keep his hands off these days, "the bedroom's always a great place to resolve differences. What do you say?" He watched her turn his offer over in her head. "Come on," he said. "We'll take a hot bath and see how we feel."

Louise climbed out of the hammock and Vittorio embraced her around the waist, as they made their way through the shrubbery. Steam from the hot lunch curled delicately into the air. Upstairs, they drew a bath in the Art Deco black and white tiled bathroom with its sunken tub, closed the door, asked not to be disturbed, and climbed in together as Caruso's *Pagliacci* serenaded the lovers from the gramophone in the first-floor drawing room.

11

As the Studebaker slowly climbed the steep, dark hill, Velma gasped at the lighted villa coming into view. In the distance, a jazz band played, the brassy sounds muffled behind six-foot-high arched bay windows. Through dips and turns, the Studebaker chugged along as Scott shifted into fourth gear, the hills and trees obscuring the estate from their view. The road wound around, Scott turned a sharp left, and again, there it was, the infamous Villa Lewaro, so named by Enrico Caruso.

Scott had contacted Paul Robeson as he had promised Velma he would. Robeson had just returned to the States from a London tour of *Show Boat*. Scott reported back to her that A'Lelia Walker, heiress of Madame C. J. Walker's fortune, was throwing a homecoming party in his honor at her villa in Irvington-on-the-Hudson.

Velma had bought a silver-beaded dress with fringes and spaghetti straps, a revealing décolletage, and a back plunging below her shoulder blades. She covered her head in a silver-beaded skullcap, with fringes dangling and swaying around her head. Her arms were draped in elbow-length white gloves, her left wrist boasting a diamond bracelet Scott had given her for Christmas, or was it her birthday? She cooled herself in the stuffy automobile by fluttering a fan of white feathers. She was squeezed between Scott and Rudy, both in black tuxedoes, white bowties, and gloves. Nobody had much to say, she guessed, because she and Rudy were nervous about meeting Robeson. Scott, she figured, resented their exclusion of him from the collaboration—though he said he didn't. Or, it was plain awkward since they all hadn't been together since the townhouse episode.

The Studebaker pulled into the circular driveway, and valets, rotating like worker ants, swung open the doors, bowed and welcomed them. They parked Pierce-Arrows, Rolls-Royces, and Packards in an immense driveway. The music from the jazz band mixed with hundreds of voices of guests milling inside and outside. Velma craned her neck to get a view of the Greek columns of the white, two-story mansion, and thought, So this is Villa Lewaro.

Entering the house, Velma thought of Gatsby's fictional estate in West Egg, Long Island, and assumed this was the type of high-society soiree Fitzgerald must have been writing about.

They walked into a drawing room where, upon a gold grand piano, a flapper danced a scandalous striptease Charleston to the drunken cheers and prodding of a dozen or so men. It was going to be a wild time tonight; she could just feel it. Every immense room, it seemed, teemed with people, laughter, and music. Studying the high gold-leaf-covered ceilings and crystal chandeliers, she imagined the house to be the size of Madison Square Garden. Scott pointed out celebrities, socialites, and luminaries. Gertrude Vanderbilt Whitney sat nearby on a chaise longue talking with someone Scott couldn't identify.

An approaching big-boned Negro woman caught their attention. She wore a lamé turban with quail feathers drooping, curving around her aristocratic chin, her dress trimmed with a mink collar and sleeves. Gliding through the maze of people, she seemed to flutter invisible wings, smiling too readily, her neck snapping back in forced laughter, puffing on a cigarette holder, and cutting the air with delicate gesticulations.

"So that's her," Velma leaned over and whispered to Scott, without breaking her gaze from the hostess.

"Yes, my dear," Scott replied. "The infamous A'Lelia Walker. Extraordinary woman. But"—he paused to light a pipe with fresh tobacco—"she's hardly the businesswoman her mother was. More adept at spending the family fortune than expanding it. She's quite the extravagant."

"I hear," Rudy added, "she's quite the eccentric."

"Believe it, my boy, believe it."

They meandered toward the august main ballroom, where chandeliers blindingly glittered. A spacious marble floor shone brilliantly, and cast dazzling reflections. Scott stopped a servant and helped himself and his companions to a second drink. Patting another on the elbow, he slipped a delectable hors d'oeuvre of caviar from the tray into his mouth. Velma paid close attention to the guests who ran the gamut from New York writers to Hollywood silent screen stars, politicians, and gangsters.

Scott had promised himself beforehand to get roaring drunk. Of late, Velma and Rudy were shutting him out. Surprised to get a call from Velma asking for the introduction to Paul Robeson, he felt he was losing his grip on his friends, who behaved as if the townhouse predicament had never happened. Rather than divide them, it seemed to bring Velma and Rudy closer, and he strongly resented it. He didn't care about being included in their insipid project, a concern Velma voiced on the telephone, because he felt superior to them as writers. He had the biggest name. At his most mediocre, he could easily outdo them at the peak of their collaborative efforts. Besides, Robeson was booked for at least another year or two, and with any luck, their project would never advance beyond the pages on which it was written.

Boy, was Rudy acting weird. Scott had anticipated a warmer reception from him, considering they'd spent no time together since that day at his house. Something was transpiring between those two—aside from their sleeping together—and Scott thought, as he grabbed a third cocktail from a passing tray, that he'd find out exactly what it was. They didn't have the decency to call and find out what or how he was doing anymore, as if they didn't need him, but didn't hesitate a moment to request a meeting with Robie. Nobody uses me, he thought venomously, smiling at them, holding Velma's hand—she did look delicious. He remembered something Rudy said that day, the last time they were all together. Apparently, it was the *second* time Velma had caught Rudy in a compromising position with another party, and he couldn't tell, between himself and Rudy, who was the principal object of her melodramatic wrath; which of the two was guilty of infidelity. When he asked Rudy, he shrugged it off as if he hadn't heard Scott's question. That's all right, he thought, watching the party's visual extravaganza begin to blur, he still had several tricks inside his top hat. And rabbits they weren't.

Velma shrieked with delight and pointed to a naked man strolling around the party with a drink in his hand. While other guests giggled and pointed, a quintet of white women approached them. They walked past Rudy and Velma, stopped at Scott, introduced themselves, and conversed with him as if he were alone. They ogled him like teenagers meeting their matinee idol, the most voluptuous among them pressed her cleavage against him. Velma gave them scathing looks, and Rudy laughed, as she grabbed Scott's arm and planted kisses on his ear and neck. The woman rolled her eyes at Velma, who felt stupid and inconsequential holding on to Scott without the courtesy of an introduction.

"Good evening," she said, sticking her hand out, "I'm Velma Brooks, novelist, poet, essayist and Scott's lover of three years. How do you do?" She smiled, hoped they got the message and elbowed Rudy, who was giggling. She reminded Scott, his drunken face sinking into the woman's tits, that they had business to attend to with the guest of honor. "It's been marvelous," she said to the quintet of lamé, sequined, and feathered women.

Entering the east wing library, Scott spotted Paul Robeson, as he talked with his wife Eslanda and playwright Eugene O'Neill. Robeson's wide, toothy smile lit up the room. He leaned against wall-length bookshelves, his presence dwarfing those around him, and his rich bass voice bellowed across the room.

"Robie!" Scott called to him from the doorway. Velma could tell by the slur that somebody was getting drunk. Robeson beckoned and Velma and Rudy exchanged a smile. Crossing their fingers, they entered the library with Scott, who hugged Robeson, kissed Eslanda on the cheek, and shook hands with O'Neill.

"Scott," Robeson said, wrapping his brawny arms around Scott's shoulders, his voice ringing like thunder. "Of course you know Gene. Gene, Virgil Scott."

"Yes," O'Neill said. "I believe we've met before."

"Robie and Essie," Scott continued, slurring, "I'd like you to meet some friends of mine. My girl, Velma Brooks, and our friend Zachary Rudolph."

"Just Rudy will do," Rudy said, excitedly extending his hand to the smiling trio.

"Are you *the* Velma Brooks of *Chameleon*?" O'Neill's eyes crinkled.

"I am."

"Marvelous work. I applaud you." O'Neill clapped his hands.

"Indeed," Robeson seconded, giving her an appraising glance. "While I was in London, it kept me in touch with the home front. Are you working on anything else?"

"As a matter of fact, that's what I wanted to talk to you about," Velma said calmly, incredulous that this was really happening— he'd read her book! She'd met, over the past few years, a sampling of New York's finest from Gershwin to DuBois. However, nobody, but nobody, compared to Paul Robeson.

"Tell us about it," Eslanda insisted, fanning herself with peacock feathers, her eyes glowing with interest.

"Well," Velma continued, "Rudy and I are co-authoring a play; a pure Negro drama with a serious theme. An entire piece without comedy or music."

"Excellent idea!" Robeson said, bowing his head in approval, his face pensive. "Have you any backers?"

"Not really," Rudy added. "That's why we're hoping you'd be interested."

"How?" Robeson asked.

"We're writing the lead role," Velma said, "with you in mind. You have the following and the establishment of a serious artist. We need someone with that kind of credibility and recognition, if you know what I mean."

"Do I ever," Robeson said, and O'Neill laughed, as if they were sharing an inside joke. "You do realize, my dear, how difficult it is?"

"Yes we do," Rudy said. "So, we figured if we could interest you, it might be easier for us to present it to potential backers. We're contemplating Broadway because of the exposure."

"Sounds like a marvelously splendid idea," Robeson said sincerely. "But, at the moment, it's more a case of bad timing."

"How's that?" Velma asked. He was far more beautiful and commanding up close; almost godlike, with a voice that could wake the dead.

"Well, I just finished up with *Show Boat* in London, and I'm back to do some concert touring. However, I'm interested; quite interested, as a matter of fact. Could you forward a draft of the script to my agent? And I'd like to set aside some time to discuss it further. Mr. Rudolph," he said, turning to Rudy, "I also enjoy your work tremendously. It would be a privilege to work with both of—"

"Yes, yes, yes," Scott interrupted, feeling ignored. "So, Robie, how do you like my literary discoveries? I make it a bloody point to surround myself with some of New York's most promising upstarts like Miss Brooks and Mr. Rudolph here; that way, I can keep an eye on my competition." He emptied the drink in his mouth.

"Well, I'm honored and flattered," Robeson continued with Velma and Rudy, "that you'd consider me for the part."

Scott felt banished from the group as the conversation bounced off and ricocheted around him. He got himself another drink. Rudy loved Gene, Gene loved Velma, Paul loved Rudy and on and on. He wanted to throw up right there on the polished marble floor. Throwing his arm around Velma—not knowing what else to do— he tried penetrating the circle but no one allowed him an edgewise remark on his own. Look at them, he thought, glancing at Velma and Rudy, they were paupers when I met them, and now they act as if they don't know me. If not for me, they wouldn't be here; how quickly they forget! His father had warned him of the proletarians. How dare they exclude him, the only American Negro novelist who basked in international visibility.

"Robie, I'll bet you can't tell," Scott interrupted in a drunken loudness, "that Rudy here is a practicing homosexual?!"

Their party, and guests in the immediate area, exchanged embarrassed glances—embarrassed for Scott. They lowered their heads, focused their attention elsewhere.

"My God, Scott!" Velma said with disgust. "What's wrong with you?"

"Here's to you, Rudy!" Scott said, mockingly, winked at him, and raised his glass in the gesture of a toast.

"Excuse me, please." Rudy walked away, half-running through the open French doors. Velma followed, calling to him, but couldn't catch up.

Into the darkness of the estate's layered landscape, he trudged through moist grass, thick brushes, and trees, and came upon a footbridge which led to a gazebo at the bottom of the incline. He crossed the bridge, and ignored the rushing brook beneath and the exotic tropical fish inhabiting the pebbled waters. Toads croaked beside the muddy banks and splashed into the brook as he hurried past. He tugged at his pant legs and sat on the gazebo steps in the enveloping darkness.

Velma, several paces behind him, could barely make out the route he'd taken. Only his white shirt and bowtie revealed him in the darkness. She stopped and glanced upward at the near full moon half hidden behind slowly drifting clouds. The scent of gardenias told her she was near a garden. The smell of soil was pungent, as was the odor of something else she assumed was skunk.

The sound of water engulfed her ears, and making out what she could in the night, she noticed an elaborate fountain, at the center of which, a winged cherub urinated onto three concrete tiers of overflowing water. She'd lost Rudy. She called his name which echoed in the pitch blackness, unanswered. The warm air was heavy with women's perfumes and men's colognes. The villa on the top of the hill shed little or no light on the surrounding estate, neither did the moon through the passing of clouds, and she tripped over something hard in the grass, and nearly fell. Glancing downward, she saw a white man, his tuxedo trousers and suspenders pulled down to his ankles, pumping a Negro woman pinned beneath him, her gown bunched up to her waist, and brown legs coiled securely around the man's pale, flat, gyrating derriere. Velma chuckled at the stark contrast of complexions, while they moaned and grunted as if she weren't there. The sight was arousing, her nipples grew hard, and she couldn't wait to get Scott home that night—or maybe . . . the couple panting in the grass gave her an idea. Remembering why she was there, she walked down the incline, approached the footbridge, removed her silver T-strap pumps, and tiptoed across. She lifted her dress and again softly called Rudy's name.

She found him at the steps of the gazebo. His face was streaked with tears in the dull moonlight. Without a word, she sat next to him. Gentle winds rustled the trees while a chorus of crickets rubbed their legs, a backdrop for the distant brass jazz and noise from the mansion on the hill. She handed him a cocktail napkin to wipe his tears, which he didn't acknowledge, and waited a long while before she spoke.

"It's such a beautiful evening," she said after a long sigh. "The moon, the wind, the crickets, the scent of gardenias—"

"I hate that son-of-a-bitch, Velma."

"No you don't—"

"Yes I do! I hate the fucking bastard! What does it all mean anyway?"

"Rudy, you should know by now how Scott—"

"How do you stand it?" he asked, gazing into the black night, trembling, refusing to look at her. "How do you put up with it?"

"Love, Rudy. What else can I tell you? It forces you to compromise the uncompromising."

"My problem exactly." He didn't care how much she knew or felt about him grieving in the dark, on the steps of a gazebo, over her man.

"In what way?" she asked.

"I hate the despicable motherfucker and yet . . . oh, never mind. It's no use."

"Go on, you need to get it off your chest," she said; then more gently, "I'm here with you, Rudy." She touched his hand.

"Well, it's no secret," he said, facing her for the first time. "I'm in love with him."

"Yes," Velma said, taking his hand in hers, and pressing it against her cheek. She'd never seen such torment in his face. "I've suspected it for a while. Here, dry your face. You're too handsome tonight for that." She understood why Rudy loved Scott and couldn't give him up. Boy, did she understand. No longer jealous of Rudy, she felt pity. Unrequited love was most tragic to her.

"You know," he said, sniffling, turning away, "sometimes I could kill him. Just drive a fucking stake through his heart. But he probably doesn't have one."

"Oh, Rudy, don't talk like that. Scott's not that bad." She threw her arms around him, and hugged him tightly, straightening his lapels, and wiping his tears.

"The things he does to you," he said, "the things he does to me, what's it all for? Why can't we leave him alone? I feel like he's got me under some warlock's spell, for chrissake!"

He wanted to be left alone, comforted by no one—namely, the woman who was getting what he wanted. He couldn't tell if she was sympathizing or gloating. He wanted to scream into the darkness, at the top of his lungs, for her to leave him alone! But, as she wiped his tears, he was glad she had followed him, and felt closer to her than ever.

Velma watched him weep and felt herself as drawn to him as she was on their fateful night of the Harlem Writers Workshop. She'd never stopped loving him. To some extent, she loved him more than Scott. It was his sensitivity and compassion and honesty, and it hurt her to see him upset like this. He was vulnerable and beautiful in the moonlight, and she looked up into the sky at the iridescent rings surrounding their lunar spotlight. It was time to stop fooling herself about her feelings toward Rudy, a penciled memory she couldn't erase. She held his hand, embraced him, and yearned for him to reciprocate. Remembering the couple rolling in the grass back up the hill, she wanted to undress him right there and ravish him on the steps of the gazebo. What would Mother say in heaven, my being in love with two men . . . who are friends? Right now, she prayed Rudy would go along for the ride, no questions asked. They'd done it once, and they could do it again. The alcohol made her courageous.

"Rudy, this may not be the best time to tell you . . . I'm aware of how you are, but somehow, I keep thinking you and I had something special. What happened to that?"

"Just one of those fly-by-night things, Velma. That's all." Oh no, dear God, not this again . . . not now.

"I think it was more than that."

"Velma, come on. That was damn near three years ago."

"I'm so confused. I love Scott, I really do, but somehow, we just don't fit in his world and he doesn't fit in ours." The headlights of a departing automobile caught her eyes and she lowered her head, avoiding the light. "I may hate myself in the morning for saying this, but . . . I never . . . stopped . . . loving you, Rudy."

"Please, things are complicated enough."

"I had to say that and get it off my chest. I can't grow old without ever having told you." She forced a laugh.

"What's so funny?"

"Oh, I don't know. Everything's so damn crazy. I'm in love with Scott; you're in love with Scott; Scott loves me; I'm in love with you. Gosh! There must be a novel in there or something, wouldn't you say? At least."

"What I'm feeling right now is far from funny. I think I'll sit here for the rest of the evening."

"And waste a rented tuxedo? Not on your life." Again, she looked at Rudy who stared ahead into the darkness. She turned his face toward her, held it for a fleeting moment, studying his expression, and wiped his tears with her napkin. Edging closer, she kissed his cheek, his chin, and tried to kiss his mouth when he broke her hold. Standing abruptly, he leaned against the gazebo railing and continued staring into nothingness.

"Rudy, why not?"

"You know why."

"But—"

"But nothing, Velma. Drop it."

They lingered for a few awkward moments, then were startled by splashing sounds. Turning around, glancing at Lewaro upon the dark hill, they watched fully clothed guests jumping and diving into the swimming pool. The muffled shrieks, laughter and applause stirred something inside Velma, and she was ready to dance and drink away the night. She also had to find Scott and make sure he and Treasure Chest were nowhere near each other; she was in no mood to kick some white woman's ass for seducing her man. This triangle bullshit had her in enough trouble already.

"Let's go," Rudy said, watching expensively attired people deliberately ruin their clothes in the pool. "I'm all right now. Let's get back to the party. Only thing left to do is get drunk. Pissy drunk!" He offered his hand. She rose, gathered her silver T-strap shoes, and took Rudy's hand. "You won't mind," Rudy continued, "if I don't leave with you two tonight?"

"I understand."

"I just can't be in the same automobile with that, that—"

"Shhh; we got what we came for, right? Come on, we'll both get drunk and celebrate," she said. "But I'm not jumping into anybody's pool, after what I paid for this dress."

12

Louise's concentration was divided between a back issue of *The New Yorker* and the chattering of women around her in the beauty shop. Peeking from beneath a veil, she watched indifferently as patrons left and entered the salon. A woman beside her engrossed in a book, raised her eyes momentarily and smiled. The beautician finished one customer and patted the chair to summon the next. "Whaddaya reading there?" the beautician asked the woman beside Louise.

"*Home to Harlem* by Claude McKay."

"Another one of them colored writers?"

"Yes. You should read it."

Louise closed *The New Yorker* and assumed her place in the vacant chair.

"How are you today, Mrs. di Bolognese?" the beautician said to Louise.

"Fine, thank you. Yourself?"

"Can't complain. Mind if I ask a question?"

"Depends."

"Are you *the* Mrs. di Bolognese—as in wife of Vittorio?"

"Yes, I am."

"I'll tell ya, some dames have all the luck. So what can I do for you today?"

"I'd like my usual manicure. But, I'm thinking of cutting my hair."

"How short?"

"Very short. A cute bob cut would look nice. What do you think?"

"You gonna cut off all this gorgeous hair?" the beautician gasped, extending a handful of Louise's wavy locks outward. "Take it from me, honey; today you cut, tomorrow you weep."

"I'll take my chances."

"Okay, you're payin' the bill." She turned her attention from Louise, and spoke to the customer whose face was buried behind *Home to Harlem.* "Really amazing how these colored people are publishing so many books these days. It's kind of nice."

"If you really want to read something that'll keep you on the edge of your seat," another customer interjected from the far side of the room, a towel wrapped round her dripping hair, "you should read the book I just finished. See these dark circles around my eyes; that's because I didn't get any sleep last night. Just couldn't put it down."

"Now, that's the kind I like," the beautician said. "What's it called?"

"*Chameleon.*"

"*Chameleon*? Hmmm, strange name. Who's it by?"

"Some colored gal named Velma Brooks," another customer intervened.

"Never heard of her," the beautician claimed, shaking her head.

"Well, you should. Especially when you hear what it's about."

Louise's head was about to be lowered into the basin for a shampoo. She stopped the beautician with her hand. "I'm sorry," Louise said, "but I'd like to hear this."

"Well," the beautician shouted across the room, "now that you've got everyone's attention, tell us what it's about."

"You just wouldn't believe it. It's about a colored lady who becomes white."

"How the hell can a colored gal turn white?" The patrons giggled and snickered.

"She doesn't really turn white, silly. She's just so fair-skinned, she decides she'll pretend to be white and see how the other half lives."

"Are you kidding me?"

"Honest to God," she said, raising an open palm. "She leaves the colored neighborhood where she grew up and moves into the white side of town. Fascinating reading. Can you imagine?"

"Sounds more like science fiction to me."

"Maybe. But, when I was a teenager, I knew a girl like that."

"Then, how'd you know she was colored?"

"Her mother used to pick her up from school. It caused more gossip than you can shake a stick at."

"You mean to say she looked as white as me or you?"

"Whiter!"

"Then how could she be colored?"

"Don't know; never asked. But the strangest thing was, her mother was black as soot."

"So, that means white women you see on the street could be colored, or any one of us here in the shop for that matter?" The beautician shook her head and turned to Louise. "Have you ever heard of such foolishness?"

"No," Louise said hoarsely. "Can't say I have."

"What's the author's name again?"

"Velma Brooks."

"Ever heard of her?" the beautician asked Louise.

"No. Never." Louise turned in her chair, blood rushing to her cheeks, and faced the gabbing customer. "You sure her name is Velma Brooks?"

"That's Thelma with a V."

An hour and a half later, Louise stepped down from the chair, admired her new cut in the mirror. She liked it, but more than that, she needed a ploy to throw off the potbellied man with the black derby who followed her. She thanked the hairdresser and dug into her purse for the veil which she used to cover her face.

"C'mon, honey," the beautician protested. "You're not gonna wear that thing, are ya?"

"Why not?" Louise asked.

"And hide that darling haircut?"

"Well, I like the way the veil—"

"Say, girls, let me have your attention for a minute, please," she shouted, turning Louise around by the shoulders to face them. "Please tell her that a hat would look wrong with this new haircut."

"I love the cut!" a voice shouted.

"It looks great. You shouldn't wear the hat."

"If I could get my hair to look like that, believe me, I'd burn every hat I own!"

"See?" the beautician added, her hands poised upon her hips. "Didn't I tell you? Don't do it, honey."

"No," Louise replied, "I think I'll wear my hat. I just love veils, don't you?"

"Okay, it's your business."

She paid the cashier, tipped the hairstylist with a five-dollar bill, and exited through the revolving door.

13

What're the odds of that?! Louise thought, headed for the bookstore.

She couldn't wait to get out of there. No longer could she stand listening to conversations about women passing for white. She felt as if the women really knew who and what she was and were testing to see how far she'd go.

What made the beautician ask her about her husband? Louise thought. She'd never asked before and though it seemed innocent enough, it was disconcerting just the same. But, when the woman leaned over and asked if she'd ever heard of Velma Brooks—*that's Thelma with a V*—she thought she'd faint. What were the odds, she thought, to be in a beauty salon where they not only talked about a book whose theme was a woman passing for white, but a book authored by her own sister? They had to be one in a million. Is fact stranger than fiction, or what? she thought, as she left the salon, leaned upon a corner building down the street, and massaged the knots in her stomach. Accepting the coincidence, she imagined that any of the other women might have been colored as well, and the thought of not being alone made her feel better.

In the stacks at Brentano's, she scanned book titles at eye level. From time to time she looked over her shoulder or toward the door, or glanced at the sidewalk. She relaxed, assuming that the man with the derby had given it a rest—at least for the day. With her veiled pillbox hat and short bob cut, she couldn't be so easily recognized. She spent ten minutes in Brentano's, but couldn't locate her sister's book. The fiction shelves were lined with every contemporary title and author under the sun. Hemingway. Hurst. Maugham. Faulkner. Even McKay. But no Brooks. About to leave and continue her search elsewhere, she first checked with the clerk.

"Excuse me," she whispered, leaning over the counter, "but do you have a new book called *Chameleon* by—"

"Velma Brooks!" the clerk replied. "I have an extra copy here behind the counter I can sell you. I always keep an extra copy of our most popular books for customers like yourself."

"Can I see it?"

"Certainly."

The clerk bent down and produced a copy. The Aaron Douglas dustcover illustration depicted diagonal lettering in a graduated spectrum which spelled out the title. Louise inspected the photograph of her sister on the back flap, below it, the words: Photograph by Carl Van Vechten. Her heart seemed to halt momentarily, and she was consumed with a sweeping ambivalence of pride and trepidation. Surely Velma hadn't written this story about her. Or could she be the mystery person who hired the private detective in the black derby? Had Vito been telling the truth all along? She read her sister's bio as the clerk, like a running motor, rambled on.

"You'll love it, miss," the clerk said, "it's an absolute must-read. The *New York Times* gave this book a good review. I'll bet you've heard plenty about *Chameleon*, huh?"

"Yes," Louise replied, examining the likeness in the photograph, running her fingers across the face. Almost two years since she last saw Velma.

"Do you know what the story's about?"

"Yes, I've heard all about it."

"Well, let me tell you." The clerk leaned over the counter and whispered as if sharing a secret. "You just wouldn't believe it," she insisted, waving her hand. "But this colored lady who's whiter than snow, whiter than you and me even, well, she changes color. Not really, because she's a human being, after all, but in a figurative sense. She's passing for white. Isn't that a witty expression? *Passing?* It's another dimension of the tragic mulatto, I'm told.

"Anyhow, I imagine Miss Brooks entitled it *Chameleon* because she's drawing an analogy between this colored woman and those awful little creatures who change color to outwit their predators, you know. Then she marries a white man who doesn't know she's—"

"How much?"

"Pardon?"

"How much?"

"How much what?"

"The book, miss, the book!"

"Oh, of course, the book. Well, that'll be two dollars and fifty cents, ma'am," the clerk replied, wounded.

Louise opened her purse and fingered through a roll of bills. "Can you change a twenty?"

"Seventeen dollars and fifty cents change coming up." She turned to press the cash-register keys. It rang and the drawer pushed out against her stomach. She turned to hand Louise her change, and she had gone, as if she'd never been there at all. "Andy!" the clerk called to the stockboy, who walked over reluctantly toward the counter with broom in hand. "Did you see that lady who was just here?" She stretched her neck over the heads in the store.

"What lady?"

"That lady, stupid. I mean, she was standing right here just a moment ago. Didn't you see her?"

"I didn't see nobody. I just been sweeping. Just doin' my job like you told me."

"But, you *must've* seen her," she exclaimed, gesticulating, mentally reliving the past few moments. "The pretty lady with the bob cut and black veil. I swear to you, she was just here a minute ago. Not that she was very friendly either, you know, kind of stuck-up. But she gave me a twenty, and I turned my back to make change. Then I turned around and she was gone. Just like that!" She snapped her fingers.

"I don't know. I didn't see no lady. Maybe you're reading too many books."

14

Turning her key into the lock, Louise tiptoed into the hollow silence of her mansion. Slipping out of her Beaute Strap shoes, she edged along the black and white diagonal tiles of the immense kitchen floor. Making certain Sara was nowhere in sight, she pulled out *Chameleon*. She adored the dustcover design—the Aaron Douglas illustration, the Van Vechten photograph on the back flap—but she had to destroy it.

Removing the dustcover, she approached the fireplace. She kissed

Velma's photograph, beheld it one last time, committed the pose to
memory and, with a match stick, set the cover aflame. She watched
it transform into a residue of ashes, and an unpleasant odor
lingered. Grabbing the brass-handled broom, she swept up the ashes
and pushed them down into the air vent. She'd instruct the butler
to empty and dispose of it tomorrow.

Now to hide the book. She frowned as she sought a safe place to
hide the book so she could retrieve it when she was alone and read
it as quickly as possible. Speaking of which, Vito should be home
any minute now. She grabbed her shoes and handbag, and ascended
the winding staircase. Hushed voices from an upstairs room trickled
down the staircase into Louise's alert ears.

"Den don't believe me," the dominant voice challenged. "Go an'
ast Sara fo' yo'sef."

"You *really* thank so?"

"I don't care how white she look, ain't no way you c' tell me she
ain't colored. Uh-uh, no way."

Louise paused on the staircase—out of view, but within
earshot—and listened further.

"Then, why Mr. B don't know she colored then?"

"Chile, Mr. B in love. White folks iz stupid when it come t' stuff
lak that. Down South, folks iz passin' alla tam."

"She do have kinda big butt, don't she?"

"An', looka dem lips. Ya evah seen lips dat big on a *real* white
lady? Well, has ya?"

"Can't say I have."

"White ladies hab thin lil, itty-bitty lips. An' sum of 'em ain't got
no lips at all."

"The mo' you talk, the mo' it make sense."

"She even smell colored. I done worked f' many a white lady an'
she don't smell lak no white lady t' me. Get up close t' her sumtam,
you see."

"Whatchu thank Mr. B do he fin' out?"

"I dunno. Mr. B wouldn't hurt a fly."

"Learn somethin' new eve'day, doncha?"

"Go ast Sara. She give ya da lowdown. Dats why her an' madam
don't git alon' too good. Sara done peeped her hol' card an' madam
sho nuff know it too. I betcha she fire Sara if she could."

"Nuh-uh. Not ef Mr. B got somethin' t' say 'bout it."

"Bet yo' ass Mr. B got somethin' t' say 'bout it. He payin' de bills
'roun' here, ain't he?"

"She can't fire Sara."

"Sara been heah longa dan alla us put togetha. Even longa dan *her*! But I tells ya rat now, plain az dis heah noze on ma face; one day, chile, one day, dem two iz gonna have it out an' dere gonna be mo' feathas flyin' dan a cacklin' henhouse. Lo'd Jesus! I sho wanna be heah t' see dat!"

"I ain't nevah knowed no colored gal name Luisa. You?"

"Shiiiit! *Luisa* my ass! Who da hell she thank she foolin' wid a name lak that!"

Louise skipped up the remainder of the staircase and stopped short. She caught her breath, regained her composure, and walked calmly into the room from which the gossip emanated. As she appeared in the doorway, the servants were startled.

"Aftanoon, ma'am."

"Nice haircut ya got dere, Mrs. B."

"I heard every word," Louise snapped, her face twisted with rage.

"Heard what?"

"You know what. I've been standing on that staircase listening to every word being said about me. Didn't hear me come in, did you?"

"No, ma'am."

"Naw, we ain't—"

"Well, you can stop what you're doing. You're both fired!"

"What?"

"Get your things and get out of here at once! I'll explain your dismissal to my husband. I can't tolerate such foolish gossip in my home. Now go!" She pointed to the staircase.

Dropping their work utensils, the servants sauntered from the room, their heads lowered. "What about what you owe us? We wanna be paid now!"

"I'll telephone your agency tomorrow. Pick up your checks there. Now, get out! You heard me, leave!"

They descended the staircase, giggling and snickering their way through the front door. Releasing a sigh, Louise listened for the door to slam before she continued. In the master bedroom, she opened the drawer of the night table. To her dismay, a revolver rested inside. Black, cold, threatening. She had never seen it before. Vito must have his reasons for owning one—more so for keeping it in the bedroom. Whatever his reason, she couldn't place the book there. She slid it beneath the mattress toward the middle of the bed. She lay on it, to be sure it couldn't be felt. She released another sigh, her heart pounding wildly, and was startled when she heard Vittorio open the front door and call her name.

BOOK FIVE

1929

A RETROSPECTIVE REVIEW

More books have been published about Negro life by both white and Negro authors than was the normal output of more than a decade in the past. . . . The proportions show the typical curve of a major American fad, and to a certain extent, this indeed it is. We shall not fully realize it until the inevitable reaction comes; when as the popular interest flags, the movement will lose thousands of supporters who are now under its spell, but who tomorrow would be equally hypnotized by the next craze.

—Alaine Locke
Opportunity, 1929

1

A typewriter sat upon a small table in the center of Velma's parlor, with a half-typed sheet of paper on the roller. Completed pages of a manuscript were neatly piled on the table beside it. Two half-filled cups of coffee sat opposite each other, gone cold some time ago. The green neon light blinked across the street while the brouhaha of a late-night party roared halfway down the block.

Rudy sat on the floor. A pencil tucked behind his ear, one in his hand, he studied a completed first draft.

Velma made fresh coffee in the kitchen, a cigarette with a long ash dangling from her lips. She heard Rudy mumble something, but was too tired to have him repeat it. "You say something?" she asked, entering the parlor with fresh cups of coffee.

"I knew it," Rudy said with exasperation, plucking the page with his finger. "This scene isn't working here. It's too contrived."

"Let me see," she said, and he handed her the few pages. He folded his hands behind his neck, and tilted it backward. "What's wrong with it?" Velma said, her eyes glued to the page.

"For one thing," Rudy said, "the understudy's character seems arbitrary to me."

"But, it's not arbitrary," Velma argued. "Like Scott says, 'If you choose it, better use it.' And we've effectively used the understudy."

"Yeah, well, the motivation of that character is still questionable."

"Oh! . . . Have you seen him lately?"

"Seen him? What're you talking about, Velma? I'm talking about the character in the play; I'm talking about motivation—"

"Well, I wasn't talking about the play." She lit a cigarette and inhaled. "I was talking about Scott."

"What about him?" Rudy didn't hide his impatience.

"Well?" Velma was embarrassed. "Have you seen him?"

"No."

"Talked to him?"

"No. Why?"

"Just asking. Don't get so—"

"Listen, Velma. We're here, or at least *I'm* here, to write a play, not true confessions. This is hardly the time or place for such—"

"Such what?"

"Far as I'm concerned, we've already said too much about Scott—"

"Okay, okay. I was just wondering."

I'll bet you were, he thought, too tired to say it.

"Look, Rudy, you're tired, I'm tired; let's just get through this and call it a night, huh? I swear, between this and the novel, my nerves are raw."

"I agree." Rudy sprang from the floor. Rubbing his hands together, he paced back and forth. "Okay, let's see what we've got so far. Act one, scene one; female protagonist is an ambitious, gifted actress, serious about her art, arrives in Harlem to do classic and serious work in the theater. Act one, scene two; she meets and falls in love with a known actor who later betrays her for a rival actress with whom she finds him in bed—"

"Is the rival actress white or Negro?" Velma asked.

"Velma, I don't know," Rudy said. "This is the part you wrote." Who else would've come up with the betrayal scene?

"Well, there's just different possibilities with either choice. I just wondered."

"Making her white could give us better possibilities. What do you think?"

"Fine with me," Velma said, lying on the floor, blowing smoke toward the neon light and watching it turn from gray-white to green.

"Okay; now," Rudy continued. "During the confrontation between the jilted lover and the actor, she loses control because she was used, or at least, she thinks she was. She picks a fight with him and slaps him—"

"You know something, Rudy?"

"What?"

Velma sat on the floor, her legs curled around her, feet tucked beneath. Coffee cup in hand, she stared ahead as if forgetting what she had to say. Rudy waited for her reply, but she said nothing. "Well?" Rudy said. "What is it now?"

"Sometimes I think," she began, "and hear me out before you say anything, okay? But sometimes, it all seems such a farce, doesn't it? I mean, I've been thinking about this for a long time and I'm afraid to talk about it in a way. Afraid of what it might really mean."

If she came up with another analysis of their triadic dynamics, he was out the door.

"Here we are writing a play," she continued. "About what we've loosely termed 'pure' Negro drama. What's Negro, Rudy? I mean, for a people who descended from Africa—although we're not literally Africans—we sure reflect Europeans more than any other culture. Think about that. How come we don't embrace Africa? You ever thought about that? Instead, we talk of Paris, London, Rome; we're really dominated by those cultures whether we admit it or not. We dress like them, talk like them, our values are westernized notions of what it's all about, and we look at everything from that perspective."

Rudy was exhausted from their twelve-hour workday. All he wanted was to finish up, go home, and climb into his Murphy bed. But while what Velma was saying had no bearing on their project, it expressed an interesting point of view. He didn't have the strength or clarity to challenge her, yet he couldn't agree.

"The whole thing hit me just recently," she continued. "It was like a spiritual awakening, a slap in the face. Of all the artistic groups in this so-called *Negro* Renaissance, none of us actually reflect ancestral Africa. Painters and sculptors do; but writers don't. Studying Barthe's work at the museum the other day really made it all click for some reason. Doesn't that strike you as odd?"

"That's a dangerously provocative thought, but roughly sixty years out of slavery, we're not doing too badly either. We must take a step at a time."

"Maybe, but it's sure something to think about. My sister's been talking about it for as long as I can remember and I just couldn't see what she meant. Guess I didn't want to."

"Is that the sister you were telling me—"

"No. That was my baby sister. She's passing. How about that?" She couldn't believe she'd actually said it to someone. As much as it muddled her head, she'd never heard the words spoken by herself to anyone outside her family.

"Seriously?" Rudy asked.

"That's what I wanted to tell you that night."

"Why didn't you?" Rudy felt wide awake now.

"Oh, I don't know. I wasn't sure of my motive. You see, I don't want people to think I wrote my novel about her, because I really didn't. It's important to me for you to believe that. I had that germ of an idea even before we met Scott or Mrs. Vanderpool. She didn't disappear until about a year later."

"She disappeared?"

"Hmmm, hmmm," Velma said, sipping her coffee. "And, I'll tell you, Rudy, I'm worried sick. We have no idea where she is. Wish I could find her somehow—"

"Why don't you? You *should* find her."

"It might not be that easy. It could ruin her life, tracking her down like that."

"Yeah, you're right. It could be quite a burden to bear."

"And all that time, I was so busy with my own career and personal life, I didn't see it coming, due to my own selfishness. Maybe, that's what Miriam saw. Mother certainly did."

"You miss your mother, don't you?"

"Yes . . . I do. Since she died, I haven't really had a family. Miriam's around, but Louise is God knows where. I've lost all sense of belonging somehow." A tear rolled down her cheek. "I'm grateful to have you though." She wiped her tear and sniffled. "You're the only person I can tell this to."

"What about Scott?"

"If I told him, he'd find a way to use it against me, probably."

"You know what you *could* do."

"What?"

"Hire a private detective to locate her. That way, you can find out without letting her know. It's safer, don't you think?"

"Believe me, I've turned that thought over so many times, it's stale. She asked us not to find her."

Everything seemed to be crumbling and disintegrating around her—family, friends, lovers, the integrity of her work. She didn't know what tomorrow would bring and, for the first time in her life, was afraid to wake up and find out.

To Rudy, she'd never looked as terrified and uncertain of where her life was headed as she did sitting in the squat position on her parlor floor. She hadn't said much, but he knew enough of the fragmented pieces that formed the porous fabric of her life. She needed a spiritual boost, a burst of laughter, something, anything, and he felt it his responsibility, as her friend, to provide it. He tried to think of uplifting, optimistic pictures to paint for her, but nothing moved with any swiftness through his mind, and the last thing he wanted to resort to was cliché.

Distracted from the silence by soft tinkly sounds in the room, they turned suddenly and noticed a pair of moths hovering, their silky, powdered wings flapping against the light bulb. Realizing what it was, they sighed, and returned to the silence.

"That's what we're all like," Rudy said.

"Like what?"

"We're just a bunch of moths drawn to the light," Rudy said, straining a chuckle. "We move blindly toward the brilliance of whatever it is we're searching for." He thought of himself, Velma, Scott, Harlem, even Velma's sister whom he'd never met. "And we're not wise enough to know that if we get too close to the red-hot center, it could kill us."

"Oh, Rudy," she said, "what am I going to do? I'm nearly thirty without a husband or children. I've lost half my family and probably Scott too—"

"Shhh, listen, Velma," Rudy suggested. "Why don't you get some sleep. You look exhausted. If there's any way I can help you, don't hesitate to let me know." Standing above her, he grasped her chin and tilted her face upward. "I mean that, Velma. I'll do whatever I can, and I think you know that."

"Rudy, you're priceless." She took his hand, kissed it, and pressed it against her cheek. "I knew I could trust your sensitivity and understanding. Who would I have if I didn't have you?" Tears slipped down her cheeks, onto Rudy's knuckles.

"Get some sleep," he whispered, then leaned forward to kiss her on the forehead. "We can finish this work in the morning."

2

Purchasing a gold bracelet at a neighborhood jeweler, Miriam haggled with the proprietor. She had never bought any real jewelry before and knew she was at a disadvantage as the man across the counter intimidated her with price comparisons and carat value. All she wanted was something nice without having to spend a great deal of money. Satisfied with the simple S chain and the dangling charm, she paid for it and asked the man to wrap it in a pretty box.

She couldn't wait to see the look on Agnes's face when she gave it to her. Miriam was shaking hands with a myriad of emotions that until Agnes, she'd never been acquainted with.

She felt like herself again. There hadn't been any problems at her job since Mrs. Greerson last spoke with her. If anything, Miriam continued to substantiate what her superiors knew about her all along; that she was an outstanding employee who loved nursing, and she moved about during her work shift with the zealous buzz of a rookie on her first hospital assignment.

She couldn't explain how she felt, but wouldn't trade it for anything in the world. It occurred to her that she'd been released from something—a darkness, a morass, an ignorance pertaining to the total working parts of her anatomy. Like inhaling the sweet breeze of a second wind, she thought, until now, she hadn't lived—not *really* lived.

Funny the way things happened. Who would've thought that she'd begin to enjoy the bitterness of bathtub gin, or allow another woman to make love to her. Good Lord! It felt good just thinking about it. People at work, even doctors, noticed something different about her, but couldn't place it. When they asked, she just smiled. She was taking it a day at a time.

Her body was alive, no longer dormant, and she thought of Agnes as Princess Charming, who awakened, with a kiss, whatever had slept inside her. Sometimes she laughed, realizing that all this had been brought about by "little" Agnes who, at one time, Miriam had thought, didn't have the gumption to wash her own face without Tommy's permission.

When Agnes returned home the day after they made love, she found that Miriam had bought her a cute Spanish lace blouse and had cooked a four-course meal. She lit candles and turned out the lights. Agnes didn't know what to make of it.

"What's all this?" Agnes asked, in a different mood than when she left that morning.

"I just wanted to do something for you," Miriam said. "It's my way of saying I love you, Agnes."

There came no reply, and this, more than Agnes's apparent apathy, caused Miriam worry.

"Don't you love me too?" Miriam asked.

"Yeah," Agnes said distantly. "I love all my friends."

The generalization bothered Miriam. But rather than pressure Agnes into giving the reply she wanted, she said nothing. When dinner was over, Agnes thanked her, yawned, and announced she was going to bed.

"You're going to bed?" Miriam asked, concealing her disappointment. She'd wanted to go to the movies, or to a nightclub, or do something, for once in her life.

"Yeah, girl. I'm exhausted."

"Well," Miriam said delicately. "You can sleep . . . in my bed . . . if you like."

"Not tonight," Agnes said. "I'm sleeping in my room . . . alone."

Miriam chose not to read anything into the sudden change of heart. Last night, Agnes was all over her like rice on newlyweds, but now she acted as if she didn't remember it. That's okay; folks got a right to their moods.

Weeks passed and in her quiet moments she recalled the man in the hospital some years ago who, because she ignored his advances, called her a bulldiker. It was alarming to think he knew something she didn't, but she concluded that he was making a flippant remark that had nothing to do with who or what she was. Every woman who refused him must be a bulldiker. Still, there was the possibility he saw something in her she refused to be aware of herself. She reconsidered her "meeting" with the UNIA officials who, nearly two years ago, asked her about her affiliation with a woman named Agnes Brown. Laughing in retrospect, she believed that her defense might have been different had all this happened before then. Nowadays, she felt ashamed for allowing them to intimidate her, ask her about her personal business, and feel they were completely justified in doing so. How easily they could throw darts. She held no grudges against their inquiry. It was expected, given the parameters of the organization. Since then, she decided it was none of their damn business. And rather than deny the charge, she might have said just that. She didn't ask what they did behind closed doors. These were her big thoughts anyway. Actually, if the situation should ever recur, she was uncertain how she'd react or what she'd say.

What did it mean being an integral part of UNIA? She didn't fancy living a double life, as Louise probably had to do before her disappearance. But now, she thought a person's sexual orientation was a petty ground upon which to be charged with misconduct, so long as it didn't infringe upon or embarrass the organization. Yes, they were expected to procreate and flourish, but there were enough folks making babies that any contribution she couldn't make wouldn't be missed. She loved and believed in the cause as much as any of them, including Garvey, and didn't feel she had to make excuses to appease them or prove her dedication. All the work she did and the time she had given should have sufficed.

Despite all that had happened in the past three years, she'd not faltered once in her vision of UNIA, the voyage to Liberia and the establishment of roots in a New World—a vision she continued to embrace although the ship lines had failed. But she'd be damned if she'd approach it as self-effacingly as she once had. Someone had opened the windows of her routine existence, letting out the stale air, and she wasn't about to shut them. UNIA could govern her politics, values, principles, virtues, and vision, but nowadays, it stopped at her bedroom door. If she didn't have any children by now, she figured they'd stop asking. She couldn't possibly give any more than she'd already given. Whenever the pressure got to her, she shifted her thoughts to Agnes which provided her strength; an audacious stance against it all that she'd never dreamed of.

She couldn't wait to see Agnes tonight. They hadn't slept together since that night, and she found herself yearning. Agnes slept in her own room, and went about her business as usual, as if nothing had happened between them. They never discussed it, and Agnes's behavior said there was nothing to discuss. Maybe there wasn't, but Miriam had a lot inside she wanted to share, and she couldn't ignore it and leave it bottled up. They were different that way. Agnes treated everything casually, and never needed to analyze or discuss anything. Miriam envied this. She had always thought of herself as the shy one. Yet now she desired to open up to it, celebrate it, and revel in it. So today, during her time between work and home, she decided to give Agnes some incentive. Not that she was trying to lure her into bed with gifts. She wanted to do something nice and thoughtful.

She wondered if Agnes would move with her to Liberia. She had barely sold her on the idea of UNIA membership, and since the meeting Tommy disrupted, Agnes hadn't returned. Considering the possible dilemma, Miriam wondered if she herself would stay in Harlem just to maintain their relationship, whatever it was becoming. God! Love did make folks do what they didn't want to do. She wanted to move to Liberia, yet it could all be jeopardized if Agnes wasn't boarding the ship. The thought frightened her.

When Miriam got home, Agnes greeted her, all dressed up to go out.

"How was your day?" Miriam asked.

"Same as yesterday and the day before," Agnes chuckled.

"Well," Miriam said, "look at you." She eyed her head to toe. "Where're you going?"

"Out for a change. Tired of sitting in this house."

"Anybody I know?" Miriam hated to ask.

"I'm just having a drink with a friend."

"Oh." Miriam began digging through her purse. "I got something for you."

"What?"

Miriam handed her the small box with a pink ribbon. Agnes opened it, much too slowly for Miriam's liking. Unwrapping the box, Agnes sighed, looked at Miriam and attempted with difficulty, to conceal her gut reaction.

"How nice," Agnes said, monotone. "You bought this for me?"

"Yes, I thought you'd like it," Miriam said, thinking Agnes could show a bit more enthusiasm. "Try it on."

Agnes did, then admired the gold around her wrist with the dangling charm. "Must've cost you a pretty penny." She undid the catch and put it back in the box.

"You don't like it," Miriam said.

"I do, but . . ."

"But what? Tell me," Miriam said, feeling panicky.

"Just that you been buying me things and I don't feel I should accept them."

"Why not?" Miriam asked.

"Because you don't have to buy me anything, Miriam."

"I know that. I just wanted to."

"Well, it's very sweet," Agnes said. "But, please, don't buy me anything else." She didn't want to hurt her friend's feelings, but since that night they slept together, Miriam was getting carried away. Stuff like this could ruin a good friendship.

Miriam felt crushed. Agnes's reaction was not at all what she had expected. And she wondered if Agnes now regretted what happened that night. A long awkward silence passed between them.

"Well, I guess I should be going," Agnes said, nervously fumbling with the gift box. She stepped around Miriam to get her jacket.

"Agnes?"

"Yes?" she said, turning around to face Miriam.

"Can we go out together sometime?"

"Sure," Agnes said. "Next week if you like."

"Are you coming home tonight?"

"Of course I'm coming home. But don't wait up."

Miriam was trying not to pry, but couldn't help it.

"How come you didn't ask if I wanted to go?" she said, trying to control the twitch in her face.

Agnes laughed. "Miriam Brooks, since when do you go out?"

"We go out to dinner sometime."

"Yeah, and we're going out next week."

Agnes placed the jewelry box in her dresser drawer, buttoned her jacket, and headed for the door. "Good night, Miriam."

"Good night, Agnes," Miriam said. "Have a good time." She watched Agnes walk out the door. She didn't know exactly, but something wasn't right. She didn't even wear the bracelet. Miriam sauntered into her bedroom, attempting to figure it all out, hoping she'd again wake up in the middle of the night with Agnes snuggled close to her.

3

Turning from Park Avenue onto Seventy-sixth Street, in his Studebaker, Scott headed for Madison Avenue. After leaving Mrs. Vanderpool's penthouse, he wondered if he'd done the right thing. Underestimating Mrs. V could bring Rudy and Velma more calamity and tribulation, both professional and personal, than either of them bargained for. His visit to the penthouse was his clandestine means of saving the only two friends he had. Naturally, Velma and Rudy might not see it that way, but then, they didn't know Mrs. V, or how shrewd and ruthless she could be.

It was his responsibility, since he had provided the introduction, to stop his friends from tying a noose around each other's necks. He'd never thought they'd get this far with their collaboration, assuming Robie wouldn't be interested. The joint venture didn't bother him as much as Velma not requesting him, her boyfriend, to be her collaborator. He couldn't stand Rudy being asked to fill shoes meant for him, her lover of almost four years. But as he had spoken in their behalf, Mrs. V promised to go easy on them. They were young, naive, and ambitious; instead of setting out to cause confusion, their motives were a bit more noble. What else could he have done? Had he not intervened, their heads would have rolled; then perhaps, when the mopping of the blood and guts was all over, Mrs. V might ask questions.

What was he going to do about Rudy? He'd taken on a role similar to Scott's father earlier in his life; an obstacle that wasn't about to yield. If not for Rudy, he and Velma would undoubtedly be married by now. It wasn't as if Velma didn't love him. Had he believed she didn't, they wouldn't have lasted these past four years. But something happened between her and Rudy—if only once—and Velma apparently hadn't shaken it or cut the strings that bound them together. Marrying her would mean adopting Rudy as their son. God only knew what she was doing with him. She included Rudy in all their activities and undoubtedly would continue to do so if he married her.

He loved Velma and Rudy, easily the two best friends he'd ever had. He wouldn't trade them for the Pulitzer Prize. There was something attractive and magnetic about handsome, gallant Rudy, though he really didn't know what he felt. And he imagined that most men, and women too, at some point in their lives, entertained such sentiments about a best friend of the same sex. But that's about as far as it went. He wanted no more to explore it than he wanted to explore poverty or destitution. Okay, so he tried to talk big during their lunch three years ago at a sidewalk café. But he never dreamed Rudy would take him up on it, be charged by it, escort him to an underground men's bar, or threaten the balance of their relationships by betraying Velma.

As an only child, he had been reared to look out for no one but himself. Without siblings with which to learn and practice the virtue of sharing, he had never absorbed the lesson. Sharing anyone he slept with was out of the question, as was sharing the spotlight of his literary reputation. Yet, he'd learned something from Velma and Rudy he'd never encountered growing up in Benjamin Scott's Boston household.

Until arriving in Harlem, he'd known little, if anything, of what it meant to be Negro. He understood the novelty he was to the white children of his boarding school. He was theirs to stare at and sometimes ridicule. And he'd learned what it meant to be Negro at Harvard, and living abroad in France, where the curiosity was ever present. The French, nevertheless, had treated him largely as an equal, a rare bird they weren't accustomed to seeing on the Rue St. Jacques.

Harlem, however, was another galaxy altogether with its own rules and mores. Never before had he seen millions of Negroes who took unequivocal pride in being just that. These people, his people, downtrodden as they were, had little else to sustain themselves other than racial pride. The word Negro, with all its historical, cultural connotations, took on new meaning, and he wished his father could somehow be forced to live here and discover that Negroes were the most genuine, upwardly mobile, resilient people on the face of the earth. Despite the odds, they possessed a buoyancy which kept them afloat on a sea of oppression. There was a tremendous amount to be said and felt about that. There was no more to be ashamed of here than in the Italian, Polish, Irish, and Jewish ghettoes below Washington Square. This is what Harlem, Velma and Rudy gave him, this priceless revelation. He held his father accountable for any remaining core of self-hatred he carried in himself. There were upper-middle-class Negroes who refused to invest their souls in self-effacing assimilation, and he wondered where his father went awry, what he was running and hiding from. Velma and Rudy put him in touch with his birthright, his heritage, and tumbled him into a cultural love affair. If, when he had arrived in 1923, he had possessed what he had since accumulated, he could have avoided alienation and, perhaps, made more friends who wouldn't, like his mates at boarding school and Harvard, think him an oddity. Those days, he didn't fit anywhere, given the stringent limits of a racially charged American society. But now, he felt whole, intact, his incongruous bits and pieces unified, peacefully cohesive. He was indebted to Velma and Rudy for that.

Velma had given him many things, and his desire to marry her was as strong as his passion to write. However, he didn't view Rudy as part of the marital picture. If Velma had anything to do with it, he suspected, she'd probably stick Rudy between them in the honeymoon bed, and that he couldn't stand for. Rudy, his best male friend, would ultimately get over him. Velma, though, might not ever stop loving Rudy.

Honking horns snapped him back to reality. Madison Avenue was clogged bumper to bumper, curb to curb. He rolled down the window, and stuck his neck out to discern the holdup. Unable to locate the problem causing the bottleneck traffic just north of Grand Central Station, he pulled his head back in, hummed a tune, and tapped his fingers upon the steering wheel.

Parking her spanking-new Rolls-Royce—an anniversary gift from her husband—Louise did a last check in the rearview mirror. Straightening her bob cut with swift hand strokes, she realized something was missing. With a silent panic, she ran her hands clumsily through her purse. Out of frustration, or disbelief that she could be so remiss, she emptied the purse's contents onto the passenger seat. How could she have forgotten something like that? For weeks now, she had meant to remind her chambermaid to place an extra veiled hat in her purse for those days when she drove to midtown. There was nothing to be done about that now, except to purchase another one.

Today, more than ever, she wanted to drive uptown and sneak a visit with her family. With new life in her womb, she needed desperately to renew family ties, have Mother welcome her home. She also wanted to see her sisters. She'd tell them, in rapid recapitulation, what she'd been doing for the last two years. Her expanding waistline and the Rolls-Royce would say it sufficiently. She was happy and doing well, except it meant close to nothing if she couldn't share it with them. From now on, she planned to see them at least once a month, until she could get her life straightened out. She couldn't wait. As soon as she could buy herself a new hat, she would head for West 141st Street. Nothing could change her mind.

She stepped into the street and smoothed out the wrinkles in her fashionable maternity outfit. Looking around her—more specifically, for the fat man with the black derby—she lowered her head, avoiding anyone's glance.

Politely, she stood back as two elderly women were leaving while she entered the millinery shop. Though the clerk tried to interest Louise in the extended line of fashionable hats from Paris and Milan—from the window, she had watched her get out of the Rolls-Royce—Louise insisted that only a plain veiled hat would do, maybe a few. Trying on several types in the counter mirror, she purchased three hats of varying colors and styles. She held on to the one which matched her outfit. She was running late. On the sidewalk, she pressed the hat firmly against her head and pulled the veil down over her face.

"Velma!" someone called her from behind. "Velma, is that you?"

Louise turned abruptly. A man she'd never seen in her life called her by her sister's name. Handsome, brown-skinned, impeccably dressed, a pipe clenched between sparkling white teeth. He leaned upon an automobile parked directly behind hers; a royal blue Studebaker Six whose fender slightly rubbed against the Rolls.

"You'll have to excuse me," the man said apologetically, slowly walking toward her. "But, you strongly favor and walk like someone

I know. Oh, I bet a lady attractive as yourself always gets opening lines like that. But, seriously, you do remind me—"

Louise scurried toward the car and ignored the man who insisted she looked familiar. Her hands trembling, she fumbled with the key, and attempted to turn the lock. Inside, she rolled up the windows and started the ignition simultaneously. The man followed her. He ran over to her side, and asked her to roll down the window. She never looked at him, as sweat dripped down her forehead. Oncoming traffic wouldn't allow her to pull off just yet as the man persisted in speaking with her. She turned her face away from him, toward the passenger side. A policeman appeared, walked toward Louise, and inquired through the rolled up passenger window, "Lady, this coon givin' you any trouble?" She affirmed the question with a nod. "Okay, buster," the policeman yelled across the roof, causing people on the sidewalk to stop and take notice. "Let's move it along, here. The lady says you're making trouble for her. What the hell're you doing down here on Madison Avenue anyway? Why don't you stay up there in Harlem where you belong!"

She used the opportunity to pull away from the curb. The Rolls lurched forward with a jerk. She put the gear in reverse and turned the steering wheel with all the strength she could muster, as perspiration drenched her armpits. Finally, her automobile joined the stream of traffic headed north. Through the rearview mirror, she watched as the policeman and the well-dressed man came to words. Now there were two reasons to be cautious: the fat man, and him. Instantly, she abandoned her plans to head uptown. She would not venture north of Central Park South, where she was meeting Vittorio for lunch.

4

"Please have a seat, Velma," Mrs. Vanderpool said, motioning toward the footstools beneath her regal chair. "Have you any idea why I asked you to tea today?"

"No I don't," Velma replied sincerely, refusing the tea.

"I'll get right to the point," Mrs. Vanderpool said, sipping her tea. "What projects are you presently working on, my dear?"

"Well," Velma said, swallowing, wondering exactly what she was getting at, "I've begun another novel, writing bits and pieces of poetry for another collection and, let's see . . . oh, yes, I helped Scott with some research for his novel."

"Is that all?"

"Yes. Why?"

"Aren't you forgetting something?" Mrs. Vanderpool arched her fading eyebrows.

"Not that I know of." Now who went behind my back and opened his mouth to this woman?

"Well, my dear, perhaps I can refresh your memory a bit." She smiled gloatingly. Velma had never known her to be so condescending—at least, not with her—but she returned the smile. Smiling, when her gut-level impulse was to jump up and grab the old bag around the throat. She had a good notion of what was coming.

"You see, Velma," Mrs. Vanderpool continued, "I believe you've let me down. Now I know I can't trust you. That, my dear, is one of the most dreadful things for me; to find out that I simply cannot trust my godchildren. It's more disillusioning than you know."

"Please get to the point," Velma said defensively, knowing what she was up against and eager to confront it.

"As you wish. Three years ago, when I first made your acquaintance, I fairly warned you that any endeavor you might contemplate against my knowledge or approval would get back to me, did I not? I fairly warned you that your old godmother has eyes in the back of her head; I'm sure you recall? . . . Yes? . . . Well, in that vein, it has painfully come to my attention that you and Mr. Rudolph have written a new play. I understand you intend to bring it to Broadway with Paul Robeson in the starring role. Now, before I proceed any further, allow me to ascertain: is the aforementioned true?"

Velma's neck stiffened. Sharp words were at the tip of her tongue. She wanted to let them out and be done with it. Tell the old woman it was none of her goddamned business *what* she was working on; that she could take her money back, and her roadster with the leather upholstery. Instead, she was calm, and reserved the rage for the rounds to come. "Yes, it's true."

So that's it, Velma thought. She found out about our project and now she wants me to sweat it out as if she caught me stealing her silverware.

Glancing around the room, she recalled the first time she'd been there with Scott and Rudy in the winter of 1926. The gigantic room, the old lady, and the servants hadn't changed, but after two successfully published books, a four-year affair with Harlem's most celebrated novelist, a mother's death, and a baby sister's disappearance, she had. She didn't need the woman anymore, and feared her discomfort about the association with her was grounded in uncertainty—beyond the contract print. Her disassociation with her would mean a substantial bite out of her income, but she didn't enjoy having this old woman looking over her shoulder whenever she decided upon a project. She'd never even considered artistic patronage, was certain Rudy hadn't either, but they went along with the plan, trusting Scott, who'd described himself as doing them a favor. And a favor it was indeed. Without the introduction to Mrs. Vanderpool, she couldn't imagine how her career might have fared. Who knew when *The Darker Sister* or *Chameleon* would have been published. But stipulations and clauses was the stop where she got off, and with no debtors breathing down her neck, this showdown in the living room of the Park Avenue penthouse couldn't have come at a more opportune time. Three years of free money was great while it lasted, but every beginning was accompanied by an end, and now, 1929 was as good an ending as any.

"I see," Mrs. Vanderpool said. "So, then—"

"Who told you—"

"It's not important who told me. The issue here is why you disobeyed."

"Disobeyed?" The taste of it was putrid.

"You went ahead when I was quite adamant about the do's and don'ts of my terms and conditions. So, what have you to say for yourself?"

"I'm going to do the play."

"Ah yes, the play in question. As I understand it, it's a polemic work of tragedy, an indictment of societal ills, a social commentary—"

"It's not full of dancing, singing, and comedy, if that's what you mean."

"You and Mr. Rudolph have every intention of doing it?"

"We'd like to. We feel the theater is inundated with comedies. No one really deals with the social ills—"

"My dear Miss Brooks, you're an artist. An artist, Miss Brooks, not a politician or statesman. Artistry, and only that, is your role in life. It's the duty of you people to produce works of art, nothing else. Leave politics to—"

"In other words, stay in my place?"

"Miss Brooks, I can't recall ever seeing you quite so ornery. You're becoming rather defensive about—"

"Yes I am. It really gets me how people like you—"

"People like me? Well, let me remind you, dear, people like me have been supporting the likes of you for the past three years. Are you so ungrateful—"

"I'm not ungrateful. Yes, you supported me, but then you got your part of the bargain too, you know. It wasn't exactly charity."

"I'll tell you what. I'll permit you and Mr. Rudolph to continue with the play, but under one condition."

"Yes?"

"You do a complete rewrite. Turn the Greek tragedy into comedy. Make people laugh instead of beating them over the head with messages. As I've said before, Negroes are gay people who exude a primitive and exotic—"

"We won't do it. We either do the play the way it's written, or we don't do it at all!"

"Oh, you're terribly mistaken, dear. Either you rewrite it to my specifications, or neither this play nor any other will ever see the light of day. I'll cut you off without a penny!"

"Lady, look at me!" Velma shouted at her. "What do you see? An African with Ubangi lips and a bone through my nose? I'm not African; I'm an American descendant of Africa, and there's a world of difference. I have no idea what you mean when you speak of exotic and primitive. I'm no more primitive than you!"

"I refuse to listen to this nonsense—"

"I've never been outside this city, much less this country, and I have no idea what Africa's like, only superficially. From what I understand, you're better traveled than anyone I know. You've seen the cultures of Africa, Brazil, and the Caribbean in all their *exotic primitiveness*. But, look around you, lady; you're on Park Avenue now. You won't see that here in America. American Negroes look just like you. We're *comparatively* more primitive than you, thank God! but we're not exactly running from hut to hut in loincloths either!"

"Well!" Mrs. Vanderpool said, appalled, her face turning red, her collapsed chest heaving. "You've certainly made up your mind about this, haven't you?"

"Yes I have."

"What do you think we should do?"

"I don't know about you, but I want out. I'm doing this play whether you like it or not. No one stands in the way of my artistic growth, lady, nobody. My integrity, both personal and professional, is at stake here!"

"Artistic growth? Personal and professional integrity?" Mrs. Vanderpool feigned a laugh which caused her to choke on phlegm and produced an unpleasant wheezing sound. "Now you've got yourself established with a little name in the big literary world. Well, let me remind you," she said, her tone becoming more stern and threatening, "of the limitations of your talent."

"What? When I published both times, you said I was one of the most promising prodigies you'd ever supported. So, which is it?" Isn't that just like white folks!

"I'm well acquainted with the sensitivity of the creative artist. I purposely avoided telling you of your literary shortcomings, because I know how upsetting that can be. However, my dear, the truth is that you're painfully limited and I wouldn't be a bit surprised if you never published again."

"I want my contract dissolved!"

"And that's it? After all I've done for you?"

"Don't pull that 'freed slave leaving the philanthropy of the plantation' routine. It's terribly dated."

"Then you may have your wish. I imagine Mr. Rudolph expresses the same desires as yourself."

"I can't speak for him." Velma paused a moment. "Did you speak with Mr. Rudolph?"

"Never mind. I believe there's nothing left for us to say to each other."

"I'll have my agent, Elizabeth Marbury, contact your lawyers in the morning. Good day, Mrs. Vanderpool."

"Well, look at you. You think you don't need me now."

"Never did. Never will."

"Whether we agree or not," Mrs. Vanderpool said, her tone sounding wounded, reconciliatory, "there's no reason to part as adversaries. Now, we're acting childish. We've been friends for three years. In all that time, your godmother never—"

"That's another thing. You're not my godmother. I'm not your godchild. Just another one of your *exotic* fantasies."

"As you wish," Mrs. Vanderpool said, rising from her thronelike chair, her hands trembling, her tone resuming its former acrimony.

"With an attitude like that, let us forget we ever knew each other. I'll be most happy to end your contract and forget I ever met you!"

"You've read my very thoughts, Mrs. Vanderpool. Good day to you too!"

5

While shaving and getting dressed, Vittorio insisted that Louise be ready to go out that night when he got home. They never did anything, he complained, hardly went anywhere, and he was bored with sitting at home. Louise could barely make out his words through the running water in the bathroom basin, as she lay in bed in the adjoining room.

"What did you say, Vito?"

"We're going out tonight."

"But I don't want to, sweetheart."

"*Cara mia*, we haven't been out of this house in ages."

"So what?" she said. "After the baby, we'll go out again."

"I don't think I can wait that long. Besides, you need the exercise."

"I get plenty of exercise every day, honey. I meet you for lunch, don't I?"

"We can't dance or listen to jazz at the Tea Garden."

In the bathroom, Vittorio's valet stood to the side holding a pan of hot water, fresh towels draped across his arm. Vittorio poked his head into the bedroom. "Tonight, be dressed, and that's that. Cabaret, dinner, dancing."

Louise didn't really object to a night out on the town; she too was a bit bored with staying home. But she couldn't tell him that she feared stepping outside the confines of anonymous safety. The only place she felt secure and unthreatened was in her home. Sometimes, she couldn't believe she'd actually married Vittorio; dreams really did come true, like Madame C. J. Walker's. She loved living as a wealthy woman, in a house whose individual rooms were larger than the entire West 141st Street apartment of her childhood. There was nothing like having more cash on hand than she could possibly spend, dining at elegant, expensive restaurants, or driving a new Rolls-Royce that was hers and hers alone. And who could object to being chauffeured, or having crepes suzette in bed, or chambermaids caring for the clothes she purchased impulsively everywhere from Lord & Taylor to Saks Fifth Avenue? Having servants to fulfill her every whim, to clean, polish, and dust the most beautiful house she'd ever seen was the only way to live. She felt safe in this exile of her own choosing. Once she stepped over the threshold and penetrated larger Manhattan, she exchanged solitude for a spin on the roulette wheel, helplessly at the mercy of whoever might spot her in a restaurant, on the street, or among a crowd, and declare *Louise! Isn't that Louise Brooks?* As it was, an unidentified gentleman called her by her sister's name on Madison Avenue, and she didn't think she could survive another such incident. It was too alarming, detrimental to her nerves. The friendly outside world, where she lived and worked before she met Vito, was now becoming an enemy in various guises. And she felt the only way to do battle was to wave her white flag and remain in her palatial prison.

She worried about the baby, not so much if the child would be healthy with two eyes, two ears, ten fingers and toes; naively, she took all that for granted. Nothing troubled her more than the child's possible complexion, hair texture, and features. Vito was a shade or two darker than she, as were his parents, and she hoped the child would favor its paternal line. She knew the tricks that genes played. She could examine her own family and attest to that. Between Mother, Father, Miriam, Velma, and herself, not two of them shared an "exact" similar complexion. Miriam at one end of the spectrum and Louise at the opposite left little or no room to predict what color her baby would be. But she couldn't upset herself over this. Chances were the child would favor Vito and his parents—thank God they were swarthy—and her anxiety, God willing, would be in vain.

As Vittorio finished dressing and bent over to kiss her good-bye on the forehead, the baby kicked. She closed her eyes and held her stomach. Vittorio smiled the classic grin of an expectant father, asked if his firstborn son was giving Mama a trying time and pressed his ear against her stomach to listen. Louise nodded her head, thinking it symbolic that whenever she worried about the baby, it moved inside her as if reacting to her innermost thoughts.

"Just remember," he reminded her. "Be ready tonight because we two are going to dance until dawn." He watched her massaging her stomach and corrected himself. "Rather, we three."

"Oh, shut up," she said playfully.

Standing before the mirror, Louise applied skillful strokes of makeup. She turned sideways and pressed both palms against her stomach. Looking up, she saw Vittorio's reflection close behind, and he wrapped both arms around her waist. "I look terrible in this dress," she complained.

"You look *bellissima*," he said, kissing her. "Just a little pregnant and it's going to get bigger than that."

"Anything to get me out."

"We haven't been out since we were married, except to a few friends' houses here and there. People ask if I got married or entered the priesthood. I miss the Cotton Club."

"Is that where we're going?" She frowned.

"Yes, why? Something wrong?"

"No, nothing," she said, consciously smoothing out her face. "You just didn't say where we were going, that's all."

"I haven't been there for over a year. I want to hear this new band everybody is talking about. Someone named Duke or something. Are you ready?"

"Almost. Just let me put on some lipstick." She painted her lips, blood-red tulips like Clara Bow's, and fastened on diamond drop earrings. Vittorio checked himself in the mirror, brushed lint from his shoulders, tugged at the tuxedo tails, the cuffs of his sleeves, and blocked his top hat. Louise sprayed her neck and wrists with a mist of Houbigant, and admired the reflection of Vittorio's widow's peak and bridged eyebrows. God, the pretty man just oozed sex!

Vittorio released the brake and slid the Rolls slowly in reverse down the circular driveway. Louise took a veiled hat from her purse and adjusted it in the rearview mirror, pulling at the sides.

She was relieved that he felt better since coming home in a bad mood that evening. She kept asking what was wrong, but he refused to talk about it. By the grimace on his face, she guessed that he and his father were at it again. Their bickering continued even while his parents stayed at the Plaza. She'd seen that look before and knew, when it came to him and Vincenzo, her reticence was appreciated. There was little she could do about their fractured relationship. She liked her father-in-law, loved her husband, and wanted to see the men get along better. Lucia was still lukewarm, which Louise could tolerate so long as the woman wasn't in her house. Whatever was wrong with Vito, he'd tell her if and when he was ready. The last thing she wanted to do was apply pressure.

Sara was suddenly proving to be quite an ally, and Louise smiled thinking about her as the Rolls purred like a kitten through the Manhattan streets. When she fired the two house staff members, she harrowingly discovered that Sara knew what she was. This placed several of their past moments in proper context. Since then, Louise found herself treating the head maid as carefully as if their roles had been reversed. Knowing Sara was privy to her secret, she humbled herself, and did nothing to ruffle the woman's feathers. Sara's loyalty to Vito rivaled Louise's. The woman could hold this obscure information over her head like a circus trainer lashing the whip at a Siberian tiger to jump through the hoop of fire. Never again did she raise her voice at Sara, or shout at her as she had that morning in the kitchen.

But, that evening when Vito came home from work a bit petulant, she was afraid to tell him that she'd accidentally broken the glass frame that held a flattering portrait of Lucia as a young woman. It sat on his nightstand, and, in her haste to select an evening dress that would best conceal her pregnancy, she knocked it over as she swung around to view herself in the mirror. She gasped, dreading his reaction, knowing how much he treasured the portrait. She didn't have time to clean it up, or purchase a new frame, because the moment it crashed on the floor, Vito turned his key in the lock and, as usual, called her name. She panicked. There was no way of convincing him that the damage was inadvertent; he knew she had every reason to despise his mother. And, as he approached the top of the stairs, and entered the bedroom, she didn't have the chance to sweep up the mess, never mind come up with an excuse. He said, "Good evening," kissed her, and pointed to the broken glass on the floor. She'd barely parted her lips, unsure of what she'd say, when Sara seemingly appeared out of nowhere.

"Sho am sorry, Mr. B," Sara said, her sudden appearance startling Louise. "I done it."

"What happened, Sara?" he asked, predictably annoyed, picking up the broken pieces from the floor.

"I was dustin' your nightstand, sir," Sara said, making it up as she went along. "An' somehow, I knocked it over by mistake. I'm sorry, sir."

He sighed heavily, sucked his tongue, and shook his head.

"That's okay, Sara. It's only the frame anyway," he said, slipping the photograph from the broken glass and splintered mahogany. "I'll just get a new one."

"I'll get it tomorrow, honey," Louise volunteered. She looked disbelievingly at Sara, who winked at her while Vittorio's back was turned.

"I'm gonna clean it up right away, Mr. B. Don't you worry about it none," Sara said, then went downstairs for the broom and dust pan.

If the woman never did anything else, Louise would always love her for that and never forget it in a million years. Maintaining their professional distance, it was comforting to know that someone in that house who knew the lie she was living was on her side anyway.

As they pulled up alongside the curb at 142nd Street and Lenox Avenue, a uniformed valet opened the door for Louise. "Hey! Well, whaddaya know! Ain't seen you for a long time! Good to see you!" He shook hands with Vittorio. Louise stepped away and walked beneath the narrow awning over the entrance, relieved beyond words that the valet was speaking to her husband and not her. Silently, she mouthed a prayer for a night without incident. After shaking hands with the valet and pressing a crisp bill in his palm, Vittorio joined his wife, wrapped his arm around her waist, and they entered the club and climbed the staircase.

"Man, we gave you up for dead!" The club's host shook Vittorio's hand repeatedly.

"No," Vittorio said. "I'm still alive. I have a wife and family now."

"You don't say. Is this the little woman?"

Vittorio introduced them. Louise shook his hand quickly, smiled crookedly, and avoided any direct eye contact. "You just in time," the host continued. "The show's about to go on. We got a new band and they cookin' up a storm!"

"So I've heard," Vittorio said.

"Enjoy the show, folks!"

The maître d' led the di Bologneses to a specially reserved table. Patrons gawked at the striking couple making their way through the packed house. Louise clutched Vittorio by the arm. They seated themselves, and ordered a seafood dish of lobster and buttered shrimp as the band slid into the opening number.

Leading the orchestra from the piano bench, playing with a kinetic, yet cool fervor, was this man they called Duke. In white tuxedo, his foot tapping and legs wobbling, he smiled, pearly white teeth gleaming below a paper-thin mustache, as his fingers jabbed at the piano keys. He glanced at the audience, then the keyboard. His blue-black, shiny hair slicked back with a part, the white tails tucked and flapping over the piano bench, he mesmerized the audience with a wailing "Harlem River Quiver," then segued into "Jungle Nights in Harlem," which seemingly caused the foundation of the building to rock.

Watching excitedly, Louise enjoyed the show. She had almost collapsed when informed of tonight's destination. How could she have been so dumb? Had she given it any thought, she would have known they'd end up here. The Cotton Club. Her old stomping grounds. Fond memories of the old chorus line, her good friend Peaches, shot back to her in rapid succession. She wondered how Peaches was faring these days as a married woman.

The place had undergone minor changes since she last saw it. The same proscenium stage with the street lamps. The same painted murals on the walls. No, it hadn't changed much at all. Other than the host at the door—who, praise Jesus, didn't recognize her—no one looked even remotely familiar. She didn't know any of the busboys, waiters, or the maître d'. Frenchie and Herman Stark were nowhere to be seen, which was just as well, and yet, they'd probably not remember her either, the turnover of chorines being what it was. So, this is what it's like, she thought, watching a Cotton Club revue from the other side; from the viewpoint of the all-white patronage.

Studying the emerging chorus line of talented, wildly limber dancers shuffling on stage in white top hats and tails, joining the Duke for a tumultuous finish, Louise was envious. She froze, gazing at these dancers, none of whom were familiar. Reminding her of the old days, an impulse surged within her. She longed to jump up—swollen stomach and all—and dance with her people, her Negro people. She had a sudden desire to come crawling back on bended knees to the sanctuary of her roots.

It was nearly two years since she'd been physically close to any Negroes—outside her domestic staff—and she felt at home. A sense of belonging settled over her with the melting softness of snowflakes. She hadn't heard Negro music like this in years—what was this fellow's name? Ellington? As the chorus line shimmied erotically, and tapped out a frenzied timestep to which her feet nearly joined in under the table, she realized just how bored she was living as a white woman. Looking like one. Studying the brown and ebony men in the orchestra beating drums, sliding trombones, and muting cornets, she wanted to release the primal scream building in her throat, jump up and shout to the club's patrons and anyone else who'd listen, that she was Negro and goddamned proud of it!

But she remained stationary, her hands clasped, and was no more visibly moved than the polite white couples who surrounded them in neighboring booths. They apparently lacked emotion, spirit, passion, soul, and she wondered how they could listen to this divine musical phrasing crossbred from gut feelings and the human need to express without blinking an eye. They were far too sterile, too placid and stiff for her liking. She marveled at the sudden realization, one she'd never achieved when, years ago, she'd danced her heart out upon that same horseshoe stage. It struck her that while she was living the good life in the land of milk and honey, she was conspicuously lacking something. It had never occurred to her before now just *how* much she missed Harlem. She took Vittorio's hand beneath the table and squeezed it. His hand was the rope that prevented her from slipping into an abyss of banished origins—the place where she belonged. She thought of Peaches, and wondered what she would say about her, Little Miss Muffet Louise.

Suddenly, she didn't want to be white anymore. Not here in the Cotton Club. But she accepted her self-imposed yoke of living as a white woman. Feeling colored.

Vittorio squeezed her hand beneath the table and felt ashamed for his somber mood earlier that evening. It wasn't Luisa's fault he and Vincenzo once again locked horns that afternoon. He couldn't tell his wife, knowing how much she worried about their tenuous relationship. It was the same story between him and Papa, and it would continue until one of them wrote his final chapter. No big deal.

His mother angered him because she wouldn't embrace Luisa and recognize her for the gem of a wife and daughter-in-law she was. He tried to talk Mama into moving back into his home before they sailed back to Palermo. He'd almost convinced Mama, even as she was packing to return home. She admitted that she might have underestimated or misjudged his wife. Then suddenly, Vincenzo decided he wasn't going anywhere, claiming the aerial view of Central Park was far better than the one from their bedroom window into a landscaped garden—he could have that in Sicily. Why couldn't the old fool just say, like a man, that he was jealous of his son. Vittorio acknowledged it as spite, pure and simple; Papa

was forever doing it to him and he knew, one day soon, he'd get
Papa back in a big way. Webster couldn't know the definition of
retribution until Vittorio played his last card in this perpetual
battle of wills.

Noticing Luisa's hand was shaky and sweaty as he held it beneath
the table, he thought it time to leave, but first asked the female
photographer to take their picture. He had a big day tomorrow,
playing the market. His Montgomery Ward stock had risen dramatically from 117 to 440 a share; RCA skyrocketed from 85 to 420,
and a seat on the New York Stock Exchange had recently been sold
for an all-time high of $625,000. Tomorrow at several board
meetings, he needed to be alert and decided that when he told his
wife the news—the stock exchange bored her silly and he loved it
when she called it *mumbo jumbo*—he'd inform her of his plans to
take the family on a European holiday beginning in Palermo, as
soon as the baby was able to travel on a ship across the Atlantic.

Late-night breezes blew a cool, crisp breath against their young
faces as they waited beneath the awning for the valet to deliver the
Rolls. Leaning against the log cabin facade, Louise thought the
evening had been marvelous. A night without incident, no unwelcome stares of vague recognition. She promised herself to purchase
a phonograph record by Duke Ellington. She gave thanks to God,
and felt foolish for trying to dissuade her husband from going out
tonight. If all she had to fear was a dire craving to be united with her
people, they could go out more often.

A group of winos huddled at a nearby fire hydrant. Crooning a
drunken blues, they passed around cheap wine and marijuana in the
semicircle. "This for the fellas in jail," one of them declared,
ceremoniously pouring a few drops into the gutter. "And, to my
partners dead and gone!"

The Rolls-Royce glided to the curb. The motor idling, the valet
emerged from the driver's seat, skipped around to the other side,
and opened the passenger door for Louise, bowing graciously. As
Louise stepped upon the running board, a man from the nearby
group of winos tugged at her elbow. His eyes were bloodshot, his
clothes wrinkled and soiled, fingernails dirty and unkempt, and
Louise winced from the body odor.

"Hey, don't I know you from somewhere, miss?" the man said.

"No, I don't think—"

"Yeah, remember that night we double-dated with Bill and
Peaches? It's me; Charles. I know it's hard to recognize me now—"

"I've never seen you before in my life."

"What's your name again? Damn! I can't remember your name," he murmured, frustrated, snapping his fingers, stomping his foot to jar the memory. "It was a long time ago, and me, you, and Bill, and Peaches, we all went over to—"

"The lady says she doesn't know you," Vittorio interceded, extending his arm, keeping the stranger's distance from his wife. "I'm sure you've made a mistake." Louise seized the opportunity to hurriedly climb into the front seat. She closed the door and stared ahead, her heartbeats rolling like a snare drum, the baby pushing against her ribs.

"Okay, okay!" Charles said, perturbed. "You ain't gotta get tough, man. Just thought I knew the lady. Shit!"

His buddy, huddled in the semicircle, called to him. "Hey, Charles, man. Come on and hit this here last taste, man. Ain't but a corner left. Leave that white lady alone, man. You know damn well you don't know her." The others laughed and cursed under their breath. "Since when you know an ofay broad with a Rolls-Royce anyhow?"

6

"Scott," Velma snapped, peering through the crack of her partially opened door. "I'm really not in the mood today. I'm very busy. Call me tomorrow." She tried closing the door, but he blocked it with his foot.

"I'd just like to see you a moment," he said, smiling. "I swear, I'll only be a moment."

She paused a second, sighed disgustedly, and contemplated the request. "Only a moment?"

"Would I lie to you?" He entered the apartment. Throughout the parlor floor, lay scattered pages of a manuscript in progress. The typewriter sat on the table in the center of the room. "Well, I see you and your sidekick are pretty busy with this project."

"What is it you want, Scott?" she said impatiently.

"Now, now, temper, temper. Aren't you even going to offer me a seat or a nice cold gin and ginger ale?" he asked, fingering randomly through the loose pages beside the typewriter, which she snatched from his touch and turned face down.

"Sitting is free. I keep no alcohol in my house. You know that. Now, what is—"

"You won't be so quick to rush me off once you hear what I have to say."

"I've been listening since you walked in."

"The oddest thing happened to me recently," he said, standing near the open window of the fire escape, glancing into the streets. Velma sat on the sofa, fingering through a stack of papers, rather than face him. "I was on Madison Avenue doing some shopping when I thought I saw you."

"Oh yeah?" she said with disinterest and didn't bother to look up.

"It was difficult as all hell to find a parking space that day on Madison Avenue, busy as it was. I've never seen that street so busy. Seems to be growing into another American success story. Horatio Alger would be so proud. Anyway, I finally found a spot. It was right behind this brand new Rolls-Royce. Absolutely beautiful machine, you should've seen it. Then the woman, apparently the owner, which I didn't know at the time, came out of a store and from the back, she looked and walked just like you."

Velma stopped shuffling papers and gave Scott her immediate, undivided attention. "What do you mean, she looked just like me?" She licked her lips.

"She had one of those new stylish haircuts women are wearing these days. Except her hair was wavy. Wasn't quite like yours—"

"A white woman?"

"She was certainly lighter-complected than yourself but I wasn't altogether convinced that she was white either; know what I mean?"

"Where did you see her?" Velma rose from the sofa as calmly and unobtrusively as possible, listening intently.

"I just told you, on Madison Avenue; oh, I guess it was around Forty-sixth Street or so."

"How long ago?"

"Aren't you listening?"

"Was she with someone—"

"No, alone. So, when I called her Velma, she—"

"You called her Velma?"

"*Ma chérie*, if you persist in playing call and response, I'll never get through this—"

"Well, what did she do when you called her Velma?" she said, remembering to downplay her excitement. She turned away from him, walked to the typewriter, picked up a pack of cigarettes, lit one, and exhaled.

"That's what I found strange," he continued. "A plain mistaken identity is usually no more than that; you apologize and get on with it. Except, she acted so bloody suspicious, it aroused my own suspicion."

"Why? What did she do?" She sucked frantically on the cigarette.

"My dear, she tore off away from me quicker than I could say 'Boo!' She practically knocked me down, running away. Her hands shook so violently as she tried getting the door opened—"

"So, why're you telling me all this? You interrupted my work to tell me this?"

"Well, it suddenly occurred to me, you know. It's certainly no bloody secret everbody's talking about your novel and its ill-fated protagonist. Here you have a colored woman who disappears from her domicile, assuming a white identity. Then she moves into white—"

"I'm somewhat familiar with the story, thank you. Get to the point." She puffed harder and quicker on the cigarette.

"Well, the point, my dear, is that I began thinking about it more and more," he replied, his tone becoming more accusatory with each uttered syllable. "And, it occurred to me that our little *Chameleon* isn't really fictitious at all, is she? Matter of fact, she could be your sister. Tell me, is that who tragic mulatto *Chameleon* really is?"

"I don't know what the hell you're talking about."

"I think you do. Do you have a sister who—"

"Have you ever heard me speak of one?"

"Can't say I have. But probably—"

"Look, Scott, I'm not like you. I don't go around conjuring up sympathy over fabricated stories about brothers and sisters I don't really have, like some people I know."

"Point for you, my dear. Bloody match point for you."

"Have you spoken with Rudy?"

"Does Rudy have information in regard to the mulatto in question—"

"I didn't say that. Just that you two are in such cahoots with each other these days, I—"

"Come on, Velma. You can tell me. My lips are sealed."

Why couldn't she tell him? she thought. It wasn't so much that she feared the inevitable connection with her fictional heroine. Digging deeper, she was ashamed, she supposed, that a sister of hers, born of the same Negro parents as herself, had betrayed her genuine origin to cross over to the other side. She rendered it far more complex than that, especially in view of Louise's trials growing up with an identity crisis. But her family background and cultural reference was so colored, so emphatically Negro, that any deviation from it brought about some sentiment of shame. She loved her sister and never passed judgment on her, but the image of shame always bounced back to haunt her. Like a lump, it stuck in her throat. It was as unwelcome as Scott's foot stuck in her doorway.

"There's nothing to tell," Velma insisted.

"You want to know what I think?"

"No, I don't want—"

"I think this woman I saw is related to you. Maybe not your sister; could be a cousin. Matter of fact, I think our novel *Chameleon* isn't really a work of fiction at all, is it, Velma? More like an exposé, wouldn't you say? Airing the family's dirty laundry."

"Please get out."

"Did I touch a nerve? I never would've suspected you, of all people, to pass off a family exposé as art. Certainly the *New York Times* would not so readily have—"

"Oh, what's the big problem? Fact is oftentimes made into fiction. It's nothing new. It's done all the time. What the hell you think your research was all about?"

"Then you admit it?"

"I admit nothing."

"I mean, even if your book is a work of fiction, it required little of your imagination to—"

"Scott, please leave."

This was turning out all wrong. Scott had stopped by with the best of intentions. Yes, he had an anecdote he wanted to share with her, a strange occurrence indeed. But, it was a transparent excuse to visit the woman he missed more than he was willing to admit. He was lonely. And actually, he didn't give a bloody rat's ass whether she knew the mystery woman or not. But after the laconic manner with which she greeted him, it all came back; his dark side and rushing tidal waves of jealousy over her and Rudy. Neither of them really visited anymore and he understood that they were busy. But, come on! Had she answered the door differently—he guessed it was her time of the month and allowed her that much—the tone of conversation could have followed a totally different path. He didn't want to fight, that's not why he'd come, but since she had tied on her boxing gloves, he wasn't going to back down either.

"You know, Mrs. V was right," he said, turning to walk away. "But then, she always is."

"About what?"

"She claims you gave quite a performance the other day at her penthouse. That you were rude and most insolent with her, an embarrassingly virulent display of behavior that just wasn't becoming. And I can't say I don't believe her. Just look at how you're behaving—"

"Did you tell her, Scott?"

"Tell her what?"

"Tell her what a jackass you tend to be; you know what."

"My dear, how quickly we forget. Why should I bloody tell her? I'm the one who secured you a meeting with Robie, your leading star, remember?" She could pinpoint the source all right, but she couldn't smell the danger, or recognize he'd just saved her bloody career. Gratification, not brusqueness, was in order.

"Just answer my question, please." She opened the door.

"Why don't you ask Rudy? I understand he and Mrs. V had quite a meeting you knew nothing about. He's your bloody collaborator, *mon coeur*, not I."

"Maybe I'll do just that." She held the door ajar, allowing him just enough space to pass. Suddenly, Scott turned around, stood in the darkness of the vestibule, and pressed his hand against the door jamb to prevent her from closing it.

Whether *Chameleon* was a work of fiction or not wasn't the issue. He couldn't attack, without further riling her, the real demons that seemed to be driving them apart. Novelists, the best of them, often weaved fiction from fact, and Velma, if it was true, had achieved it most admirably. But somehow, the book being based on a real person, not having come completely from an imaginative concept, made her work less threatening since the public continued to celebrate it, while his last novel had long ago disappeared from the retail bookshelves.

He wanted so desperately to hold her, kiss her, nibble on her left nipple—it was bigger than the right—or maybe pull down her panties and bury his face in Miss Kitty's whiskers. *Remember me!*

But pride forbade him. Why couldn't she realize she was in error, apologize, and ask him to stay? He needed her. Didn't she love him anymore?

"Velma," he began, standing beneath the door frame, his tone becoming tender and submissive. "What's happening to us?"

"I don't know, Scott," she said, refusing to look at him, chiding herself for being in the shittiest of moods that had little to do with him. Life wasn't so spiffy for her these days with all that was crumbling around her, the last blow of which was the meeting with Mrs. Vanderpool who, beginning next month, would substantially decrease her income. She couldn't tell who divulged the secret to the old woman, and accepted that she'd probably never learn the identity of the culprit. Men had a way of protecting each other fiercely. They loved and honored one another with a fraternal loyalty that taught her that women couldn't possibly ever love and protect them any more than they loved and protected themselves. The covenant of male loyalty couldn't be penetrated. And they labeled the likes of Rudy homosexuals?

Chaos disarranged her mind like a Picasso painting. Her perceptions were dulled. She needed to figure things out, and didn't need the unsolicited, disruptive company of anyone, not even Scott, until she could wade through the muck and achieve some much needed clarity.

"I love you, Velma," Scott said, walking down the dark vestibule.

"I love you too," she said, closing her door. Rudy must have told Scott about Louise. He couldn't have seen her on Madison Avenue. I never believed him for one damn moment, she thought.

7

Miriam wandered aimlessly through the streets, oblivious to sights and sounds unfolding around her. She passed by the Dunbar National Bank. It was the first Negro-owned financial institution where, she read in the *Amsterdam News* late last year, John D. Rockefeller held seventy-five percent of the stock, when originally it was supposed to be fifty. God only knew why that thought ran through her head, but studying the bank sign made her think of Velma. Dunbar was Velma's favorite poet while she was a student at Barnard, and Miriam thought of calling her. Locating a public telephone, she dropped the coins into the black box, and dialed the number. The line was busy. She waited a minute or so and redialed. The telephone rang several times, and Miriam suspected that either she wasn't home, or she wouldn't answer because she was working. Then again, she might have stepped out to the grocery. Miriam hung up after the tenth ring, sighed, glanced at the Kid Chocolate poster above her, and thought, the last thing Race people needed was to be pulverizing each other in the boxing ring for the financial gain of avaricious white folks.

She didn't know what to do with herself. Heading southward toward her former address at West 141st Street, she thought of stopping by to say hello to the new family who'd since moved in. Uncertain of what she expected when she got there, she reasoned that seeing the apartment again might lend her some sense of stability, a fading landmark of her past with which she needed to touch base. West 141st Street seemed to be the sole anchor in her life these days. She had no idea what to do about Agnes.

None of the pieces in her life seemed to fit anymore, and she was tiring of the roller-coaster ride, dipping and soaring through days of the week. Today was promising, tomorrow doomed, and this situation with Agnes was going nowhere much too quickly. Agnes hadn't changed, so Miriam thought the fault might be with herself. Agnes had guided her blindfolded into a maze, then abandoned her. Subject to mood shifts like anybody else, Agnes was still basically the same Agnes she'd always known. No more, no less. Miriam thought it her problem because she wanted more. Worse, she expected it. She had tasted the fatted calf and diligently searched for the banquet. Except, no one told her that the last of the grapes, wine, and poultry had been consumed, and all that remained were crumbs.

There were times, much too often these days, when she wished nothing had happened between them. Now that something profoundly alive moved within her, there was nowhere for it to go. Had she not allowed Agnes to seduce her, she wouldn't be groping through her mental morass. Ignorance truly was bliss. She had been perfectly content when she kept her body and emotions to herself. She'd given Agnes more than breasts and vagina. She had handed herself over on a silver platter to the woman, and if Agnes didn't plan to feast upon the sum of her physical, emotional, intellectual, and spiritual parts, she could hand the platter back. When Miriam thought about it though, maybe Agnes did, and Miriam's stubbornness refused to take it back.

It got to the point Miriam would sit in Agnes's room when she wasn't there and spray her perfume to evoke her presence. It required sampling several bottles until Miriam found the one Agnes wore that night. All that were left were the scent and the memory which pulled at her. As the weeks progressed, she'd taken to rummaging through Agnes's private things, looking for telephone numbers of gentlemen callers, her fingers lifting this, unfolding that, for some logical explanation as to why Agnes was acting this way. She found nothing. The gold bracelet continued to sit in its box in Agnes's dresser drawer. There was nothing left for Miriam to do. If the woman wouldn't accept the ultimate gift she'd ever bought anyone, then there was little hope.

Heading home after work increasingly became a trial. She took to roaming aimlessly through the streets, not unlike today, until her legs refused to carry her farther, and she surrendered by taking a subway, which wasn't necessary, given the close proximity of her home to the hospital. Her eating habits were poor, sleep and bowel movements irregular, and it amazed her to think how emotional, spiritual shortcomings could manifest themselves in the physical. This was all new to her. Agnes was her first love.

As she turned the corner and passed by the Lafayette Theatre, she was struck by a resolution that hit her in the face like a hailstorm. Agnes would have to move. Miriam had gotten used to sharing living quarters; the extra money she saved while Agnes footed half the bills she deposited in her Dunbar Bank account. But she had survived before Agnes and would continue to do so. Like most Race people, she wore survival the way white women draped minks around their collars. She and Agnes had to untie the knots that strung them along. She didn't fancy presenting Agnes with an ultimatum, but no one was going to watch over and look out for Miriam like Miriam. Agnes certainly did whatever she pleased, with little thought to whom or what she was involving, so Miriam viewed it as an example to follow. She had to quit stewing in the caldron of self-pity.

As she walked up the staircase at West 141st Street, childhood and coming-of-age memories rang back to her. She recalled the day when, as she was playing outside with Louise, a bunch of neighborhood children harassed them and accused them of not being sisters. She saw Velma, at the foot of the staircase, giddy over some cute boy from down the street. It was always a boy their parents didn't like—a different one every month—who had Velma so wound up that she scribbled his name in school textbooks and all over the pages of her diary. She could almost smell the clash of cosmetic and food odors. She knocked on the door. A woman not much younger than she answered. Two small boys peeked at Miriam from behind their mother's skirt.

"Yes? Can I help you?" the woman said, her door cracked.

"Yes, ma'am," Miriam replied. "I don't know how to say this, but I was wondering if I . . . well, you see, I used to live here, and . . ." She looked over the woman's shoulder at the new coat of paint; a color Mother wouldn't have chosen. The curtains, furniture, the beauty parlor, everything was gone, and she barely recognized the room.

"Yes?" The woman looked confused.

"What I'm trying to say is that I grew up here before the war and I was wondering if I could just see the place again."

"What you wanna see?"

"Nothing in particular, just . . ." She was becoming discouraged, at a loss for a rational explanation. If she couldn't impart to the woman why she'd come, perhaps she didn't know herself. "Nevermind ma'am. I didn't mean to bother you." She turned and walked down the staircase.

"Miss . . . oh miss," the woman called. "It's all right. You can come in and look around if you like."

"No, that's okay, really. But it's mighty kind of you," Miriam said, continuing down the stairs, at which the woman looked more confused than before, and closed her door.

She turned her key in the lock, mentally rehearsing the words she hoped wouldn't fail her when she needed them. Agnes wasn't home, which somehow made her feel she had the advantage. Advantage over what? At least she'd have the chance to settle down, get comfortable, maybe take a bath, and kick her thoughts about one more round. Before she got undressed, she considered entering Agnes's room to sneak a whiff of the perfume her nostrils craved. The door was closed, and as she approached it, she heard moans and groans and squeaking bedsprings that sounded like the night they were together. She knocked, listened, and the moaning continued. "Agnes, you in there?"

"Yes!" Agnes shouted back, her panting voice muffled through the door. "Don't come in," Agnes warned. "I'm not alone."

An urge swelled within Miriam to cry, protest and kick down the door all at the same time. Silently, she walked away, wishing Agnes could sense the storm raging within her. Was this jealousy? Was this what it felt like? Her stomach sizzled and her head pounded from the back to her temples. Her breath came quicker, and mustering all the restraint she could summon at a moment's notice, she nearly tied her hands behind her back to stop herself from breaking plates and glasses in her cupboard. In her mind's eye, she watched herself kicking the bedroom door open. And then what? Demand that Agnes pursue her sexual fulfillment elsewhere in a seedy hotel? Declare that the apartment was off limits for fucking? Insist that they couldn't engage in sexual activity with anybody in the apartment but each other?

She walked into her bedroom, closed the door, lay across her bed, and wrapped a pillow around her ears. Fantasy got the better of her in this moment of desperation, and she pictured Agnes throwing open her bedroom door, kicking her partner out of the house. She heard Agnes explaining that she loved Miriam, and what they were doing behind closed doors was terribly wrong and unfaithful. She saw Agnes slamming the door shut on whoever had yanked her from the virtue of fidelity. Then she saw Agnes place the gold bracelet around her wrist and run, blinded by tears, into Miriam's room and beg her forgiveness. How could she have been such an imbecile? Could Miriam find it in her heart to forgive her?

The fantasy didn't help much, and was interrupted by the creaking of Agnes's bedroom door. Miriam got out of bed, tiptoed across the floor, and pressed her ear to the door. Agnes's voice and laughter dominated, but Miriam could hear the undertones of bass, which belonged to a man. She toyed with the idea of cracking the door to see who the hell it was laying up in her house doing what she couldn't do. She decided against it, then remembered this was her apartment and she could do as she damn well pleased. Despite her shame at her small-mindedness, she opened the door and stepped into the parlor. She couldn't believe her eyes.

"What are you doing here?" she asked, watching that slob fasten his trousers, and zip himself up.

"Hey!" Tommy said. "Long time no see."

She couldn't believe her eyes, and to some extent wished she hadn't opened her bedroom door. After all Agnes had been through with him, she was still dabbing in yesteryear's leftovers. Miriam was appalled, but did everything not to show it. She pretended to be going to the bathroom, when Tommy stopped her.

"Ain't you gonna even speak?"

Miriam rolled her eyes, yanked her arm from his grip, continued toward the bathroom, and stopped when she glimpsed Agnes wrapping her nakedness inside a bathrobe.

"How're you doing, Miriam?" she asked.

A million responses raced through Miriam's head, and she consciously censored the words about to fall from her lips. "Not as good as some people, I reckon."

She could tell Agnes was embarrassed. And for the first time, she didn't care about Agnes's feelings. Miriam washed her hands in the bathroom, then marched truculently into the kitchen where she banged around pots and pans, opening and slamming cupboards, not knowing what the hell she was doing in there. She wasn't about to cook anything. Hell, she wasn't even hungry. Agnes stepped into the kitchen, her arms folded to keep the bathrobe closed, and asked if she needed help. Miriam looked at her, and again, rolled her eyes. Never before had Agnes offered help when she threw together the evening meal. She wanted to demand that Tommy leave, but knew she had no right to, since Agnes paid half the rent. Agnes got the message, turned from the kitchen, and reentered the parlor where Tommy whistled Ethel Waters's "Am I Blue?" She heard Agnes whisper to Tommy but couldn't make out the words.

"Why?" Tommy said, from the other room. "You pay half the rent, doncha?"

She heard Agnes whisper again, followed by smoochy kisses, which, Miriam assumed, was Tommy's way of letting her know to whom Agnes belonged. Agnes promised to call him tomorrow, then closed the door. It was Miriam's cue to demand answers to questions screaming inside her. Every part of her body trembled, and to steady herself was to keep mobile.

She walked into the parlor, ignoring Agnes, who stood near the door. She absentmindedly picked up magazines and newspapers on the coffee table—anything to occupy her hands.

"So," Miriam began, as casually as possible, though her voice cracked. She cleared her throat. "You and Tommy back together?"

"We're friends again," Agnes said, walking toward her in the parlor, "if that's what you mean."

"He finally found out where you live," Miriam said, as if talking with herself, her fingers working overtime as she hastily turned pages looking for nothing.

"Actually," Agnes said. "I found him."

"You what?" She stopped flipping pages.

"Yeah. I kind of missed him and . . . you know."

"No, I don't."

"What's wrong with you, Miriam? For weeks, you been walking around here like you done lost your best friend or something."

The accuracy of her allegation pierced Miriam's heart. "Yeah," she said pensively, "I guess I have."

"No, you haven't," Agnes said. "I'm still your best friend."

"If you say so."

"You want something more, don't you, Miriam?"

"Want what? I don't want anything."

"Yes you do," Agnes said, thinking the night she slept with this woman had to be one of the most unwise moves she'd ever made. She wanted to comfort her, knowing her heart was hurting, looking more pitiful than the day her mother passed. And yet, to merely touch her would be an even bigger mistake. "What is it you want from me?"

"Nothing." She flipped the pages.

"If you didn't, you wouldn't be walking around here dragging your face along the floor."

"So what do you want me to say?" Miriam shouted, throwing down the magazine. "I think you and Tommy being back together is great? Okay, then I'll say it. I'm so happy for you and Tommy, okay?" She surprised even herself with the stream of sarcasm.

"Miriam? You're jealous?"

"Didn't I just say how happy I am for you?"

Agnes looked at her quizzically, watching Miriam's bottom lip tremble. An eerie silence grabbed hold of the parlor, and she could hear next-door neighbors through the wall, laughing at a radio program.

"Well, Miriam, I don't know what to say—"

"What to say? You could begin by telling me why we did what we did—"

"Sex, Miriam," Agnes said. "It's okay to say it. We had sex."

"Okay, okay. But then what happened?"

"Miriam, I love you. I'd never do anything to hurt you. Never. I just felt sorry for you, I guess."

"I don't want your sympathy."

"I didn't mean it that way. But, here you were, a woman a little bit older than me, you had never been with anybody and it just kind of happened somehow. You were in such pain, I wanted to make you feel good. I know what it's like to need love too. I was glad I was releasing something in you. I mean, I did it because I wanted to, but if I ever thought for one moment, that you wanted to make it permanent . . . I wouldn't have."

"So, you do this all the time when people are in pain—love them and leave them?"

"It was just something we both wanted at the time. Folks get lonely, you know. I never stopped loving you because of it, but I don't want to be . . . involved either."

The words cut Miriam, just sliced her up like a razor. Now that she'd heard it, she had to get past it and on with her life. If only she could take the first step.

"You don't like . . . women anymore?"

"I guess not."

"You lived with a woman before and said it was better. That's more than I ever did. Why can't you . . . be . . . you know . . . that way with me?"

"Because I love somebody else. Miriam, don't make me say this—"

"You said you liked the woman better—"

"If I liked it better, would I have left with Tommy?"

Miriam felt her face sagging into her lap.

"So Tommy's back in, and I'm out, is that it?"

"Miriam, you know I love Tommy. He straightened out his life. And you know he's my main nigger—"

"And that's another thing; don't use that word!" Oh, how sweet it could be if her only problem with Agnes was the word nigger. "I hate that word and I wish you wouldn't use it around me."

"Colored people use it all the time; it ain't the same as white folks—"

"Nigger is nigger. Don't matter much who's saying it. I'm sorry, Agnes, to be putting you through all this. Really I am. I do wish you the best with . . . Tommy . . . if that's what you want. Good night, I'll see you in the morning."

"Miriam."

"Yes?" She stopped but wouldn't turn around.

"I'll be moving out in a month or two. Just thought you'd want to know."

Miriam continued toward the bedroom. Pushing through the

door, she decided that this was only round one. Agnes had to come to her senses. She couldn't go back to that trap. Had she gone mad? That man was going to piss all over her and swear it was raining. She wasn't giving Agnes up without a fight, knowing she was waging battle with a sword against an army of aimed rifles. She had to fight it, especially since that low-life weasel Tommy was the cowardly opponent.

8

"I understand you met with Mrs. Vanderpool," Velma said, her arms folded, standing over Rudy who sat on her sofa.

"Yes, I did," Rudy replied, not sure what she was driving at.

"And?"

"And what? You called me in the middle of an afternoon nap, and this is the emergency? Velma, I don't like your tone. I get the feeling you're accusing me of something."

Since she had thrown Scott out a couple of hours earlier, her rage had since increased exponentially. The knuckles and palms of her hands itched mercilessly to physically strike out at something or someone. Before Scott's arrival, she hadn't considered calling Rudy. Mother was known to say that misery loved company, and shamefully, she assumed that was why he sat there in her parlor. He was no more the source of her woes—well, maybe a little—than the inanimate typewriter sitting in the center of her parlor. Yet she had to strike or crush something or somebody, and until she did, the unleashed fury would turn on her and devour her internally. Part of her sympathized with Rudy, who sat before her a child reprimanded by the disciplinarian. Now that the bottle which contained her anger was uncorked, she had to let it flow. She hardly fancied herself a maenad, and derived no pleasure from it. But since the curtain went up on Act One, she felt determined to play out the scene.

"You're aware she found out?" she asked.

"Of course I'm aware."

"Who told you?"

"She did."

"Then you did meet with her?"

"I just said that, but—"

"Did you tell her, Rudy?"

"I really must be going." He stood, but Velma pushed him back down. "What in God's good earth makes you think I told her anything?" he pleaded.

"Who else would've done it?"

"It wasn't me. Did you forget this play is my project as much as yours? Why would I cut my own throat?"

"Rudy, don't make me spell out motivation. There could be several reasons why—"

"Oh yeah, just name one. I'd like to hear you come up with one of these motivations!"

"G. Virgil Scott!"

"I swear, Velma, I don't get it."

"Don't give me that. You've already betrayed my confidence to Scott—"

"I did not!"

"Yes you did. And you've already confessed that you're in love with him. You said so yourself in A'Lelia Walker's gazebo that night. Not that I needed the confession, you understand."

"So, you think I betrayed you to Mrs. Vanderpool because I'm in love with—"

"Why not? I can just imagine how frustrating it all must be for you. You're in love with a man who's in love with me. I think you'd do just about anything to get Scott from me. You really wish you were me, don't—"

"This is becoming more Proustian by the moment."

"And if that's not bad enough, you went and told him about my sister too. The one and only secret I've ever told anyone, and like nothing, you ran and told my *fucking* secret to Scott of all people—"

"I didn't tell Scott a damn thing!"

"Oh no? Well, he certainly had the story all figured out. What gets me is how you both protect each other; this Underground Society of Male Loyalty. You protect him, he protects you. This afternoon, just before you came over, before I threw the jackass out on his ear, he claimed he saw my sister on Madison Avenue. Pretty damn original, wouldn't you say? And, first I believed him. Just like I always believe everything he says. Then it occurred to me: I told Rudy! If all this happened before I told you, Rudy, I swear I'd believe you. But, as you can see, you don't have a case—not a credible one, anyway. And, that Madison Avenue story. My God! I mean, that's pretty damn original. My sister driving a Rolls-Royce," she said sarcastically. "That's certainly more clever than anything I could write."

There was nothing in the world to convince him that she sincerely believed, for one moment, any one word of what she was charging. How could she place blind faith in the allegation that he'd run back to Scott with the story of a missing, passing sister she'd specifically asked him not to say anything about, or report to Mrs. Vanderpool to undermine her? It was far too preposterous for a response, and he hated himself for dignifying her claim with one. Didn't they consummate their secret partnership with a sealed promise? Didn't that count for something? Would she believe him if he swore upon an open Bible? Sometimes, friendship doesn't count for shit! In some twisted way, he pitied her, knowing her life was a near shambles these days. But he'd be damned if he'd sit in her parlor as her whipping boy. If he did that every time he had problems, he'd have no friends. If she kept it up, she wouldn't either. No matter what she said, he knew she was punishing him for the mere fact that he refused to sleep with her, or reciprocate love the way she wanted him to. Women had this insatiable need to control and manipulate, and he wasn't her pawn to be moved and lifted across the chess board of her design. He adored women platonically, they made for the best of friends, the ultimate confidantes, but he felt blessed that he no longer slept with them. He had to get the hell out of there, and quickly. Had he known, or barely sniffed the nature of her "emergency," he wouldn't have budged from his Murphy bed. As it was, she'd awakened him from a wet dream he was having about Scott—is that the irony of all ironies?—and he'd rushed over here like a damn fool just to be called a traitor, a usurper, damn near. He despised fighting with this woman, this supposed friend of his, and if he never exchanged another shout or swear word with her, it would be too goddamn soon.

"Listen to you, Velma," Rudy said, shaking his head. "You're beginning to sound just like Scott. I'm going home. When you calm down, give me a call," he grunted, walking briskly toward the door. "Seems no matter what I say, I'm guilty as charged without trial. Take my word for it, dictatorship hardly becomes you."

"Don't you walk away from me when I'm talking to you!"

Rudy stopped at the door and Velma rushed after him, halting in time to avoid a bodily collision. He opened the door. She closed it. He opened it again. She kicked it closed with her foot.

"I'm not finished with you yet, Mr. Rudolph. Just who the hell do you think you are anyway? First you sleep with me. Then hand me some bullshit like, 'Oh, poor Velma, I didn't mean for you to fall in love with me, but that's just the way I am!' So, I get myself another man and you run after him too. No sooner than my back's turned, you're climbing into the sheets with him just like the other man I caught you with—"

"You're a fine one to talk! You slept with the both of us too! That doesn't exactly make you—"

"Why did you do it, Rudy? Why?"

"I didn't tell Scott or Mrs. Vanderpool—"

"Why did you ever sleep with me?" She poked her index finger repeatedly against his chest.

"You really want to know why?" he said, his voice growing hoarse.

"Only for the past four years!"

"Something about you really excited me sexually that night, *one million* years ago. Call it the moment's impulse, if you will, or impetuousness at its worst—"

"So you sacrificed me to atone for your homosexual guilt! Just to convince yourself that you weren't a sexual misfit—"

"Okay, goddamn it! I did it because I needed to write a tediously heterosexual love scene. You were my source of research! Okay? Now, are you satisfied—"

Velma's trembling hand swept upward before she could stop herself, and landed across his face. He held his cheek, staring at her in disbelief.

"Feel better?" he said, rubbing his cheek. "I love you too."

"How's that for research?"

"You realize what just happened here? Now it's all come full circle for you, hasn't it?" He tried laughing, stroking his cheek. "You just lived out your own play. Remember? Female protagonist feels betrayed by lead actor and slaps him across the face? When we went over the first draft together, I had no idea it was a prophecy." He walked through the door and down to the vestibule. "See you later."

9

Vittorio received a message from his mother summoning him to the Plaza. After Sara gave him the information, he rushed out of the house and headed for midtown as quickly as the automobile would deliver him. Mama had finally, finally come to her senses, not about to let Papa dissuade her, and he couldn't wait to hear it with his own ears.

When he arrived, he was told by Papa that she was taking a nap. He had raced to their hotel immediately after getting the message and wondered how she could be asleep so quickly. He didn't like the way this sounded.

He and Papa, alone, were awkward with each other. Lucia was the bridge across the gap between them. Papa asked him to be seated and he sat, looking out the window over Central Park. He knew that Mama hadn't called at all. Papa called and used Mama's name, knowing Vittorio wouldn't otherwise respond.

As Papa paced uneasily before him, Vittorio wondered what the old man was about to say. They virtually never spoke or exchanged pleasantries. Whatever the reason he'd been summoned, Vittorio knew it had to be absolutely necessary, and held his breath as Papa began to speak.

"We're sailing in two weeks," Vincenzo said, without directly facing him. "Won't you come back with Mama and me?" Vincenzo stood over his son, and leaned on one hand against the mantelpiece. "The stock market is losing and gaining as much as ten, fifteen, even twenty points a day. I won't let you do it!"

"*Let* me do what?"

"I can't let you slit your own throat."

"It's my throat to slit, Papa."

"I know, Vittorio—"

"And *my* money—"

"Which you got from me—"

"Which I turned into sound investments that have since tripled, old man."

Five minutes, that's all it had been, five minutes, and already father and son were volleying taunts. Papa could never say what was on his mind. Vittorio believed he was jealous of his success. He'd proved to be a far wiser businessman than Vincenzo. His father could no longer tell him what to do. Relinquishing that kind of power and being surpassed as a tycoon was a bitter pill for Papa to swallow. In Palermo, Papa was a big man. Here in America, no one. The son had grown richer and more prosperous than the father, and this would be the death of him.

"I don't know, my son," Papa continued. "The signs are there if you care to read them. It's got Mama and me very anxious. Too many people are purchasing stocks on margin, taking a loan for the rest. When those prices drop and the loans are called in, it can only mean trouble."

"I'll talk with Mama. Maybe she'll see—"

"Talk with Mama? Vittorio, this is her idea. She's scared to death. All she wants is to sail back to Sicily. But we want you to bring Luisa. Have your baby on Sicilian soil."

Mama couldn't leave just yet! Vittorio thought. She had to delay her voyage a few more weeks. The baby's arrival was too close, and if she left, abandoning her first born grandchild, he would never forgive her.

"Papa, I've told you before," he said willfully in English, "I'm American now."

"Speak Italian," Vincenzo insisted.

"All this time you've been here, old man," Vittorio said, "you should know some English by now. That's your whole problem, you never try to expand."

"You're still Italian!"

"And American!"

"Your mama said it before, and even *I* thought she was exaggerating. But she sees how this America has done something to your head." He leaned forward and poked Vittorio's skull with a forefinger. "This country has changed you, Vittorio. You're not the same anymore."

"Papa, what does the stock market have to do with America?"

"Everything!"

"Maybe it's easy for you. But what about me? I have loyalties, Papa. Can't I make you understand I'm not in this alone?"

"Loyalties to whom?"

"My investors!"

"You're more loyal to them than to me, is that it, Vittorio? These

American investors you speak so highly of, are they more important than me? I'm your father! More than that, you wouldn't have had the capital for those investments if it wasn't for me!"

Here we go again! "It's not that clear cut. Stop talking about it like it's a simple matter of me getting up and sailing back to Sicily. If every one of my investors did what you're asking me to do, we'd be having trouble a lot sooner, no? We're capital investors, Papa. We have faith. You've got to have faith! To pull out is unpatriotic, un-American!"

"I don't know," Vincenzo said, shaking his head, staring into the fireplace. He pulled a handkerchief from a back pocket and covered his face with it, mopping the perspiration. "I try to guide you. I tell you only what I think is best. I'm accustomed to the old ways, Vittorio. You don't respect the old ways anymore. What's happened to you?"

"I got out from under your shadow, your claws. That's what happened."

"My shadow? My claws?"

"Yes, you know. 'Do this, Vittorio. Do that, Vittorio. Lick my boots, Vittorio. I made all the money around here, remember that, Vittorio.' That's a shadow, Papa. That's what I got away from."

"So, on top of everything else, you're ungrateful too?"

"Ungrateful? Don't forget, old man, I paid you back every last lira you ever loaned me—with interest. I turned that money into something. That's not ungrateful, Papa!"

"Things have been too easy for you, my son. That's your problem. Mama and I made everything too easy."

"That again! Don't you even know why I came to America? You think I left home because I wanted to?"

"With the crazy thoughts you keep, how could I know—"

"Because I needed to get away, Papa. From you, from that small-town life you always—"

"And we took good care of you! We made sure our only son wouldn't starve in a strange country. Gave you more spending money than the average man could hope for in a lifetime. And, this is how you repay us. Loyalty to strangers."

"Papa, before we even—"

"Are you coming with us? Yes or no?"

"How can you—"

"Yes or no, Vittorio?"

Vittorio hung his head and stared at the floor. Flexing his fist, punching the flesh of his open palm, he shook his head. "No, Papa, I can't. You're backing me against a wall here."

"I'm trying to save your life."

"No, you're not. You're trying to save yours. Because if I don't return, Mama will never forgive you, and that's what we're really talking about here, isn't it?"

"Your arrogance shocks me," Vincenzo said.

"Like father, like son, no?"

"Why is everything I say such a personal affront?"

"You're leaving before your first grandchild is born; isn't that personal? Can't you wait?"

"This is your mama's idea—"

"Mama! You put everything on Mama, don't you; everything you don't have the balls to own up to. Admit it; let's get it all out in the open once and for all. You've always been jealous of Mama's love for me, haven't you?" Vittorio said, raising his voice.

"Vittorio, please. Mama's sleeping—"

"Come on, old man, you're jealous, huh?"

"I feel I don't know you anymore—"

"You never did."

"So, you're not coming back with us?"

"What do you think?"

"That's all I want to know. Mama and I have lots of packing to do. I just hope you're not too *loyal* to see us off from the pier, my son!"

Vittorio looked at his father looking back at him. The old man appeared desperate. His face was red, his clenched fists trembled. His paunch was pressed against the fireplace, and suddenly, he looked aged beyond his years. Had his son not been sitting there, he would have released the tears welling up in his eyes. For the first time in years, Vittorio wanted to touch him. They hadn't since the wedding. Yet, he felt weighted in the chair, unable to make that move and reach across the void, terrified of Papa's rejection.

He stood up, walked across the floor, stopped behind his father whose back faced him. Vittorio tried to say something, but the vocal chords failed him. He attempted to touch him, but paralysis stopped him. Slowly, he lifted his hand, looked again at his father, changed his mind and left quietly through the front door.

10

"We could get in a lot of trouble for this, you know, Velma."

"We can't worry about that now. We agreed to do it, Rudy, so come on."

The Atlantic, a majestic shimmering mass of royal blue in motion, stretched before them in the distance, as their bare feet sank into the sand. The noon sun directly overhead cast a diamond-like brilliance on the breaking ripples. Dotted with multicolored yachts and a handful of small boats, the tide rolled with a roar, building momentum, and crashed at the sands, the white foam receding.

White, pasty and reddened bodies against the whiteness of the sand basked in the rays. Spread-eagled over blankets or hiding beneath angular umbrellas, beachers slept, applied suntan oil, screamed at unruly children, and read books. Others stared at the colored couple making their way toward a deserted spot.

Baskets and blanket in hand, Velma and Rudy trudged across the burning-hot granules. Velma wore a red, trendy one-piece bathing suit, Rudy, blue trunks fastened with a buckle and a striped T-shirt as required by law. They strutted with forced obliviousness past the dozens of curious eyes focused on them. Claiming a spot, they emptied their burdened arms of everything save the blanket. They unfolded and pulled it apart at opposite ends, while the sea breeze snapped it like a sheet on a clothesline. They placed it down and tucked the corners into the sand.

A few of their neighbors stood and pointed at the colored couple. "I don't know about this, Velma," Rudy whispered, placing their belongings on the blanket. "Look how they're staring at us, for chrissake!"

"Just pay them no mind," she insisted, giggling. "We have as much right as anybody to sunbathe wherever we want. Shit, Rudy, this is 1929!"

"Okay, okay. I just hope you know what you're doing."

"What *I'm* doing? We're both doing it, Rudy. We can hide behind typewriters for the next ten years, but we have to take a stand at some point. Writing about it just isn't enough anymore. God, how I wish that wasn't true, but it is."

"You're right," Rudy said defeatedly. "I don't even know why I'm saying it. I know you're—"

"If you're that shaky about it, you can leave. I won't make you—"

"And leave you here alone? No!"

"Then, relax and do me a favor."

"What?"

"Pass me the suntan oil, please."

"Velma, can't you wait—"

"Please."

"Gosh, if I had half your guts." He handed it to her, and looked around for reactions, as she applied it to her arms.

"We like to get dark just like they do," she said to no one in particular, pouring the oil in her palm, spreading it from her shoulder to her wrist. "Any crime in that?" Scattered laughter and exchanges of hushed whispering filled her ears. Beachers stood for a better view, displaying glances of shock and outrage. Velma ignored them. "Rudy, come over here so you can put some on too."

"None for me, thanks. I'm black enough."

"What the hell's that supposed to mean? See, that's what I'm talking about," she said, scoldingly shaking the suntan oil at him. "What's wrong with being black anyway?"

"Just a figure of speech, Velma. Figure of speech."

"Is it? Let's hope so."

"Velma, for as long as I can remember—"

"Rudy, please. Let's not argue; we just made up. I don't have an argument left in me, I swear."

"Good. Neither do I."

Once again, she had called Rudy to apologize for her behavior. She didn't mean to slap him, but the results of what she felt were mixed. One part of her hurt more deeply after striking out. She loved Rudy so. He was the one friend who stuck with her through thick and thin. Another part of her was relieved she'd done it. Slapping him did make her feel better. It was a purging of all that was bottled up inside her. She couldn't remember what the hell she'd been angry about. Stunned by her own violent reaction, she stood paralyzed as Rudy became swallowed up by the darkness of her vestibule. As she heard his footfalls fade, she called him back, went inside, slammed her door shut, and cried like a baby. She feared it was the last time she'd see him. A world without Rudy? She couldn't even consider it, and waited until he got home before calling with her tearful apology.

A few days later, she came up with this beach idea, and asked for Rudy's participation. This was her friend, the man who could accept her apology as well as an invitation to possibly getting himself lynched. They were trying to do what their literature could not. Scott, in a millennium of Sundays, would never even dream it.

Rudy found it easy to forgive her. He blamed himself, blamed his libido, blamed his unbridled, unfulfilled yearnings. She was frustrated, he knew, because he wouldn't sleep with her, a frustration he could understand. Perhaps he didn't deserve the slap, but he had brought it upon himself. He accepted her apology, even laughed about it out loud on the way home that day, thinking he might have done the same thing if a friend of his had played a ruthless game to chase his lover.

Velma lay down on the blanket, closed her eyes, and exposed her face to the sun. Like Nefertiti before the mummification. Rudy picked a bruised peach from the basket. "So, you think we'll get in trouble for this?" he said.

"Doesn't the sun feel wonderful, Rudy? You should lie down—"

"You hear me?"

"What'd you say?"

"I don't believe we're doing this—"

"Believe it, Rudy. We're here now—"

"Excuse me!" A white man with a washboard stomach, and firm pectoral muscles, his face riddled with freckles, approached their blanket. Velma peeked at him through one squinting eye. Closing it, she resumed her conversation with Rudy.

"After reading the papers day after day, I think it's the least we could—"

"I said, excuse me!" the stranger insisted.

"Can we help you, sir?" she said, lifting herself on her elbows.

"You can help yourself, lady," the man said.

"Oh?" she asked. "How's that?"

"I think you got the wrong beach."

"The *wrong* beach?" She feigned surprise, looking toward the incoming waves, and shaded her eyes with her hand. "Looks to me like a beach. How about you, Rudy? Does this look like a beach?"

"But this ain't the colored beach, lady."

"It must be. This is Black's Beach, and we're here, aren't we?"

"What kind of man are you?" He turned his mounting anger to Rudy. "You gonna sit there and let your wife do the talking for you? Aren't you man enough—"

"For one thing," Velma interrupted, "he's not my husband, and for another, we're not moving. So, save your breath, mister, because—"

"Look, lady, I don't mind so much for myself, but what about my kids?"

"What about them?" she asked.

"They, well . . . they—"

"They never saw colored people before?"

"Lady, you're gonna force my hand. Can't you see you're not wanted here? You'll be sorry for this. Don't say I didn't warn you!" He stormed away with a grunt, sand kicking up at his heels.

"Velma, c'mon, we'd better go!" Rudy said.

"You can go if you want, but," she insisted, resuming her former position, "I'm going to get some sleep."

"Velma, you've got to be crazy! You know what they'll do to us? For all we know, you could've just told off the Grand Wizard of the Ku Klux Klan! Velma! You listening? You can't be asleep that fast. Velma!"

Rain fell in slanted fury from an intensely lit magenta sky. Hitting the pavement, the raindrops transformed into crawling, scurrying insects. Women screamed and ran, clutching children to their breasts. Automobiles collided, resounding in loud crashes, the shattering of windshields and headlights. Velma tried to run but was unable to move quickly. Her movements were delayed in a frustrating slow motion. She looked for Mother, her sisters, her house; the one in which she grew up. A team of wild horses charged in a mad gallop down Lenox Avenue. Hooked to a carriage carrying a dark, floral wreathed casket, they halted at the magenta sky. Lightning bolts whipping the pavement before their hooves caused them to whinny, and raise up on their hind legs. Snapping the reins from the carriage, they galloped away, the casket falling and tumbling to the ground. Oncoming automobiles blew shrieking horns, swerved, careened, and slammed brakes to avoid collision. Tires screamed louder than hysterical, shouting women. CRASH! The hideous sound of exploding wood dissuaded Velma from looking. Suddenly, the casket was before her, resting on the steps of her apartment. Skipping over it, she ran into the darkness and waited. Running up the stairs, she threw open the door. It creaked on its hinges, and slammed against the wall with a thud! The apartment was vacant. Little furniture remained; mostly cobwebs. She was startled by a baby's cry. On the stove, wrapped in newspaper, a newborn infant screamed and kicked, the face turning red. She grabbed the child and called to Mother! Miriam! Louise! No one answered. She heard voices; Mother's and Louise's. They laughed hysterically, but Velma couldn't see them. Their laughter rang in every room in the abandoned house. Back through the door she fled, clutching the baby in her arms. Pausing in the vestibule, she checked the infant, making certain it was unharmed. The infant's face transformed to that of an old woman's. The face laughed. The casket blocked her passage. It was shut tight, lying perpendicular to the street. With slow, cautious steps, she descended the stairs when the lid opened suddenly. A hand popped out, half flesh, half skeleton. It grabbed both her ankles in one grip, causing her to trip and fall. The laughing infant with the old woman's face fell from her arms, and rolled into the street. A partially decomposed body emerged from the casket, stood over her sprawled body, and grabbed her by the arms. She pulled away screaming. The cadaver, a partially decomposed body of a woman, tried to lift her, yanking her from the ground by both arms.

Velma became nebulously aware of screeching sea gulls flying overhead in a circular ritual. Blurred images focused. Salty sea air penetrated her nostrils. A policeman tugged at her arms, trying to lift her. She bolted upright, looking around her. Rudy was being escorted from the beach by two policemen, one on each arm. Crowds of nosy beachers huddled around the blanket, staring, pointing, calling her a nigger bitch. "Come on, lady," the policeman demanded in a brogue. "Just get your stuff and let's go. Don't give us any trouble!"

"Where're you taking me?"

"To jail; where else?"

"For what?"

"Look lady, you break the law, you go to jail!"

As she was carted away by the policemen, cooperating without further protest, the crowd applauded, whistled and cheered the arresting officers.

11

The chauffeur-driven limousine pulled into the circular driveway. Vittorio sat in the front passenger seat. Behind him, a weathered, debilitated Louise rested a frail hand upon a flattened stomach. Beside her, a uniformed nurse cuddled an infant whose face was partially covered.

The limousine halted and Salvatore clicked the emergency brake. Getting out, he walked to Louise's side, opened the door, and offered his hand. Down the driveway, Jasper, the gardener, pushed a wheelchair toward her which she refused with a wave of the hand. Vittorio hooked his arm around her, and the nurse, the blue-blanketed bundle cradled in her arms, followed closely behind.

Inside the nursery along the west wing of the English Tudor-style mansion, where there had been months of detailed, meticulous preparation, the entire staff huddled around the small but elaborate crib, babbling in baby talk, trying to amuse the infant. Sara smiled widest of all.

"Look jus' lak Mr. B to me!" Jasper said.

"Uh-uh," Sara disagreed. "Spittin' image a his mama."

"That boy don't look lak his mama," Jasper argued. "Looka from over this here side—"

"The boy has a name," Vittorio said, smiling the smile of a first-time father. "His name's Angelo Vittorio. Now, come, you all have work to do."

What better timing, Vittorio thought, than to have his first child born the day after Mama's and Papa's inauspicious departure. He was so enraged with both of them, he was happy to see them sail back to Palermo.

As they packed the last of their luggage and souvenirs, Mama volunteered a disturbing confession that momentarily caused him to despise her as much as he loved her.

"I hired a private detective," Lucia told her son. "And to my misfortune, I found no evidence to hold against Luisa."

Vittorio was stunned and remembered Luisa's claim that she was being followed. He had thought she was being silly and hysterical. He sat down on the sofa to contemplate Mama's admission.

"Why do you look so pale?" Lucia asked. "You should feel relieved. I'm the one disappointed. I surrender. I'm ready to move back into your home, except that now Papa won't hear of changing our ship reservations."

If ever there was a time when he wanted to inflict physical abuse upon Mama, this was it. Struggling through tears he wouldn't release in Papa's presence, he said, "Why couldn't you take my word at face value? I told you before there's nothing wrong or suspicious about my wife. Why can't I make you believe that?"

He chided her for not crediting him with his own good common sense; as if Luisa were lying about something and he were blindly protecting her. Mama attempted to console him with the thought that she was only looking out for his welfare, and reiterated that he should have been ecstatic instead of moping. He wanted to scream at her. And he knew that if he said any more, he would utter ugly and regrettable words. If she were in his house, he would have asked her to leave.

He had very little to say while accompanying them to the pier. He changed his mind about bringing the baby to visit them in Palermo. He had never felt so viscerally wounded, so uprooted and alienated from them. Their American trip had proven disastrous, and it would be months, maybe years, before he could speak to Mama again with a civil tongue.

Driving home, he needed Luisa badly. He wanted to lay his head in her lap and weep uncontrollably. She was the only remaining bastion of family, his sole comfort, the anchor that maintained his stability. He had lost Mama and their closeness. Luisa was all he had left. Yes, he thought, shoving his Latin masculine pride aside, when I get home, I'll need my loving, devoted wife. Luisa would have to become an oversized handkerchief into which he'd weep.

When he got home, he found out that she'd gone into labor a half hour before his arrival.

It was a difficult birth, the single most stamina-challenging ordeal Louise had ever experienced in her life. Her pregnancy, as pregnancies went, had not been a bad one. The family obstetrician assured her an easy, effortless delivery. He foresaw no complications. What does he know? Louise remembered thinking. He never gave birth to anything.

It was early evening when the initial throes of labor assaulted her womb; multiple claws gnawing at her uterus. Her stomach contracted, her joints and ribs ached, and sweat glistened across her forehead. She tried rising and couldn't, not without pain. She kicked and screamed until somebody responded to her. Her breathing shifted and Sara prepared cold cloths, and mopped her forehead, while she held her hand and hummed "Jacob's Ladder."

"Tha's all right, honey," Sara said. "You scream your pretty head off if that make you feel betta. I knows what it like. Got five of my own." She hummed louder and rubbed Louise's stomach.

Vittorio arrived home with tears in his eyes, but forgot his pain when he realized what was happening with Luisa. He charged into the bedroom like a wild man. She wailed and laughed deliriously, tears pouring down her face, and pulled him to her, frightened out of her wits. He tried to soothe her, but she couldn't control herself. They embraced, rocking back and forth, their tears falling upon each other's shoulders, and he felt they were passing each other's mental and physical anguish between them, to and fro, like a relay baton.

"She might not make it," her doctor whispered to his colleague once they got her to the hospital. "We may be able to save the baby, but it looks risky."

Drowsy, she heard the words clearly. She was aware of nothing else.

In recovery, she was awakened by Vittorio with a bouquet of calla lilies and the whispered announcement she'd given birth to a healthy, beautiful boy. A nurse walked into the private room, carrying a wrapped bundle in her arms. She placed it in Louise's arms and Louise cried. Vittorio hugged them both, wife and child, and a tear rolled down his cheek. Louise fingered the baby's shiny curls, and traced the lines of his peaceful, pale face, kissing him repeatedly, deciding out loud he had his father's nose, his large hands, and his benevolent manner. Vittorio kissed her forehead, unwrapped the blanket, and kissed the bottoms of Angelo's pink, wrinkled feet.

Next day, the young couple rattled off grandiose plans for their child. He would be this, taught how to say that. Together, they blueprinted the enchanted life in which he would be indulged. The silver spoon was grandly awaiting. They planned to sail to Palermo in the coming months so he could visit his grandparents. Little Angelo, as infant, would travel to the faraway birthplace of his father, while Louise, in her entire life, had barely been outside New York. Her child would be christened and taught how to speak Italian for the summers he'd spend in Sicily. Indeed, their plans were well thought out and lavish. How exciting to bring home the first child who would grow up on the estate. What Vittorio didn't say was that they'd probably travel around the European continent, and never, ever stop in Palermo.

"You know, sweetheart," she began, "one day, I found a revolver upstairs in your drawer. I want you to get rid of it right away. I won't have a loaded gun around my child. Why do you have a gun anyway?" This had been on her mind for a while and she thought now was the time to mention it.

"Don't worry," he consoled her. "I got it for a very good reason. It's just a way to protect my family if we were ever in trouble . . . you know, prowlers, that sort of thing."

"Prowlers?" Louise asked. "Why would anyone want to rob us—"

"We have money," Vittorio cut her off. "Don't we? That's enough reason to break into our home. If you have money, consider yourself a target. People in this country do anything for money. Anything to get rich."

"I guess you're right," Louise gave in. "I never thought of it that way before."

"I know," Vittorio assured her. "A man's got a right to protect his family best way he knows how. You, I, and Angelo Vittorio have a wonderful life ahead of us. And, I won't let anything or anyone stop that. Not anything!"

He uttered it with such conviction, he frightened her.

Lying at home in her bed with the infant sleeping peacefully beside her, she watched Sara fold bed linen while the staff, of their own initiative, waited on her hand and foot. She was pleased to have Sara look after her and didn't know what she'd do without her. Outside her husband and family, Sara had become her most valued asset. She wished they could verbalize what Sara already knew about her but felt it was totally unnecessary and very much out of place. Studying Angelo beside her as he bunched up his face, she counted her blessings relative to his health. She felt satisfied, indebted even, that his complexion was rather fair. Angelo Vittorio was the spitting image of his father. God was good. And her incessant worries had been in vain.

Sara hummed, glancing at Angelo Vittorio sporadically, hoping he'd wake up so she could hold him. She thanked God for Mrs. B's safe delivery, and the fact that her Madam had pulled through as Sara had told her she would. She adored this family, and knew she'd grow to love Angelo like one of her own.

Sara considered herself blessed. She had the best boss in Mr. B that any domestic could hope for. Among her friends and neighbors who were also domestics, she was a target of envy. Nobody else's boss occasionally sent her home in the family limousine. Mr. B did. And none of them received extra cash, or well-prepared food to take home to their children. What's more, he didn't seem to hate colored folks like most rich people. Mr. B never called her anything but Sara; nor did he insult Jasper or anybody else in his employ, no matter how short-tempered he got.

She'd come to love or, more accurately, admire Mrs. B as well, though initially, she hadn't liked her. But what Sara had construed from Mrs. B as highfalutin and dicty, actually boiled down to plain insecurity and nervousness. The poor woman was more shaken than a prisoner before a death squad, and it provoked Sara to look closely, in search of clues.

She couldn't pinpoint what it was, the evidence so subtle, but she realized Mrs. B was colored when she examined her physical contours—first of all her protruding buttocks. It was the way Mrs. B walked, the regal carriage she had, like most colored women Sara knew, including herself. And Mrs. B looked no more white to her than other high-yellow colored women she knew. On top of which, and this was the ultimate giveaway, Mrs. B had a colored temper. Arguing with her was like going blow for blow with a neighbor, or someone in her family. That was a colored woman's tongue in her mouth. There were no white women who could get angry like that. Sara couldn't explain it, and could easily reduce herself to a bumbling idiot on a witness stand if asked to prove it before a judge and jury in a court of law. Everything folks knew, couldn't always be put into words, but she knew the difference between a colored and white woman. *It take one t' know one.* But working for a lady as colored as herself—a rarity, to say the least—she discovered that she was jealous of Mrs. B.

Nobody worked harder and tried elevating herself more than Sara, who'd fled the South to find a better life. She worked her fingers raw, went to church, prided herself on honesty, diligence, responsibility and loyalty, and all it ever got her was cleaning somebody's floors and washing their laundry.

All that aside and having passed, she felt ashamed for begrudging Mrs. B her happiness. After their run-in in the kitchen, Mrs. B had quieted down and never again raised her voice at Sara. Given the opportunity, if Sara could change color and marry a rich, loving white man—not that she was ashamed of being dark—there would be nothing in the world to stop her either. Recognizing herself in Mrs. B, connecting with the bond and desire they shared to rise above the twentieth-century Negro condition, she couldn't blame her for choosing the easy way out. Negroes, far too often, lashed out at each other like crabs in a barrel, and while they all aspired to liberate themselves from the rut, they sometimes didn't share the exultation when one of them made it out alive. She a colored woman jus' lak me, Sara thought, an' here I is tryin' t' give grief t' one of my own, an' we's sisters! And she resolved, in private repentance, to do everything in her power to protect madam.

She had made the mistake of telling the maid Mrs. B had since fired who, against Sara's request, went blabbing her lips about it to everybody damn near, except Mr. B himself. Served her right, Sara thought. But Mrs. B was so well liked by all the servants, they assumed a similar, quiet vigilance over her. Jasper, Bessie and everybody else guarded Mrs. B fiercely, much in the way Mrs. B maternally guarded that pretty little baby sleeping beside her. Sara was proud that one of them had "made it," whether she was living a lie or not.

12

Sitting handcuffed in a red bathing suit was no way to be. But considering what she and Rudy had done, Velma thought they were probably lucky.

She bit one policeman on the wrist to break his hold, and as his partner charged her, she aborted his heroics by kicking him in the jewels. "Wild nigger bitch!" the arresting officer screamed in pain, as he grabbed himself and doubled over. His partner, nursing the fresh teeth marks on his wrist, slapped the handcuffs on her, and reported to his sergeant that she was the troublemaker and did all the big, bad talking. "A real tough dame," he said, "but we'll show her!" And, to some extent, they did. As he walked away, to lick his wound in the infirmary, he took one glance at Velma's imprisoned hands and said, "Niggers look best in chains. Whether it's around your neck, your wrists, or ankles. It's kinda like jigga-boo jewelry."

She was worried sick about Rudy, not knowing where they had taken him. They wouldn't tell her and she hoped he wasn't somewhere in a sealed-off room, handcuffed to a chair, while officers practiced punt kicks on his beautiful face. Whatever happened to him, she felt completely responsible. Rudy might *really* never speak to her again. But what he said to the arresting officer made her proud, even surprised her.

Handcuffed, Rudy leaned against the sergeant's desk as they booked him. He was calm—a contrast to Velma's storminess—and he spoke evenly, eloquently, without perturbation, providing the booking information like a student reciting Keats before the class. As they were about to take him away, Rudy turned to the officer and said matter-of-factly, "It just puzzles me," he began, smiling graciously and humbly, "that you, as a white man in this great country of ours, with all the career opportunities available to you—which is *everything!*—it just baffles the dickens out of me that the only thing you could turn out to be is a police officer—" He was barely finished with his snide observation when the policeman slugged him, knocking him to the floor. Then they dragged him out of the station and into the waiting paddy wagon. "And your courage, when the opponent is at a disadvantage, must be unsurpassed!" he added, as his legs dragged along the floor.

Watching her friend being dragged like wild, captured game caused Velma to choke with tears. But she refused to display any semblance of fear, submission or vulnerability in their presence. This was the single most humiliating chapter in her life. Had she been a slave, she wouldn't have survived this long.

She thought again about the nightmare she had during her short beach nap before being awakened to the angry, scarlet faces of the blue-clad policemen. They didn't know who they were arresting, but they were sure to find out. She counted her blessings though. They'd witnessed the Red Summer of 1919. They'd seen Negroes maimed and murdered without reason, for actions far less provocative than theirs.

After booking her, they threw her into a cell where one woman screamed herself fire-engine red, and no one demanded that she shut up. Another made goo-goo eyes at her, winking intermittently, fondling her own breasts, licking her lips and sucking her thumb. Velma ignored her. She wrapped her fingers around the iron bars and hoped that the woman would keep her lewd suggestions to her side of the cell. Then there was the whiner. Curling herself in a corner like a cat, she moaned and whined throughout the night like a feline in heat. Probably frightened to death, Velma thought, the poor thing. Maybe as frightened as Velma herself. She struggled to maintain a tough exterior. It seemed to be working. Just look tough, she kept reminding herself.

When morning came, she woke to the stench of human excrement. The nightmare had stayed with her throughout the night. She flipped and tossed it over and over in her mind. She tried to decipher it. What did it mean? Her Freudian and Jungian theories from her Barnard days failed her. Was that Florence Mills's floral wreathed casket? The one she witnessed through Mother's bedroom window? And that baby? Who was it? To whom did it belong? Was it hers? A symbolic sign of a yearning in her womb? She recalled its face turning old and wrinkled. And the voices, Mother's and Louise's, laughing deliriously as she had heard them do many times. She felt like the inside joke being shared between Mother and Louise in the nightmare. As if they could see her, the manner in which she panicked, the desperation with which she called out their names. Mother's dead, she thought. Does that mean Louise is too? Oh my God! As the partially decomposed body tackled her around the ankles, hovered above her as if about to consume her whole, and shook her by the arms like a rag doll, she was awakened. She woke from one nightmare and assumed her position in the next. What could be said, or possibly hoped for, about the society which applauded an innocent Negro couple's being carted off to jail merely for sunbathing.

The one telephone call she was allowed to make the next day was the most dreadful call she'd ever made. Whom could she call to post bail for her? She knew the Van Vechtens, the Knopfs, or her agent would, but the embarrassment of asking overwhelmed her. She wasn't ashamed of her two-bit political activism, but she didn't feel close enough to any of them, except her agent, who often wasn't home. And when she dialed her one allotted telephone call, the party had to be there.

She thought of Scott, who also might not be at home. But there was the possibility that he'd ask too many questions. He might not sympathize with her, insisting that knowingly and willingly, she had walked head on into this trouble. And she remembered how rude she'd been to him last time, kicking him out of her apartment. Scott forgot nothing. Vindictiveness was the sort of thing he thrived on and seemingly lived for.

Rudy, had he not been involved, would have rescued her for certain, no questions asked. She felt a maternal pride in his heroics, despite his well-founded trepidation and intimidation. He even refused to leave her alone on the beach. Sitting in her cell, watching this motley bunch of misfits, she understood the meaning of true friendship.

One person was left, a thought which made her cringe. But she had to do it. What alternatives did she have but to face the music, whether she felt like dancing or not. There was one person who without doubt had the cash lying around and was always home.

The telephone rang nearly fifteen times in the Park Avenue penthouse. With my luck, she thought, the old bitch has gone on an extended vacation to some obscure, *primitive* crevice on the globe. Worse, she probably died. Velma decided to hang up around the fifteenth ring—indeed, she'd been counting—when she heard a click. The maid finally answered, panting, out of breath. She could picture the domestics scurrying about, carrying out their duties, too preoccupied to stop as the telephone rang off its hook. And the old lady. She probably sat upon her throne with the dignity and pomp of Queen Victoria. She was much too busy sipping tea and delegating work.

Velma was surprised—no, shocked at Mrs. Vanderpool's calm reaction. The old woman sounded so accommodating, so sympathetic. She would have hugged her wrinkled neck had she been standing within reach. Suddenly, she felt shame for having spoken with her in the manner she did last time.

"Just relax," Mrs. Vanderpool consoled her. "Things could be much worse."

They already were, Velma felt, but she wasn't about to tell the old woman that. She would say nothing, not a blessed thing. Not from the interior of a city jail while in search of bail money she wouldn't. Velma tried to explain. Mrs. Vanderpool interrupted her.

"It doesn't matter," she said. "These things happen. Sit tight and I'll send someone for you. What'd you say the address was again?"

Velma smiled. Her heart began to beat the pulse of a second chance. And she was on the verge of rambling off *Thank you's* and *I'll never forget you for this, Mrs. Vanderpool!* when her fears were realized.

"It just goes to show you," Mrs. Vanderpool scolded. "You never know when you might need someone. And, if I'm not mistaken, you ranted about here in my penthouse about how much you don't need me. But, my dear, as you can see, you need me more than you care to admit. I always knew something like this would happen. It might've been weeks, maybe months, perhaps a year. But I knew something like this would happen. It's not the first time. I can bet every penny I have, that in some form, you'd come running back to your kind, forgiving godmother. Now, you may correct me if I'm wrong . . ."

Velma wanted to tell her to go to hell! Take her money and shove it up her old, wrinkled ass. Bail or no bail, Velma had meant what she said to Mrs. Vanderpool that last time. Every word of it. Nobody exercised that much control over her.

But Velma swallowed her words, which felt like poison dripping down her throat. She cleared her head of all the clever rebuttals she might have bounced back with, providing no further rope to hang herself. She ended the call with a mere, "Thank you, Mrs. Vanderpool. I appreciate it more than you know."

"Oh my dear," Mrs. Vanderpool concluded before hanging up, "I'll just bet you do!"

Scott was the last person she had expected to come for her. She assumed the old woman would send a maid or the butler. Entering the jailhouse as if he owned it, his face and manner sympathetic, he was a sight for sleepless eyes. She couldn't remember being more elated to see him. The desk sergeant couldn't concentrate on the paperwork for staring at this well-dressed, articulate Negro of letters before him posting bail. The sergeant stared them out the door. His mouth gaped, he scratched his balding head.

Heading homeward in the Studebaker, after inquiring about Rudy, and being told that he'd already been released, Velma used the opportunity to say what had been tugging at her heart for some time now. Hadn't she promised Mother on her deathbed? Didn't she want it as much as Mother?

"Come on, Scott," she suggested, cashing in on the moment's impulse. Her heart pounded like a bass drum. "Let's do it!"

"Do what?" he said. "Surely you don't mean have sex right here in the automobile."

"Of course not. Why don't we get married? We've been together for almost four years. What else is there? We don't even have to have a big, formal wedding—"

"It's simply out of the question," he said. "Why on earth would you want to marry me?" He wanted marriage as much as she, but first he had to listen to her reasons.

"Scott, I know we have our problems, but the fact remains, I still love you. I can help you. You can help me. We'll help each other. Can't be much different from the way things are already. We certainly see a lot of each other—well, we did. We're intellectually compatible and we have great sex. And you still love me, don't you?" God, she thought, I sound so desperate.

Scott said nothing immediately. He's going to let me stew, she thought. Now that I've made myself vulnerable to him again like a groveling fool. But then he cleared his throat and took Velma's hand in his. "I'm really flattered," he began, and kissed her hand. "Of course I'm still in love with you. That's why I bothered to come. I've never loved anyone or anything more." He paused, stopped at a red light, and continued. "But the situation being what it is, it could be terribly risky. There are just too many things we have to work out. I need time to pull myself together and take inventory of what we have between us. I need to work out these thoughts and feelings that boil inside me. But thank you just the same, Velma. I'm bloody flattered, really I am. I never would've suspected in a thousand years, that you'd ask *me* to marry you. But I just can't. If we married, we'd only be headed for the ruination of a treasured friendship. And I only have two." He hoped she was reading between the lines; picking up on the subtext he didn't have the courage to delineate. Bright as she was, he didn't have to spell the main reason out for her. "You're the best thing to ever happen to me, on many levels. But I need—"

"What you need," Velma interjected, "is a good, strong woman to take care of you. Someone who knows you and can help you. Children are good for that too." She thought of her nightmare. "Why don't we have a child? We could make fabulous babies, Scott," she said, forcing herself to laugh when she didn't want to. "I don't know; maybe I'm panicking. I'll be thirty soon. And if I don't get a move on it, I won't be able to bear children. And probably, I won't be eligible for marriage either."

"You really want to get married?" he asked, excited by the idea. He was happy to have been her rescuer from jail. She didn't know that he'd sprung for the bail, not Mrs. Vanderpool, who had merely called him. He felt nothing in particular regarding the Black's Beach incident, except pride at Velma's sinewy spirit.

"Yes, I want to get married," she said. "We already are in so many ways. Just picture it, Scott. We could move to Connecticut, buy a home, and raise our family." She began chuckling, a little embarrassed at revealing her preconceived notions of the family portrait.

She'd never shared these fantasies with him. "Imagine our son. He'll be just like you. We'll send him to boarding school and Harvard, like his father, and we'll groom him to be a poet. A combination of Dunbar and Hughes—we could throw in Cullen for you. Couldn't you just see it?"

Scott grinned. "What about daughters? Won't we have a little Velma too?"

"Of course," she said sanguinely, believing she was finally winning him over. "She'll go to Barnard like her mommy, or maybe Radcliffe. And you and I could write from a cottage buried deep in the woods or on a beach. I don't care, so long as we're together. Imagine it—George Virgil the second, and Elvira Louise."

"You've already picked out the names?" Scott laughed.

"Of course!" she said, happier at that moment than she'd ever been.

"Just like a woman," he said.

Scott studied her, and without warning, pulled the automobile up to the curb. Then he held her hand and face, and looked into her eyes. She had no idea what he was going to say, unable to interpret his gaze, but she assumed he was going to make the proposal official for her, like any woman in love would want.

"You really want to do this?" he asked.

"Why do you keep asking me that? Yes, yes, a thousand times, yes!"

Never breaking his gaze from her, he swallowed, sensing the deciding power of what he was about to ask. It could be the most important, most pressing question of his life.

"Velma, I'm going to ask you something," he began. "And I need your absolute honesty. Understand? No matter how difficult it might be, if you're not honest with me now when I most need it, I'll never forgive you."

"Yes, darling," she said, holding his face. Traffic zoomed past them. Scott had a forlorn desperation in his eyes.

"Look me in the eyes," he said, "and tell me you don't love Rudy."

"I do love Rudy; he's my best friend," she said, her eyes straying from his. He turned her head back to face him.

"Of course you love him; I love him too. But tell me you're not *in* love with him. Can you?"

She looked in his eyes and felt as if she were gazing into God's on Judgment Day. Her stomach knotted, she bit her lip and accepted that she had to give him a truthful answer without a speck of doubt or dishonesty, and knew, as he knew, that she couldn't. If she told him the truth, the marriage was off, and she, more than he, would understand. Never before had she felt so put upon and so desired by Scott. She was both flattered and terrified. If she lied and told him what he obviously needed to hear, she'd pay dearly and would have only herself to blame when the marriage was a disaster.

Rather than perjure herself, she said nothing. She loved and respected Scott too much to trivialize his needs out of her own selfishness. She suddenly turned tacit after having been so garrulous.

"Just as I thought," he said, releasing her hand and face. He kissed her paternally on the forehead, pressed her head against his chest, shifted the gear into first, and continued up Eighth Avenue. "Thanks for your honesty. You just saved my life."

At least she'd given it her best shot, hoping Mother, wherever she was, recognized her efforts. And for the moment, she despised and blamed herself for her lack of commitment in the face of a decision that meant everything to her and Scott.

She thought of Roland. He'd been pretty quick to marry someone else after she broke up with him. That was ten years ago. But for the first time since, she gave sincere thought to what Roland must have felt. He was so eager to tie the knot. She had set her sights on becoming a writer. The price one paid. The law of retribution seemed to be viciously at work. She felt she was getting her just due. What she'd done to Roland, someone had now done to her. I must remember this feeling, she advised herself, sitting silently beside Scott. I must remember this and use it in my writing.

13

Louise enviously watched the private nurse change Angelo's diaper. Nearly eight months she carried her unborn child, nurtured it, spoke to it, felt it kick in response, and the nurse seemed to be enjoying the fruit of Louise's labors. Everybody wants to hold, cuddle, and feed the baby, she thought. Nobody wants to share the agony, just the ecstasy. The nurse was Vito's brainchild, since he himself had been reared by nurses and governesses. But Louise felt there was nothing the nurse could do that the mother couldn't. Moreover, she feared that the first time Angelo said "Ma-ma," it might be to the nurse. She could hardly bear to think of it.

"I'll take him," Louise said, nudging the nurse aside, completing the diapering. The woman'll never know if she has a job or not, she thought. "Why don't you take the day off."

"But, madam—"

"I insist."

Though he'd already had his bath, she bathed him again and brushed his shiny locks of black, silky hair: Vito's hair. She expected her husband home about noon. The weather was beautiful and balmy. She took him into the garden, swung him in the hammock, and sang soft lullabies. "Go to sleep, my baby, my baby, my baby. . . ." She guarded him from mosquitoes, picked flowers to tickle his bare stomach and the pink bottoms of his feet. He laughed and kicked and dribbled and gurgled.

"Yes, my darling boy, that's right . . . you're Mommy's beautiful boy . . . the most beautiful boy in the whole world."

Sara was observing them through the kitchen window. When Vittorio arrived, he brought toys and candy for the child.

"I know he's too young for this," he told Louise, who glanced at him with a skeptical eye. "But I wanted to buy them for him anyway. I can't help myself."

"He's getting big, isn't he?" Louise said, as Vittorio bounced the child on his lap.

"Don't do that. You'll make him sick. And don't touch his head. His skull isn't fully formed yet."

"Who do you think he looks like?"

"Just like you, Vito. Don't you think?"

"Let's have more, now!" He began waltzing through the garden, leading his son, cradled in his arms. "Let's have more babies, Luisa."

"How many more?" She agreed, but she didn't want to raise a tribe, not after that last delivery.

"Oh, I don't know. At least give him a little sister."

"Wouldn't that be sweet?"

"Luisa," Vittorio said, kissing her and the baby. "I love being a father. I love you. I didn't begin to live until you . . . and him."

"I know, sweetheart." She watched him, happier than she'd ever seen him. "I love you too."

*   *   *

After lunch, Louise put Angelo to sleep in the nursery and retired to her own bedroom to finish rereading *Chameleon* in privacy. With about a chapter and a half remaining, she wondered if her sister had written this story about her. She hadn't read the novel again for nearly a year. It remained hidden beneath the mattress, and occasionally she forgot it was there. But today was an ideal afternoon for reading.

As she lay on the bed, riveted to her sister's cliffhanging plot, one of the servants broke a glass while cleaning. The crash startled her, and the book fell from her hands and landed on the floor. She picked it up, and the dedication page stared her directly in the face. She'd never bothered to read it before. Her eyes crawled across the words: *In Loving Memory of Elvira Murchison Brooks 1880–1927.* She wailed so loudly, one of the servants heard her and came running to see if something had happened to her or the baby. Louise quickly hid the book behind her back.

"You all right, ma'am?" the servant asked.

"Yes, yes, I'm fine."

"The baby too? You sho?" the servant asked again, noticing the tears inching down her cheeks.

"Yes, really. I'm okay. You may go."

The remainder of the day she spent sobbing, dabbing her eyes, blowing her nose into an entire box of tissues, hugging Angelo fiercely, and making excuses to Sara and the staff that she was fine. They could see that she was distraught. Sara called her employer.

Vito came home immediately. He sat on the bed, and placed his arms around his weeping wife. He'd never seen her cry like this before.

"*Cara mia*, what's wrong?"

"I don't know," Louise whispered. "I don't feel good." She shook her head, while her husband watched perplexedly.

"Get dressed," he said. "I'm taking you to see Dr. Santucci."

"What for?" Louise asked.

"Maybe he can tell us what's wrong."

She dressed, and they drove across town to visit her obstetrician. Vittorio informed the doctor that his wife was suddenly, chronically in tears.

"Postnatal depression happens to most new mothers," Dr. Santucci said to the young couple in his private office. "It's nothing unusual."

Louise stopped weeping and listened to the doctor.

"Mothers feel an anxiety and depression relating to several biological factors," he said. "They're worried about their bodies losing shape, varicose veins popping up in the back of their legs, that sort of thing."

"See, honey," Vittorio said, taking Louise's hand and rubbing it.

"I'll prescribe something you can have filled at the pharmacy," Dr. Santucci said. "Don't worry. She'll be just fine."

Louise could have reached across the desk and kissed the doctor as he came up with an explanation for her. She herself had never heard of postnatal depression. They left and Vittorio took her to the nearest pharmacist to have the prescription filled and he promised to monitor her dosage. It made her love him that much more, when she otherwise felt she couldn't possibly love him any more than she did.

14

Night rain beat a crackling rhythm on Rudy's fire escape and windowsills. The parlor was lit with waning candles. Rudy sat opposite Scott in unnerving silence, his head turned away, buried in his hands. Their shadows flickered, looming large, black, and jerky on the wall.

"I know," Scott scoffed, waiting for Rudy to pull himself together. "Or at least I can imagine that you're tormented by your sexuality which makes you, how can I aptly phrase it? . . . comparatively abnormal—"

"Abnormal?" He looked at Scott through the fingers covering his face.

"I did say 'comparatively.' Now don't misunderstand me. I'm the first to sympathize with your plight, but my word, boy, you can't go through life suspecting that every man who smiles at you is guilty of the same carnal drive as yourself. I mean, it's preposterous. Surely you agree?" He puffed on his pipe.

"For someone supposedly 'normal,' " Rudy said, "you sure possess an uncanny curiosity about sexual 'abnormality,' as you so *aptly* phrase it, don't you?"

"What can I possibly say? I've never known a homosexual before—at least, not personally. I have questions and curiosities like the next man. Is that so strange?"

"No. But *you* are."

"Well," Scott said, rising, brushing his arms of God knows what, noticing the black eye Rudy was trying to conceal. "We're not getting anywhere with this. Here you've summoned me to your flat, and all you do is accuse me, then sulk behind your—"

"I'm sick and tired of you making me feel I've imagined everything."

"Haven't you?" Scott said, hunching his shoulders.

"What happened here that night at dinner, was that my imagination? Or, did I imagine being in your bed?"

"But nothing happened. I just wanted to see how far you'd go—"

"No! How far *you'd* go, until you-know-who came charging through the door to your rescue. How goddamn convenient for you. Saved by the bell."

"You see," Scott said, walking toward the door. "There you go again—"

"Don't move until I'm finished."

"I thought you were—"

"Scott, remember the day I took you to the gentlemen's bar? Remember? I took you there for a reason. Before that, you were always the big shot, so in control of everything, so unintimidated, and your reaction really shocked me at first. I didn't understand the way you shit in your pants when I took you there, but now I do. You became powerless like a child afraid of the dark, afraid of what you might see. And I loved it. You were like putty in my hands. There was an exchange of power; I had power over you because you were in my element. The same way you hold power over me—Velma too, for that matter. Yeah, it occurred to me, you were in my element; that same element you want to indulge in, the one you flirt with whimsically. On the other hand, in *your* element, I'm powerless. Wherever we go or whatever we do, I'm always victim to your power because you dominate everything and everybody. You'll have it no other way. Introducing us to people like O'Neill, Robeson, Mrs. Vanderpool, the entire goddamn Manhattan society at your fingertips. Well, I'll tell you quite frankly, if I had my choice, I prefer you weak and powerless."

"I said I was sorry for the remark in front of Robie and Gene—"

"That's not what bothered me. After a few drinks, you were

attacking in me what you see in yourself." Scott sat, exasperated, defeated. Rudy stood and began pacing, his shadow jumping from one wall to the next.

The rain came harder now, splashing from the fire escape and windowsills onto the floor. A gust of wind snuffed out two or three candle stubs, and Rudy wished the same wind could blow out the candle burning within him. How apropos, he thought, the precipitation coming down in buckets, and yet it was no match for the water he resisted in the rims of his eyes, nor the electrical storm raging in his heart. From where he stood, he could smell the spiciness of Scott's cologne, and wondered why moist air sharpened the sense of smell. Watching Scott, he felt a love-and-hate ambivalence in the pit of his stomach, as he glided from one emotion to the next, then back again.

"Are you quite through—"

"I despise people like you," Rudy said, feeling used, abandoned and ultimately discarded. The cycle he had been locked into, falling in and out of unrequited love with best friends from high school through college, had taken its toll. "From nowhere, you come out of the woodwork and exploit my feelings for some childish flirtation because you're not really man enough to put both feet in the water. You can't face who you really are. Whether you're Negro or white. Whether you want women or men. Like a vampire, you emerge only at night, then stalk the likes of me. Feasting on my blood. My *fucking* blood!

"When the sun rises, you vanish out of sight, escaping any possible harsh judgment. You turn over in your coffin inside the grave you've so conveniently dug for yourself—"

"I love Velma. What do you want me to—"

"Velma! Hah! That's a fucking laugh! You hide behind her. She's only your refuge. You know what Velma . . . I'll tell you what . . . you know what Velma is to you? Her role is that of the gravedigger. She shovels the dirt over you night after night. That way you can't see. You relish a tentative blindness, so you won't have to look at yourself and who and what you *really* are. Haven't you ever wondered why vampires are afraid of mirrors? Then, and only then, you slip without notice into your so-called place of rest; your so-called respectable station in society, leaving me, the *abnormal*, to bear the stones of persecution. Oh yes, I remember so well. At the gentlemen's bar, you even went so far as to say 'Ignore them, and they'll go away! Remember that? The two English *pansies* who saw right through you? But you'd like that, huh? You'd like for all the pansies to fly away and leave you to your repressed decadence. Is that on target? Wait, it gets better.

"That's what I symbolize to you, isn't it? I mean, when the dust settles, that's really what it's all about, isn't it? I know you'd like me to go away and leave you uncorrupted. That is, until you're ready for me again. But listen to this, and listen good," he warned, bending down, pressing his face against Scott's, feeling violently and sexually charged. "I'm not going away, you got that? I'm not one of your fictional characters who'll disappear with the closing of a book. I'm here to stay, baby. Even more, I'm here to remind you. You like that? I refuse to let you ignore me or evade me. So just consider me a permanent fixture. There's a lot of healing that twisted mind of yours could use, and whether you like it or not, your first step in that healing is me. The game begins and ends here, with me—"

"How can I get it through your head that I'm attracted to women—"

"You like men too! What do you think, I'm stupid? I'm pretty *worldly* my goddamn self, you know. And I'm fucking fed up with being your cute, little homosexual fellow whose subdued, kind nature you discern as weakness!"

"I've heard enough!" Scott rose again, glanced around, and wondered why Rudy had improved his grooming and wardrobe but not his bohemian apartment.

"What do you plan to do about it?" Rudy asked.

"Go home and make myself a drink."

"Ah yes, the drink. The infamous gin and ginger ale. If you've heard a word of anything I've said here tonight, maybe you wouldn't have to drink so much."

"I hope we understand each other now," Scott said, opening the door, pausing. "Maybe now, we can—"

"Scott?"

"What?"

"Don't bullshit the bullshitter, okay?"

"Take care of that eye, Rudy," Scott said, glancing at Rudy's swollen eye.

"Don't worry about my eye," Rudy replied. "When you come to your senses, I have something for you to take care of." He closed his door and, for the first time, locked it.

* * *

The bar behind the alcove seemed to call his name, but Scott steered clear of it.

He hadn't touched a drop since Paul Robeson's homecoming party at Walker's Lewaro estate. He hadn't meant to insult Rudy at the party. The words sprang from his lips before his mind could abort the passing thought. Velma was right. He drank too much. And if it got in the way of his two best relationships, then he had to do something, and quickly.

Sitting on the blue velvet sofa, he opened Faulkner's *The Sound and the Fury* and climbed inside Benjy's mentally retarded reveries. He couldn't concentrate. The room felt damp, drafty, and there was an annoying, incessant drip of water outside on his fire escape.

Rudy had his wires crossed. Okay, so he had flirted dangerously close with him once or twice, but Scott never gave him the go-ahead to fall desperately in love. He couldn't love Rudy that way. He wanted to comfort himself with *Let him believe what he wants to believe.* Three or four years ago, he wouldn't have cared what anguish and romantic agony Rudy was putting himself through. As his friend, it wasn't that simple.

What was he going to do about Velma? What was he going to do about any of it? He sought the answers with far more vigor than he sought the characters, plot and voice of his next novel. Velma couldn't marry him. Or was it that he wouldn't marry her? He had come to depend on her, but he knew it was coming to a close. He felt it in his bones. Pressing her head against his chest in the Studebaker, he had never felt farther away from her—unable to reach and touch and make the contact that could shift their lopsided suspension. He loved her, but she couldn't wholeheartedly love him because of Rudy. Rudy couldn't reciprocate her love, but, rather, handed it over to Scott. The entire situation had escaped the levers of control, and as it unraveled before them, everyone's worst fears were being realized. There had to be a novel in it somewhere, a piece he couldn't write until viewing it all from hindsight. First, he needed to detach himself from the tied, twisted, overlapping strings which bound them together. Whatever happened to the good times? They drank, danced, and crashed every party in Manhattan from Harlem to the Village, and he hadn't noticed until now that playtime was over. It was time to live real life.

If he and Velma couldn't marry, then what remained? Carry on as they'd been? No, they'd choke, stifle and smother one another as each of them clawed and gasped for air.

Staring across the room at his mother's photograph on the wall, he felt remorseful. He hadn't written her in a long while, since he met Velma. He needed her now. He picked up the telephone to call Massachusetts, then reconsidered, avoiding the possibility of his father answering. Walking to his credenza, he sat down, pulled out some paper, dated it, and began composing what would be a lengthy letter to his mother. He was stumped by the second sentence. There was so much to say, he didn't know where to begin. He put down the pen, and thought *Fuck it!*

Rising, he crossed the room, entered the alcove, and mixed himself a drink. The liquor smelled and tasted magnificent, either because it had been sitting there so long, or because his tongue had forgotten how friendly it once was. After three drinks, he clicked on the gramophone and played Bessie Smith's "Empty Bed Blues." It reminded him of Velma and the night he visited her and lied about having read her book. He'd since read it, and was quite proud of her. Although he never bothered to tell her. He sat her picture before him, turned the glass up to his mouth and wept himself into a drunken snore.

15

All babies get darker as they grow . . .

Vittorio sat alone in Giuseppe's, frantically biting his nails, listening to reports on the radio. Many of his stock holdings were drastically changing position; gaining and losing as much as ten points per day. He realized that Papa's forecast was possibly coming to pass, but chose to shove the thought aside. He absentmindedly stabbed his fork into the cooling linguini. He couldn't eat, and listened to Herbert Hoover on the radio. He felt as if Hoover were talking directly to him, while addressing the nation regarding economic ruin. His voice traveled the air waves so that Vittorio di Bolognese alone, wherever he was, would hear and heed the warning.

Part of him snickered at the old man. Vittorio was among the so-called crusty, blue-blooded financiers Hoover vituperatively attacked. But he didn't care. He was one among the many hustling young stockbrokers who lobbied against the President; a part of an elite fraternity of Wall Street giants who all but controlled the financial direction of an entire nation. If Hoover knew what was good for him, Vittorio thought, he'd hand over the reins and grant them absolute power. There was no cause for panic.

Refusing to listen further to this hogwash broadcast, he wiped his mouth with the linen napkin and placed it beside his linguini. Leaving a tip, taking a last sip of wine, he put on his hat, and climbed into the limousine as Salvatore closed the door behind him.

In his dark mood, he decided upon a sneak visit to his wife and son. Whenever life became coarse and choppy, solace could always be found with his family. He was scheduled for an RCA stockholders' meeting this afternoon to discuss the emergency situation lurking on the horizon. But he'd be a little late today. They couldn't start without him.

He was concerned about Luisa, who continued to cry off and on throughout the days. The prescription had not done much good. He hoped this afternoon she was in a more peaceful state of mind. She didn't deserve tears and anguish.

He hadn't heard from his parents since their departure, nor did he care. They'd need him before he them. Willing to strike a compromise, he couldn't see his way clearly to one which suited both parties. Each parent disapproved something about his life, and until they rectified their prejudiced attitudes, he wanted little to do with them.

Arriving home, he asked Sara about his wife's whereabouts, and she pointed to the garden. Louise was bouncing Angelo in her lap, and he assumed she was in a better mood. Studying the child as he walked into the garden, he noticed something, a nuance, something unidentifiable he couldn't place his finger on. Something he'd not noticed before.

He kissed his wife and son, sat at the patio table, and stared into space.

"Darling, what's wrong?" she asked.

"Nothing," he said, unwilling to burden her with his financial woes. As he stuck out his arms, she passed his son to him. He held him toward the sun and noticed that the child was getting darker, alarmingly so. His thick hair was becoming coarse, like Sara's.

"*Cara mia*, isn't Angelo getting a little dark?" he said, comparing the child's complexion with Luisa's and his own. The baby was a shade darker than them already.

"All babies get darker as they grow," she said nervously. "It's nothing unusual." Her lip twitched and he saw it.

"Yes it is!" he barked with an adamance that startled her. "It's *very* unusual! Doesn't it seem strange to you? He's darker than both of us—"

"Sweetheart, what's wrong?" Louise said, noticing that he'd come home in an uncharacteristically bad mood. It must have been the stock market again, she thought, recalling the headlines in the *Wall Street Journal* that morning.

"I said, nothing's wrong."

"You sure?"

"Luisa, look at this child. Whose nose and lips are these . . . and his hair? You think the hospital made a mistake and gave us the wrong baby?"

"There's no mistake," Louise replied weakly, distant bells clanging in her head, her temples throbbing. "He's ours. A mother knows."

"I don't think so," he challenged.

"It's your stocks again, isn't it?"

"What makes you say that?"

"Well, you're in a bad mood—"

"Oh, God," he said.

"What's the matter?" she asked, holding her breath.

"I just remembered. I've got a meeting this afternoon, and I should be going." He stood and passed the baby back to her, unable to take his eyes off the boy's face and hair. "This baby doesn't look like me—"

"Sure he does," Louise claimed, wishing he'd stop. "Can't you see the resemblance? He's you all over."

"No!" Vittorio scoffed, and started back toward the house. "I don't think so. We'll talk about it later tonight when I get home. Luisa, there's something terribly wrong here."

16

Tossing and turning in a fitful sleep, Miriam rolled over and squinted at the clock. Father's sepia-toned photograph stared down at her from the wall. She wished she could be just a photograph on somebody's wall or table. She could smile from behind a glass and wooden frame and mean it, watching life happen around her, without having to actually live it. There was an insufferable racket throughout the apartment building, and uncharacteristically, she'd decided to sleep in on this cold and wet Saturday morning. Except she hadn't planned on fathers arguing, babies crying, children yelling and screaming, and mothers banging cupboard doors shut. She usually got up with the sun and never heard so much as a toilet flush before noon.

She started to get up, then thought, for what? There was nothing she planned to do today. She turned over and listened to the rain. The sun needn't show its face on her account. Closing her eyes, she was startled by a crashing noise. Her first thought was that someone, somewhere within the three-story building, had broken a dish. Then she realized that the sound was coming from her own apartment.

Getting out of bed, wrapping a bathrobe around her body, she wondered what Agnes could be doing this early on Saturday morning. Cracking open her door, she peeked outside, and two rooms away, saw Agnes and Tommy picking up the pieces of a vase. The front door was opened, and it appeared that Tommy had been going in and out. Part of her wanted to rush into the room, bitch and complain that he was disturbing her sleep and throw him out with the trash. Another part of her wanted to climb back into bed so she wouldn't have to face either of them. Striking a compromise, she walked into the parlor, past them.

"Good morning," Agnes said. "Hope we're not disturbing you."

"Mornin'," Miriam said. There wasn't a damn thing good about it.

"How you doin'?" Tommy said.

Miriam continued toward the bathroom though there was nothing in that room she wanted or needed. She could feel their eyes following her as she whisked past.

In the bathroom, she closed the door, sat on the toilet and thought of ways to circumvent Agnes's moving out. Agnes hadn't mentioned it since that night, but neither had she stopped seeing Tommy. She even took to spending nights, sometimes days with him. Since the last discussion, Miriam had not bothered to raise the subject again. Not that she didn't feel the urge, she just recognized the futility. She didn't understand Agnes's motives. How could somebody give that much of herself and remain uncommitted? It could only mean trouble when folks hopped around from bed to bed like some kind of sexual philanthropist. Since their discussion, she'd since allowed her sorrow and chagrin to give way to anger and resentment. Agnes had begun to impress her as a user. She bounced around from place to place as it suited her. When it got too hot and complicated, she was on to the next victim. Much as she despised him, Miriam aligned herself with Tommy nowadays to some extent. He too, regardless of how he'd treated Agnes, had been abandoned. And judging by what Agnes was doing to her, she imagined that Agnes had possibly brought it all on herself. She considered how she'd leaped from Tommy's aunt's bed into his, then into Miriam's. Miriam felt little sympathy for what was in store for Agnes. She was destined to reap what she'd so unscrupulously sown, and Miriam didn't feel sorry for her, not one bit, not anymore. And yet, if Agnes were to recant her decisions and remain with Miriam, she'd take her back, no questions asked. This dichotomy made her furious with herself; hypocrisy rated low on her measuring stick of virtues. Sitting on the toilet seat, she waited until she could no longer hear Tommy, then flushed the toilet, ran water in the basin, shut it off, and emerged. Walking past Agnes who was entering her bedroom, Miriam stopped and followed her inside.

"When you think you'll be moved out?" Miriam asked.

"Few more days," Agnes said. "I'm just trying to get some of these things—"

"Have you found a place already?"

"Yes."

"Where?"

"Tommy's—"

"You're moving in with him too, huh?" she asked, eyeing the jewelry box with the bracelet Agnes never bothered to wear.

"Yes, Miriam." Agnes was tiring of her thousand questions, especially when she wouldn't accept the answers.

"Well, I wish y'all the best of luck," Miriam said, without

meaning a word of it. She hesitated, struggling with an urge of sheer pettiness. She'd be ashamed of herself in the morning, but if she walked out of this room without doing it, she'd never forgive herself.

"I guess you won't be needing this where you're going," she said, picking up the jewelry box and slipping it in her pocket before Agnes could protest. The woman was leaving with her heart. She wouldn't take the gold too.

"I thought you gave it to me," Agnes said.

"You never wore it."

"That's not the principle."

"Then what is, Agnes? Huh? What is the principle? Girl, don't talk to me about principle."

Miriam walked back into her bedroom, slammed the door shut, and crawled into bed. Turning over and closing her eyes to recapture the state of unconsciousness, she heard Tommy reentering the apartment, talking loudly as if he wanted the entire building to hear him.

"You tell her?" he asked Agnes.

"Tell her what?" Agnes said.

"Where you're moving?"

"Yeah. Tommy, lower your voice. Miriam's trying to sleep."

"Hey, she ain't the only one paying rent here."

That was it! That was the second time she'd heard him say that. In and of itself, it was no more than a verity she didn't need to get upset about. But she did. She was looking for a reason to give him a piece of her mind. She'd been wanting to ever since the night he gave her his telephone number at Liberty Hall.

She jumped out of bed, wrapped herself inside the bathrobe, and opened her door. Even better, she saw Tommy moving a lamp out of the apartment. Her lamp. And she charged into the room with such force that he did a double take.

"Hey, slow down, lady."

"Slow down, my ass," Miriam said. "Where you think you're taking that?"

"Agnes is moving," he said sarcastically. "Didn't you know?"

"Yeah," she replied. "*Agnes* is moving, not my damn lamp!"

"This ain't yours—"

"Yes it is," Agnes said, rushing out of her bedroom to stand between them. "This is Miriam's."

"Well, all right, shit," Tommy said. "She ain't got to bite my fuckin' head off about it neither."

"Bite your—" Miriam said, cutting herself short, glaring at him as if she hadn't heard him correctly. "You got a lot of nerve coming in here on Saturday morning, talking like you're out in the streets. Some people do work and sleep, you know."

"Hey lady, I'm sorry, okay?"

"You sure are," Miriam said. "Before, I was 'sweet thing,' now I'm 'lady.' You just don't realize how sorry you are."

"What the fuck's that supposed to mean?"

"Don't cuss in my house," Miriam said, knowing they weren't scratching the surface of what truly made them enemies. She turned to walk away before somebody got hurt.

"That's the trouble with you bulldikers, man. You always try—"

"Who're you calling a bulldiker?" Miriam said.

"The pants fit, wear 'em," he said snidely, smiling wickedly.

"Get out of my house," she said, pointing to the door. "Now!"

"Yeah," Tommy said. "No wonder you wouldn't let me touch you. You were too busy trying to fuck my woman. Anybody ever mistake you for a man?"

"No," Miriam said. "Anybody ever mistake *you* for one?"

Tommy looked at Agnes who looked at Miriam.

"You're just mad because Agnes is leaving, that's all; jealous because you love her and she don't want your ass. She told me all about it because she loves me . . ."

Miriam, without considering it, balled her fists and charged him. She pounded him in the face, the neck, the chest, anywhere. He tried holding her arms, blocking her blows. Agnes got involved and the three of them shouted at and cursed one another. Agnes separated them and pushed Miriam back, sat her down, and shoved Tommy into her bedroom and closed the door.

"Miriam Brooks?" Agnes said, panting. "What the hell's wrong with you?"

Miriam didn't answer. Sitting on the sofa panting and wheezing as Agnes's body loomed over her, she wanted to attack her too. Reach down her throat and retrieve her heart which Agnes had chewed up and swallowed whole. Enough was goddamn enough! She wanted her solitude back. Without roommates and their trifling lovers disturbing her once uneventful, but peaceful, existence, she wanted her former life back intact. As Miriam and Agnes listened to each other breathe heavily, not a word cut the thick silence between them. Miriam got up, closed her bathrobe and walked toward her bedroom. Without looking back, she said, "I want you to move." She opened the bedroom door. "As soon as possible."

17

Sitting alone in Smalls Paradise at table number three, Vittorio watched a wavy-haired beauty pass his table; the same table where he had met Luisa. Gulping his fourth drink in half an hour, as the orchestra played, he regarded the beauty studying him from across the room. She blew him a kiss. He winked and raised his drink toward her before emptying it. Then he snapped his fingers and ordered another. He knew she wanted him. Already she had passed his table at least eight times.

A trio of golddiggers approached his table and smiled coquettishly as if they had rehearsed. They giggled incessantly, deliberately leaning forward to reveal cleavage. He raised his glass to them, though his vision was so blurred he could barely make them out. He didn't know what the hell they were saying to him, but he pulled out his pen and gave them what they came for. Clumsily ripping a cocktail napkin into three parts, he scribbled his telephone number, encouraged them to call, and added, "If a woman answers, ask for Vito." He asked them each for a kiss and they obliged him. He knew there were lipstick prints on his face. That was how he wanted it. They promised to call, then lost themselves in the fog of smoke and live music.

He noticed a Negro woman in the distance smiling at him from across the dance floor. To Vittorio, she was easily the most beautiful of all the women there. Gorgeous beyond words, her teeth sparkled when she smiled, and her tits seemed to be jumping out of her tight dress, with an ass that turned the corner a moment after the rest of her had. Flirting back with her, he wondered, sitting at table number three where he had met his wife, if he would ever bed a colored woman. Harlem's nightlife was fraught with breathtaking Negro women who could tempt the most faithful and xenophobic of men. One day, he thought, he'd have to test the waters and discover what savages they were in bed. He'd heard the stories, even at Princeton, and believed them, thinking it not for him. Maybe another time. He didn't see himself rolling in pagan lust with a colored broad. One night, perhaps if he was drunk enough . . .

The wavy-haired beauty passed his table for the ninth time. She stopped, seated herself without invitation and whispered in his ear. He summoned a waiter, paid the bill, then stood to escort the woman through the front door into his parked limousine.

In the backseat, he sat stoically. His head was spinning, his stomach queasy, as she climbed all over him, thrusting her hand down his trousers. He did nothing but hold on to his seat as the limousine jerked and rocked its way to the Plaza. While the woman tried having him in the backseat, Salvatore watched them through the rearview mirror, his face perplexed. That much Vittorio could see, and he ordered the chauffeur to keep his eyes on the road and out of the backseat.

She wouldn't shut up during the ride. Her loquaciousness was getting on his nerves and he toyed with the idea of putting her out at the next corner. Had the limousine not pulled up in front of the Plaza when it did, he might have. Pulling her antsy hands from inside his trousers, he told the woman to behave herself; there'd be plenty of time for that.

As Vittorio and the woman walked through the lobby toward the registration desk to reserve a suite, the clerk hesitated. He knew she wasn't Vittorio's wife. He saw them together every week. Mr. di Bolognese didn't strike him as a philanderer. Vittorio read it in his eyes, paid the bill and quietly said, "What are you looking at? Huh? Don't look at me that way."

In the suite, they undressed, the woman never shutting up for one moment. She tried taking him in her mouth and he pushed her away. He viewed her as a tramp, a vulgar slut who must have done that to every man she was with. He liked oral sex. But there was a time and manner in which to do everything. She tried wiping the lipstick prints from his face, but he stopped her hand.

This just wasn't working out. He was too drunk to keep an erection. Taking his time, he thought of Luisa's nakedness, her supple breasts and thighs, the forest of her sweet smelling pubic hair, and then he began to come alive. The woman tried kissing him and he turned away. She touched his penis and he removed her hand. Mounting her, he despised her for being there with him, knowing he was a married man with family. He hated himself for taking her there and again realized why he'd chosen Luisa.

"I understand," she said, "that the Tea Garden downstairs is a snazzy place to eat. But," she said, transparently, "*I've* never eaten there."

Golddiggers! Goddamn golddiggers, he thought, and rolled over on his back, his erection once again failing him. Just what in God's name am I doing here? he thought. She was a flapper; one of the women who paraded around town with her boots unbuckled, letting her leather flaps fly as she walked. She was beautiful, but she wasn't Luisa. She placed her head on his chest and he winced.

"What the hell's wrong with you?" she asked, fed up with this guy who picked her up and acted as if he'd never been with a woman. Hmmm, she thought, everything she'd heard about the hot-shot dago playboy wasn't true. He kept going soft and wouldn't let her help him out. He never answered her question; just lay there like a beached whale, staring up at the ceiling. She eyed his manhood and thought, What a waste! She couldn't be sure, but it looked as if there were tears in the corners of his eyes. Bending over, she kissed his tears.

"Get out!" he screamed, jumping out of bed, which frightened her so, she thought he was a maniac. "Get out, you fucking tramp!" he yelled again, ashamed for using four-letter words that rarely entered his thoughts.

She nearly tripped over herself getting dressed. He lay down in bed, and she was sure he was weeping now. She thought of asking him to zip her up, but feared he might put a knife in her back. Writing down her telephone number, she put it on the lamp table near the door and whispered, "Call me sometime when you feel *up* to it." She couldn't resist the pun. From the table beside the bed, he grabbed a small vase and threw it at her. "I said, get the fuck out!" The vase sailed across the room, barely missing her, and shattered against the door as she closed it behind her.

Turning over on his stomach, he wept into the pillow.

Downstairs in the lobby, he stumbled past the desk clerk, dug into his wallet and threw him a fifty-dollar bill.

In the limousine, traveling through what seemed a lifetime to get home, he saw his chauffeur watching him again through the rearview mirror.

"I told you before, Salvatore, don't look at me like that," he said weakly. He'd tried to pay Luisa back for what she'd done and couldn't, for the life of him, go through with it.

She cried all the time these days. She woke up crying, went to bed crying, and he didn't know what the hell was wrong with her. Vittorio listened intently to the family obstetrician. It was all new to him, this postnatal depression. He knew nothing about a woman's body beyond the obvious. But he trusted Dr. Santucci, which was why he delegated to him the care of his wife and the delivery of his firstborn. He was *paisano*. What was there not to trust? Watching her take the medication, stringently following doctor's orders, Vittorio monitored Luisa. He pitied her, though he didn't understand this female problem she was having. He wanted his wife back.

Though he said nothing to Luisa yet, he strongly suspected her of infidelity. It was the decade when white women openly explored the legend of Negro men who purportedly satisfied them in a way white men couldn't. Vittorio thought himself extraordinarily endowed—some women couldn't take him—and if Luisa was seeking sex outside the marriage, she must be a nymphomaniac.

She must've been fucking a nigger! he deduced, the thought so provocative, he wanted to put his revolver to her head and that of her secret Harlem lover. Never before had he had the slightest reason to suspect she was unfaithful, but with all the free time she had shopping, lunching and whatever else, he didn't know for sure what she was doing, or with whom she was doing it. Mama's hiring of a private detective inspired him. But he could never go through with it. While he was wheeling and dealing, providing a secure financial net for his family, ensuring their economic stability, she was running around fucking some nigger. He couldn't prove it, but she must have. The night he met her, she was with a colored guy. And that half-colored baby lying in the nursery of his Tudor mansion wasn't his. That much he knew. He couldn't bring himself to say it, to confront her, since it was difficult for him to believe. The words hadn't fully formed in his head, and in accusing her, he had to be unequivocally certain of his allegation. He had to figure out what was going on between them. He waited for her to come to him and confess her sin. Time was passing; she didn't have much left.

There would be no more calla lilies.

She's crying, he figured, because she knew she'd had a colored man and the guilt consumed her. Maybe he was a longtime lover. Maybe he was an afternoon fling. In either case, she got pregnant with somebody else's child and let him believe it was his. She made a fool of him.

When he came home late and drunk, which he'd done every night for a week, she said nothing. That, for him, was proof of her guilt. He was never known to have more than two drinks at any one time, usually table wine. Now, he drank anything, so he wouldn't have to go home sober. Part of him wanted her to say something, so they could get it out in the open and end it. The past week had been the worst of his life.

Pulling into the circular driveway, he dreaded climbing into bed with her and yet, couldn't keep himself apart from her naked satin body sprawled across black silk sheets. In happier days, he couldn't tell which was softer, the sheets or Luisa. Getting out of the limousine, he remembered one last, important thing.

From a backseat compartment, he pulled out a bag containing lipstick and expensive perfume. He took off his shirt, dabbed at his mouth with the lipstick, and planted prints on his collar. Putting the shirt back on, retying his bowtie, he sprayed a cloud of perfume around him while Salvatore watched through the rearview mirror with a disdainful look on his face.

He got out, bade Salvatore a good evening—or good morning, as it were—turned his key in the lock, and sauntered drunkenly upstairs.

Hearing his footsteps on the staircase, Louise feigned sleep, listening to her heart pound in her eardrums. He got undressed without turning on the light. She smelled women and liquor on him. He climbed into bed with his back toward her. She touched him and he moved away.

18

Velma slumped down in the seat of her roadster. She was parked down the street from Miriam's apartment on Eighth Avenue, puffing a cigarette out of boredom. She watched the first cracks of light penetrating the inky, rapidly transforming darkness. Stars disappeared, twinkling their finest, final moment, melting against an emerging blue sky, and the muses of poetry came to mind. She stifled a yawn, wiped a tear squeezing from her eye, and embraced herself, warding off the morning chill. The sun cast its first rays, the tentacles of an immense, golden insect.

She had grown bored with lying in bed, unable to sleep, listening to the same old phonograph record. She tried to concentrate on a good book which did everything but lull her to sleep. So, she got up at thirteen minutes to four and dressed. She climbed into the roadster and drove aimlessly throughout Manhattan, smoking herself ragged.

She drove to the Brooklyn Bridge. She sat on the Manhattan side and marveled at it. She thought about Roebling, the bridge's engineer who died before it was completed, and how he could transform his genius into form and function *and* art in a single stroke. Could her literature benefit mankind as this bridge did? Were readers really listening to what she had to say? Did they listen to anybody ever? If so, why were she and Rudy arrested for sunbathing? Why did Louise have to pass for white? Why did Miriam want to move to Liberia?

She heard their felicitous voices. Scott's. Rudy's. Hers. Remembering that once upon a good time, she was tempted to cross the bridge and stand at the center where they enjoyed their midnight picnic back in '25. Life then was marvelous, full of wonderful surprises, gaiety, carefree laughter. She wanted to travel back in time, start over, do things differently. Four years ago, Mother was alive and Louise was somewhere they could find her. It was a time when Scott couldn't keep his hands off her and he carried the key which opened the golden doors to all Manhattan's riches and twentieth-century luminaries. Folks don't realize how good they have it, she thought, until they have it no more.

She thought of Scott's novels. They'd gotten better over time. The stereotypical women that haunted the first book became more whole in the fourth novel. She couldn't help but think that his four-year affair with her had something to do with it. Now she understood why *Prodigal*, his first novel, had made such a splash. Beyond Toomer's *Cane*, Scott had been critically hailed because his story was one, she felt certain, that a white American readership had never before heard. She herself hadn't read such a poignantly moving and diverse piece authored by a Negro.

It was the first time she'd read a story about an upper-middle-class Negro child coming of age at the turn of the century. He had studied French with a tutor, and classical piano with a European virtuoso and he was victimized by a tyrannical father who practiced law. After graduating from Harvard, the protagonist sailed for Paris where he became a novelist contrary to his father's wish that he follow his own footsteps. Rather than spend a summer, as he'd promised his parents, the fledgling writer remained in Paris for years. He sold his first book, then returned to the States—Harlem.

Such a "unique" vision must have knocked the critics on their pompous asses. A Negro alienated by his own people, history and culture stunned their sensibilities. They lapped it up. It wasn't unusual to Velma for a Negro family to be professional, upper-middle class, and well-traveled, but to literary critics it was. She understood all the critical noise they created over it. Hoping her second novel, about to go to press, made half the impact of Scott's, she worried about the publishing industry's dismal forecast.

The gossip raced through the literary community like wildfire and the proof lay in the editors' slush piles and rejection letters. As quickly as the New Negro vanguard had burst to life, so it was choking to a quicker death. Lots of writers were feeling the crunch. Scott's publisher stood uncommitted on his latest effort. Rudy couldn't find a publisher at all for his third. And her publisher made no commitments beyond this second book. Agents were no longer seeking new Negro clients with the back-stabbing competitiveness as they once had. White readers were yawning, patting their mouths in sheer boredom, as they searched for fresher voices. Whatever they sought, Negroes no longer had it. Not anymore. Not for now. The choir was being silenced, voice by voice.

She thought again of walking the bridge, just to recapture that magical night. Instead, she got back in the roadster and drove by Scott's by way of Edgecombe Avenue's "Sugar Hill" overlooking Harlem from a rocky cliff. She wanted to knock on his door. Recalling the night Scott stopped by her flat after midnight, she felt she owed him one. She still loved him and cursed herself for singlehandedly fouling up an almost marriage. She feared she'd never, ever find someone like him again—one of the century's brightest, most brilliant minds.

Opening the door to get out, she heard a door close down the street, followed by footsteps. She saw Rudy walking down Scott's steps. He paused on the sidewalk, looked both ways, and started home, she guessed. She slumped down in the seat and asked herself whether or not she should call him and offer a lift. Rudy would suspect her of spying. The suspicion would be there, expressed or not, and she couldn't blame him.

After he disappeared around the corner, she turned on the ignition and glanced up at Scott's window, watching the light go out. She pulled off and headed for West 141st Street which she drove up and down several times, then decided she'd go to Miriam's. Only Miriam's company could calm her, as she thought of Scott, Rudy, and Louise. Where was Louise? Miriam couldn't know anything more than she, but she still needed to be with family. It had been too long.

Parked in front of Miriam's apartment, she watched an iceman emerge from his truck. She opened the door, crushed the cigarette beneath her heel and walked slowly up the staircase, the wind flapping the edges of her coat. She pushed the oval-shaped, beveled glass covered with the translucent white café curtains, and was startled by a dog's barking. She knocked on the door. A woman, whom Velma obviously had disturbed from a sound sleep, cracked the door, her mouth stretched in a yawn. She rubbed her eyes, squinted repeatedly, and scratched her backside. "Can I help you?"

"I'm looking for Miriam."

"You know what time of morning it is?"

"Yes, I'm sorry."

"It's all right. I had to get up anyway." She opened the door and let her in.

"You must be Agnes," Velma said, extending her hand. "I'm Velma, Miriam's sister."

"Oh yes," Agnes said, yawning again. "I've heard a lot about you. Aren't you the famous writer?"

"Well, I don't know about famous—"

"Girl, don't be modest. It's nice to see a colored girl doing something like that."

Agnes led Velma into the parlor and asked her to make herself comfortable. She knocked on Miriam's bedroom door, entered, then came back out. "I told her you're here," Agnes said. "She'll be right out."

Newspapers and magazines like *The New Masses* were scattered across the table. Large brown suitcases were situated in the middle of the floor. Dust particles, caught in the beams of morning sunlight, rolled across the hardwood floors like miniature bundles of tumbleweed. Velma wondered to whom the suitcases belonged, and where they were going.

"Velma! Velma, is that you?" Miriam poked her sleepy head through the door.

"Miriam!" Velma stood, her face breaking into a smile.

   Miriam rushed to her and threw her arms around Velma, squeezing her tightly. Rocking back and forth in their embrace, Miriam
wiped tears of happiness from the corners of her half-closed eyes.
Miriam pushed away, holding her at arm's length. "You looking
good, girl!"

   "I look like shit. I didn't get a moment's sleep last night." Velma
touched Miriam's face, brushing her fingers across her gaunt
cheekbones. "You've lost weight."

   "That ain't all I lost. Make yourself comfortable while I splash
some water on my face and make us some coffee."

   "I'm glad I came."

   "You should be," Miriam said, tying her bathrobe. "We ain't seen
each other in months."

   "I hope you don't mind. I drove around and around—"

   "You're driving?"

   "Yeah, I drove around half the night and parked across the street
but waited until daylight."

   "I'm so glad to see you," Miriam said, clearing the table of papers.

   "Excuse me," Agnes said, reappearing from the bathroom.
"Miriam, could I speak to you for a moment?"

   "Yeah," Miriam said, scratching her wild-looking hair, clutching
the lapels of her bathrobe. "Velma, this here's Agnes—"

   "Yes, we've met," Velma said, smiling.

   Miriam followed Agnes into the bedroom and shut the door.
Velma turned and looked out the windows into the street. Whispering floated from behind the closed door, filling the morning
quiet. Though she couldn't make out the words, a static tension
seemed to ignite the air, and she wondered how Miriam was getting
along with her roommate. The door opened and Miriam reemerged,
her lips pursed.

   "Going somewhere?" Velma indicated the luggage with a nod of
her head.

   "No, not me." Miriam busied herself with the coffee and Velma
followed her into the kitchen. "So, tell me, how you been? You
kinda famous now. I read your book and I swear, I'm so proud of
you."

   "Thanks."

   "How do you like your coffee? Cream and—"

   "Black for now."

   "Black it is." Miriam carried two steaming cups into the parlor.
Velma followed, her arms folded. Miriam sat one cup down and,

with a sweep of the arm, cleared the coffee table of papers. She neatly stacked a pile of leaflets and shoved them to the side. Velma studied her. Something was wrong.

"You happy, Miriam?" Velma asked, sipping her coffee, studying her sister.

"About as happy as I'm ever going to be, I guess." She sipped her coffee, scolding herself for sipping too soon. She blew the surface, holding the cup with both hands. "How's that man of yours? What's his name? He ask you to marry him yet?"

"Scott. No, he didn't . . . well, in a way, I guess he did." There were several holes in the story Velma had to fill in for her. Now wasn't the time.

"And?"

"No, we're not getting married."

"Oh, I'm sorry. That's too bad."

"I asked *him*, actually."

"Did you? You know what they say; it's not a lady's place to—"

"Who the hell ever said I was a lady."

"Not me, ma'am, that's for sure." Miriam laughed.

"Miriam," Velma began, placing the cup on the table, folding her hands. "Recently, I had this nightmare about—"

"Louise."

"How'd you know?"

"She's been on my mind a lot too. You worried about her?"

"Worried isn't the right—"

"I know what you mean, girl. I think about her all the time. Where she is, if she's all right—" Miriam cut herself short with a quick sip of coffee as Agnes reentered the room fully clothed.

"I'm leaving for a couple of hours," Agnes said. "But I'll be back for the rest of my things."

"You need some help?" Miriam volunteered.

"Thanks, but no. I think I got it under control."

"How are you going to carry all—"

"Don't worry; I called a taxi. See you later." She picked up one suitcase and carried it to the door. "Nice meeting you, Velma."

"Nice meeting you too," Velma said, her eyes darting from Agnes to Miriam. Agnes picked up the luggage and left. Velma waited a sufficient time, then asked. "Everything okay?"

"Yeah," Miriam replied, distantly. "Why?" She stared at the door Agnes just closed, trying not to think about it but rather enjoy the good tidings her sister brought.

"I don't know," Velma said. "It just seemed a little tense in here."

"Everything's fine and dandy. You're here, aren't you?"

"Somebody told me they saw Louise," Velma said, "or rather, a woman who looked like me and answered to my name. This person said she was driving a Rolls-Royce and—"

"What? Then you know something?"

"I'm not sure. I mean, I don't know if I could trust the source."

"Is the person close to you?"

"You could say that. But this person's integrity is sometimes questionable. First I believed it, then I had reason not to. I just don't know."

Miriam paused with the question she was about to ask. She didn't want her sister to get the wrong idea. She was just curious. "Velma?"

"Hmm hmm?"

"Did you write your book about . . . well . . . you know . . . Louise?"

"No. I didn't. And you can imagine the irony I felt once she disappeared. Actually, I began that story while she was working at the Cotton Club. I'm not the only colored woman writer who wrote about passing. Larsen and Fauset did too."

"I was just wondering." Miriam sipped her coffee. "What're we going to do?"

"Anybody's guess. Hurry up and wait. I mean this person might've really seen Louise, but I've caught this person in lies before. You know how it is when you want to believe something but can't." She looked to Miriam who stared at the door and knew too painfully what Velma meant. She caught Miriam staring fixedly at the door. "Miriam!"

"I'm sorry; what'd you say?"

Velma hesitated. Miriam was acting weird. "Where's your mind this morning?"

"Oh, I'm listening. I'm just . . . well, nothing. Go on, what were you saying?"

"Well . . ." Velma said, glancing at the door to see what Miriam was looking at, "I got this so-called story about Louise driving a Rolls-Royce, and if I hadn't told my friend Rudy—you remember Rudy—"

"I love that woman. . . ." Miriam wept. She couldn't help it. This was one hell of a way to tell her sister something like this, but nothing mattered anymore.

"I'm sure you do," Velma said, perplexed. "You were roommates now for—what was it?—almost two years—"

"I'm *in* love with her."

"What?"

"She broke my heart," Miriam wept.

"You've loved her all this time?"

Miriam nodded her head, burying her wet eyes behind her hands.

Velma was shocked, a trifle repulsed. She struggled against being judgmental. She wondered how long Miriam had been this way, and suddenly understood why she had never dated men after George. She'd gotten used to homosexuals, but she never thought for a moment that one could be blood-related. After Rudy, and catching him and Scott together in a compromising position, nobody's sexuality surprised her anymore. Damn near everybody was suspect. Miriam's sudden confession also explained the packed luggage, the tension in the room so thick she could lick it. She had a barrage of questions and didn't know where to begin. It didn't matter now. Her sister needed her, and this was no time to ask the who, what, when, where, why and how. She hadn't seen Miriam cry that hard when Mother passed. Some sister she was, Velma thought about herself. She couldn't see that she had a sister who loved women, and another who would one day disappear and pass for white. Her nose was so deep in her work and what Scott and Rudy were doing, she never had a clue.

"I wanted to tell you," Miriam said. "So many times. I just didn't know how to tell you what I didn't know . . . myself really. You shocked?"

"No, yes, I don't know, I mean, hell yes, I'm shocked."

"That's why I never told you."

"Oh, Miriam, I'm sorry. I just—"

"That's why there was never a 'mystery' beau as you used to put it."

Velma put the pieces together. Any fool could.

"She left you, didn't she?"

"You saw it yourself."

"You must be terribly hurt, Miriam. I'm glad I'm here."

"It's really something, you know, Velma," she said, sniffling. "I'm hurt because," her voice cracked, trailed a bit, and a lump enlarged in her throat, "she left me for another man. Not just any man. Some no-'count bum who doesn't treat her half as good as I did." Tears rolled down her face. Her chest heaved and her shoulders vibrated. "He beats her, takes her money, disrespects her, and she runs to him. Leaves me here flat with nothing. And she started this whole thing between us. Now what I got?"

For years, she couldn't tell Velma that she didn't like men; not that she liked women. She loved Agnes but wasn't sure if her passion extended beyond her. Velma always read her like the books her nose was forever buried inside, and Miriam felt certain Velma knew before this telling, but had been allowing Miriam to admit it of her own volition. Right now, with everything colliding inside her, she didn't care what Velma thought, or if she blamed her for loving another woman. Velma had Scott because she needed to be loved. Hell, she had Rudy too. Big sister was no different.

"You always have me . . . and you have your medical and organizational work." Velma didn't think that helped much. She didn't know what else to say.

Miriam tried to laugh, the whining sound still in her voice. "The UNIA?" she said, shaking her head, tears splashing on the floor. "I had such hopes, such steadfast beliefs and"—she sniffled, wiping her nose with her palm—"it's all over but the shouting. I'm sure you heard all about it."

"Garvey's exile?"

"And the whole damn organization fell apart at the seams, though we tried holding on. It's really something how folks'll cut each other's throats for a little bit of power and rank. Everybody wants to be the chief, but nobody wants to be Indians . . . nobody, except me," she said, trying to laugh.

"But I can see you're still politically active," Velma said, wrapping her arms around Miriam to comfort her.

"It ain't quite the same. I'm checking out the Communists to see what they have to offer colored people. I just can't help myself. It's in my blood, just like writing's in yours."

They started laughing, about what they didn't know. Much of it emanated from nervousness and anxiety. Miriam wiped her eyes and dabbed at her runny nose. "Oh, Velma, I've missed you so much. I'm so glad you're here." She hugged her sister.

Velma held her tightly, wiping her sister's tears. "Me too."

"What're we going to do?"

"We won't be out of touch with each other for too long anymore. We've said it before, but this time, I mean it. That's for certain—"

"I mean Louise. What can we do about her?"

"I don't know, Miriam. I just don't know. But we'll think of something."

Velma looked at the chair; the chair where Louise sat last time she saw her. She choked up, but wouldn't allow herself a good cry. She'd done enough crying in the last several weeks. She didn't have a tear left. She watched and listened to her sister grieve over a broken heart and could understand; man or woman, black or white, love was love, and a broken heart a broken heart. She wondered how she could grow up with a woman, close in age, side by side, share everything with her from tooth powder to stockings to underwear to secrets, sleep in the same room, know her naked body as she knew her own, and yet not *really* know a goddamn thing about her at all.

19

Nodding at the kitchen table while Sara cleaned around her, Louise became alert, as Vittorio finally came downstairs. Nearly eleven-thirty; he was going to work later every morning. Pressing the cup of cold coffee to her mouth to conceal trembling lips, she watched him enter the kitchen, his face unshaven, eyes bloodshot. He looked at her, about to bid her good morning, then looked past her to Sara.

"Good morning," he said in a monotone, grabbing a glass of orange juice.

"Good morning," Louise said, wanting to humble herself. She wanted her husband back.

"Good mornin', Mr. B," Sara said, watching Mr. B painstakingly avoid his wife, as Mrs. B twitched in her chair to be acknowledged by him.

Vittorio pressed his hands against his head. "Sara, I'm terribly hung over," he said. "What you got for this?"

Prepared as always, Sara reached into her apron pocket and handed him two aspirins. She cracked two eggs into a glass, added Tabasco sauce, a dash of pepper, shook it, and handed it to him. He looked skeptically at the glass, sniffed it, and shivered.

"You wanna feel betta, doncha?" Sara said. He nodded. "Well then?"

He turned the glass to his lips, swallowed the concoction in one gulp, exhaled, grimaced, fanned his mouth, then belched without excusing himself. Putting on his coat, he asked Sara to inform Salvatore that he was about ready. Picking up the *Wall Street Journal* from the table, he turned to leave.

Louise's heart sank. It was the seventh or eighth morning straight that he left without the usual good-byes, smiles, and kisses. Watching him move away from her, she had to say something.

"Vito?" she said weakly, her voice cracking.

"Yes?" he asked, and stopped, without turning to face her.

She didn't know what to say.

"Is Angelo Vittorio awake?"

"Don't call him Vittorio."

"Is . . . Angelo awake?"

"I saw the nurse changing him when I got up."

Please turn around and look at me, she thought, please. He turned the knob and stepped over the threshold.

"Vito!"

"What?"

"Today Angelo's four months old. I was thinking of having a party for him tonight. . . . Will you be home early?"

"Yes, I'll be here," he said, closing the door.

"Vito—" He was gone.

She wearily climbed the stairs, entered the nursery, Angelo kicking and gurgling as she came in. Cradling him against her breast, she rocked him, laid him down beside her on the nurse's bed, and struggled to keep from crying.

She had fallen asleep in the nursery and jumped upon hearing the front door slam. She knew it was Vittorio, who had left barely a couple of hours ago. She could tell he was sober by the sound of his footsteps on the stairs. She smoothed out her hair, rubbed sleep from her eyes and picked up the baby, waking him from a sound sleep. The footsteps neared the master bedroom, stopped, turned and headed for the nursery. Her heart pounded wildly.

The door creaked open and he stepped inside. He said nothing. Just crossed the room and stared out the window. Angelo gurgled and tangled his hands in his mother's hair, saliva bubbles popping in his mouth. The quiet tension was too much to bear. She was about to say something, anything, when Vittorio spoke first.

"Luisa, I need to speak with you in the bedroom."

"Sure," she said calmly, her heart bursting through her flesh. "Let me tuck Angelo in first."

"Hurry up!" he shouted, then stormed out of the room and slammed the door.

Louise's hands shook; the baby kept slipping from her grip. Her breathing increased rapidly. She sat on the bed to catch her breath before facing her husband, wiping perspiration from her forehead, the October breeze blowing in the room. Angelo lay in the crib, playing with the rattle Daddy had bought him, gurgling and making smacking noises. Louise took a deep breath before standing up on legs that could barely support her.

She walked slowly down the spacious foyer, into the bedroom where she slept with her husband, their former love nest. From the nursery to the master bedroom—it would be the longest walk of her life.

She found an impatient, pacing Vito rubbing his hands together, mumbling under his breath in Italian. He's probably cursing and swearing, she thought, entering quietly. She knew that mumbling. His accent always thickened when he was angry.

"Sit down," he said. "I want to ask you something. And tell me the truth. Don't lie to me!" he threatened, maintaining a cool exterior, a visible explosion glowing in his eyes.

"First of all," he began, "I want you to know I wouldn't ask you this if I wasn't almost certain that I'm right. We've been married, what is it, almost two years now? and I've never, not once, Luisa, even slightly suspected you of being unfaithful to me. You hear me?" he screamed, halting in his tracks.

"Y-y-yes!" she stuttered in a whisper.

"Then, look at me when I talk to you!" He continued pacing, his hands behind his back. "I've never entertained the slightest idea that you could be taking a lover. Haven't I given you everything? Diamonds, furs, a comfortable home with servants? Haven't I made you happy? Are you tired of me? Tell me, Luisa, I need to know. You tired of me? You want somebody else?"

"Vito, there's no one else. I swear to you."

"You tell me," he continued, "that Angelo in there is yours. Well, if he's yours, then who's his father? That's a half-colored baby, can't you see that? You have a colored lover somewhere?"

"Of course I don't have a lover," she pleaded. "You know I love you. I do, more than anything. Angelo's yours. Please don't say he isn't."

He looked at her as if awaiting further explanation. The one she'd given apparently wasn't sufficient.

"You're upset," she said. "You're under lots of pressure lately with your stocks fluctuating. It's making you nervous and you haven't been yourself lately."

The look on his face said that her attempt fell short. Very short. He'd already decided what he would or wouldn't believe.

"Tonight, I'm sleeping alone in a guest room," he said. "Tell me the truth about your lover . . . that nigger! What's his name? Where does he live?"

She said nothing, but sat, tight-lipped and idiotic. God! he thought, she couldn't even reveal his name or whereabouts, and her loyalties to him—whoever the nigger was—far surpassed her loyalties to her own husband. Considering the travesty of their nuptials, the irrevocability of a blessed Catholic union, he wouldn't allow himself to think of divorce. She'd committed the utmost sin; his calla lily turned adulteress. She had fallen from grace.

"You do realize," he said, containing the rage within him, the impulse to slam her against the wall, "that you've sinned. For this, you'll burn in hell!" He turned to leave before his urges got the best of him. He nearly ran down the stairs, and slammed the front door behind him.

That evening, while Sara busied herself with Angelo's party preparations, Louise was upstairs putting on Vito's favorite dress, and spraying herself with his favorite perfume. Recalling their confrontation earlier that afternoon when he called her an adulteress made her cringe. Before the mirror, she rehearsed telling him the truth, checking mannered expressions with each uttered syllable, knowing she couldn't bring herself to do it. Watching her own reflection wasn't convincing, and she wondered how the hell she was going to persuade him.

The telephone rang, and she rushed down the hall to answer it, praying it was him.

"Don't worry, Sara!" she yelled downstairs. "I got it!" She picked up the receiver, panting. "Hello?"

"Hello."

"May I help you?"

"I'm looking for Vito."

"He's not here right now. Can I take a message—"

Click!

Outraged, she hung up the telephone. It was the sixth night in a row that women had called the house, asking for her husband. She knew they weren't calling about business, and was tired of girlish giggling on the other end. Unable to stand any more, she had to tell him the explosive truth.

By seven-thirty, she was sitting downstairs at the kitchen table with Sara and Angelo. Everything was ready—everything except Vittorio who should have been home two hours ago. Baby-blue crepe paper decorated the room. Sara had baked a lovely birthday cake and stuck four blue candles within the frosted words: Happy Birthday, Baby Angelo.

The grandfather clock in the adjoining library ticked and struck eight chimes. There were no sounds, save the ticking and Angelo amusing himself, squirming restlessly in Louise's arms, as she and Sara exchanged vexed glances, and listened to each other breathe. They all wore party hats, and there remained one for which there was no head to strap it around. Louise stared at the empty chair and knew that tonight, there'd be no surprise toys or clever gadgets for Angelo. Jerkily, her eyes bounced from the empty seat to Sara to the extra piece of birthday cake to the birthday hat to the decorations to Angelo. She wanted to smash the grandfather clock and stop the ticking.

"Maybe Mr. B forget," Sara said, and the break in the silence made Louise jump. Sara touched her to steady her. "Sometime he git so busy, he plum forget," Sara said, knowing he hadn't forgotten, but trying to ease the tension in the room and put madam at ease. Mrs. B was in trouble, deep trouble, way in over her head, she knew. Sara felt virtually as nervous as Mrs. B did. Loving and caring for her employers, distantly involved in the ups and downs of their marriage, she hoped for the best, but expected the worst. Overhearing their argument earlier that afternoon when Mr. B accused his wife of sleeping around, she listened to Mr. B say *nigger* for the first time ever that she could remember. She realized that he had it all wrong. Just like white folks, she thought, grabbing for the head when all they got is the ass! There were so many things she wanted to say to madam, but knew would be out of place. And even if she did, then what? Sara couldn't protect her from the cement block about to fall and crush her. The house was too quiet, unnervingly so, and Sara wished that the house staff hadn't yet gone home. Sitting at the table with madam and Angelo as a family member rather than as domestic help, she wanted to talk, laugh, and possibly disperse the gray clouds suspended over her employer's head. Except madam didn't say much, mostly bit her lip, glancing at the clock every two minutes, and giving one-word answers. Sara wished that Angelo could talk beyond his gurgling, so she could release the tension mounting inside her. She didn't want to be there when Mr. B got home. No siree, ma'am! It hurt her to watch or listen to them quarrel. This was the part Sara despised most about her job. She was hired to cook, clean and supervise, but inevitably she got caught up in people's private lives which she then carried home like the free food Mr. B gave away.

"Let me take him for a while, ma'am," she said to madam, who was not staring into space. Angelo, sensing his mother's tension, began to get cranky and started to cry. Louise gladly handed her the child, loving Sara for being there.

Louise had always known this whole thing could backfire, but she had never expected Vito to accuse her of adultery. That was far worse than living a lie. Once she told him of her double life, which she obviously had to do, maybe he'd understand. She had no way to gauge his reaction, but what was there to lose that she hadn't already lost?

She hated this race thing—*and* the God who created it. She'd shown God and Vito what a dedicated, loyal, loving wife and mother she could be. Didn't she get merit points for that? Paying her dues, living the curse of a colored woman who looked white, couldn't. God give her a break? Why, despite all His majestic wisdom, mercy and kindness, was He so grossly insensitive to her plight? Hadn't she had her share of tribulation? What did she ever do to warrant His wrath?

It was her punishment, her just due. She knew and accepted it as such. God was paying her back. Looking like a white woman. Secretly living as one. Yes, God was playing a nasty trick on her.

20

. . . But you can't fool God!

As Louise sat in her hot bath, her eyes closed, struggling to relax, the words shot back to her from her past. She'd forgotten Mother's words, spoken nearly twenty years before, until now. She thought of Mother dying while she, ignorant of the fact, gallivanted about Manhattan, shopping at Bonwit Teller and Lord & Taylor, lunching at the Plaza Tea Garden. It made her want to submerge her head in the tub of water and end it all.

Oh my God! she thought, bolting upright in the tub, the mint-scented water swishing and heaving until it overflowed onto the floor. She recalled the medium's foretelling that she'd someday meet a wealthy man, fall in love, and marry. *But there be problems!* She could still see the wrinkled woman's toothless dark gums, her face merging with the darkness. She'd invited Louise back for a second reading, but Louise had thought her fatuous and stupid. Now, she thought herself stupid for not taking heed.

Later, stretched across the black silk sheets on her bed, she wished she had a friend. Isolating herself in this corner of the city, avoiding new friendships, wearing veils, and glancing over her shoulder had caused her to lose touch with the outside. Beyond Vito, she didn't have a friend in the world. If only there was someone she could call, a shoulder to cry upon, a listening ear to bend, a warm body to embrace.

Glancing at the clock which read 2:47, she sighed at the cold, empty spot beside her. She couldn't blame him; he'd done nothing wrong. Thinking of Angelo, she got out of bed and went to his nursery. The child slept, his tiny chest rising and falling, his mouth and eyes flinching, his fists balled tautly. How lucky infants are, she thought. He was oblivious to all that was plaguing their home. The house could have collapsed and Angelo wouldn't have known. She envied him, her child, this bundle that had pushed his way out of her. Remembering Dr. Santucci whispering to his assistant about the prospect of losing her to save the baby, she realized she had almost lost her life to give Angelo his. And, in some way, she wished she had. Even though the baby's arrival was, in retrospect, a burning match tossed upon her house of straw, now that he was here, she wouldn't have it any other way. She promised herself to prepare him for and teach him the wicked racial ways of the world, and not skirt the issue as Mother had done with her. God bless her, though, Louise thought. But she had learned from Mother's mistakes and planned not to make them with Angelo.

She heard Vito struggling with his key in the lock, and she ran, quietly as possible, down the foyer into her bedroom. She pulled off her bathrobe, nearly ripping it in her haste, kicked off her slippers and climbed into bed. Pulling the sheets and blanket up to her neck, she rolled over, and turned out the light. She closed her eyes and attempted to breathe normally, when he kicked open the bedroom door. She could smell the liquor and the perfume, and pitied what he was putting himself through.

"You awake?"

She pretended to be asleep, then changed her mind.

"Yes."

"Good. We need to talk."

He switched on the light, covered his eyes from the brightness, and sat on the edge of the bed.

"I've come to a decision. I think you should hear it."

"I'm listening." She raised herself up and stared sympathetically. His hair was uncombed, and her heart stood still, examining blatant lipstick prints from his forehead to his stomach. It just wasn't like him.

"What's done is done; there's nothing we can do about that now," he said. "I'm Catholic, so my hands are very much tied, you see. I don't know what else to do."

He raised both hands, brought them down, and slapped his thighs. "I can't divorce you. That would be against the Church. I would be excommunicated. I can't leave you. I have a son in there who isn't even mine, yet I feel I should take care of him. I don't know why, I just do. It's not his fault. He's only a baby. But I've decided that we'll no longer sleep together. You can have this bedroom if you want. I don't. Too many memories. Too many reminders," he said, waving his hand across his face as if swatting at a mosquito. "Everything will be the same as always," he said, belching, rising up from the bed. "Everything except you and I. You live your life. I'll live mine. Good night!"

"Wait, Vito, please," she pleaded, getting out of bed. "I have something to tell you."

"So, *now* you're ready to confess. It takes all this to make you—"

"It's not what you think." She swallowed deeply before continuing. "Vito, I love you very much," she said, tears streaming down her face. "I've always loved you. I've never been with anybody else. Only you. I was a virgin when I met you and I've never had anyone else. You must believe that . . . Oh, Vito, this is so difficult for me, please don't look at me like that, please. I know you thought what you did because of the baby, but he's ours, Vito. He is! He's yours and mine. Please don't deny that. And—"

"Spare me the tears and get to the point!"

"I'm not . . . really . . . Italian. I'm—"

"What did you say? You're not what?"

"No, Vito, I'm not." Her voice trembled and spittle crawled down her chin.

"Then what the hell are you?"

"There were so many times I wanted to tell you, but I just couldn't. I didn't want to lose you. I couldn't. I gave up everything for you, Vito, *everything!* My family, my friends, my work, everything! I knew that if I told you that day at Giuseppe's you wouldn't—"

"What are you?" His eyes widened with a glare that pierced her. Suddenly, he seemed sober. "Even better, *who* are you?"

"My real name is Louise. Not Luisa, not Anna Luisa. I—"

"What the hell are you?" He stood, backing away from her.

"Vito—"

"What are you? That's all I want to know!"

"Colored . . ."

"What?" He wasn't certain he'd heard her correctly.

"Yes."

"What did you just say?"

"I'm colored!" she screamed, covering her ears.

"Oh, God . . . oh no . . . you're lying . . . you can't be—"

"Vito, I am." She nodded, waiting for him to take it all in, to sort through the incoherence of what she'd said and make order of it. She imagined how confusing it all must be for him. "So you see, things can be the way they were. Now you understand that I wasn't unfaithful to you. Look at me, Vito, I'm no different. I'm the same person as before. You never would've known if I hadn't told you." She walked toward him, needing to be embraced, to hear him forgive her. "Vito, please hold me. Please—"

He pushed her away with such force she landed on the floor.

"You mean to tell me you're a nigger?" His tone was low and ominous. "Oh my God, is that what you're saying? My child is a half-breed? Oh my God! God, please help me!"

He yanked a table lamp, pulling the plug from the socket, and smashed it against the wall. Tables, chairs, the jewelry box, bottles of perfume—anything he could get his hands on—sailed across the room. The crashing, the breaking, the shattering of glass woke Angelo. She wanted to run and comfort him but she was frozen, terrified of what Vittorio might do next, afraid he might take the revolver from the drawer. The bedroom was a shambles. She observed him from the floor where he had thrown her; he seemed all-powerful.

"No wonder Mama didn't like you!" he shouted, ripping up the bed sheets and smashing mirrors. "She saw right through you, didn't she? No wonder she hired that private detective. And, you know what? I told Mama I never wanted to speak to her again. I said I never wanted to even see her unless she apologized! It's all your fault!" He stormed from the bedroom. She jumped up from the floor and followed him, pleading. He turned quickly and ripped the satin nightgown with a jerk, then slapped her across the face with the back of his hand.

"Don't you touch me! I don't even know you!" he warned, moving away from her.

He stopped, turned, walked toward her, his fists clenched, his face twisted with rage, then changed his mind. Turning around, he stumbled away. He dropped to his knees in the foyer, curled his body into a fetal position and sobbed violently, his shoulders shaking. Breathless, he uttered hoarsely, his face to the floor, "Call a taxi. Get your things and get out of my house. Don't take anything you didn't come here with," he demanded wearily.

"Where will I go? I have nowhere to go! What about Angelo—"

"You hear me! I said get out before I kill you!"

21

On the rooftop overlooking the ledge, Velma smoked a cigarette, resting her elbows upon the fire escape ladder. Pigeons cooed, flapping their wings on the ledge below. Arms folded, she strolled to each side of the roof, her feet sticking to the tar with each step. To the west, a half-moon reflected on the peaceful waters of the Hudson. Late October winds blew and she heard the trees rustling, as her eyes followed the river's southward course.

The skyline was silhouetted and twinkling with lights. In amazement, she pondered the rapid births of skyscrapers bridging the steel landscape of this thriving metropolis. People the world over flock to view this skyline, and I have the entire panoramic view free of charge from a Harlem rooftop.

The sudden shattering of glass broke her thoughts. Startled

pigeons took flight, their wings flapping in frenzy. She ran to the other side of the roof.

An automobile, its wheels screeching from around the corner, stopped in front of one of the neighborhood speakeasies. Three men emerged, slammed the doors, and ran toward a basement door. They forced their way inside, and in seconds, women and men fled into the streets, scattering in all directions. Shouting, muffled voices rang into the still of the night. Velma watched and tried to listen. The three men began rolling kegs out onto the sidewalk. They struck the kegs with clubs and alcohol spurted like geysers, flowing into the gutter. Countless kegs were rolled out. A man, his hands raised above his head, was escorted out by one of the arresting officers. Preoccupied with the smashing of kegs and bottles, the others failed to see the speakeasy owner lower one of his hands. Reaching inside his vest with a slow, unobtrusive movement, he produced a revolver and shot the arresting officer. He shot another. Then he fled down the street in the shadows while the policeman fired shots into the dark.

Velma ran downstairs to her apartment. She closed the door and sat in the darkness, panting. The neon sign across the street buzzed, flashed, and lit her face with its green and red hues, as she fumbled for a cigarette. The clock read a quarter past four.

She had had a sleepless night. She ran herself a bath, made a cup of tea. Even Bessie Smith seemed to lack the cradle magic to lull her to sleep. Scott was on her mind.

She pulled her rickety typewriter with the sticking keys to the center of the floor, and tried to rework scenes in the play she and Rudy had written. That didn't work. She pulled out a short story she'd begun some days ago, but ended up staring blankly at the empty page in the typewriter. She decided to read.

Someone banged at the door. A persistent, heavy-handed knock which caused her to jump. Who the hell was that? Could it be Scott calling for a dose of wanton sex? She hoped not; hardly in the mood. Could it be Rudy at four-thirty in the morning? It wasn't like Rudy.

Worse, maybe it was that man, the speakeasy owner who shot two plainclothes policemen in cold blood and fled for his life down the street? Was he seeking refuge in a random apartment? Would he force a gun in her face as she trustingly opened the door? The banging sounded again. A woman's voice softly called her name. She ran to the door. As she opened it, shock and disbelief gripped her. She gasped and covered her mouth with both hands.

Louise stood in the vestibule, leaning one hand against the door frame. Her face bore a purple bruise. Her hair was short, tangled, disarrayed. In bedroom slippers and a torn nightgown inside a mink coat, she trembled, her swollen lip quivering as she spoke.

"Can I come in?"

Velma pulled her close, and squeezed her tightly, tears running down her cheeks. "Oh my God! Baby, what happened to you? Where have you been? You all right?" She closed the door, led her sister by the waist, and sat her down on the sofa. She reached for the lamp. Louise held her arm back.

"Louise . . ." Velma said again, rubbing her sister's hand.

Louise sat speechless, staring straight ahead. Velma didn't know what to do, what to say. A thousand questions raced through her mind. She didn't know where to begin. She just wanted to comfort her.

"How'd you get here?" Velma asked.

"Taxi," Louise replied, hesitated, swallowed, then continued. "I know," she said sobbing, "that you're surprised to see me." She could barely speak. "And, I wouldn't blame you if you didn't let me stay—"

"Oh no, baby," Velma said. She could feel her pain and it hurt to look into her eyes. Velma held her again.

"Velma," Louise said, "everything went wrong. Everything! He accused me of cheating on him. I've never seen him like that before. H-h-h-he t-t-told me to—"

"Baby, take your time, just take your time. You're all upset now. Take a deep breath and tell me what happened. Who's 'he'?"

Louise paused, staring blankly out the window. The neon lit her face while she fumbled with her hands. "I have a baby, Velma."

"A baby?"

"He told me I couldn't take my baby. What am I going to do? I have to get my son back. Oh God, please help me, please!" She wept, folding herself into her lap. Velma rushed to the bathroom, grabbed a handful of tissues and handed them to her. She sat again and pulled Louise toward her, resting her disheveled head on her chest, and rocked her like an infant. She examined the torn pink satin nightgown, silk bathrobe, satin slippers, mink coat, and thought about the Rolls-Royce Scott had said he saw her driving. She was grateful to have her back alive and safe, and thanked God for another one of His miracles.

"You have any liquor here?" Louise asked.

"No, baby, I don't keep liquor—"

"Got a cigarette?" Louise sniffled.

"Yes," Velma said, wondering when her baby sister started smoking.

The cigarette vibrated in Louise's lips. She lit it with unsteady hands, tried to inhale and choked, having never smoked before now. Velma patted her on the back.

"You don't need that cigarette—"

"You've got to help me get my baby back! I can't sleep knowing he's in that house with him! He might hurt my baby!"

"Where is he? The baby?"

"He's home with . . ." her voice trailed off. Vittorio's name wouldn't form in her throat. "I've got to get him. I need your help. Will you?"

"Shhh, shhh." She stroked Louise's hair, rubbed the purple bruise on her cheek. "Of course I'll help you. Let me get dressed."

"No! Not now. He's still there. Tomorrow, first thing—"

"You know I'll help you." She cleared her bed of typewritten pages and books. "You need some sleep. You don't look well."

Walking her to the bed, she sat her down while Louise whispered to herself. Velma removed her coat, slid the slippers off her feet, took off the torn nightgown. Louise stared blankly, like a mannequin passively being disrobed. Velma went to the closet and pulled one of her nightgowns from a hanger. Bending over Louise's naked body, she pushed her arm through the sleeve. Velma dressed her, much as she had when she was a little girl. She fluffed the pillow. Then grabbing Louise's ankles, she elongated her legs. She pulled the blankets over her sister's scented body, and tucked her in.

"Oh God! Don't let him hurt my baby!" Louise cried.

"Shhh, shhh. Get some rest, sweetheart. Don't you even worry. We'll get your baby."

22

As he lay face up on the floor, Vittorio's head throbbed, as the morning sun caused him to squint. His nostrils flared at the clashing perfumes in the air. Licking his dry lips, he tasted lipstick, more perfume, soured bourbon, and suddenly wondered where he was. Eyelids sticky, he struggled to open them. He couldn't discern the figures huddled over him at first. Then he recognized Sara. As he slowly opened the second eye, Jasper loomed above him, his expression full of pity. He raised his head; the room spun. Needles seemed to prick his skull, and his stomach bubbled with sourness. Resting on his elbows, he saw the remnants of war in the bedroom and remembered last night.

"Jasper, Joseph," Salvatore said, "you get his legs, and I'll grab his arms. Okay, on the count of three."

They peeled his body from the floor, carried him to the bed.

"Put me down!" Vittorio demanded, his limp head pressed against Salvatore's stomach. He tried wiggling his ankles loose from Jasper and Joseph. "Get your hands off me!"

Sara disappeared downstairs to fetch aspirin and one of her hangover concoctions.

Lying face up, Vittorio watched through blurred vision, as the staff surveyed the leveled surroundings and shook their heads, their jaws suspended, eyes popping out of their sockets. He heard Bessie and a few of the other women suck their tongues, and mumble, "Hmm, hmm, hmm, Lord . . ."

Jasper the gardener, and Joseph the butler were a trifle annoyed at Mr. B's outburst. The least he could have done was thank rather than scold them. It wasn't their fault he was too stupid to know a colored woman when he saw one.

Sara wondered where Mrs. B had gone, as she handed Vittorio the hangover remedy. Their mess of a bedroom looked like one of several abandoned lots in her neighborhood. She thanked God that Angelo, crying fitfully with his nurse, was all right. He probably wondered where his mother was. Sara couldn't believe Mr. B had done all this himself. It frightened her to think he had it inside him.

She just hoped he hadn't harmed his wife in the process. As he handed her the empty glass, she mouthed a silent prayer.

Bessie and others began cleaning up the mess, their heels crunching upon broken glass. They swept the glass, turned tables and chairs upright, straightened crooked mirrors, and picked up feathers from shredded pillows.

"Get the hell out of here!" Vittorio shouted. "Bessie, put that down! Did I ask anybody to clean this? No!"

They all stopped to stare at him. He seemed deranged.

"Salvatore!" Vittorio yelled. "Get the limousine. I have business to attend to at noon. Salvatore, you hear me?"

"*Si, signore,*" Salvatore said.

"Mr. B," Sara spoke up, clearing her throat. "It ain't none of my business, but I don't think you in no kinda shape t' be going out nowhere today—"

"You're right, Sara," Vittorio said, rising, walking past her into the adjoining bathroom. "It's none of your goddamn business!"

23

October 24. Black Thursday. Twelve noon.

Vapor from his nostrils formed circles of fog on the glass, as Vittorio leaned his throbbing head against the window. The limousine was parked near Wall Street and he eyed the crowd swarming the steps of the New York Stock Exchange. Salvatore, at the steering wheel, chewed gum, whistled a tune, and cleaned his fingernails.

The doors of the New York Stock Exchange flew open, and what appeared to be hundreds upon hundreds of mad dashers scrambled out, hurling themselves down the steps in a frenzy. Some tripped; others fell over them. Bankers. Brokers. Investors rushed to the bank. Grown men openly cried, oblivious to the stampede. Automobiles slammed on brakes and honked their horns. Some of the crowd climbed over the hoods, over roofs, dodging bumper fenders. A wealthy woman, staggering as if too overwhelmed to continue further, attempted to rip her mink coat in portions—snatching a piece here, a piece there. "Three hundred dollars! Please, anybody! I need to cover my margin!" she pleaded. Panic, like a wide broom, swept the sidewalks of Wall Street. An awesome economic Armageddon was upon them.

Unable to face any more, Vittorio nodded to his driver and Salvatore lurched the limousine from the curb. He made a U-turn to avoid the panic ahead. Vittorio stared through the window. He had not washed, shaved, or combed his hair, and could smell himself. A tear rolled down his cheek as he helplessly endured this third, nightmarish blow. First his parents, then Luisa, and now this. All that he'd lived for was slipping through his fingers.

What would he do now? Where could he go? Papa had warned him. Mama had warned him. He couldn't bear hearing, *I told you so!* But what else was there left to do? Go back to Palermo, his tail between his legs? Papa would love that. Vittorio had been born into wealth and privilege. He'd never known a moment of want or sacrifice. Hunger, poverty and the blue-collar proletarians were merely intellectual concepts he observed from a distance. He had grown up in a Palermo villa, and studied at Princeton. Now *he* was poor. *Poor!* He'd lost his stocks, savings, nearly everything! All that remained would, in time, be gone. The limousine, the Tudor house, the exorbitant furnishings, and the servants would become yesterday's news.

The signs are there if you care to read them . . . Okay, Papa, you win. You always do. How did I ever think I could outsmart you anyway? he said to himself. Had he known then what he knew now, he would have boarded the ship twenty-four hours before them—his money in his pocket. Too late for that now.

And Luisa. He still loved her and wished things were different. How could she have lied to him? Did she really love him? Or was she just another golddigger, as Mama accused her of being? No. She loved me. It was love. I know the difference.

He had married a colored woman, bought her jewels, furs, a house, a Rolls-Royce, shared his bed with her. Who'd believe it? In some twisted way, he wished she had been a mere adulteress. Angelo did favor him. Negro blood or not. Luisa, his lovely calla lily turned burdensome. She became a cross he'd have to bear for the rest of his life.

Looking back, he could understand why she had been so secretive about her address and telephone number; why she was with the colored guy when he first saw her at Smalls Paradise; why she had no friends or family present at the wedding. Was she really an orphan? And that bum who approached Luisa outside the Cotton Club, did he really know her?

In a low voice, he instructed Salvatore to park in front of Trinity Church.

"But, signore, it isn't a Catholic Church."

Inside, he walked through the drafty, hollow-sounding hall, down the aisle. His footfalls echoed. The air was chilly, even with his heavy overcoat, cold for late October. Genuflecting, he made a sign of the cross. Tears stinging his eyes, he bowed his head to the floor. The last time he was in a church must have been for Angelo's christening. Before that, his wedding. The thought made him wail uncontrollably and he couldn't catch his breath. In his native tongue, he pleaded with the Almighty, staring up into the face of a seemingly indifferent Christ Jesus. Through quivering lips, he called out God's name. Confessing his sins aloud, he banged both fists upon the altar and begged for one more chance. He held onto the pew as if blinded by the light, as he turned to leave.

He wanted Luisa to hold him. She might have deceived him, but he'd fooled her too. He'd tortured her with the belief that there were other women. He'd been intimate with no one else, wanted no one else. Luisa was his life, the only woman to satisfy him. But he still had his pride. Things couldn't be turned around now. Had there been no baby, she'd still be living that lie.

"Where else can I take you, signore?" Salvatore said, bringing Vittorio out of his fog. "Will you be meeting the signora today?"

"You are never to mention her again!" Vittorio grunted. "Understood? Never!"

24

"What do you want?" Rudy asked, speaking through the crack of his door.

"May I come in?"

"I'm very busy, Scott." He sighed disgustedly, looking at the floor, avoiding Scott's eyes. "What can I help you with?"

"I was in the neighborhood," Scott said, removing his fedora and fanning himself with it. "Thought I'd drop in."

"Listen, Scott, I'm very busy."

"I can see that," Scott said, rising on tiptoes, looking over Rudy's shoulder. "I won't be a minute."

Rudy walked away, leaving the door ajar, and Scott pushed it open with his foot. Rudy sat down at the typewriter, typing out the thought he had been composing before the interruption.

"What're you working on?" Scott asked.

"The play," Rudy replied, never looking directly at him.

"Oh? I thought you were done with that some time ago."

"Rewrites, Scott. Ever heard of rewrites?"

Scott smiled with a trace of sadness. He made himself comfortable on the sofa, crossed his legs, and fanned himself with the fedora. "I can't say I blame you for being angry with—"

"Angry? Who's angry?"

"Go ahead. I suppose you have the right. God knows—"

"The right? I have the right to kick your pompous ass out of here if you don't state your business in two—"

"I came to say good-bye."

"Good riddance, Scott. Catch you on—"

"I'm leaving, Rudy."

"There's the door."

"I'm sailing for Europe tomorrow morning."

"What?" Rudy gave him full attention, his tone and attitude changing.

"That's why I'm here. I came to say good-bye."

"Europe?"

"I need to get away, Rudy. Things are turning sour here. The newspapers are warning of an impending depression—"

"Why Europe?"

"Well, Paris specifically. I'm too distracted here in New York. I was terribly productive living in France. Besides, I have literary contacts—"

"You're leaving for good?"

"I'm afraid so."

"I'll never see you again?"

"No time soon, I'm afraid. Unless you come to Paris."

"Oh, Scott." Rudy was both elated and melancholy.

"What's the matter? You look like you've lost your best friend."

"I guess I just have."

"Am I *really* one of your best friends?"

"In some peculiar way . . . yes."

"I thought you'd be all too pleased to see me go."

"I guess I am. But . . . I'm not so sure. This is quite a surprise. Why can't you write here?"

"It's not the same. You see, I want to be a writer. Not a Negro writer, not an American writer; just a writer. With all our collective successes and literary triumphs, we're still considered Negro writers, disparagingly so. Editors say they're looking for different material, new and fresh material. But they're not. If Negroes hadn't written about racial strife in America, they wouldn't have published us. Now they won't even publish that. They're bored with us, Rudy. Paris isn't like that. At least, not yet."

Rudy couldn't believe his ears. For months, he'd tried devising a foolproof plan to rid himself of Scott. He thought of not seeing him, or moving back to Jersey City, changing his address and telephone number, until he was over him. Loving Scott was like walking against a seventy-mile-per-hour wind. He didn't have the heart and guts to follow through on any of his plans, and felt as if the whole world was surging forward without him, while he stewed in a pot of unrequited emotion. He fluctuated from one extreme to another, arm-wrestling with what he wanted, as opposed to what he needed—or didn't need.

Now suddenly, the decision was being made for him. He listened to Scott's words of farewell. He was terrified and tried not to show it.

"So you're leaving for another continent," Rudy whispered, as if to himself, scratching his head. "What about your townhouse—"

"I've sold mostly everything."

"Everything?"

"Had to do it quickly before money gets real tight."

"Well, Velma and I are finishing up with our project and we're planning—"

"Rudy, my dear boy, don't you see how futile that is? If what the newspapers say is true, there'll be no money to produce your play. There won't be any for white playwrights. Where do you think that leaves you?"

"I like to think more optimistically."

"That's all well and good. Hardly pragmatic."

"So, what did Velma have to say?"

"About what?"

"About this. Your leaving."

"She doesn't know yet."

"When will you tell her? A postcard from the Champs-Elysées?"

"Did you know she asked me to marry her?"

"No. I can only assume your answer."

"Do me a great favor, Rudy?"

"Depends."

"I don't believe I can face her. I want to marry her too, but . . . well, let's just say, it wouldn't work."

"You want *me* to tell her?"

"If you'd be kind enough—"

"Oh no. Uh-uh. Tell her yourself. Don't be such a coward for once in your goddamn life!"

"It's not cowardice. I just can't bear . . ."

"Just tell her."

"I don't think she'd be very happy about the sudden news."

"Well," Rudy said. "Find out. Be a man. Tell her exactly what you're telling me."

"She's an extraordinary woman, you know," Scott said, as if reflecting on memory or deep thought from the past. "She has to be the sweetest, most tolerant, most sensitive—"

"That's all the more reason to tell her. You owe her that."

"That's just it. I've never cared about anyone the way I've cared about her. Any other woman, I wouldn't have given it a second thought. But, I care about Velma, tremendously so. I've hurt too many people already."

"I'll drink to that."

"Will you do it?"

"No. I'd be the worst person to tell her. She might think I'm gloating, laughing in her face. Even worse, what do you think she'd say? You came to say good-bye to me and not her. No, thanks. I've had my share of fights with Velma—"

"She won't think that. She's a sensible woman. You know that."

"I don't know, Scott. That's asking a lot."

"Well then," Scott said, rising, placing the fedora on his head. "I gave it my best shot. I really must be going. Last-minute packing, you know." He walked to the door and turned the knob.

Scott had expected as much—or as little. He had no right to ask Rudy to do his dirty work, and yet he couldn't face Velma either. It was a matter of choosing the lesser of two evils. As though she had died, Scott wanted to remember her as she had been the last time they were together in the Studebaker, kicking around the prospect of marriage. From his viewpoint, she turned *him* down. To bid her farewell would only open the wounds, throw salt on raw, festering sentiments. Seeing her again, he might marry her anyway, casting all his well-founded justifications and reasonings aside, regretting it the following morning, then holding it against her for the rest of her life. He'd never cried over a woman before—hoped never to again—and it scared him.

If she decided to visit him in Paris—*sans* Rudy—they could start anew; maybe, do it the second time, the way it should have been done the first.

"So, this is it, huh?" Rudy said sadly.

"I imagine so." Scott shrugged his shoulders. "This is it."

"I'll miss you." Rudy walked toward him. "You know, you're probably the strangest, one of the most despicable people I've ever known. And yet, I still like you. I don't know why, but I do."

"It's been great, Rudy."

"Yeah, a million fucking laughs."

"We had good times, didn't we?"

"Yeah, I guess we did. And now . . ."

"Now what?"

"It's all over. One third of our trinity is sailing across the Atlantic. Probably never to be seen or heard from again. Take care of yourself. Drop me a line, all that kind of stuff."

"We'll see each other again." He sincerely hoped as much.

"You think so?" Rudy chuckled.

"I'm certain of it. Come to Paris any time you feel like. You're always welcome."

"After I get you out of my system first . . . then . . . maybe."

Rudy offered his hand to shake a final farewell. Scott ignored it and embraced him. Rudy's arms hung limply at his side, not wanting to hug him back. "Oh, what the hell!" He hugged Scott tightly. They stood near the open door for a long time, embracing in silence. Scott held Rudy by the sides of his face, studied him, planted a paternal kiss on his forehead, then turned quickly and walked through the door.

"*Au revoir, mon bon ami,*" Scott's voice echoed, resounding in the dark hallway.

"Good-bye," Rudy said loud enough for no one but himself to hear. His arms folded, legs crossed, he leaned against the door jamb, knowing he couldn't continue with his rewrite this evening. He watched Scott walk away, sensing his thumping heart tucked in Scott's back pocket with his Studebaker keys.

25

"It's all over, isn't it, Rudy?" Velma made a right turn.

"How're you keeping up, kid?"

She shrugged her shoulders. "Okay, I guess. You?"

"I don't know. My father's dying. My mother wants me home for Thanksgiving. What're you going to do with yourself?"

"After I drop you off, have lunch."

Velma parked a block away from Grand Central Station. She dropped the car keys into her purse, and started to get out.

"Wait." Rudy stopped her. "I have a few minutes before my train. Let's sit awhile."

She closed the door and rested her purse next to Rudy's rope-fastened suitcase. Tilting their heads backward, they stared partly at the gray sky and partly at a melancholy yet bustling Forty-second Street before them. The ominous weather complemented the depressed economy and the solemn expressions of midtown commuters.

"What're you thinking, Velma?"

"Oh, I don't know. How bad things are going to get."

Rudy hesitated with his next question. "You miss Scott?"

"Of course. I wonder where he is and what he's doing right at this moment."

"Hunting down two Parisian facsimiles of us. God help them. You're not angry? His not saying good-bye, I mean?"

"It's vintage Scott, if you think about it. Expect the unexpected."

"If Scott asked, would you ever go to Paris to be with him?"

"He did ask. He wrote me a letter last week. I'm sailing for Paris in March."

"Sorry I had to be the one to tell you."

"After I phoned his house for days and pounded on his door, somebody had to. I'm glad it was you." She sat up straight and faced him. "Rudy, I'm really sorry I slapped you."

"Naa. A good slap's healthy every now and again. Besides, after the episode at Scott's house that day, I thought you'd never forgive me."

"It's funny, you know . . ." She didn't know if she should say it or not, but felt compelled to. "I was never really angry with you . . . about Scott . . . not really. It didn't matter so much what you might or might not be doing with him." She sighed and looked away. "What mattered was what you weren't doing with me."

"You have an uncanny sense of flattery, Velma."

"We'll be in touch?"

"Of course. I'm only a river away."

How he hated farewells; the sentimentality, the lumps in the throat, the gloomy prospect of the end of an era, the awkwardness. He had every reason to expect to see her as much as he had been. But then, folks expected the stock market to be insoluble. Expectation, for him, was an enemy.

He loved and adored this woman, his best friend of four years, more than he'd loved any woman. Jersey City was a stone's throw from Harlem, but it wasn't the same as living a few blocks apart. And with Scott gone, it would all be off balance somehow.

Much of him didn't want to and couldn't leave her—his sister, lover, mother, confidante, colleague, running buddy—their ties so sinewy. For four years, she had wished him to be heterosexual. Looking at her beautiful face against the gray, drab surroundings, a purple iris in a field of dandelions, feeling so powerfully what he did for her, now he thought, If only she were a man . . .

"What're we going to do about the play?" Velma asked.

"I don't know. What can we do? The curtains are closing. There's no more money. No jobs. White folks are bored with us. Just like that," he said, snapping his finger, jerking his head. "They've stopped beating the tom-tom." He chuckled. "We were primitive, dancing children, dancing to the beat until time ran out. The drums have been silenced. The jungle is unnervingly quiet." He rolled down his window and shouted, "Sorry folks, there'll be no more dancing today!" He laughed until his face turned red. Velma started laughing too, hysterically so.

"What'd you think?" Velma said. "White folks would be in love with us forever?"

They howled, guffawing so loudly, they drowned out the sound of traffic. She wiped a suspended tear from the corner of her eye, thinking Rudy's metaphoric sensibility always gave words to the inarticulate, and placed the chaotic into proper prospective. She'd miss that.

They embraced within the echoing halls of Grand Central Station. The P.A. system announced arrival, departure times, and platforms.

"My voice in the rain," she said.

"What's that?" He released her, looking into her face.

"That's how I always think of you. The day I met you on Fifth Avenue near 138th Street. Remember? You came to my rescue after I was laughed out of the Harlem Writers Workshop, and called my name in the rain. A voice in the rain. There's a poem in there somewhere. . . ."

Rudy hugged and kissed her again. "Take care of yourself, hear?" He walked backward and waved, Velma shrinking from his sight.

"Say hello to Jersey for me." She waved languidly.

"Do me a favor!" he shouted, cupping his mouth with a hand.

"Anything, my darling!" she shouted back.

"Don't stop dancing, whatever you do!"

"What?" she shouted over the roar of trains. "I can't hear you!"

"Dancing! Don't stop dancing!"

"I love you, Rudy!"

Rudy turned with a skip and ran toward the platform. Sadness swelled within her, filling her chest. Simultaneously, she surrendered to a vague sense of freedom. A flock of doves took flight.

26

The restless sky cracked the whip of thunder. Clouds rolled into a gray conspiracy, joined, and blocked out the blue heavens. Lightning flashed. Rain splashed Vittorio's bedroom window. Ravenous and unshaven, he opened his window hoping to be struck by lightning.

Broken glass and shattered lamps covered the bedroom floor. Feathers of shredded pillows were everywhere. Dripping multiscents of perfumes stained the walls.

The rain then stopped and he was disappointed.

He fondled his bearded face, stroked his unkempt hair, and headed for Angelo's nursery. Passing the top of the staircase, he heard Sara downstairs working diligently and uninterrupted as ever.

A jolly Angelo kicked the blankets. He balled a dimpled fist into his mouth, rubbing itching gums, and saliva ran down through his fingers. Seeing his father, he slapped his hands against the crib bedding, the way he splashed water during his bath. Raising his heel and slamming it down, he threw a rattle from the crib onto the floor.

Vittorio picked up the rattle, and placed it back. Then he picked up Angelo and rocked him, pressing the child's head to his shoulder. The perfumed newness of a baby's skin clashed with the stench of a grown, unwashed man. He rubbed Angelo's head, the part Luisa told him never to touch.

Standing before a mirror, he turned the child's face against his. Moving closer to the mirror, he stared fixedly at the stark resemblance: deep-set brown eyes, widow's peak, the shape of the eyebrows. Angelo favored a photograph of himself as a baby; the one Mama kept in an elaborate frame at her bedside. Angelo smiled and specks of teeth emerged from his bottom gum.

Placing him back in the crib, Vittorio watched him in silence, the way he had watched him at the hospital when he was still pasty white, barely twenty-four hours old. He bent down into the crib and kissed Angelo's forehead, his cheeks, his balled-up, dimpled fists, the balls of his feet. "*Figlio mio*," he whispered, ashamed for having denied him as his own. "Angelo Vittorio, *figlio mio*."

He walked back to his bedroom and stood amid the ruins. The mattress was halfway on the floor, with a book hidden beneath; a novel called *Chameleon* by Velma Brooks. It had to be Luisa's. But why had she put it there?

He sat near the window, and sized up the landscaped garden that, in a matter of weeks, would no longer be his. From the floor, he picked up the smashed photograph of himself and Luisa at the Cotton Club, her smile crooked, her stomach bulging. The crisp, early November wind blew, and his nostrils picked up a passing stench. He turned and noticed the wilting calla lilies in a vase. The petals were yellowing, shriveled and the water cloudy, with a layer of scum at the surface. He held the photograph and ran his forefinger across Luisa's face.

Taking a stick match, he lit it and placed it in an ashtray as the fire did to the emulsion what Luisa had done to him. But a gust of wind pushed through his window and blew the fire out.

He picked up a wilting calla lily from the vase, glancing down into the garden, eyeing the hammock, and traced the flower along the curves of his face. With his free hand, he reached across to his night table, opened the drawer, pulled out the revolver, and pressed it to his ear.

His hand unsteady, he moved the revolver upward toward his temple, then brought it down to his mouth. Nervously, he placed the barrel between his lips, and slid it over his warm tongue, flinching at the cold taste of sweet death.

As he pulled the trigger—at the last minute changing his mind—the gun went off still, the barrel dropping downward toward his torso. The impact sent him whirling backward and the chair toppled over, his body slumping to one side. Blood splattered the walls and the windows. In shock, his lips moved. Not a sound escaped.

27

Quietly distraught, Louise didn't say much, and when she did, she whispered. Velma knew it would be a long time before she recovered emotionally—from what, Velma still didn't know—and she feared that her sister might never overcome whatever she'd been through. Meantime, the burden lay upon Velma and Miriam to bring Louise out of her trance, so she could get on with her life.

"Louise?" Velma faced her, steering the roadster.

"Hmmm?" Louise's eyes focused on the road, and she puffed the cigarette with such vengeance, Velma could barely see her through the smoke.

"I want to ask you something," Velma began. "But if you don't want to answer, you don't have to, okay?"

"Hmmm hmmm."

"Did a man call you by my name on Madison Avenue?"

There followed a long silence.

"Yes," she replied, so softly Velma could barely hear.

"What did he say to you?"

"He just mistook me for you and apologized."

"What did he look like?"

"Very good-looking . . ." Louise said, her thoughts drifting.

"And . . . let me see if I remember . . . oh yes, he was well-dressed. . . . Why? Who was he?"

"That was Scott, my beau. Let me ask; what were you driving?"

Louise sighed heavily. "A Rolls-Royce."

God! Velma thought. The man was telling her the truth and she called him and Rudy liars. Shame kicked her in the stomach.

"What did you say to him?"

Louise wanted to talk, but her mind was elsewhere. She didn't know what to expect when she got home. There was no way of knowing if Vito would really try to kill her if she returned. She couldn't rest until Angelo was safely in her arms. She had a right to take him with her. But if Vito was there, it might not be that simple.

Velma's jaw dropped as she pulled into the circular driveway. She surveyed the neighborhood, the manicured lawns and hedges, the immense red brick Tudor building. *My God!*

They got out, walked toward the door, and there it was. Louise's Rolls-Royce. She nearly gasped but stopped herself for fear of upsetting Louise. From West 141st Street to this! Velma thought, Girl, I might've disappeared myself!

They rang the bell several times and Velma held Louise's hand, noticing that she bit her lip so fiercely, it started to bleed. The longer they waited, the more visibly nervous Louise became. Velma herself shook from the vibration of holding Louise's hand.

Standing and ringing repeatedly, Louise thought Vito was upstairs in the window watching them, perhaps laughing, not about to let them in. Shifting their weight from one leg to the other, they rang incessantly, staring at each other in silence.

Deciding no one was home, they turned to leave, when a hand frisked the knob. Louise was ecstatic and terrified. The last lock was unfastened and Sara opened the door.

"Mrs. B!" she screamed with elation, and Louise ran to her.

They embraced each other and cried, as Velma stood to the side admiring their kinship.

"Oh, Mrs. B," Sara said, wiping her face of tears. "I was so worried about you. We didn't know what happened. You all right?"

"Yes, Sara," Louise said. "I'm fine. This is my sister Velma; Velma, Sara."

Sara extended her hand. Velma bypassed it and hugged her too, figuring she'd been an ally to her sister.

They stepped inside, and Velma couldn't believe her eyes. The

house was laid out in tasteful Art Deco; the living room was twice the size of her entire apartment—hers and Rudy's together. It was dark. Lights were out, shutters and curtains drawn, and the air, damp and drafty.

"Where's my baby?" Louise asked, heading toward the staircase.

"Mrs. B," Sara said hesitantly. "He upstairs but . . ." She paused and sat down.

"What's the matter?" Louise asked.

"It's about Mr. B."

"What happened?"

"Well, you gonna see a lotta mess when you go upstairs. Mr. B . . . well, he try t' kill hisself. . . ."

"What?!" Louise gasped, the knot in her stomach pulling tighter.

"He all right now. Just shot hisself in the shoulder—"

"Where is he?"

"In the hospital. They say he be jus' fine. . . ." She turned away and wiped her eyes. "I jus' thought you should know."

Louise walked up the staircase slowly. She was happy to retrieve her son without protest, but the guilt over Vito weighed heavily on her shoulders.

"Honey," Velma said to her sister. "You want me to come with you?"

"No," Louise said, shaking her head. "I'd rather go alone."

At the top of the stairs, she hesitated, then walked into the nursery. Upon seeing her, Angelo kicked and gurgled animatedly. She picked him up, pressed him to her, and kissed him repeatedly while tears ran down her cheeks. She was so tired of crying, it seemed to dominate her waking hours nowadays, but she couldn't help herself. Angelo made smacking noises and baby talk, and Louise answered him the way she used to, noticing the teeth pushing through his bottom gum.

"Yes, my darling sweetheart. Mommy's come to take you home. She wouldn't forget about you."

Carrying him, she cautiously approached the master bedroom, noticing several rooms throughout the house had been closed off. Covering the child's eyes, she saw the blood. The partially burned photograph of herself and Vito. The blood-splattered calla lilies. She felt she had a lifetime of repentance ahead of her to atone for this.

She walked downstairs, and Velma jumped up at the sight of her nephew. Running to Louise, she took Angelo from her arms, kissed him and spoke in baby talk, remembering her dream on the beach about the infant whose face turned old in her arms.

"I'm your aunt Velma," she said, noticing what a happy, good-natured baby he was. "And looka those teeth. This boy's so big," she said over her shoulder to Louise and Sara. "He's about ready to get a job."

"Isn't he beautiful?" Louise said.

"Of course," Velma said. "He's a Brooks boy. First we've had since Father," she added, marveling at the concordant mixture of his bloodlines. An Italian Negro, she thought, remembering jokes whereby, allegedly, there wasn't much difference between the two.

"Come give yo' aunt Sara some sugar," Sara said, kissing his dimpled fists. "Honey, me an' Angelo done got t' be good friends, ain't we, sugar?"

"Sara," Louise said, sitting down beside Velma. "What happened to the baby when they took . . . you know, his father?"

"Firs' thing I done," Sara said, careful not to recount gruesome details, "was call the pohlice. An' I was worried about them comin' t' git him in time, 'cause I didn't know if Mr. B was alive or what. Befo' the pohlice come, I didn't know what t' do. The baby here was screamin' his head off from the gunshot, it scared him so. Me too. But then, I remembered. When the pohlice come, they woulda took him since I only works here. An' they come runnin' in a hurry too, chile. I ain't never seen no pohlice come so fast. They don't come that quick in Harlem, tha's fo' sho. Five pohlice cars, can you imagine that?

"Anyway, I hid Angelo afta I quiet him down some. Rooms done been closed off upstairs, an' I wrap him up, put him in there, an' locked the do'. Good thing too, 'cause when they git here, they ast a whole buncha questions. I say I don't know nothin', I jus' works fo' the man. When they saw the nursery, they come ast me where the baby was. I say the baby gone wid his mama, lak ev'ry child 'sposed t' be. An' I'm prayin' t' God that the chile be still. If he start up cryin' again, there wasn't nothin' his aunt Sara could do. I tol' 'em I didn't have no key to the locked rooms. I jus' works fo' the man.

"So, afta they lef' an' took Mr. B t' the hospital, I got that chile an' hightail it outa here in case they comes back. I took him home and fed him, did ev'rythang, then brang him back wid me in the mornin'. I ain't been doin' much work aroun' here lately . . . you know . . . wid all tha's goin' on, but I been steady waitin' on you, ma'am. I knew you be back t' git yo' chile. I knows. Got five o' my own."

"Sara," Louise said. "You did that for me?"

"Sho," Sara said. "We's both womens with chirren, right? An' we's both . . . colored too. We gots t' look out fo' each other. Ain't nobody gonna do it fo' us, right?"

Louise kissed Sara. She didn't know what to say.

"If I didn't," Sara continued, "they woulda throw that chile in a home fo' chirren quicka than I could blink. They thinks people lak me is stupid; you shoulda heard how they talks wid me. But I was one step ahead o' them."

"You're here alone?" Louise asked. "Where's Jasper and Bessie and—"

"They gone, ma'am. I guess you know Mr. B stone broke. I let them go. I hate t' do it, but what else I'm gonna do?"

"Velma, would you help me get some things from upstairs, please?" Louise said.

"Sure," Velma said, passing Angelo to Sara.

The sight of the bedroom rendered Velma speechless. The blood, the mess, the closet bulging with sequins, lamé, silk and furs. The diamonds, rubies and pearls strewn across the floor. She couldn't believe her eyes.

"There's my book," Velma said.

"Did you . . . write that . . . about me?" Louise asked.

"Of course not," Velma said.

"If not for that," Louise said, "I wouldn't know . . . about Mother. How did it happen?"

"Don't worry about that now," Velma said. "I'll tell you later."

They packed her belongings in the roadster while Sara amused Angelo.

After Sara dressed the baby in warm November clothing, she held him, thinking she might never see him again.

"What will you say to my husband?" Louise asked Sara.

"About what?"

"Well, when he comes back, he'll find Angelo gone—"

"You his mama. A chile belong wid his mama. If it was me, I hope somebody do that fo' me."

"Sara," Louise said, kissing and hugging her again, "you're a miracle. You're my guardian angel and I don't know how to repay you—"

"I got an idea," Sara said.

"What's that? Anything, you name it."

"Could you bring the baby by t' see me sometime . . . in Harlem. I wants t' keep in touch, if you don't mind," she said.

"Yes, I'll bring him. I'd be more than happy to."

They bade tearful farewells and the sisters started for the automobile. Velma's roadster didn't look the same against the shining Rolls.

"One mo' thang," Sara said. "I almos' forgot." Reaching into her apron pocket, she produced several hundred dollars. "This here the money Mr. B give me t' run this house. You an' Angelo should have it."

"But what about—"

"Honey, ain't you heard? We's knee deep in a depression an' you gonna need it. Go on, take it, it belong t' you."

Louise looked hesitantly to Velma.

"Go on, girl," Velma said. "You better take that money."

Louise took the money, and handed her back two hundred-dollar bills.

"Oh no, ma'am," Sara said, throwing up her hands. "I couldn't take—"

"I insist," Louise said, and squeezed the two bills into Sara's clenched fist.

"Thank you, ma'am. You come see yo' aunt Sara," she said to Angelo, as Louise and Velma climbed into the automobile. Sara waved goodbye, holding back the tears, then slowly closed the door.

Velma started pulling off.

"Wait," Louise said. "I just want to look at this house a moment. I'll never see it again."

Velma let the car idle and waited for Louise to nod before she turned out of the driveway and headed for Harlem.

S U N S E T

Velma paused to contemplate a problem she was having with a short story, and began staring at the bare Christmas tree in the corner of the room. Writing is too painful and demanding, she thought, Why did it choose me?

She walked to the crib and checked on her nephew. He was a delightful and welcome distraction for her. Miriam and Louise had gone Christmas shopping. Louise and Velma had since moved in with Miriam and today Velma took the opportunity to work and be alone with the baby. He was sound asleep though and she wished for him to stir—any excuse to pick him up.

She stared into his face, felt the love she had for him and her sisters, and sensed Mother's spirit hovering over them in the parlor, like the warmth of a winter's fire.

She eyed the typewriter, the page tucked inside the roller, the completed papers piled neatly beside it, and smiled at the prospect that she'd be joining Scott in Paris in the spring. *Paris!* She couldn't wait. The manuscript on her desk brought Rudy to mind. She had spoken with him two days ago, and they agreed to spend Christmas together. She was counting the days. She could see his lanky body moving away from her into the fog of Grand Central Station as in a dream. Taking mental inventory of the work she'd done and the volumes she was yet to produce, she heard him calling to her through the mist, *Don't stop dancing!*